Louise Welsh

Louise Welsh is the author of six highly acclaimed novels, including *The Cutting Room* and *The Girl on the Stairs*. She has been the recipient of several awards. *A Lovely Way to Burn* is the first novel in the *Plague Times* trilogy.

Praise for *A Lovely Way to Burn*

"A terrifying journey into the possible . . . *A Lovely Way to Burn* gripped and chilled me in equal measure." —Val McDermid

"I was with Louise Welsh's gutsy gripping heroine Stevie Flint every terrifying step of the way." —Kirsty Wark

"I read it in two sittings, pausing only to sleep and dream about it. Gripping, perfectly paced and beautifully written." —Erin Kelly

"This intelligent thriller creates an alarmingly convincing picture of London on the brink of disintegration." —Andrew Taylor, *The Spectator*

"Welsh plays brilliantly on our worst fears, and the pace never lets up. Seriously scary." —*The Times*

"A thrillingly dystopian mystery." —*Guardian*

"This is a novel rich in the kind of iridescent word painting that has long been Welsh's speciality . . . readers will be impatient for the second in the trilogy." —*Independent*

A LOVELY WAY TO BURN

Also by Louise Welsh

The Cutting Room
The Bullet Trick
Naming the Bones
Tamburlaine Must Die
The Girl on the Stairs

A LOVELY WAY TO BURN

Louise Welsh

Quercus

New York • London

Quercus

New York • London

© 2015 by Louise Welsh
First published in the United States by Quercus in 2016

ISBN 978-1-68144-462-8

Library of Congress Control Number: 2016930921

Distributed in the United States and Canada by
Hachette Book Group
1290 Avenue of the Americas
New York, NY 10104

Manufactured in the United States

10 9 8 7 6 5 4 3 2 1

www.quercus.com

For Zoë Wicomb

. . . love is strong as death;
jealousy is cruel as the grave:
the coals thereof are coals of fire,
which hath a most vehement flame.

—The Song of Solomon

Prologue

London witnessed three shootings that summer, by men who were part of the Establishment. The first was the Right Honorable Terry Blackwell, Tory MP for Hove who, instead of going to his constituency as planned, sat in a deck chair on the balcony of his Thames-side apartment one sweltering Saturday in June and shot dead six tourists.

The first five were neatly dispatched, with shots to their heads. Terry Blackwell had been a sniper in his army days, and tourists, ambling by the river in bright summer clothes, were easy targets. The sixth was running for cover when Blackwell hit her in her right knee. He waited until the girl, Marina Salzirnisa from Latvia (visiting the city for a language class that her father hoped would improve her English), had almost dragged herself to the safety of a café, and then shot her four more times, wounding her in her left knee, both thighs, and finishing with a shot to the spine that wasn't guaranteed to kill her, but did.

After Marina, the MP had lost his touch, or perhaps people had simply succeeded in running for their lives, because although Terry Blackwell kept the streets and buildings in range pinned down for the rest of the day, he didn't kill, or even wound, anyone else. Around six o'clock he botched his own shot to the head, lingering on alone, on the floor of his apartment, where the Rapid

Response Team eventually found him. Police negotiators had located Blackwell's ex-wife, Cynthia, and later there was speculation in the press that it had been her voice on the answering machine, telling Blackwell she still loved him, that had prompted the MP's coup de grâce.

Toward the end of June, John Gillespie, a hedge-fund manager for the Royal Bank of Scotland, let rip in an Underground car on the Circle line with a gun he had concealed in his briefcase. Gillespie was known for his canny ability for risk assessment and had chosen a not-quite-full car between rush hours. He managed to kill all fifteen occupants before the train reached its next station. Gillespie waited for the doors to open, and the oncoming passengers to see the carnage, before turning the gun on himself. Witness statements mentioned the banker's smart suit and neatly knotted tie, the professional smile he gave as he pulled the trigger.

The following week the Reverend Matthew Sheppard, vicar of St. Alban's parish church in Ealing, mounted the altar, took a shotgun from beneath his cassock and attempted to gun down his congregation. St. Alban's worshippers were aging, and had it been a normal Sunday, the Reverend Sheppard might have succeeded in sending them all to what they presumably believed was a better place. But it was the week of Aimee Albright's christening and the church was packed almost to capacity. Aimee's Uncle Paul, who had never been good enough to turn professional but had captained his local cricket team for the past eight years, bowled his hymnbook full square at Sheppard and knocked the gun from his grasp. Aimee's father was wounded in the shoulder, but he and two of his brothers managed to wrestle the vicar who, now that he was unarmed, seemed dazed, to the floor. The Reverend Sheppard had remained dazed to the point of catatonia, right up to the moment when he succeeded in hanging himself with a sheet in the prison cell where he was on suicide watch.

On the surface, the shootings were nothing to do with what happened later, but they stuck in Stevie Flint's mind. Their details returned to her during the months ahead and she would begin to think of them as a portent of what was to come, a sign that the city was beginning to turn on itself.

One

S tevie Flint had lived in London for seven years. She no longer had the soundtrack to the movie of her life playing in
her head, but had only just turned thirty and could still appreciate the buzz of the city as it headed toward night. She walked
out of Tottenham Court Road Underground station, noticing
a faintly sulfurous tinge to the air. Stevie shaded her eyes with
Jackie O sunglasses, suddenly remembering Jasmine's, the only
smart dress shop in her hometown, its window screened with
yellow cellophane to protect gowns from a rarely existent sun.
London had a hint of yellow to it today, she decided, a septic
glare. She set out in what she hoped was the right direction for
the private members' club Simon had suggested. Her new sandals were too high for a long hike but she had traced her route
earlier on Google Maps and been reassured that she could walk
the distance without too much damage to her feet.

Soho was full of pubs and all of them were full. Drinkers had
spilled out on to the pavements, and it seemed that everywhere
there were pretty girls and men in suits, minus ties, all of them
talking and laughing and all with a glass in their hands. Stevie
caught snatches of conversation as she passed:

". . . smooth, like a billiard ball into a pocket . . ."

". . . six down and he refuses to call in a . . ."

". . . I told her if she don't like it she can . . ."

". . . that's me done in Deptford."

Stevie stepped on to the road to avoid a crush of bodies and felt the skirt of her dress flutter in the slipstream of a passing moped. There was dust and laughter and gas in air that had been breathed in and breathed out, breathed in and breathed out; it was better not to think about how many times because that might set her to thinking about the water she drank, or how much of the heat currently broiling the city came from the sun, and how much radiated from the strangers pressed around her.

Stevie paused, unsure if she was in the right street after all. She took a deep breath, feeling the air hot and tarry against the back of her throat. Her shift had ended at three that morning and a headache threatened at the back of her eyes. A drunk man in shirtsleeves slid free of the crowd and put an arm around her. She felt his body heat, the sweat of his underarms touching the back of her neck. "Do you want another one, just like the other one?" the stranger whispered in her ear, his hop-scented breath warm against her face. Stevie would like to have slipped off one of her new sandals and stabbed its heel in his eye, but instead she gave the drunk a shove in the ribs and wriggled free of his grasp. He called after her, "Was it something I said?" She heard his friends laughing, and fought the urge to go back and tip their pints from their hands.

"See how much you laugh then."

Stevie realized she had said the words out loud and glanced around to check if anyone had noticed, but she was alone on a crowded London street, and if anyone had, they paid her no mind.

Perhaps it was the incident with the drunk that made Stevie lose her way, or maybe it was her usual lack of direction that snared her in the maze of Soho streets. She called Simon, and when he didn't pick up, left a message, making an effort not to sound irritated. After all, it was she who was late and it wasn't Simon's fault that her bare sole was blistering. Stevie checked the route on her iPhone, retraced her steps, and finally found the club, a discreet doorway with only a number to distinguish it.

The interior was self-consciously stylish, a dimly lit retro-Nordic exercise in design that would hang around for a few years, then be revamped in response to some new trend. Usually it amused her that Simon, a man whose business relied on cleanliness and precision, liked these desperately trendy dives, but they had not seen each other all week and tonight she would have preferred somewhere more intimate.

Stevie smiled at the hostess, gave her name and watched the girl's green-lacquered fingernail trace a path down the list of reservations. It wasn't really a members' club, just somewhere that people who had decided they wanted to be fashionable paid to get a table. The hostess's finger paused and she put a tick next to Stevie's name. Simon's name was slanted beside hers, unadorned by ticks: *Dr. Simon Sharkey.*

"Am I the first?"

The receptionist was signaling for a waiter to show Stevie to a table. She turned to reply, and Stevie thought she saw a ghost of recognition flit across her face. The girl would work late too, Stevie realized, and for a moment she glimpsed a life not so different from her own: the high heels kicked off beside the couch, the calorie-counted snack eaten by the glow of the computer, the TV murmuring on, barely watched.

"Yes," said the hostess, her smile wider than before. "You're the first."

The smile told Stevie that the girl couldn't place her. But no one had ever admitted to guessing where they knew her from, even when Stevie told them.

By the time she had finished her second glass of wine Stevie knew Simon wasn't going to turn up, but she ordered a third anyway. She didn't bother to glance again at the bars on her phone. She had already checked them and knew that the signal in the club was fine. The door opened and two girls in short summer dresses entered. They were laughing, but the sound of their laughter and high heels was drowned by the heavy beat of the music.

Something had probably come up. Things had come up already in the time she and Simon had known each other, his job made that inevitable, but he had always called, or gotten someone to call for him.

The two girls were buying drinks. Their skin and dresses were stained yellow for a moment and then shifted to pink, violet, aqua as the mood lights embedded below the bar's glowing surface drifted through the spectrum. The barman turned toward the gantry, lifting a hand to his mouth to cover a cough, and as if in response, one of the girls also started coughing and raised a handkerchief to her mouth. The other girl said something that made all three of them laugh again.

Stevie glanced at the five-minutes-fast clock above the bar. Her friend Joanie had been more available since her split with Derek. There was still time to call her and arrange to meet for a drink. She would be full of outrage at Simon's defection, and that would help to put it in perspective.

On a video above the bar a rapper and his crew were making bad-boy gestures, while a group of skinny girls with inflated breasts and improbable rears paraded behind them in high heels and bikinis. The rapper squatted low, his knees scissored far apart, and pulled the camera close to his face. Stevie thought he was repeating *"ho," "ho," "ho," "ho," "ho," "ho," "ho . . ."* but the club was noisy and she might have been mistaken.

The understanding crease in Joanie's brow would be too much tonight, Stevie decided. Maybe later she would be able to indulge in a postmortem, but for now she would leave her relationship with Simon on ice.

Stevie slipped her cell into her bag and slid from her seat, leaving the unfinished glass on the table and trying not to care that she had been stood up. She had done her own share of letting-down in the past, and there was still the chance that something had happened at the hospital, something so quick and so urgent that there had not been time for Simon to call her.

The barman's grin was bright and consoling, the hostess's smile sympathetic. Stevie's smile outshone them both, but their pity embarrassed her, and it was an effort to make her eyes sparkle the way Joanie had taught her. She stepped from the bar into the warm evening haze of London in summer, and retraced her steps to the Underground station. This was their first broken date, but recently Simon had been prone to absences, even when they were together. Stevie had made a vow never to ask a man what he was thinking, but Simon's long silences and distant gaze had tempted her to break it. Now she thought she knew what had been on his mind. She had been bored with the places where he liked them to meet. Simon, it seemed, had been tired of her.

Stevie swiped her Oyster card and took the stairs down to the Central line platform. A breeze gusted from somewhere in the network of tunnels, rippling the skirt of her dress, touching the sensitive skin of her thighs. She clenched her hands, enjoying the dig of her nails against her palm. When Simon called, she would forgive their thwarted date; tell him it had been nice, but it was time for them both to move on.

A train rattled into the station. Stevie waited for the doors to breathe open. The carriage was almost full and she had already taken a seat beside a teenage boy before she realized that he was bent under the weight of a summer cold. The boy coughed, not bothering to cover his mouth. Stevie considered moving, but stayed where she was and fished her phone from her bag. There were no missed calls. She switched it off, trying not to care. An abandoned *Evening Standard* was crumpled on the floor by her feet, the MP, the vicar, and the banker splashed across its front page. Sometimes it seemed as if civilization rested on a slender thread.

Stevie forced herself to smile. She had been looking forward to seeing Simon, to sitting across the table from him, both of them aware of each other's skin and of what would follow later in the cool of his apartment; the doors to the balcony open, the curtains shifting in the breeze as their bodies moved together in the bedroom. Disappointment was tempting her to get things out of proportion. Simon might yet have a good excuse for not turning up, and even if he didn't, all that had happened was a man she liked had let her down. It wasn't as if anyone had died.

Two

They were selling toasters, fucking toasters, at six in the morning. Stevie slid a slice of white bread into each of the four slots and pulled the lever down gently, mindful of the model she had broken in rehearsal. Beside her Joanie chirped, "I like my toast nice and crispy, not burned but well-fired. My husband Derek, he likes his golden brown . . ."

Beneath the studio lights Joanie's skin had a golden-brown shimmer, enhanced, Stevie suspected, by some product Joanie had sold herself. Joanie was the best kind of salesperson, one who fell in love with the merchandise, and then sold it on with a sincerity that was impossible to fake.

Stevie said, "So with the Dual Action Toaster you can each have your toast the way you like it, and still sit down to breakfast together."

"Exactly." Joanie was beaming as if she had just discovered the secret to happiness in the crumb tray. "And we all know how important it is for families to eat together."

Stevie said, "Especially in the morning." And Joanie grinned at her. They were playing what Stevie thought of as their retro-porno-roles: Joanie the experienced but well-preserved housewife, initiating Stevie (newly married, not sure how to keep both her man and her sanity) into the ways of the world.

"Yes," Joanie said. "Especially in the morning. Derek's shifts are unpredictable but when we can, we sit down together in the morning, even if it's only for ten minutes."

Derek had left Joanie for Francesca, a special constable he had been assigned to train, and Stevie wasn't sure if her friend's constant references to him on air were wishful thinking, sales technique, or an act of revenge. Joanie had once told her that Derek's squad took turns to record the show. Joanie thought it sweet of them, Stevie suspected elaborate bullying. The tally on the LED board behind the cameras was climbing, but not quickly enough. The sales information appeared onscreen, Stevie read out the order number again, then the camera was back on her, and she was back on camera.

The toast sprang from the toaster, one slice as pale as it had gone in, the other a shade short of charcoal. Joanie said, "That was quick, wasn't it?" in her horny housewife's voice. "Just enough time to make a pot of tea while you wait. My Derek can't start the day without a cup of tea."

Stevie lifted up the slices of toast, ebony and ivory, for the camera to zoom in on, almost dropping them as the heat seared her fingertips.

"Whoops." Sometimes it amazed her how good she had gotten at not swearing on air. "That is most definitely toasted."

Joanie produced some butter and a knife. "Well, I don't know about you, but I'm ready for some breakfast."

Sales were speeding up as people across the country, in Leicester, Glasgow, Manchester, Cardiff, and beyond, got out of bed, turned on their TVs, reached for their credit cards, and dialed in their orders. Joanie let out a moan as she chewed her toast, overdoing it now.

Rachel, the producer of *Shop TV*, spoke into Stevie's head-piece: "Try not to choke and then read out some of the tweets and e-mails."

Stevie bit into her carbonized slice, aware of the camera zooming in on her mouth. They were a man down today and Hector the cameraman was pulling a double shift. The bags under his eyes were a purple shade of black that Stevie would have described as damson if she had been selling them. She rolled her eyes and said, "Mmm, that's perfect," sincere as a straying politician squeezing his wife at the garden gate. Hector shook his head and she tried not to laugh.

"E-mails and tweets," Rachel repeated in her ear and Stevie glanced at the autocue. "Shelley in Hastings has bought three Dual Action Toasters, one for each of her children. She's gearing up for a day in the garden. Good idea, Shelley, I think it's going to be another hot one. Maybe some Melba toast and a Pimm's on the lawn this afternoon?"

Bed, she thought. *Bed, bed, bed.*

"Nice link," Rachel said in her ear.

Stevie said, "Rowan in Southend-on-Sea has tweeted to say that the sun is shining and she can see the sea from her living room window. And Hannah in Berwick thinks the Dual Action Toaster might just save her marriage."

The words were coming easily now, she and Joanie part of a conversation with the unseen viewers.

"Lesley in Edinburgh has bought a Dual Action Toaster," Joanie said. "Lesley's e-mailed to say her hubby likes his toast cremated but she . . ."

Their sales were climbing on the LED display. Across the studio, out of camera range, two technicians were setting up the next line: beaded batwing sweaters, gaudy outsize numbers, ideal for the larger lady who didn't mind drawing attention to herself.

"I had an aunty who lived in Southend," Stevie said. "Starlings used to swarm off the pier and swoop across the bay. Sometimes they turned the sky black."

"Too creepy, Stevie. Keep away from swarms of black birds," Rachel whispered. There was a faint echo of laughter in the production booth, harsh, like static on the line, but she was on a roll now. "I don't know if the camera's picking this up, but the Dual Action Toaster has a lovely matte sheen, so it will fit with your decor whether you're an up-to-date techno kind of person, or prefer the traditional, country kitchen look."

"I'm definitely a country kitchen kind of girl," Joanie said, looking as if she was about to let the washing machine repairman bend her over her stripped pine units.

Their chat always circled back to the toasters, as viewers knew it must. Sometimes Stevie wondered if the audience bought their wares just to keep the presenters in a job. She said, "Just a few of these really unique items left. Do *you* have one of those households where everyone likes their toast done a different way? If you do, then this is the ideal solution."

Over on the other side of the studio, Aliah shimmered onto the fresh set, wearing a copper-and-green sweater patterned with banana leaves, like some jungle nightmare.

Joanie said, "I've reserved one of these for myself. Derek likes his toast golden brown . . ." The gold-brown skin on her arms glistened, and across the studio Aliah bobbed and turned, practicing her twirls, the sequins on her top glittering like a mirror ball beneath the lights.

Stevie felt the heat of the parking lot pavement through the soles of her sneakers, the surface sticky and pliant beneath her feet. It was the seventh week of the watering ban and the air was dry and gritty against her skin. She walked toward her Mini, rummaging in her bag for her sunglasses, remembering too late that she had left them on the hall table in her apartment.

"Shit."

Stevie shaded her eyes with one hand and in the other she carried the jacket she had been wearing when she had arrived at the studio in the cool of midnight. She hadn't bothered to cleanse her face of the makeup she had worn for the broadcast. She imagined it melting from her face in one smooth mask: café au lait skin and red lips, a flutter of mascara trimming wide-set eye sockets, minus her brown eyes. The thought was grotesque. Stevie pressed her fingers to her forehead. Her headache was back, and the sun, surely too high in the sky for eight in the morning, felt strong enough to burn her eyeballs from her head.

The air inside the car made her cough. Stevie opened all of its doors, and sat in the driver's seat with her feet on the ground, hoping she wasn't coming down with something. She checked her phone for missed calls. In the two days since Simon's no-show, irritation had given way to anger, which had in turn been replaced by a faint prickle of doubt. Stevie dialed Simon's landline, feeling like a stalker. The answering machine kicked in, and she hung up. There was no point in calling his cell. She had left enough messages there already.

They had never talked much about their friends and family. Stevie remembered a brother who lived in Thailand, a father who had traveled a lot to America on business. Was Simon's father still alive? She knew that his mother had died when he was a boy. He kept a photograph of her on the chest of drawers in his bedroom, a studio portrait of a smartly dressed woman hidden behind her makeup. Stevie couldn't recall Simon mentioning any particular friends, but then neither had she. It had been part of the pleasure of their encounters, their disconnection with the rest of her life. She did know where he worked though. Simon had referred to St. Thomas's Hospital more often than Joanie mentioned Derek.

"Are you all right?"

Stevie looked up, shading her eyes. She hadn't noticed the security guard approaching the Mini and now the sun's glare was conspiring with the shadows thrown by his uniform cap, so that she could barely make out his features.

"I'm fine." She had been grinning for hours and it was an effort, but Stevie managed to raise a faint smile. "Just letting the car cool down before I drive off."

"It's going to be another hot one."

The guard spoke with an accent, Polish or Russian. It made him sound like a movie villain, the Mr. Big of a human trafficking ring. He moved into the shadow thrown by the car and she saw his face, pale and thin, the kind of skin that needed to be careful of the sun.

"I should get going. It's been a long night." Stevie swung her legs into the car and closed the door, then, in case it had seemed like an unfriendly gesture, she rolled down the window and said, "You're new here. Is Preston on vacation?"

"No." Sweat was beading the man's forehead. He took a hankie from his pocket and wiped his eyes. "Preston's sick. I'm Jirí, I usually work days. That's how come we've never met before."

"Well, good to meet you now."

Stevie turned on the ignition and the engine growled to life, but instead of stepping away from the car Jirí moved closer.

"I watch you. On television."

She wanted to be gone, somehow to cut out the journey home and arrive magically in bed, freshly showered and tucked between clean sheets, but Stevie resurrected another small smile.

"I would have thought you'd get enough of this place at work."

"When I got the job I wanted to see what kind of shows they made and then I got hooked." He grinned, revealing a gold tooth behind his left incisor. "You're my favorite."

Jirí squatted down and put his fingertips on the edge of the car window, as if settling in for a long conversation. His nails were broad and slightly ridged.

"Thanks." Stevie pulled her seat belt across her body, but didn't fasten it. "I'd better go or my boyfriend will wonder what's happened to me."

The security guard slid his hands from the window and rocked gently on his heels.

"You never mention him."

"What?"

"On the program, the other woman talks about her husband, but you never mention your boyfriend."

"No, I don't, do I?" She put her hands on the steering wheel. "It's been a long night. I really must go."

Jirí rose slowly to his full height. He was tall, Stevie noticed, six two, or thereabouts. She put the Mini into gear and he stepped to one side as she guided it from the space. Stevie raised a hand in farewell and the guard said something, which was lost in the throb of the engine. He might merely have been telling her to have a good day, but Stevie thought she heard him mutter, "Fucking bitch," as the car pulled away. She glanced in the rearview mirror before she turned out of the gate and saw him standing in the empty parking space, watching her go, a long, black shadow stretched out behind him.

Stevie pulled the car over, a mile down the road. She used her iPhone to find the number of St. Thomas's Hospital, dialed the switchboard, asked to be put through to the surgical department and then, after waiting for a long time, asked to speak to Dr. Simon Sharkey.

"Dr. Sharkey's on vacation until the end of the week." Stevie sensed the business of the hospital going on in the background, and heard the impatience in the woman's voice. "Can I help you?"

"No," she reassured the voice, it was nothing anyone could help her with.

Stevie forgot about the bed she had craved for the past three hours and drove through the early-morning traffic to Simon's apartment.

Three

S imon lived in an ex-council high-rise in Poplar that had been sold to private developers and upgraded into luxury apartments. There were things the new architects had been powerless to convert, and traces of the social housing it had once been lingered on. The building's elevators and doorways had been designed with the proportions of the 1960s working classes in mind, and they remained on the economical side for the Übermensch who had displaced them. The covered walkways that had been calculated to encourage social exchange were vaguely embarrassing to the new occupants, who were forced to avert their gaze when they passed each other.

Stevie ducked her head as she went past the security cameras in the entrance lobby and took the elevator to the twentieth floor. Her intention was to put her keys through Simon's letter box, no note, no nothing; the keys themselves would tell him all he needed to know. But she hesitated when she reached his front door.

Simon's toiletries had been assuredly male, and so Stevie had brought her own lotions, shampoos, and cosmetics, all of them expensive. She had also left a dress in his closet, a red-and-purple silk sheath that she had bought in New York. She rang the doorbell and when there was no response, turned the key in the lock and let herself in.

Her first thought was that it was even hotter inside than it had been out in the sunshine and that Simon had forgotten to empty the trashcan. She closed the door gently behind her but the lock refused to catch and it slid open. Stevie swore softly under her breath. Simon had been reminding himself to get the warped doorjamb fixed ever since she had met him. That was the kind of girlfriend he needed, one who dealt with domestic hassles, leaving him free to cure the sick. She locked the door to keep it closed and was struck by a sudden impulse to laugh.

Everything she had come to collect was in the bedroom, but Stevie ignored it and entered the long sitting-cum-dining room with its ultramodern kitchen. The room was cast in half-light, and though Stevie had decided not to touch anything, she went over to the glass doors that led out on to the balcony and drew the curtains wide.

She could see the Olympic Park, where the old docks had once been, and the city's other new landmarks, the Gherkin and the Shard, in the distance, cutting free of the skyline. Stevie stepped out on to the balcony, enjoying the sensation of the outdoors against her skin. She looked down at the manicured green encircling Simon's apartment block and at the bus stop beyond it, crowded with old-age pensioners, young braves, and glamorous mums. Simon had joked about the benefit of having a bus stop by your gate. But Stevie had grown up in a small council apartment in a town that resented no longer being a village, and she had wondered why a surgeon inclined to fast cars, silk-lined suits, and taster menus would want to live somewhere ringed by housing estates.

"Because it's real life," Simon had said. "The closest most of my colleagues get to a mugging is stitching a victim back together. I might meet one on my way home." And he had laughed.

A haze of pollution shimmered against the horizon. Stevie's throat felt raw and she raised a hand to her neck, to check if her glands were inflamed. She would go straight to bed when she got home, or else she would be unfit for tonight's show.

It was strange being alone in Simon's apartment without his knowledge, dangerous and powerful. All at once she understood why teenage burglars lingered in the homes they robbed, raiding the fridge, scrawling obscenities on walls, wreaking damage. Stevie stepped back into the sitting room, sliding the glass doors closed behind her. The smell was worse after her brief exposure to fresh air. The festering garbage can would be a nice welcome for Simon when he came back from wherever he had gone. She noticed the answering machine blinking with the weight of her messages and pressed play, but the voice on the recording belonged to a man.

Simon, if you're there, pick up please. The voice was English, upper class, and tight with anger, or anxiety. *Simon, pick up the phone.* Whoever it was didn't say anything else, but she could hear the man breathing on the other end of the line, waiting until the recording cut out. There were a couple of silent calls after that, which might or might not have been her, and then the messages she had been waiting on, her own voice stiff and nowhere near as relaxed as she had imagined, asking Simon if he was okay. She erased them, and after a moment's indecision, her hand trembling above the delete button, wiped the stranger's message and the silent calls too. As soon as she had done it, Stevie felt ashamed. She didn't mind Simon knowing she had collected her things from his apartment, but the thought of him discovering that she had listened to his messages made her cringe. She drew the curtains, plunging the room back in gloom, and went through to Simon's bedroom.

The bedroom blinds were also down, but she knew her way around and didn't bother to raise them. The smell was worse in here, and Stevie wondered if it was something to do with the drains rather than a neglected trashcan. There was a framed photograph on the wall, of a younger Simon standing in front of what looked like a university building, with his arms around two men. Each of the trio had floppy hair and a reckless smile. Simon was a good twenty years younger, but the generous mouth, a little too wide for his face, and high cheekbones that hinted at a Slavic connection somewhere in his family, gave a glimpse of the man he would become. Stevie turned the picture to the wall. She hadn't minded that Simon had never introduced her to his friends, but now she supposed that she should have seen it as a sign.

She went into the en suite, ignoring the tumbled quilt and pillows heaped on the bed. They were another mark of how little she had known Simon, the man who had appeared neat to the point of obsession.

Stevie caught sight of her face in the bathroom mirror, drawn and slightly wild, and knew she should never have come. She shoved her toiletries into her bag anyway, feeling a prickle on the back of her neck as if someone was watching her.

"Wrong," she whispered to her reflection. "Sometimes you are just so wrong."

She felt the urge to giggle creeping up on her again. If she got away without being discovered she would tell Joanie, and they would laugh about it together. After all, she reassured herself, what she was doing was no crazier than some of Joanie's adventures in the wake of Derek's betrayal.

Stevie glanced in the mirror again. She had left the bathroom door open and could see the reflection of the bedroom beyond, the chair with Simon's clothes neatly folded over its arms, his mother's photograph angled on the chest of drawers, and above it the room re-reflected in the vanity mirror; the unmade bed with its familiar white duvet, the ugly abstract painting she would have persuaded him to replace if they had ever become a couple. The bed tempted her, but Stevie opened the cabinet above the basin, found the perfume she had stored there, and swung the mirrored door home.

The air seemed to leave her lungs and she dropped the bottle of scent into the sink where it shattered against the porcelain. Stevie ignored it. She paused, and then opened the cabinet again, slowly angling the mirror, until she captured the room as she had seen it in the flash of its swinging door.

Stevie took in the scene, with a gasp that seemed to draw all the air in the room into her body. Simon lay cowled in the duvet, his mouth slightly open, his eyes almost, but not quite, closed. His face was peaceful. Were it not for the awkward hang of his head and his skin's *eau de Nil* tinge, Stevie might have thought he was sleeping. The scent of her perfume mingled citrus and musk with the sweet-foul smell of decay, and she knew immediately that Simon was dead.

Four

The following hours had the unreal atmosphere of a movie watched while drifting in and out of consciousness on a red-eye flight. Stevie called the emergency services and sat in Simon's living room until the police and paramedics arrived. She watched with dead eyes as the paramedics carried in a stretcher and what she supposed was a body bag.

"So you don't live here?" The policeman had asked the same question already, but perhaps asking everything twice was part of the procedure. They were sitting opposite each other in the lounge. Someone had opened the curtains and Stevie could see the sky, blue and heat-hazed beyond the window. She wanted to drag the throw from the back of the couch, swaddle herself in it and sleep. She took a sip of the water someone had given her and tried to focus.

"No," she said. "I don't live here."

The policeman wrote something down on the form he had rested on the arm of his chair. He was in his late forties, with creased eyes and a weathered face that made him look like a countryman, but his accent was the East End of barrow boys and futures traders.

"And Dr. Sharkey gave you keys to his apartment?"

"Yes."

She had placed the keys on the coffee table between them and now she touched them lightly with her fingertips to show that she was leaving them there. She had strung them on a key ring, a red plastic heart that Simon joked made them look like the keys to a love-hotel bedroom. "How would you know?" she had asked, and Simon had winked.

A paramedic called the policeman through to the bedroom and they had a murmured conversation. Stevie closed her eyes. Simon was dead and she had found him. She thought of how it must have been: the empty apartment, her voice on the answering machine, hard and impatient while he lay curled up, beyond hearing, on the bed in the next room.

The armchair creaked as the policeman settled his bulk back into it. Stevie looked up. The policeman's skin was pale beneath his tan, his eyes dark with lost sleep, and she wondered if he too was coming to the end of a long shift.

"It appears that Dr. Sharkey died of natural causes, but as you'd expect we have to wait for the coroner's report for official confirmation." He leaned forward, his hands clasped together, striving for an intimacy neither of them felt, and she saw that his forehead was speckled with tiny globules of sweat. "Just to be clear, there was no drugs paraphernalia, no bottles of alcohol, no note, nothing you cleaned up to save his relatives extra grief?"

The answering machine messages she had wiped snagged in Stevie's mind, but she said, "No. Nothing like that." Her bag lay at her feet, full of the toiletries she had come to collect. She didn't want them anymore, would never be able to smell that brand of perfume again without remembering the whiff of decay she had mistaken for an overripe trashcan. "I don't understand what you mean by natural causes. Simon was only in his early forties. He went to the gym three times a week."

"Like I said, we can't be sure of anything until we hear from the coroner, but sadly it's not as unusual as you might think. Young, healthy men do occasionally have heart attacks, or slip away in their sleep for no apparent reason."

"No apparent reason." She repeated his words under her breath, remembering a soccer player falling to the field during an international match, felled by a heart attack. And hadn't there been a girl in her class at school whose brother had been found dead in his bed by his mother? Stevie hadn't thought of him in years. She said, "You've come across this before?"

"Once or twice." His face told her nothing. "The only consolation is it's peaceful. It looks like he fell asleep and didn't wake up."

The policeman placed the statement he had written on her behalf on the coffee table and she signed without bothering to read it.

"I'm sorry for your loss," he said as he walked her to the door.

"We'd only been going out for four months," Stevie said. "I can't even tell you who you should be contacting."

"In that case it was good of you to call us." The policeman took a hankie from his pants pocket and dabbed some of the sweat from his face. He glanced back into the apartment, perhaps checking that the paramedics weren't about to begin maneuvering Simon's body through the hallway before she was gone. "Plenty of people would have walked out the door and saved themselves the trouble of all this."

"Is that what you would have done?"

The policeman considered for a moment, and Stevie realized it was the real man, not the uniform, who was about to speak.

"No," he said. "I would have done exactly what you did. But I'm in the job. I know how things go. Some people take fright at the thought of the authorities. They'd rather disappear, or call it in anonymously."

"I waited in the living room," she said, and suddenly it seemed terrible that she had left Simon alone, after all those days and nights of being on his own. "I didn't stay with him."

"It wouldn't have made any difference. The fact that you called us might, though, to his loved ones." The policeman covered his mouth with his hand and coughed. "Sorry, allergies." He touched his handkerchief to his forehead again and asked, "What about you? You've had a shock. Is there someone at home to look after you?"

"I live alone, but it's okay, I'm used to it."

"Me too," the policeman said. "No one to find me either."

Five

Stevie took off her clothes, stuffed them in the washing machine and pulled on her bathrobe. Her apartment was hot, and she poured herself a glass of water. The surface of the liquid trembled and it was difficult to raise the glass to her mouth. She remembered that there was some Valium at the back of the cutlery drawer, left over from when her mother had died. Stevie found the packet, swallowed two pills, then climbed into the shower and turned the water up as hot as she could stand it. She closed her eyes and raised her face to the spray, letting it drench her hair, trying to empty her mind of everything, except the sensation of the water pounding against her flesh.

Later, she wrapped herself in her bathrobe and called the station to tell them she was sick and wouldn't be able to appear tonight, and very possibly not the following night either. Then, to her surprise, she was sick, gut-wrenchingly, jaw-stretchingly, horribly sick. Her bowels clenched and she realized that her body was determined to expel everything from its system.

When it was through Stevie drank a little water, pulled on an old pair of pajamas, and climbed into bed. The room seemed to tip and she saw Simon's face again. His mouth had been slightly open, his lips pulled back, showing his teeth. Another wave of nausea washed over her. She ran to the bathroom, only just making it in time.

A long, sleepless day was followed by a feverish night punctuated by nightmares. She became part of a floating world, a place without edges or gravity, where nothing was bound to the earth and objects and people drifted free of time and place. She saw Joanie and Derek, dressed up for a night on the town, and knew that they too were dead. The new security guard put his hand up her skirt and whispered that she was a stuck-up bitch and he was going to give her another one, just like the other one. The sun turned orange and a voice in her head, that wasn't her own, told her it meant that she was going to die.

Sometime in the early hours Simon walked into her bedroom. He was wearing the doctor's coat she had never seen him in and was fully restored. She noticed the red Bic in his breast pocket and the careless line of ink above it, where Simon had replaced the pen minus its cap. He gave her a smile and then opened the door and left. It was these details that spooked her when she woke: the line of ink, the closing door.

There was vomit smeared, nuclear yellow, on the pillowcase. Stevie pushed the pillow under the bed and stumbled to the kitchen, the dreams still tugging at her consciousness. There was vomit in her hair, but she was too weak to shower again. She tried to comb it out with her fingertips and then stuck her head under the tap. The cold water scalded her skin. She drank some and immediately threw up in the sink. Her ribs ached worse than when she had been swept overboard during a white water raft race and tumbled half a mile downstream, slamming against riverbed boulders all the way. The memory of the water, its centrifugal force, made Stevie dizzy and she threw up again.

She found a plastic bowl, set it by the bed, and continued to retch into it long after she had forgotten to try and keep herself hydrated. She slept again and woke to the knowledge that she had soiled herself. Stevie dragged the sheet from the bed, wiping herself as clean as she could with its hem, and crawled on to the bare mattress. There was a noise in her head like a telegraph machine in some old movie, and she realized that her teeth were chattering. Recent nights had been too warm for anything but a sheet, and she had packed her duvet away weeks ago. Now she pulled it from the blanket box at the end of the bed and drew it over herself, not bothering to find a cover for it. A telephone was ringing somewhere far away, but it seemed more remote than her dreams, and it didn't occur to Stevie to answer it.

The next time Stevie soiled herself she cried, but all she produced were dry sobs she didn't have the energy to maintain. She kicked the duvet from the bed and pulled on her bathrobe. Her movements were all instinct now, memories of how she should act.

She woke and turned over, wondering why she was so cold.

Her mother stroked her cheek and sang a song Stevie had forgotten, her mother's voice stretching the tune the way it always did.

There was a dog in the room. She could hear it panting. The room was black, the dog hidden in the darkness, but Stevie saw the gleam of its eyes and knew that it was waiting for her to fall asleep.

She had to stay awake.

She closed her eyes and slept.

She slept.

She slept.

She slept.

She woke, wondering where she was.

She turned over, closed her eyes and slept.

Her mother was at her bedside again, her face old and yellow, the way it had been toward the end. She touched Stevie's face and said, "I would like to have died in my own bed." Stevie said, "I know," and closed her eyes.

Shewokeandsleptandwokeandsleptandwoketofindherthings floatingaroundthebedroomthenewdressshehadboughtlastweek itsarmsswayingintimetoabeatshecouldn'thearandthenperhaps couldthesoundofherheartcreakingoninherchestthenecklaces andbraceletshadescapedtheirboxandwereexplodinglikeslo- mofireworksshewatchedthemfascinatedshoeshoesshoesboots shoesandsandalsspanthroughtheairherpantiesbrasandtights gotintotheactthepairofstockingsshehadboughtasatreatfor Simonbuthaddecidedwereaclichétangledtogetherthenapart teasinglyhewouldhavelikedthemthedogwasinthedarkagain pantingreadytopounceassoonasshecloseddhereyesshewascold coldcoldandshoutedtohermothertoclosethewindowbuther motherwasdeadandthewindowalreadylockedandboltedto keepherclothesfromflyingawayitwasdarkandthenthesunshone throughhurtinghereyessherolledoverandsleptagainrolledover andsleptwoketothedarkandthenthesunlightrolledoverandslept.

Stevie dropped her bathrobe beside the shower, and stepped naked into the spray. Her body was covered in an angry, red rash that was starting to blister. She remembered radiation victims she had glimpsed in a documentary about Japan. The stained gown lay at her feet, like a dead thing. The atomic bomb had vaporized people, leaving their shadows fixed to the ground.

She abandoned the gown on the floor of the cubicle, wrapped herself in a towel and fell into bed in the guest room she used as an office. The urge to be sick surged over her again, but her stomach was empty and all she produced were painful heaves. Her body clenched as if it wanted to expel her internal organs and she groaned out loud. It occurred to Stevie again that she might die and she thought vaguely of phoning a doctor, but she was tired and weak, and gave herself over to Fate more passively than she would have thought possible. Somewhere a cell phone was ringing. She wished that Simon would answer it so the noise would stop. A deep and dreamless sleep that was a kind of death overtook her.

Six

S tevie woke, stiff and thirsty, unsure of how long she had been asleep. She took another shower. The rash was still there, but it was less angry, the blisters that had made her think of radiation sickness already fading of their own accord. She rubbed the blandest moisturizer she could find on to her skin, extra gently around her ribs, which were still tender from throwing up, and pulled on an old tracksuit, soft and baggy from over-washing. Stevie texted Joanie to ask her to let the station know that it would be a day or two more before she could return, then she lay down on the couch, dragged a throw over herself, and fell back to sleep.

Later she made herself a cup of weak black tea and turned on the television. Later still she put together a pot of noodle soup from a pack she found at the back of the cupboard. Stevie ate cautiously, unsure if she would be able to keep it down, but to her surprise she found that she was starving, and it was an effort not to wolf another bowl.

The act of eating seemed to wear her out and she curled up on the couch again, thinking about the soiled sheets and pillowcases she had stuffed beneath the bed, but lacking the strength to do anything about them. She remembered the hang of Simon's head, the sneer of the smile that was his and not his.

Stevie woke to the sound of Big Ben and the frantic jingle that announced the news. The headline story was of a cache of bomb-making material found in the home of a white supremacist somewhere in the Midlands. Stevie muted the sound, pulled her hair back, shoved her feet into her sneakers and padded down to the shops beneath her apartment. It was cool outside. The stars were hidden by the sodium glow of the streetlamps but she thought she could feel their presence sharp and prickly in the firmament. She didn't believe in God or an afterlife, but her mind was so full of Simon that it was as if she could feel him, standing just beyond her sightline, watching to see what she would do next.

"I don't fucking know what I'll do," Stevie whispered, and then felt bad, though Simon would have laughed.

She bought a pint of milk, drank a glassful, and went to bed in the spare room.

Stevie checked her cell phone the next morning and discovered a screed of missed calls and texts. She spooled through them, wincing at the sight of Rachel the station producer's number, repeated over and over like a warning. Then she curled up on the couch and turned on the television again. The bomb-making story had given way to an explosion in a fireworks factory somewhere in the Far East, the sound was too low for her to hear where. She worked her way through her messages, looking for Joanie's name, wondering if her friend had mislaid yet another phone. Stevie wanted to tell Joanie about Simon, to dilute the shock of his death by saying it out loud.

The doorbell pealed, loud and insistent, ringing on longer than was polite. Stevie muttered, "Speak of the Devil and smell smoke." She padded through to the hallway, wondering how bad the apartment smelled and hoping Joanie didn't have a bottle of Cava tucked in her bag. The bell rang again and she shouted, "I'm coming," in a voice that sounded torn.

The woman at the door was a little older than Stevie. She was dressed in a no-nonsense navy business suit and a frothy white blouse that made her look top-heavy.

"I'm looking for Steven Flint."

She held a large handbag, decorated with unnecessary gold chains and buckles and stamped with the Chanel logo, in front of her, as if preparing to ward off an attack, or perhaps launch one of her own.

Stevie took a step backward, keeping a hand on the door, ready to close it. She said, "I'm sorry, I don't buy things on the doorstep," even though she instinctively knew the woman wasn't out to sell her anything.

"I'm not here to try and persuade you to change gas suppliers." The woman's laugh was harsh and incredulous, but there was an edge to it that told Stevie she was nervous. "This is the right address?" She took a piece of paper from her pocket and looked at it. "Steven Flint does live here?"

"What do you want?"

The woman hesitated and an expression that might have been sympathy flitted across her face. "Are you his wife?"

"I'm Stevie Flint."

It wasn't the first time her name had led people astray. When she was a journalist, before the Internet had closed the newspaper she was working for and made all but freelance work (and precious little of that) impossible, it had occasionally opened doors.

The woman looked confused. "I was expecting a man."

"No, Stephanie Flint, Stevie for short."

The woman stared at her, and Stevie was reminded of a computer rebooting after a tricky download.

"I'm Julia Sharkey, Dr. Julia Sharkey, Simon Sharkey's cousin." She faltered again. "He asked me to give you something." And a single tear trickled down the side of her cheek.

Stevie made them both a coffee, though she knew she wouldn't be able to stomach hers, and they went through to the lounge. She saw Julia Sharkey taking in the room: the cream rug and the Heal's couch; the Timorous Beasties blinds; the coffee table that was like the one Stevie preferred in John Lewis, but was actually from IKEA; the 1960s Ercol sideboard she had found on eBay.

The news was still running silently on the television. A shot of people in white cotton surgical masks crowding a city square somewhere in Asia cut to a view of a hospital ward, failing bodies laid out on rows of beds. Stevie lifted the remote and killed the screen dead.

She had opened a window and turned on the fan, but was sure that the smell of her own illness still permeated the apartment. As if to prove her right, Julia Sharkey said, "You've been unwell?"

Stevie wanted Simon's cousin to deliver whatever it was he had left for her and then leave. But she summoned a smile and said, "Yes, I'm still a bit shaky, but I think the worst is over."

Julia Sharkey got up from her seat, crossed to where Stevie was sitting, and placed her hands either side of Stevie's neck. "Tilt your head back for me, please." Her palms were cool and smooth, their pressure a comfort against Stevie's skin. Julia's fingers pressed a pathway along Stevie's neck, and then slid toward her clavicles, gently kneading the soft tissue at the base of her throat. Her perfume was a blend of bright floral notes Stevie couldn't identify. She said, "Tell me your symptoms."

"Vomiting, diarrhea, fever. I thought I had Ebola." Stevie gave a small laugh. "I had lots of bad dreams—I suppose you might expect those under the circumstances—and a horrible rash."

The uncertain woman who had faltered in the doorway had given way to an assured professional. Dr. Sharkey asked, "Do you mind if I take a look?"

"No." Stevie lifted the top of her tracksuit and exposed her stomach. "It's a lot better than it was. The blisters have almost gone."

"I can see that." The doctor looked at her skin without touching her and then nodded at Stevie to cover up again. "Exactly how long was it from onset to recovery?"

"I don't know exactly. I didn't feel too clever when I left work, but I was coming off night shift and I never feel very clever after that. I was sick for the first time when I got home. I was probably laid up for between fifty-two and sixty hours, if you count it from then."

"And you feel okay now?"

"Like I said, a bit shaky, but basically I think I'm fine. I thought it was a reaction to the shock of Simon's death."

Stevie waited for the other woman to give her diagnosis, but Julia Sharkey simply said, "Well, you certainly look like you're on the road to recovery." She crossed her legs, giving a quick glimpse of the red soles of her Louboutins, and pushed her coffee cup out of reach, as if ensuring that she didn't absently take a sip. "The police told me that it was you who found Simon's body."

"Yes."

Stevie cradled her cup between her hands; the smell of the coffee revived the memory of her nausea, but the fan had made the room a little chilly, and the feel of the warm china against her palms was comforting.

"I wondered why you hadn't gotten in touch with us, Simon's family, but if you were unwell that would explain it."

Stevie rubbed at a stain on the thigh of her tracksuit pants.

"Simon didn't talk much about his family." She closed her eyes for a moment. When she opened them Julia Sharkey was still sitting in the armchair opposite, the cup of untouched coffee in front of her. "We hadn't been going out for very long. I'm sure he would have introduced us eventually, if we'd stayed together, but I'm afraid that even if I had been well enough, I wouldn't have known who to get in touch with."

"We weren't close." Julia Sharkey shrugged as if to indicate that was just the way things went sometimes. "Both Simon's and my parents are dead, and Simon's brother lives in Thailand. I have a family of my own, two girls, and I work as a GP. When you combine all that, there isn't much time for anything else. And Simon was always very busy at the hospital." Her voice was businesslike, but she drew a tissue from the cuff of her sleeve and wiped away another tear. "I hadn't seen him for at least a year. We had lunch together, just the two of us, somewhere near St. Thomas's. He told me he was going to get married and have a family of his own. All he needed to do was find the right girl." She looked up. "Had he found her?"

Stevie said, "I don't know. We liked each other a lot, but it was too soon to tell."

Julia Sharkey nodded. Stevie saw how pale she was and wondered if she too were coming down with something, or if grief had sucked the color from the doctor's skin.

"That's a shame. I would have liked to think of him being happy before . . ." The sentence trailed away as she dabbed at her eyes. "I'm sorry. It's been a bit of a shock."

"I think he was happy. He found his work fulfilling." Stevie brushed a stray hair from her eyes, searching for a way to describe how things had been between them. "We enjoyed each other's company."

They had enjoyed being in bed together. Everything else had led toward or from that, their two bodies moving together.

Perhaps Julia Sharkey saw it in Stevie's eyes because she sighed and tucked the tissue back in her sleeve. She pulled an envelope from her handbag and handed it to Stevie.

"I found it in the tea caddy. A perfect hiding place for something you don't want to be overlooked, don't you think?"

"Yes." Stevie turned the envelope over in her hands. Her name and address were neatly printed on the outside in Simon's clear, undoctorly hand. "The perfect place."

Julia Sharkey got to her feet, as if eager to be gone now that her task had been accomplished. She said, "If it's a suicide note, I'd rather not know."

Stevie followed her into the hallway.

"The policeman said Simon died of natural causes."

"Yes." Julia Sharkey paused at the front door and turned to look at her. "And so it probably was. But don't forget, Simon was a doctor, and we doctors have a way with death. If he'd wanted to, he could have killed himself quietly and neatly."

Stevie put a hand against the wall to steady herself.

"However neat it was, someone had to find him."

"True, but if he did do it, and there's no evidence that he did, at least he showed some consideration." Julia Sharkey leaned her back against the door. Her skin was the color of old bone, her eyes hollow shadows. "I've seen too many messy suicides to think of them as anything other than acts of revenge." She forced a smile. "Sorry, that's what being a GP does to you." Julia opened the door and stepped into the lobby. "I'm not sure when the funeral will be, there has to be an inquest first, but I'll let you know. I expect a lot of Simon's friends and colleagues will turn out for it. I posted the news on his Facebook page and we've already had condolences from as far away as Hong Kong. He had a talent for friendship."

"I didn't really know any of his friends. We hadn't gotten to that stage."

"No." Julia stared down the lobby, past the doors to other apartments, toward the stairs. "The police said you surrendered your keys to Simon's place to them."

The word "surrendered" felt like an accusation. Stevie said, "I volunteered them. The police gave me a receipt."

"Of course, but is there any possibility you picked up his set?" Julia looked her in the eye. "By mistake?"

"Finding Simon's body was one of the most horrible experiences of my life. The last place I'd want to go is back to his apartment."

"I didn't mean to imply you'd done anything wrong. It's just that I've not been able to find Simon's keys, or his cell phone. I thought it might help me be sure I'd been in touch with everyone who needs to know, but it seems to have vanished."

Julia Sharkey was one of those women who never meant to imply anything, Stevie decided, but who was adept at making insinuations all the same.

"I have no idea where his cell might be, but Simon always hung his keys on the hook next to the door. He was meticulous about keeping them in the same place. The first time I stayed the night he made a point of telling me where they were. I teased him and asked if he thought I might make a run for it. But Simon was serious. He said he'd seen a family of four who died of smoke inhalation in a house fire when he was a junior doctor. They were found in the hallway, crumpled against the front door, mom, dad, and two kids. The keys were in the father's jacket, upstairs in the bedroom."

"Typical doctor." Julia Sharkey smiled sadly. "We develop obsessions from our patients' tragedies, as if their misfortunes might help prolong our own lives. What we should realize is, death comes for us all eventually. The day before the police contacted me about Simon I admitted four previously healthy patients to the hospital with the same symptoms you exhibited. One of them passed away, another looks like he may not make it. But here you are, hale and hearty." Julia Sharkey glanced at her watch and the shadows caught her face again, showing the hollows beneath her cheekbones, the sockets sunk in her skull. "I'm sorry, I've got to go. I took sick leave when I heard about Simon's death, but the hospital called this afternoon and asked me to cut it short. I managed to buy enough time to keep my promise to the girls that I'd pick them up them from school. They consider it a great treat to see me at the school gate, which makes me feel rather guilty."

"Are you saying that what I had was serious?"

Julia shrugged. "There's certainly a nasty virus doing the rounds—as usual the media are making a big thing of it—but you're young and in good basic health, so probably not. If you were old, or suffering from an underlying condition, it might be a different story. The main thing is you recovered." She took Stevie's hands in hers and gave them a brief squeeze. Her palms were slightly damp. "I'm glad Simon had you in his life." Julia gave a wry smile. "When I saw your name on the envelope and assumed you were a man, it crossed my mind that he might have been gay. Not that I would have cared about that, but he was always so private, I thought maybe he had killed himself out of some kind of misplaced shame. I'm not sure I could have stood that."

"So you do think he killed himself?"

"I think I'm just doing what I've seen countless relatives do, trying to attach some kind of meaning to death. Maybe that's why I'm fixating on his missing keys and telephone, to distract myself from the pointlessness of everything." Julia settled her oversized handbag on her arm and her brow furrowed as if something had occurred to her. "If Simon was feeling unwell he very possibly locked the door and put them somewhere he wouldn't normally."

"Yes," said Stevie. She remembered the damaged doorjamb and the necessity of locking the door to keep it closed. "I'm sure they'll turn up, eventually. Things usually do."

Seven

Stevie put the coffee cups in the dishwasher, poured herself a glass of water and went back through to the lounge. The seat of the armchair was rumpled where Julia Sharkey had sat. She smoothed all trace of her visitor away, lay down on the couch and took Simon's letter from the pocket of her sweat suit.

It was sealed in an ordinary, white envelope. She ran a fingertip across her name and address, handwritten by Simon before he died. It occurred to Stevie that Julia must believe his death was suicide, whatever she had said about the lack of evidence. Why otherwise would Simon have left a hidden note addressed to her? He had known he was going to die, guessed it would be Stevie who would find him, and left the note as an apology, somewhere it would be found by his cousin, rather than by the police.

"What if they'd made me a cup of tea? You didn't think of that, did you, you selfish bastard?"

Stevie flung the letter across the lounge and turned on the television.

Ten minutes later she muted the screen, crossed the room, and picked up the letter. Part of her wanted to put it in the kitchen sink and burn it, like microfilm that must be disposed of in a spy movie, but Stevie knew she would regret it. She turned her back on the TV screen where Naomi was demonstrating a range of bracelets and necklaces made from semiprecious stones, and went through to the spare bedroom.

The bed was still unmade, and smelled faintly of sweat. She stripped the sheets, left them in a mound on the floor, and opened the window. A pile of catalogs featuring forthcoming products was heaped on her desk. Stevie pushed them to one side. She had hung a framed poster above her workspace when she moved in, the alphabet in several fonts, pretty enough to be decorative, boring enough not to distract her too much. She sat staring at the print without seeing it, and then placed Simon's letter in front of her. Her fingertips touched her name again. She could feel the indents beneath the letters where Simon had pressed hard as he wrote. How strange that the pressure he had exerted should still persist, when the man himself was dead. Stevie slit the seal, unfolded the sheet of paper inside and started to read.

Dear Stevie,

I've never written you a love letter. I wish I was correcting that oversight now, but this is a letter I hope you never have to open. If you are reading it, it means I'm lying low and have an important request to make.

I have left a package in the loft space of your apartment. My plan is to collect it myself without your ever knowing, but if circumstances make that impossible, I beg you to conceal it in your most frivolous bag and deliver it unopened to Mr. Malcolm Reah at St. Thomas's. Do not entrust it to anyone else, no matter how polite, kind, or authoritative they are. It may be that something has already happened and that your first instinct is to turn to the police. Please don't. Malcolm will know what to do. He finishes his rounds at 3pm on weekdays and then goes directly to the ward office to write up his notes. Please deliver it to him there at your first opportunity.

I am about to set out for a meeting that I hope will make all of this superfluous but, if it doesn't go as I intend, and I somehow wash up somewhere without a phone signal, I want to make sure that you get the package into the right hands.

I'm not used to writing from the heart, but I want you to know that you mean more than sex to me (and you know how important I consider sex). It seems a little crass to write this in extremis, but I hope we have a future together.

Stevie, you are clever, persuasive, persistent, and resourceful, and have enough nous to know that doing the right thing doesn't always mean doing the obvious thing. Please make sure Malcolm Reah gets the package. It will sound melodramatic, but you might just save my life.

<u>All</u> My Love,
Simon

Beneath his signature, in a wilder, more impulsive hand, Simon had scrawled,

Trust no one except Reah.

Stevie was surprised to find that she was crying. It had been unfair of Simon to write to her of the future just before he died. It was as if he had taken a portion of her life with him.

She took a tissue from the box on her desk and wiped her eyes. Simon hadn't committed suicide, that much was clear. The letter didn't mean he hadn't died of natural causes though; weird coincidences did happen and stress could lead to sudden heart attacks, everyone knew that.

She reread the letter through a swim of tears. Her first thought was that Simon had misjudged her, and that she would leave the package where it was, telephone the police, and show them the letter. Perhaps she could ask for the officer who had interviewed her after she had reported Simon's death. He had been sympathetic, in a weary way. There was a phone on the corner of her desk. She reached out a hand and touched it.

Stevie pushed back the desk chair, went through to the hallway, dragged the stepladder from the cloakroom cupboard, and set it beneath the small ceiling hatch that led to the loft space. If the package was hidden there she would telephone the police. No one would blame her for checking first.

The ladder's rungs were cold against her bare feet. Stevie tipped the hatch open and put her head and shoulders into the loft. It was dark and spidery and she was forced to go back down and find a flashlight. She pointed its beam into the blackness and saw a shape, dark and flat, resting on one of the ceiling joists, beyond arm's reach.

"Fuck, Simon," Stevie whispered. "You're not exactly making things easy for me."

The days in bed had weakened her, and it took all of her strength to haul herself into the crawlspace that separated her ceiling from the apartment above. She lay there for a moment, gathering her resources, and then stuck the flashlight in her mouth and started to pull herself along one of the beams on her belly. Simon must have used a pole of some kind to push the package out of reach. He would never have fit his body into the tight space. A tiny fleck of darkness scuttled away from her. Stevie gasped, but the flashlight in her mouth stopped her from crying out.

The telephone started to ring down in the apartment below and Stevie remembered she had forgotten to call the TV station. She took the flashlight from between her teeth.

"Shit, shit, fuck, fuck, fuck, shit."

The beam of light swept the length of the narrow space. It was like being buried alive, sandwiched there in the dark. Something touched Stevie's face. She gasped and flung a hand out, but she had come too far to turn back.

Now that she was closer she could see that the package was oblong and wrapped in a plastic bag. Stevie stretched out, gripped the edge of the plastic with her fingertips and pulled it slowly toward her. "Got you." She grasped it tightly with both hands. She had expected the package to contain some kind of manuscript, but it was too hard-edged and heavy to be papers. Stevie edged her way backward until she was able to lower herself back, out of the hatch. Her feet groped for the ladder. It occurred to her that it would be ironic if she were to fall now and end up in the morgue beside Simon, but she managed the transition safely and set her burden on the top step.

The plastic bag was grimed with dust and cobwebs. She peeled it free to reveal a laptop zipped in an anonymous slipcase. Stevie tossed the empty plastic bag back into the loft, slotted the hatch cover back in place and carried the laptop down with her, realizing she was as filthy as the bag she had discarded.

She stripped off her tracksuit, went naked into the spare bedroom and set the laptop on her desk. There was nothing for it but to call the police; anything else would be foolish. She unzipped the slipcase and slid the laptop free. Simon had been devoted to a slim ultra-fast tablet, small enough to slip into his jacket pocket. This machine reminded her of her own computer, top of the line a few years ago, but not up-to-date enough for someone as techno-chic as Simon. Stevie opened the lid, pressed the power button, and watched the screen glow into life. The manufacturer's logo sailed toward her, followed by Windows' four-colored pane. The display shifted to black, Stevie saw her own naked torso reflected in it for an instant, and then the start page invited her to enter the password.

She typed in different variations of Simon's name, St. Thomas's Hospital, her own name, his cousin's name. Each try elicited an irritating wobble on the screen.

"Simon, you are really pissing me off now," Stevie muttered. She was going to have to stop these whispered appeals to the dead, especially when it seemed she had never really known the living man.

Eight

Stevie turned off the laptop, pulled on clean underwear, a pair of jeans, and a T-shirt, took the telephone through to the sitting room and called the TV station, hoping to God it wasn't Rachel who was producing the show that night.

"Hello?"

Rachel had recently abandoned the mockney accent she had cultivated for years and reverted back to the clear, well-formed vowels of public school and Oxford. Her *hello* hung in the air like a challenge.

"Rachel, it's me, I'm sorry I didn't call earlier but . . ." Stevie paused, unsure of what to say.

"But you know I run a relaxed ship and that it's easy come easy go around here?"

"I asked Joanie to call you. My boyfriend died and I've been throwing up for the past few days."

There was a pause on the line, and then Rachel said, "I didn't know you had a boyfriend."

"I don't anymore. I found him dead in his bed on Wednesday."

"I'm sorry." Rachel's voice was surprisingly gentle. "I had a cousin who accidentally took an overdose at a party. My sister and I found her the following morning. It was horrible."

"It wasn't drugs. He was a doctor."

"Either way it's a tragedy."

Rachel's tone suggested that doctors were far from being above suspicion.

"He didn't do drugs." Stevie wasn't sure why she was so anxious to labor the point. "The police think it was something called sudden adult death syndrome. You go to sleep and never wake up."

Rachel sighed. "I was about to send someone around to check on you."

"To check on me?"

"You live on your own, you called in sick, and then we heard nothing, complete radio silence. I got young Precious to call, but you didn't pick up. I was worried."

"I'm touched." Stevie silently cursed Joanie. She was probably off on one of the short-lived romantic adventures that had become a feature of her life since her Derek's defection.

"I'm genuinely sorry to hear about your boyfriend, Stevie," Rachel continued. "Believe me I wouldn't do this if I had any choice, but you're on shift tonight."

Stevie closed her eyes and took a deep breath. She had calculated the consequences of walking out on her job so many times that the urge to tell *Shop TV* to shove it automatically conjured the aura of unpaid bills and lawyers' letters. But proximity to death had made her reckless. She opened her eyes.

"Rachel, Simon died. I found him. I don't think I can go on live television and pretend to be wet about whatever crap it is we're punting tonight. Cut me bit of slack, just this once, please."

"I would love to, believe me I sympathize. I'll never forget finding my cousin Charlotte, it took me years to get over it. I'm not sure my sister ever recovered, but we're three presenters down, including Joanie who's in the hospital."

The guilt that had sat on Stevie since she had discovered Simon screwed itself tighter in her stomach.

"What's wrong with Joanie?"

"The same thing that's wrong with the rest of them, only more so, sickness, vomiting, diarrhea, high fever, hot and cold sweats. Don't you watch the news?"

"I told you, I was sick. I thought it was the shock of finding Simon."

"The great washed and unwashed of London are going down with the bug, as are a good portion of Paris, New York, and anywhere else you care to mention. People have died. That's why I was going to send someone around to check on you. I was worried you might have shuffled off this mortal coil."

For the first time Stevie thought she could detect a note of panic beneath Rachel's classy bonhomie. She walked to the window. The parade of shops in the street below looked as busy as ever. Rachel had a reputation for exaggerating, but she wouldn't lie about Joanie being in the hospital.

"Do you think that might have been what got your boy?" the producer asked.

It was on the tip of her tongue to tell Rachel that Simon hadn't been her boy, not really, but Stevie merely said, "No, I don't think so."

"If you can get here for seven, I'll get Precious to go over the briefings with you, and you can go on at eight."

"I look like shit."

"We'll all look like shit by then. I'm covering for Brian, and then doing my own gig tonight. Put your trust in makeup, darling. You'll look a million dollars by the time you go on." Now that everything had been settled, the producer was back to her usual brisk self. "I'll e-mail you the product lineup so you're not entirely in the dark when you arrive. We've got some top-notch stuff."

Rachel always described their merchandise as "top-notch stuff." Joanie, whose father and grandfather had worked the markets, called it swag.

Stevie asked, "Which hospital is Joanie in?"

"I'm not sure, hang on." Rachel had a muffled exchange with someone and then came back on the line. "St. Thomas's. She's in intensive care, but I'd keep away if I were you. This thing seems to be catching and we can't afford to lose another presenter."

"You forget I've already had it."

"That doesn't necessarily mean you're immune. My cousin Charlotte thought she was immune. Look where it got her."

Nine

Rachel had spoken as if London was in meltdown, but the Jubilee line showed no sign of crisis. The carriage was full and Stevie was forced to stand, her body just one of many sardined together, hurtling through the depths. Perhaps the trains were brightly lit to take people's minds off how dark the tunnels outside really were. The Underground car's fluorescence drained the passengers' complexions of any luster. The dark skin of the business-suited man beside her had turned gray, and the woman leaning against the pole by the door had taken on a jaded sheen that reminded Stevie of the print of Tretchikoff's green lady that had hung in her grandmother's hallway.

Stevie felt the weight of the city above her and wondered how deep beneath the ground she was. *West Hampstead . . . Finchley Road . . . Swiss Cottage . . . St. John's Wood . . .* The automated announcer declared the stations in her machine-plummy voice, not bothering to warn them to *mind the gap.* Londoners didn't dwell on the people who had died on the Underground: the workers sacrificed to its construction, the suicides and careless drunks crushed against the tracks, the terrorist bombings, Jean Charles de Menezes murdered by police marksmen. They walked past the memorial to those who had died in the King's Cross fire without a glance, because to remember too often would be crippling. Londoners were the blood of the city, and the city went on, regardless of the Black Death, the Great Fire, the Blitz, and terrorist bombings. It was only occasionally, when the train stopped between stations, that passengers caught each other's eye and wondered if their luck had run out.

Simon's laptop was in a satchel slung across Stevie's body. The weight of it pulled at her shoulder blade. The carriage shuddered to a halt and an elderly man's hand grazed her right breast. He gave her a half smile that might have been an apology or an invitation. Stevie's foot tensed with the urge to stamp on his toes but she merely shifted her bag to her other side, making a barrier between them.

Stevie thought she could scent the lingering smell of her illness beneath the blend of body odors and rubber that permeated the car. A droplet of sweat slid down her spine and she hoped her shirt wouldn't cling to it. She noticed an ex-member of the Cabinet further down the train. Cartoonists had made a feature of his hair, which was usually gelled in a blond quiff, but it had lost its bounce and was slumped greasily against his forehead. Stevie wondered how he dared to use public transport in the wake of failing wars, austerity, and job cuts, and then she spotted the trio shadowing him, men whose sharp suits needed no padding to broaden their shoulders. They looked tired, as if a life of being on the alert had taken its toll.

The Underground train dashed to a halt and the robot voice announced: *Westminster*. Stevie squeezed from the carriage, joining the stream of bodies making their way along the platform and into the corridors that led to the escalators. The station was a hundred or so years old, but the original interior had vanished beneath a monumental steel-and-concrete façade designed to remind travelers that this was a feat of engineering, a miracle to rival flesh and blood.

Stevie stepped on to one of the upward-bound escalators, aware of other bodies being ferried upward and downward in the vast hallway. The whoosh and rattle of the trains was still audible beyond the hum of the escalators, but otherwise the station was surprisingly quiet, as if this was a place where machines held sway and men and women held their tongues.

She imagined the noise that would fill the station if all of their thoughts became words, the racket of it. The idea felt like a hangover from her fever. Stevie gripped the moving banister and looked up toward the exit. The angle of the stairwell was dizzying.

Then, suddenly, the hum of the machine world was fractured by shouting. Stevie looked across the rows of escalators and saw a man tumbling down the metal steps, limp-limbed and flailing. Somewhere, someone must have hit the emergency button because the staircase stalled. People reached toward him, trying to stop his progress, but the man's body had gathered momentum. He crashed into a woman on the stairs below; she fell too, and then it seemed that a shoal of people were falling.

A couple of youths managed to leap on to the banisters, but gravity was faster than even gym-fit commuters and other people were caught in the descent. Stevie had watched countless movie villains tumble to their deaths, but cinema hadn't prepared her for the chaos of it, or the sound of bone on metal that seemed to rise above the shouting. Her escalator juddered to a halt and she stood, frozen, unsure of what to do. The screaming died into sobs and agitated chatter, and she heard a train rush into the station. Down below, people were gathering. Someone was crying. Someone else shouted for a doctor. And then slowly, unbelievably, the line of people on the stairway ahead of Stevie started to move, and she moved with them, climbing out of the Underground toward the light.

She overheard a passing teenager, who might have been Italian, say, "He was swaying and then he fell. I saw him. It was too quick to do anything. What could I do? I was on the other staircase."

A cockney voice answered, "Nah, mate, he was pushed. I saw it with my own eyes. A white man pushed him down the steps."

"He's got the sickness," said an elderly lady. "That's how it hits you. One moment you're okay, the next you're dead."

"It was gravity got him," the cockney youth said. "It never lets up for a moment."

Then they were outside, embraced by the ever-present rumble of traffic and the stale city air that not even the river could freshen. For an instant the commuters, newly released from the world below, were distinct from the pedestrians aboveground, as if their mortality had risen to the surface with them and left its mark. Then they dispersed, and were absorbed into London's careless anonymity, taking the memory of the falling man with them.

Stevie wove her way between the tourists who crammed the streets around Westminster, viewing the sites through the lenses of their cameras. The satchel containing the laptop banged against her thigh. An ambulance was trying to force its way through the traffic toward the Underground station, its sirens screaming. It was agonizing, the sound of the sirens, its thwarted progress. She looked away, at the Thames and the looming Houses of Parliament. They seemed unreal, like a backdrop rolled out for a low-budget movie that needed a quick establishing shot. This was what tourists imagined when they thought of the city: Big Ben and red buses, the London Eye and bobbies with silly helmets. And it was all there waiting for them.

But did they see the rest? Stevie wondered. The street people and tense demos, the cheap chicken fryers whose sleeping bags lay bundled in the back of the shop, the men and women hanging around King's Cross with a kind word and the offer of a bed for the night to runaways they would soon put to work?

Maybe the tourists did see, and felt as helpless as she did. It was a globalized world after all, and there was no reason to imagine that their capital cities were any different. The screams of the people falling were still in her mind. Stevie felt a sudden urge to go back, but didn't break her stride as she crossed Westminster Bridge. Simon had trusted her to deliver the laptop. It was the only service she could do for him now.

Ten

St. Thomas's Hospital was gray and dirty against the blue sky. The filth of the city clung to its once white façade as if drawn there by the sickness within. Stevie felt a familiar sense of dread, but she walked through the automatic doors and into the foyer.

Inside, St. Thomas's looked more like a small mall than a hospital. A line ran all the way from the tills in the Marks & Spencer concession to the bunches of two-for-three-pounds roses and serviceable carnations stationed in buckets at its door. The entrance hall was busy with workers on their lunch breaks but Stevie caught glimpses of the building's real purpose among the crowd.

A thin man with a stethoscope draped around his neck stood by the elevators, talking on his cell phone. Two women in green scrubs chatted as they walked toward the exit. A policeman shook his head and laughed at something an ambulance driver had just told him. Stevie thought she could spot some relatives of patients too. Tired-looking low-wattage ghosts of themselves, hoarding their energy for those moments when they needed to dredge up a healing smile or their heart's blood.

Stevie went to the reception desk and explained that she was looking for Mr. Reah. "I think he'll be in one of the children's wards."

The receptionist consulted her computer. Stevie stared at a poster on the wall behind the desk.

COUGHING
VOMITING
DIARRHEA
RASH
SWOLLEN GLANDS

If you experience a combination of three or more of these symptoms, avoid sharing them with your friends and family.

OBSERVE GOOD HYGIENE
CATCH COUGHS IN A DISPOSABLE TISSUE
DO NOT PREPARE FOOD FOR OTHERS
WASH YOUR HANDS FREQUENTLY
STAY AT HOME

CALL 0800 669 9961

The receptionist looked up at her.

"You're in the wrong building. You want the private part of the hospital."

Stevie thought she sensed disapproval in the other woman's voice, but perhaps she was just hearing an echo of her own surprise. Simon had never mentioned that he did private work. Stevie had imagined him tending sick children regardless of their parents' means. She covered her disappointment with a smile and asked if it would be possible to visit Joan Caniparoli.

"I was told she was in intensive care." Stevie's voice was salesgirl-bright. "But I think there's a good chance she'll be out of there by now."

The receptionist asked her to spell Joanie's second name and rattled it into the computer keyboard.

Her eyes met Stevie's. "Are you a relative?"

"A friend."

"I'm afraid Mrs. Caniparoli is still in intensive care." This time there was sympathy in the woman's voice. "That means only close relatives are allowed to visit."

Stevie wanted to tell the woman that she saw more of Joanie than any of her relatives did, but the reception telephone buzzed. The receptionist answered it and returned her attention to her computer screen, looking for whatever the person on the other end of the line needed to know.

Stevie followed the directions to the private wing. There was a flutter of apprehension in her stomach, a quickening of the feeling she still got just before the studio clock hit the hour and they went on air. She glanced at her cell phone and then switched it off. It was 2:45 p.m. so she should be in good time for the end of Mr. Reah's rounds. Stevie straightened her back, trying to assume the air of someone who had a right to prowl hospital corridors. If anyone asked her what she was up to, she would tell them the truth. She was delivering a laptop from the recently deceased Dr. Simon Sharkey to Mr. Reah. What could be more reasonable? After that she would go to intensive care and tell whatever lies she needed to, the same way Joanie would if Stevie was lying alone in a hospital bed.

She shifted her bag, transferring the weight of the computer to her other shoulder, and wondered how Joanie would look. The thought conjured a memory of Julia Sharkey's gaunt cheekbones, the wry smile in the skull face.

"We doctors have a way with death."

Stevie hoped, for Joanie's sake, that they had a way with life too.

Eleven

Stevie washed her hands with the antibacterial gel from the dispenser in the corridor and pulled at the door to the children's ward. It refused to open. She tried pushing and then pulled again, but it stood firm against her.

"What did you expect me to do, Simon?" she muttered beneath her breath. "Use a battering ram?"

There was a security pad on the wall, similar to the one she swiped her identity card on at the television station. She thought again of Simon's letter, his appeal to her ingenuity. But she was powerless against locks and electronic alarms.

Footsteps sounded in the corridor behind her. Stevie could tell it was a man by the confident length of his stride and the flat sound his shoes made against the floor. She took a step backward, fished out the small handbag she had slipped into her satchel with the laptop and started rummaging in it. When the stranger was almost upon her, she tipped the bag's contents, a jumble of receipts, pens, card wallet, purse and cosmetics, on to the floor.

"Damn." The case of an Yves Saint Laurent lipstick had cracked when it hit the ground, and her curse wasn't entirely an act. Stevie crouched and started gathering up the muddle of stuff. "I'm sorry."

She had hoped the newcomer might bend and help her pick up the spilled contents, but she could feel him standing behind her. Stevie glanced up and saw a tall, broad-shouldered man in a white coat staring down at her. His brown eyes were shielded by glasses, but his stiff posture was as impatient as a clicking finger.

"I'm sorry." She got to her feet, apologizing again. "You're in a hurry." Stevie read the name card pinned to his lapel as she stood up: *Dr. Ahumibe.* The doctor's expression was stern, but his eyes did a quick flit, down, then up her body. Stevie smiled, forcing herself not to show too many teeth. Face-to-face selling required more subtlety than the brash, late-night TV pitches she was used to giving. "Can you tell me where to find Mr. Reah, please? I was meant to meet him after his rounds, but I seem to have lost my bearings."

Dr. Ahumibe closed his eyes for a second. His expression was tight, like that of a man who knew he was reaching the end of his tether, but was determined to stay in control.

"I'm sorry," Stevie said again. "It's a big hospital, easy to get lost."

The doctor opened his eyes. He swiped the door and ushered her into the ward.

"Are you a close colleague of Mr. Reah?" His voice was deep and upper class, touched with a hint of an accent she couldn't quite identify.

"No." The question startled her.

"A friend?"

"We haven't met before."

"That's good." He took off his glasses and dragged a hand across his face. Stevie's calves felt tight, the way they did after a long run, and some instinct told her to turn around and walk away, but she stayed where she was. The doctor replaced his glasses. "I'm sorry to have to tell you that Mr. Reah is dead."

"Dead?" Stevie repeated the word, as if saying it would make death more real. "When?"

"Yesterday."

The edges of the ward seemed to sharpen. She saw the gray floor, the doors to the private patients' rooms, the nurses' station midway down the corridor, everything sure and distinct.

"Was it an accident?"

"No, it wasn't an accident. But it was sudden." He glanced at his watch. "I'm sorry, but you'll appreciate we're working at full capacity. The ward is two doctors down and the hospital as a whole is facing a massive challenge. Perhaps I can point you toward someone else who can help you?"

Stevie took a step backward. The smell of the hospital was in her nostrils; the scent of her illness filtered through a chemical wash, harsh and sweet.

"No, it's fine, thanks."

She turned to go but there must have been something furtive about the way she moved, because the doctor gripped her by the wrist, keeping her there.

"Are you a journalist?"

Stevie wondered why the presence of a journalist would spook him. She forced another smile. "No." There was a move she had learned in self-defense classes when she was a student—a chop to the attacker's forearm, designed to hit a nerve and release his grasp—but force was always the last resort. She lowered her voice and whispered, "Let go of my arm. You're hurting me."

"It's not acceptable for people like you to go wandering around in search of an angle or a scoop, or whatever it is you call it." The doctor kept his voice low, but his words were like bullets. "This is a hospital. The children on this ward are extremely sick. Some of them are dying. Is that a big enough story for you?"

A piece of spittle had landed on Stevie's cheek. She resisted the urge to wipe it away.

"You have a good instinct for professions. I used to be a journalist but I haven't worked as one for quite a while. My name is Stephanie Flint. I was Simon Sharkey's girlfriend. He asked me to deliver something to Mr. Reah."

The doctor let go of her arm, as if her skin had suddenly scalded him, but a note of suspicion still colored his voice.

"Simon never mentioned you."

"We hadn't been going out for very long."

"So why the subterfuge?"

"Simon probably thought it wasn't your business who he went out with."

The doctor touched her arm.

"That's not what I meant. Why didn't you tell me who you are?" His anger had vanished and his voice was gentle.

Stevie couldn't tell him about the letter from beyond the dead, the trouble Simon had gone to, hiding the laptop in her loft, the resolution she had made to follow his instructions.

"Simon was insistent that I deliver the package to Mr. Reah personally. I didn't realize I had to introduce myself."

"What's in it?"

"I don't know."

Ahumibe was still staring at Stevie as if she was a ghost. His face was gaunt, but there was a hint of flesh around his jowls that suggested he might recently have lost weight. He sighed and she saw him making an effort to return to himself.

"I would have gotten in touch to pass on my condolences to you, if I'd known." He shook his head. "Simon always joked that he was married to medicine. Are you organizing the funeral?"

"No, a cousin is taking care of his estate."

His estate. Stevie didn't think she had ever used the phrase before. It sounded like an expression lifted from a Victorian novel, not anything that could be relevant to her.

"I see." The doctor gave her a weary smile and she saw that he was handsome. "I'm John Ahumibe. I was a friend of Simon's. Whatever this package is, if it's hospital property then it must be returned. I can make sure that it finds the right home."

Stevie drew the bag closer to her.

"That's kind of you, but Simon was insistent that it went to Mr. Reah personally."

Dr. Ahumibe's voice was patient. "Sadly that is no longer possible."

"Then I'll pass it to his executor. She can decide what to do next."

Dr. Ahumibe gave a swift look down the ward.

"Come with me." He touched Stevie's elbow and led her into a small office off the main ward, shutting the door. The room was clean and white, but it appeared that whoever occupied it had been suddenly called away; papers were splayed across the desk, a half-drunk cup of coffee abandoned beside them.

Stevie asked, "Was this Mr. Reah's office?"

"Mr. Reah generally wrote up his notes in here, but the room wasn't for his exclusive use. We're pushed for space, like everywhere else in the hospital." He gave a rueful, upside-down smile. "Everywhere else in the city."

"What did he die of?"

Dr. Ahumibe put his hands in the pockets of his white coat and leaned against the desk, staring down at his shoes.

"I don't know." He raised his head and looked at Stevie. "Nobody knows, but people are dying from it. Hospitals might not be the healthiest places to be right now."

"Are they ever?" She meant it as a joke, but her voice broke on the final word. "Sorry." Stevie massaged her temples with her fingertips, wishing she could stop apologizing. "It's been a long day." She thought of Joanie in intensive care, remembered the man falling from the Underground escalator and the old lady saying, "He's got the sickness." She asked, "How serious is it?"

"No one's sure yet." Dr. Ahumibe pulled out a chair from beneath the desk. "Sit down." She sat and he squatted level with her, scrutinizing her face. "You're pale. Do you feel feverish?"

"I'm fine." No one had stood so close to her for days. Not since Joanie had greeted her with a kiss before they last went on air. "I saw an accident on the way here and I'm a bit hospital-phobic, that's all." The doctor smelled like Simon, Stevie realized, the same scent of soap and long hospital hours. "Plus I've been indoors for the last few days. I came down with something after I found Simon. It laid me out. I think I'm still recovering."

She pulled away from him and Dr. Ahumibe sank into another chair, his feet planted wide apart, body hunched forward, his brown eyes still fixed on hers. His hair was black and neatly shorn, showing the shape of his skull, the swell of the back of his head.

"You found him?"

"Yes."

She thought he was going to ask her about it, but he said, "It's hard to believe." His skin looked muddy with tiredness.

"I know." She had seen Simon's body with her own eyes, but it seemed impossible that the flesh that had held her flesh was easing into decay. No, she reminded herself, the decay had been stalled. His body was in a freezer somewhere, awaiting a postmortem. Dr. Ahumibe's brow puckered with deliberate concentration or concern, she wasn't sure which.

"Tell me your symptoms."

Stevie listed the horrors that had pursued her. The doctor nodded from time to time, as if to show she was confirming what he already knew. When she had finished he said, "And you feel okay now?"

"A little weak, prone to queasiness, but basically fine."

He nodded, his face closed and careful.

"It's good to meet a survivor."

"Surely only people who are already weak are in real danger." The words made her sound like a eugenicist and she added, "I mean old and very young people, or people who are already ill."

"Mr. Reah was a hale-and-hearty fifty-five." The doctor clasped his hands together.

"And Simon? Is that what killed him?"

Dr. Ahumibe looked away from her, toward a small window high on the exterior wall and a glimpse of blue sky. Stevie followed his gaze and thought how like a prison cell the room was.

"No. From what I heard, Simon died of something else." He ran a hand across his skull. "Simon and I had known each other a long time. We worked together here, and as part of the same small team in private practice. That's why I was surprised he hadn't mentioned you. Whatever it was he wanted you deliver to Mr. Reah, he would have trusted me with it, now that Malcolm's gone."

Stevie hesitated. Simon's letter was insistent that she trust no one except Reah. But Reah was dead and Dr. John Ahumibe had a tired, anxious air that made her want to confide in him. Behind her a door opened.

"You're needed on the ward." The nurse who had entered was dark and pretty, with black hair that looked as if it would break into a riot of curls, were it not besieged by a barricade of pins.

Ahumibe gave her a small nod and got to his feet.

"Two seconds." He looked at Stevie, his eyes mild and unreadable. "Why not open the package here and make up your mind once you've seen what's in it?"

Dr. Ahumibe had the sort of voice designed to soothe frightened patients, or to gently break bad news, but the reasonableness of it recalled Simon's letter. He had told her not to entrust the laptop *to anyone else, no matter how polite, kind or authoritative.* Stevie slung her satchel over her shoulder.

"I'll call if it's anything belonging to the hospital."

The nurse was still standing in the doorway, watching them as if they were part of some play. Her good looks and neat figure were marred by her sour expression.

"Excuse me," Stevie said. "I need to go."

For a second Stevie thought the other woman was going to block her way, but she held the door open.

"Miss Flint." Dr. Ahumibe followed them out of the room. "I'm afraid I'm going to have to ask you to stay a little longer." He glanced at the nurse. "Miss Flint may have survived the virus."

The nurse looked at her. Stevie saw that her irises were almost pure black, her eyes shadowed with lack of sleep.

"You had it?"

Stevie shrugged. "I'm not sure."

The nurse started to say something, but the ward doors opened and a thin man wearing a creased white coat over an equally crumpled blue shirt and chinos strode toward them. The new arrival was almost as tall as Dr. Ahumibe and as pale and blond as the other man was dark. Dr. Ahumibe said, "Miss Flint's had the virus and lived to tell the tale."

The man turned his Weimaraner eyes on her, his face keen and intelligent.

"In that case you could be a rather useful young woman." He smiled. "I wonder if you would oblige us with a few samples. Don't worry, they'll be painless."

Stevie could see a couple of nurses at the nurses' station looking at them, wondering what the huddle was about. She wanted to leave, but the thought of Joanie stalled her. The idea that the solution might lie in her blood was strangely nauseating, but if she could help, then she would.

"I have to go to work later. I'm happy to give you whatever samples you need but I'm afraid I can't hang around."

"In that case, Nurse Webb will take you down to the lab." The pale man looked at Dr. Ahumibe. "Makes more sense for them to take whatever samples they need there." He nodded to the nurse and put an arm around his colleague's shoulder, steering him away from the two women without waiting for an answer. "Do you have a moment? I've got to dash off and pick up William in a minute."

Dr. Ahumibe murmured, "Miss Flint was Simon's girlfriend." The newcomer's eyes glanced back at her, sharp and quick as a scalpel. Dr. Ahumibe added, "She dropped in to deliver something from Simon to Malcolm but . . ." He let the sentence trail away.

"O-h." The newcomer dragged out the vowel, like a politician trying to buy time before answering a tricky question. He let go of Ahumibe's shoulder and took Stevie's hand in his. "I'm Alexander Buchanan, the pharmacist in the team. Please accept my condolences. In our profession you have to press on, regardless of personal feelings, but please believe me, everyone is devastated by Simon's death." The pharmacist's hands were warm and dry and there was genuine regret in his expression. "I'm happy to take responsibility for whatever it was Simon wanted to pass on to Mr. Reah."

Stevie looked at the doors lining the ward. Behind each one were beds bearing small, sick bodies. She returned her gaze to the doctors. Their white coats were clean, but they spoke to her of blood and infection.

"I'll pass the package to Simon's cousin. She's his executor and a doctor, so she'll know what to do with it."

"Whatever you think best." Buchanan took a notebook and a ballpoint pen from the pocket of his white coat and handed them to her. "Do you mind leaving me a note of where we can contact you?" His smile was apologetic. "As Simon's friends and colleagues, we're keen to pin down the exact cause of his death. At present it all seems a bit vague. I assume you'd like to be alerted to whatever we come up with."

"Of course."

Stevie scribbled down *Shop TV*'s address and her cell number, and handed it back to Buchanan.

Nurse Webb said, "Follow me," and walked toward the exit. Stevie trailed her through the double doors and out into the corridor. The nurse went on, but Stevie paused and looked through the glass doors, back into the ward.

Ahumibe and Buchanan were still standing there, deep in conversation. Beyond them stood the closed doors of the sick children's rooms. She wondered why the doctors didn't go to them.

"It's this way."

Nurse Webb's voice echoed, tired and impatient, along the hallway. Stevie turned and hurried after her.

Twelve

Nurse Webb resembled a small gymnast in her white scrubs and tennis shoes, lithe and strong, able to pull more than her own weight. Stevie matched her pace, keeping an arm's length between them. A glow of resentment surrounded the other woman, like a radiation field it would be unwise to enter.

Two stretcher-laden carts, each with an orderly at their head, exited an elevator at the end of the corridor and trundled toward them. Nurse Webb hurried on, neatly negotiating the procession, but Stevie felt the same panic that sometimes overtook her at the sound of a siren when she was driving through crowded traffic. She stepped to one side, flattening herself against the wall, and let them pass.

A woman of about her age lay motionless beneath a white sheet on the first stretcher. The woman's blond hair was cut in a neat asymmetrical bob. Her lips were cracked and pale, her eyelids tinged with blue. The woman's eyebrows were dark. Stevie caught herself noting the detail and thinking that the contrast in colors was too much. She censored the thought almost as it occurred, but she saw a blur of lipstick smeared on the woman's mouth, mascara crusting her eyelashes, and realized that, earlier that morning, the woman had been well enough to examine her own features in the mirror and apply her makeup. Stevie's eyes met the porter's and he looked away.

The second stretcher was ferrying a young girl. A sequined clasp pinned her long black hair on the top of the girl's head; her skin was sallow and sheened with sweat. Her mother and father followed behind, the mother's pink shalwar kamiz looking festive and out of place in a hospital corridor, her father's beard and military bearing lending him the air of a Russian tsar. Stevie saw the husband take his wife by the hand, and dropped her gaze, wondering if it was anxiety that had drained the couple's faces, or if they were wilting beneath the same sickness that had felled their daughter.

She caught up with Nurse Webb at the elevator. The other woman looked at her for the first time since they had left the ward and Stevie saw again the tiredness blighting her eyes.

"Were you really going out with Dr. Sharkey?"

"Yes."

The elevator rumbled down the shaft toward them.

"I'm sorry for your loss." The nurse's voice was flat and free of emotion, as if she had learned the condoling phrase by rote. "It must have been a shock."

Stevie saw again Simon's face in the mirror, the awkward angle of his head, the line of spittle trailing from his mouth.

"Yes, it was a shock."

The elevator doors opened, and they were met with the stares of the people cramped inside, whey-faced and packed together as if in an upright tomb. Nurse Webb put an arm on Stevie's elbow and stepped smartly forward, taking Stevie with her. The elevator's inhabitants squeezed impossibly closer to make room for them. They traveled downward in a fog of sweat and recycled breath. The elevator shed occupants at each floor, like a metaphor for the randomness of death, until Stevie was left alone with Nurse Webb, but it wasn't until they stepped out into the cool of a deserted basement corridor that the nurse spoke again.

"Dr. Sharkey was a good surgeon. He saved a lot of children's lives."

It sounded like an accusation, and Stevie wondered if the nurse thought Simon might still be alive if he had found a girlfriend who had known how to take proper care of him. She said, "Simon spoke about the hospital a lot, but it was generally funny stories, the human things that happened." She smiled at the irony of it. "It's only now that I realize I was never really clear what Simon did. I knew he was a surgeon, I knew he worked with sick kids, but he never talked about the details."

"You didn't know about his cerebral palsy work?" The hint of accusation was back in the nurse's voice.

"No."

Nurse Webb's small chin jutted out. She reminded Stevie of the war memorial in her home town: a female Victory, her triumph tempered by the death of so many gallant youths.

"Dr. Sharkey was modest about it, but he was part of a major breakthrough in treating the condition."

Simon had liked chic restaurants and loud nightclubs that made her ears ring the next morning. He had liked her to bite his shoulders when they made love, and to leave marks so that he could remember it later. He was a member of a carpool with access to a series of sports cars that drew pedestrians' stares. Simon's being a surgeon had seemed part of his glamour. He had encouraged her to see him that way, Stevie realized, and she wondered if that was the reason he had kept her separate from his family and friends.

They had been walking along the corridor all this while and had now reached a set of double doors. Stevie followed Nurse Webb through them, into a room that reminded her of the television studio just before a program went live, every member of the crew focused on their task, working against the seconds, with a determination that left no room for panic.

Nurse Webb seemed to lose her poise for a moment. She hesitated, as if unsure of who to talk to, but then a woman in a white coat looked up from her task and asked, "Yes?"

"I've brought Miss Flint down to have her blood tested." Nurse Webb produced a form Stevie didn't remember anyone filling out. "Dr. Ahumibe called ahead to let you know we were on our way."

The woman's hair was neatly tied back in a ponytail but she touched a hand to her forehead as if expecting to push away some stray strands.

"Who did he speak to?"

"I'm not sure."

"In that case, I suggest you find out."

"Miss Flint thinks she's survived the virus. Dr. Ahumibe thought it might be worth taking some samples from her."

"That's a lot of speculation." The woman's voice had a Liverpudlian lilt. Her skin was pale gold beneath the harsh fluorescent lights. Her hand went to her temple again, smoothing her already smooth hair. "But I guess speculation is pretty much all that we have at the moment." She took the form from Nurse Webb and glanced at Stevie. "I'm Dr. Chu. How do you feel?"

"Okay. A lot better than I did."

"Good." Dr. Chu's grin reminded Stevie of the smiles she forced after hours of late-night selling, but her glance was sharp enough to cut through flesh and into bone. "If you don't mind waiting here for a moment, I'll see if I can get someone to do the deed."

"I can do it if you like."

Nurse Webb was wearing her war-memorial expression again, sweetly noble and ready to sacrifice someone else's blood.

"Are you sure?" Dr. Chu unlocked a metal cabinet and took out a cellophane-wrapped syringe, not giving the nurse time to change her mind. She smiled at Stevie. "We may want to hang on to you for a little while."

"I have to go to work." Stevie hated the combination of apology and panic in her voice. "I'll come back if you need me, but I can't hang around much longer."

"Ah yes, work." Dr. Chu looked at her as if she was an interesting sample it might be worth putting under the microscope. "The sky may be falling on our heads, but the wheels of commerce grind inexorably on." She turned her attention back to Nurse Webb. "You really think she has had it?"

The nurse shrugged. "That's why Dr. Ahumibe sent her down."

"Okay, I'll go and speak with Mr. James."

Dr. Chu turned her back on them and returned to the mysterious busyness of the lab.

Nurse Webb pulled out a chair. There was nothing to stop Stevie from walking out of the room and then out of the hospital, but she sat down, tucking the bag with Simon's precious computer in it between her feet. The thought of the needle piercing her skin made her feel sick. She asked, "Those children in the ward upstairs, where I was to meet Mr. Reah, do they all have cerebral palsy?"

"Some of them." Nurse Webb tore open an antibacterial wipe. "Roll up your sleeve, please."

Stevie unfastened the cuff of her thin cotton shirt and pushed the sleeve up as far as it would go. She held out her arm and the nurse swabbed the crook of her elbow.

"At least you've got good-sized veins."

Stevie wondered at the "at least," but she said, "That's the best compliment I've had in a while." The antiseptic was cold against her skin and she swallowed a gasp. "Will the children in the ward still get cured, even though Simon won't be there to help them?"

Nurse Webb broke the seal on the syringe's cellophane packet. "It's not as easy as that. I'm afraid there isn't a straightforward cure."

She fastened a tourniquet around Stevie's upper arm.

"But the breakthrough he made will still help them?"

"This will be easier if you don't look." Stevie turned her head to look up at the ceiling and steeled herself against the needle's sting. She felt Nurse Webb's fingers firm against her flesh, and then the burn of the needle as it pierced her skin. "Don't worry." The nurse's voice was unexpectedly soothing. "We don't need much." Stevie felt the nurse attach something else to the puncture and then the fluid being drawn from her body. Nurse Webb repeated, "Look away," but Stevie glanced at her arm and saw her blood sliding through a transparent tube into a sealed bag. A drop of moisture landed on her arm. She looked up and saw that the other woman's face was shiny with perspiration. Nurse Webb said, "Dr. Sharkey was part of a team. He'll be sadly missed, but they should be able to continue without him."

They sat for a while in silence. Stevie stared at the satchel between her feet until she felt the nurse's cool fingers against her skin. "Hold that until the bleeding stops." The nurse pressed a cotton-wool pad to the wound.

Stevie did as she was told, her fingers dark against the whiteness of the cotton wool. Some of the polish had peeled from her nails. She should have made time for a manicure before this evening's program but she would have to rely on whoever was on makeup to touch up her nail polish instead.

She asked, "Did Simon's team offer their treatment on the National Health Service?"

Nurse Webb held up the bag of blood, checking its seal. The hospital lights shone redly against it.

"Unfortunately the treatment is too expensive to roll out on the NHS. It can only be obtained privately."

"So it's only available to children with rich parents?"

Nurse Webb gave the bag a last check and labeled it.

"The only way to make the treatment cheap enough for the National Health Service was to develop it, and the only way to do that is through private practice." She dumped the needle she had used on Stevie in a trashcan marked *Sharps*. "Dr. Sharkey could have lived entirely off his private earnings, but he continued to work for the NHS as well."

Stevie pressed the pad to her arm, trying to displace the nausea in her stomach with a more manageable pain.

"But he profited from sick children."

"No." Nurse Webb sounded exasperated. "He helped sick children. Without Dr. Sharkey and his team the treatment wouldn't exist. You were going out with him. You know he was a good man."

"Yes," Stevie said.

The large apartment made sense now, the over-the-top cars and overpriced restaurants too. She lifted the cotton-wool pad. The puncture mark was bold against her skin, but the blood had congealed, and a bruise was already forming. She could see Dr. Chu walking toward them from the other side of the department, deep in conversation with a tall sandy-haired man. Dr. Chu nodded in her direction, they stopped, and the man said something to the doctor that made her glance again at Stevie.

Nurse Webb said, "Dr. Sharkey made a lot of sacrifices for his profession. Whatever he earned, it was less than he deserved." There was a catch in her voice, a threat of tears. "You should be glad he enjoyed life while he could."

"I am." Stevie was watching the tall man now. He was on the telephone, talking intently to someone. He glanced in her direction, caught her gaze and quickly looked away. Stevie wondered if he was speaking to Dr. Ahumibe and what had made her think that he might be. She said, "Why would they want to keep me here?"

"If you survived the virus, there might be tests that we can do that could help us find a vaccine."

"Are there other survivors here?"

Dr. Chu was back at their side. She took a notepad from her pocket and wrote something in it. "We've taken samples from a few." She turned to Nurse Webb. "I think we can manage from here."

The nurse hesitated. Stevie saw the sweat on her forehead glisten beneath the harsh fluorescent lights and asked, "Are you okay?"

Nurse Webb gave a curt nod, but her attention was focused on Dr. Chu.

"You should keep her until you find an antidote."

Across the ward, as if on cue, someone stumbled. There was the sound of smashing glass and a flutter of activity, but although they both glanced in its direction neither Dr. Chu nor Nurse Webb moved to help.

"Thank you, nurse." The doctor touched Nurse Webb's arm and her voice softened. "Don't worry. We're not the only ones working on this. Labs all over the world are pooling their resources."

The nurse stepped closer to Dr. Chu and Stevie saw the doctor take an involuntary step backward. She wiped a hand across her face and held it up, displaying the slick of moisture across her palm.

Dr. Chu said, "Nurse, if you are feeling unwell, follow procedure and take yourself to quarantine."

Nurse Webb's hand was still raised and for a moment Stevie thought she was going to touch the doctor's face. But then she turned and walked slowly from the room, letting the door swing shut behind her.

"Will she be all right?"

Dr. Chu was still staring at the door, as if unsure of whether she should go after the nurse.

"Do you mean will she live?"

The starkness of the question shook Stevie, but she was surprised to realize that it was exactly what she had meant.

"I suppose so."

The doctor looked at her. "I've been doing my homework. In the fourteenth century sixty percent of Europe's population died from plague. It's a myth that it was caused by rats. The truth is, we still don't really know what it was. Of those that survived, there wasn't anyone who hadn't lost someone close to them. Many lost their entire families."

"This isn't anything like that though, is it?"

The doctor looked away. She lifted her hand to her hair again. This time a few strands had escaped. She tucked them back in place.

"It's impossible to know."

"You said labs across the world are working on it. Surely someone will find an antidote?"

"Perhaps, but there's not a physician alive who isn't regularly reminded that we've failed to find an effective cure for the common cold." Dr. Chu glanced toward where the tall, sandy-haired man was standing. He had put the phone down and was beckoning to her. "I think Mr. James needs me. Is there anyone waiting at home for you? Children?"

"Why?"

"It might be useful if you could hang around for a bit longer." She gave Stevie's arm a reassuring squeeze. "Don't worry. I'll make sure you're kept in one piece."

Stevie watched Dr. Chu cross the room to where Mr. James was waiting and saw him hand the doctor a piece of paper. She scanned its contents quickly and the two began to talk in low murmurs. Mr. James looked at Stevie. Dr. Chu followed his gaze and then they stepped closer, like conspirators toward the end of an intrigue.

Stevie flung her bag over her shoulder, stepped smartly through the double doors and walked out of the department. She thought she heard a shout behind her and upped her pace, sprinting along the corridor until she found a fire escape. She took the stairs as fast as she could, feeling the blood pounding in her head, and blessing all the dark, wet winter mornings when she had forced herself out of bed and into her running gear. When she was sure that the clatter on the metal staircase was caused by her footsteps alone, Stevie paused on a landing, bending forward, panting hard until she recovered her breath. Then she stepped out into the silence of a deserted hospital corridor. A sign on the wall pointed toward intensive care. She glanced in her bag at the laptop and then walked in that direction.

Thirteen

Joanie had once told Stevie that she believed in alien abductions. She looked like the subject of an alien experiment now, webbed in a network of tubes so dense and complex they might be outgrowths of her body. Joanie's golden-brown glow had sunk to a sallow beige. Her eyes were closed and caved deep in their sockets, like the absent eyes of a death mask. Stevie whispered her name, "Joanie," and a voice behind her said, "It's no good, she can't hear you."

Joanie's husband Derek had lost the grifter's swagger that had sometimes made him seem a more likely candidate for prison than the police force. He stepped into the room and stood at the end of the bed with his head bowed, as if he was about to say a prayer.

Stevie asked, "What's wrong with her?"

"Out on the streets they're calling it the sweats." Derek turned to face her. He had taken off his uniform jacket and rolled up the sleeves of his white shirt, but kept his stab vest on. He looked as if he was broiling beneath its weight. "In here they don't know what to call it. I suppose they'll come up with a bunch of letters and numbers that won't mean much to the rest of us. The sweats seems as good a name as any to me."

Stevie had spent a fair bit of time in Derek's company when he and Joanie had been together. They had gone out for drinks, shared meals, once even spent a weekend together in a rented cottage in Dorset, but Stevie had never really been alone with her friend's husband. She hadn't seen him at all since he had told Joanie that he couldn't help it if he loved someone else.

Stevie had heard the story so often it had almost become part of her own stock of memories: Joanie turning to greet her husband as he stepped into the bedroom, her recent purchases laid out on the counterpane; the cold beer she had uncapped for him untouched on the bedside table; Derek muttering accusations and excuses, not daring to meet Joanie's eye as he bundled his clothes into the sports bag he used for soccer practice; his voice breaking as he said goodbye; the look he gave Joanie before he walked out of their bedroom and then out of the house for the last time; the bottle of beer still sweating cold on the table.

"Why are you here, Derek?"

"I'm still her husband. Joanie always hated doctors. She'd be terrified if she knew she was in the hospital."

Less than a week ago Joanie had been her usual sweet-vain self, dragging Derek into their on-air sales pitch, pretending she did it to humiliate him, though she and Stevie both knew it was her own form of SOS, an appeal for him to come home.

"Doesn't Francesca mind?"

Derek ran a handkerchief over his number-one buzz cut.

"I don't suppose she knows I'm here. Her mom stays out in Norfolk; she took off and drove up there. We were meant to be going on vacation, first week with her mom, second week on a barge, but all leave's canceled and . . ."

He let the sentence trail away, but his eyes were on Joanie's slight figure draped in tubes on the bed.

Stevie asked, "Will she be okay?"

Derek's shrug was miserable.

"Joanie's one of the lucky ones. She caught it early and got hooked up to all this." Derek gestured toward the paraphernalia weaving its way in and around Joanie's bed. "There's people who look to be in the same state, lying on stretchers in the ER." He looked at Stevie, his round face blotched with pink, a flush of broken veins high on his cheekbones. She could imagine him as a child, a boy who had come off worst in a playground fight and was trying hard not to cry. He said, "Joanie's not the dying-young type. She doesn't even like to leave a party early."

Stevie looked at the slender shape beneath the sheets and wished her friend hadn't lost so much weight. She reached out a hand to touch Joanie's face, but Derek caught it in his own. "Best not." He was wearing a pair of leather gloves at odds with the warm weather.

Stevie slipped free of his grip.

"What do the doctors say?"

"Fuck all. I thought Afghanistan was the worst I'd see, snipers hiding Christ knows where, picking men off one by one." He gave Stevie a small smile, an apology for swearing in front of her. "But at least we knew what we were fighting. This thing?" Derek shook his head. "It really is fucking invisible."

More than once Joanie had arrived at work, weary from waking to her husband's screams, complaining that if only Derek would talk about his war he might stop fighting it in his sleep. Mention of it now felt like an appeal for sympathy, as disconcerting as the regular beeps coming from the machines Joanie was wired up to. It made Stevie want to hurt him. She said, "So, will you join Francesca in Nottingham?"

"Norfolk," Derek corrected. "Go AWOL? Not my style." He glanced at Joanie and gave a battle-weary smile that was sweet with regret. "Not usually. But if I were you I'd think about taking a bit of a vacation until all this blows over."

"I've got things I need to do here."

"It's your funeral." Derek let out a quick bark of laughter, loud in the small room. "My last review said I was lacking in diplomatic skills. I guess they were right."

Stevie had only ever tolerated her friend's husband. He was too brash, too black-and-white in his judgments for her to warm to him, but the sight of Joanie, laid out on the bed, made her wish that he would reassure her, in the same definite voice that was inclined to hold forth on the benefits of CCTV and the need for women to stay sober if they wanted to avoid being raped, that everything would be okay. She resisted an urge to touch his arm.

There was a commotion of activity in the corridor outside. They both looked in its direction, but neither of them made a move. Derek said, "I'd better get going before someone notices I'm not where I should be."

It was Stevie's cue to leave him alone with his wife. She shouldered her bag.

"Can't you get compassionate leave?"

"I told you. All leave's canceled. We're men down and the sweats has meant we're in demand."

Stevie thought of Simon's poor body, lying in a freezer in a morgue somewhere. She had seen such things on television and could imagine how it would be.

"What's happening to ongoing investigations?"

Derek snorted.

"We're fire-fighting. There's precious little real police work happening."

"What about sudden deaths?" She faltered and then said the word that had been lurking in the back of her mind since she had read Simon's letter. "Murders? Surely they can't be set aside?"

Derek narrowed his eyes. Stevie thought he was going to ask if she had a particular case in mind, but then he sighed and said, "The thing about murder is that it's already happened."

"Murder is murder, whenever it occurs."

"I agree with you, but it's a question of scale. Real life isn't like the movies. Most murderers aren't serial killers; they kill once, usually by accident, sometimes by design, generally because they were drunk, or stupid." He glanced again at the bed where Joanie lay, her breathing shallow. "What's one death compared to thousands? A tragedy for their loved ones, sure, but it's like I told you, we're in a war. Different rules apply. We may not be able to halt the sweats from spreading, but we can do our best to keep order." A new insistence entered his voice and he reverted to the Derek she recognized, a firm man, sure of himself and the grubbiness of the world. "Do yourself a favor and get home well before dark. You know how London is, a fucking pressure cooker. The Met and the fire service are under-capacity, and it's ninety degrees in the shade. Before you know it, the Muslim Brotherhood and the English Defence League will be getting ready to mess each other up, not to mention all the other nutcases who like to come out when the sun shines. Tonight could be one of those nights when it all kicks off."

Fourteen

Perhaps it was the five years she had spent as a newspaper journalist, under the command of deadline-obsessed editors, which made Stevie ignore Derek's advice and go directly to the TV station. Or maybe it was the feeling that without Joanie or Simon she had nowhere else to go.

She was scheduled to knock off at midnight, but Rachel had trouble putting the next shift together, and so Stevie worked on. The program passed in a haze of distorted time. She had had no chance to review the products before she went on air, and they seemed to increase in strangeness as the night progressed, like a succession of confused dreams grafted on to a sleepless night. Toward the end Stevie thought she might be getting sick again, but it was only tiredness, combined with the late hour and the heat of the lights, all of it pressing on the strain of the day. Rachel had not been able to find a replacement for Joanie, and so Stevie presented the show on her own, watching the sales numbers' staccato climb, poor ghosts of their usual tallies. Aliah had neither called nor turned up but Precious, the production assistant, agreed to ignore union rules and take her place. Her frozen grin and self-conscious dips and twirls, in a series of outfits a size too small for her, added to the strangeness of the night.

Some time around 2:00 a.m. Rachel opened a bottle of wine. The producer's steady sips sounded in Stevie's earpiece. She heard Rachel's voice grow heavy and recognized her longing for sleep. It was odd, Stevie thought, how they forged on as if they had been charged with a vital mission, but when the program drew to its close and the remnants of the next shift were in place, she felt suddenly, ridiculously elated, like a soldier whose squad had survived a bloody battle unscathed. They had gotten through the night.

Stevie high-fived Dave the cameraman, gave Precious a hug, and made an elaborate bow to the production booth. Rachel saluted the team through the glass, laying her headphones carefully on the desk, as if they were worth a million dollars. Stevie watched her slide free of the controls, saying a few words to the producer who was taking her place. There was something off-kilter about the way Rachel was moving, an awkwardness Stevie hoped was down to the empty bottle of wine abandoned on the production desk.

"I think we got away with that."

Rachel's voice was hoarse with drink, fatigue, and something else. She opened her arms wide and Stevie met her embrace. She smelled the decay lacing the sweet-sour scent of cheap white wine on the producer's breath, saw the sweat sticking her hair to her face and knew that Rachel was ill. She forced herself not to pull free.

"Can I give you a lift home?"

"No thanks, darling." Rachel gave her a last squeeze and let go. "I'm going to bunk down here. You probably should, too, if we're going on air tomorrow."

Rachel's smile was ghastly. She had always been slender but now her flesh had been sucked close to her bones. Stevie forced herself not to look away from Rachel's expensive grin, the capped teeth set in the jolly skull. She said, "You should go home."

The producer didn't bother to answer. She linked an arm through Stevie's and they walked together to the dressing room she usually shared with Joanie. Inside, Rachel flung herself on to a chair and brought her face close to the mirror, scrutinizing her reflection.

"And I thought you looked bad." She ran a hand through her untidy bleach-blond bob, looked at the clump of hair that came away in her fingers and let it drop to the floor. "Well, you know what they say, the show must go on."

"Must it?"

Stevie unlocked the locker she had never bothered to use before and took out her bag. She glanced quickly inside to make sure Simon's computer was still there, though the weight of it had already reassured her.

Rachel's eyes met Stevie's in the mirror. "Of course the show must go on. It's more important now than ever."

Stevie slipped out of the dress and tights she had worn for the broadcast and pulled on a vest, jeans, and a long-sleeved cotton shirt. "We barely had enough people to put out a broadcast tonight." She kicked off her high heels and slid her feet into a pair of leather pumps. A scream was forming in her head but she kept her voice soft and reassuring, as if talking to a nervous animal she wanted to placate. "The next shift is struggling even more than we did." She took her jacket from the coat stand and pulled it on. "I'm guessing that by tomorrow morning anyone well enough to work will have left the city or be lying low until this passes." She put a hand on Rachel's shoulder. The producer's T-shirt was damp with sweat. Stevie wondered how long it would be before nausea joined the shakes that were making her tremble. "Let me take you to the hospital. We've been on air for hours. They may have found something to fix whatever this is."

Rachel swiveled the chair around and looked Stevie in the face. "People are calling it the sweats."

"I know."

"I Googled it while we were on air. There are all kinds of crazy theories about where it came from." Rachel sounded as if she was at a dinner party, relating a scandal that had just hit the social media. "Top of the list is China, with the former Soviet Republics and the United States joint second. Racists are blaming it on Africa or the Arabs. Socialists point at capitalist greed and capitalists at labor laws and moral degeneracy. Of course, religious fundamentalists of all persuasions think the Day of Judgment has finally arrived." Rachel grinned. "They seem to be positively relishing the whole thing. But the bottom line is there's no cure. People either get better, or they die. You got better. I will too, if I keep on working."

Rachel's eyes glowed with enthusiasm and she looked like a witch Stevie remembered from a book she had read as a child, beautiful in her deathliness. "You know how I am, Stevie," she continued. "As soon as I go on vacation I fall prey to some malady or other. My father was the same. He worked for over fifty years with barely a day off sick in his life. He retired at the age of seventy-five and six months later he was dead." Rachel's voice took on a pleading quality. "Even if the others let us down, we can put out some kind of broadcast tomorrow, just the two of us. I'll operate the camera, and you can present the same products we showed tonight. It was decent enough trash, don't you think?"

Stevie searched her memory for the name of Rachel's latest boyfriend and drew a blank.

"Is there anyone at your place?"

"I tried Nigel's landline and his cell phone. He's not answering." Rachel's laugh was harsh. "Nobody's answering."

"In that case, if you won't go to the hospital, I'll take you home with me."

"You've always had contempt for what we do, haven't you?" The sweat was standing out on Rachel's forehead now, but her voice was surprisingly strong. "Even though it's made you a good living for five years."

The suddenness of the attack surprised Stevie, but Rachel had always been a tactician, able to coax or cajole in order to get her own way. She would have made an ideal general for a heroic losing army, ready to rally her troops on a long fight to the death.

"That's crap."

"At least have the honesty to admit it." The producer let out a snort. "You think all we do is sell swag to a bunch of halfwits."

Stevie had thought it was what they both believed, but she whispered, "I don't."

"Don't you?" Rachel took a handful of tissues from the box on the dressing table and wiped her face. "I'm surprised, because that is what we do. We sell shit no one needs to people stupid enough to buy it. We're not breakfast TV or *Newsnight*, not even our biggest fans could claim that we're an essential service, but we go into thousands of viewers' homes every day. Some of them have so little in their lives they think of our presenters, of Joanie and you, God help them, as friends. Are you really willing to let them down?"

"There's nothing I can do for them."

Rachel's face creased into a horrid parody of a smile. She had aged in the course of the night and the summer-blond cut that had been model-sharp at the start of the program seemed to mock her decay.

"Come on, Stevie, you wanted to be in show business, remember?"

"No I didn't. I wanted to be a journalist."

"You wanted to show off." Rachel held her arms wide. "All the world's a stage, and all the men and women in it merely players.

They each have their entrances and their exits. Let's make our exits in good style."

"I may be a show-off." It was true. Stevie knew her looks were both her secret strength and her kryptonite. They were the reason she had landed a TV sales job so vacuous she wanted to return to journalism, and so cushy she had never found the strength to leave. "But I don't consider selling necklaces that are meant to make you look thin, tabletop donut fryers, or face cream that's guaranteed to fill in wrinkles, as going out in good style."

Rachel closed her eyes for a moment. When she opened them she had summoned the remnants of the charm that had made her such a feared operator. "If you keep selling, you'll reassure our viewers that everything is still okay." Her stare was as intense as a Scientologist hoping to win her first conversion, and Stevie remembered the craziness that had reputedly gotten Rachel fired from the BBC. "Whatever happens next, you'll give them a sense of normality."

Stevie caught a glimpse of how it might be, her own face bright and sunny, beaming into living rooms occupied by the dead and dying.

"It's you who wants the sense of normality, Rachel. If I carry on, I'll only be lying to our viewers. We need to face the fact that everything's not okay. Forget about your sales targets."

Rachel's last remnants of poise deserted her and she shouted, "This is nothing to do with sales targets."

"In that case let me take you home."

The producer pulled herself to her feet. She was still wearing the high heels that were part of the ditzy camouflage she used to wrong-foot men into thinking she was approachable, and she staggered a little.

"If you're going to fuck off, at least have the grace to do it quickly."

Stevie felt dizzy with the urge to race from the room, but she held her ground.

"You're not well."

"No shit Sherlock, you should have been a detective." Rachel stumbled forward, like a child's nightmare of a scarecrow come to life. Stevie put out a steadying hand, but the producer grabbed a jar of moisturizer from the dressing table and flung it at her. The heavy pot hit Stevie on the forehead and she reeled, almost dropping her bag. Rachel hissed, "Go on, fuck off and live."

Stevie touched her forehead. A lump was already rising where the jar had hit her, but the skin felt unbroken.

"Rachel . . ."

The producer kept her fevered stare on Stevie. She reached a hand backward to the dressing table, searching blindly for another missile.

"I'd be careful if I were you. I never knew how much the dying hate the living." Rachel's hand had found a clutch of nail-polish bottles. "They'll take you with them if they can."

She fired one of the bottles of polish at Stevie's head. It missed, bounced off the door and smashed against the tiled floor, a slow leaking red.

"Christ, I'm trying to help you."

Rachel selected another bottle from her arsenal.

"I may have the sweats but I'm not so desperate I need your help."

This time the polish was the pale blue of a Mediterranean sky. It spread across the floor like a promise of summer. Stevie jerked open the changing-room door and slammed it behind her. The sound of the producer's laughter followed her down the corridor.

The lights that normally illuminated the parking lot were out. Stevie stood for a moment on the back steps of the studio, letting her eyes adjust to the dark, thinking of Joanie, alone in her nest of tubes and wires. Joanie had a sweetness that made people want to please her. She would have managed to persuade Rachel to go to the hospital. Stevie wondered if she should go back and try again, but stepped out into the gloom of the forecourt, her pumps silent against the pavement. Tiredness and the shock of Rachel's attack had chilled her. She took a silk scarf from her jacket pocket and wrapped it around her neck.

Alone with Rachel, in the brightly lit changing room, it had seemed as if they were on the brink of the world's end, but now she could see a chain of car headlights driving along the highway in the distance. A plane passed overhead on its way to Stansted or Heathrow. She stopped and watched its landing lights blinking until it slipped into the darkness. Stevie took a deep breath and smelled freshly mown grass. She was alive in a world where people still cut their lawns. She let out a long, shivering sob of relief. She would go back, tell Rachel that they had both succumbed to mass hysteria and persuade her to go to the hospital.

As Stevie turned to retrace her steps she glimpsed a figure, dark against the blackness. A hand reached out and grabbed her satchel. Stevie snatched it free and ducked his blow, hooking the bag's strap over her head, stringing it fast across her body. She spun in the direction of her Mini and ran, reaching into her pocket for her keys, but her assailant was swift. He caught her by the shoulder. Stevie dug her elbow backward, aiming at the vulnerable point in his stomach, letting out a yell that stayed in her throat, sudden and airless, held there by a pair of strong hands twisting her scarf tight around her neck. Her heel made contact with her attacker's shin and he swore: "You fucking bitch." Her kick seemed to spur him on. He wrapped his arm tight around her neck and leaned backward, still gripping her scarf. His free fist slammed into her solar plexus and he lifted her from the ground, taking her weight on his chest and raising her up, Stevie realized, so that he could let her drop, and allow gravity to do the work of breaking her neck. She kicked out again, but he had levered her free of the range of his body and her legs pedaled uselessly in the air. Her face was touching his. She felt his breath, warm and ragged, close as a lover's. Wool bristled against her cheek and she guessed that he was wearing a balaclava. She wanted to pull it free, but her hands were intent on scrambling against his arm, desperate to tear his grip from her throat.

The muscles in her legs were screaming. Stevie kicked out again, summoning all the stamina wrung from years of spin classes and Pilates sessions. White spots flashed on her retinas. She bucked and buckled, hearing the man's heavy breathing, knowing that he was growing tired too, and that her only chance was to unbalance him and bring them both down. She was losing consciousness. The laptop battered against her groin and she wished she had surrendered the bag rather than fastening it around her body. She had survived the sweats only to die for Simon's secret, without ever discovering what it was.

Stevie hit the pavement hard. The man's weight was upon her and she wriggled like a netted fish, struggling to pull herself loose. Someone was shouting in a language she didn't understand. A boot hit her in the ribs and something gave, but she knew somehow that the kick had been meant for her assailant. Stevie grabbed the balaclava, dragged it off the man and rolled free of the fight. She scrambled to her feet. One of her shoes had gotten lost in the struggle. She tore the other one off and threw it at the man on the ground.

Jirí was on top of him now, putting his fist into her attacker's face. The security guard's body interrupted her view of the man, but she got an impression of broad, pale features beneath a shock of bright hair. Jirí looked up at her, ghost-white in the dark, and shouted, "Run!" Stevie held on to her battered ribs and made for her car, pressing the key fob in her pocket, sobbing with relief at the electronic beep that told her the doors were unlocked. Someone was shouting behind her, but Stevie didn't look back. She scrambled behind the wheel, locked the door and fumbled her keys into the ignition, swearing at her own clumsiness. The engine caught. Stevie shifted the Mini into gear, reversed out of the space and skidded across the parking lot, turning the head-lights to full beam.

The security guard was alone on the pavement, clutching his bloodied face and trying to get to his feet. Stevie swerved around him and caught her attacker in the shaft of her headlights. She saw his face, his open mouth and panicked eyes, and knew she had never seen him before, but that she would recognize him again. Stevie pressed her foot hard on the accelerator, hearing the engine whine as she ripped through the gears. "Fucking bastard." Her lips moved but her throat was raw, and no sound came out. The man was zigzagging now, trying to evade the beam of light. Stevie lost him for a second, *fuckfuckfuckfuckfuck*, and then caught his dark shape running across the grass verge that edged the parking lot. She bumped the Mini over the curb and slammed on the brakes as the perimeter fence loomed in front of her. Stevie's chest hit the steering wheel and she swore again, a spray of spit and invective, as she saw the man scale the railings that secured the station and boost himself over the top. Her assailant gave one quick look back at her and then he was gone.

Stevie had no memory of switching off the engine, or of leaving the car, but she was outside. Her hands were gripping the metal bars of the fence, and she was staring through them at the empty road beyond. The grass was wet against her bare feet, her satchel still strung across her body.

"I'm sorry, he got away." Blood and saliva thickened Jiri's accent. She turned and saw him standing behind her. His nose was bleeding and blood drenched the front of his white shirt. He raised a hand to his face; the other clutched his cap. "Are you okay?"

"He was trying to kill me."

"It looked that way." The security guard turned away, spat into the grass, coughed and spat again. Stevie found a tissue in her pocket and passed it to him. "Thanks." Jirí dabbed at his face but the tissue was too insubstantial and he untucked his shirt from his pants and used its hem to wipe off the worst of the blood. "What is he? A jealous boyfriend?"

He made it sound as if such things were only to be expected.

"No," Stevie said. "My boyfriend's dead."

Jirí shook his head. The blood was still leaking from his nose and he dabbed at it again with his bloodied shirt. His uniform pants were too wide for him and he had belted them tight to take up the slack. Stevie said, "I need to go."

"That man, did he kill him? Your boyfriend?"

The threads of car headlights still glimmered in the distance but they no longer seemed reassuring. It was three in the morning, yet they were lined up on the highway as if a midmorning rush hour had been stalled by roadworks.

"No, he was unwell."

Stevie thought Jirí would ask whether Simon had fallen victim to the sweats but the security guard merely looked at the ground and said, "I am sorry."

It was quiet in the parking lot after the shouts of the fight and the roar of the car engine, but the smell of gas still hung, dark and chemical, in the air. It reached into her lungs, and then slipped down to her belly, evoking a memory of long car rides and travel sickness. Stevie bent over and threw up in the grass. Jirí took a step backward.

"Are you sick?"

"No. I had it but I'm okay now." She wiped her mouth with the back of her hand. "I got hit in the stomach."

She didn't want to say that it was his boot that had found her ribs by mistake.

"Why do you say you 'had it?' What did you have?"

"You don't know?"

He looked bemused. "Why should I know?"

"There's a sickness, a virus, people are calling it the sweats. It's been in the newspapers, on television, people are dying."

"I don't see so much television, I watch your show and movies on DVD, and I study, that is all. After the summer I go back to university." News of the virus seemed to have no impact on the guard. He asked, "Why did he attack you?"

Stevie's hand tightened around her bag. "I don't know."

"There are crazy people about. Probably he saw your program and decided to become a stalker. I feel bad I didn't see him before he attacked you. You want me to call the police?"

"No thanks. I'll go to a police station on my way home." Stevie forced a smile. "I think you might have saved my life."

Jirí said, "You don't owe me nothing." He transferred his uniform cap from one hand to another. "You shouldn't be alone while he is still out there."

There was a proprietorial note in the guard's voice that made her uneasy. The car keys were still in her hand. Stevie braced herself.

"Don't worry. I'll be okay."

"You should let me drive you."

"I told you, I'll be fine." She opened the door and slid into the driver's seat. The security guard was at her window and she was reminded of the first time they had met. She had been desperate to go home then too, but he had held her there, using her politeness against her. This time, though, she owed him. Stevie wound down the window and asked, "How about you? Will you be okay?"

"Of course. I hope he comes back. I will be ready for him." Jirí crouched down, as he had before, his face level with hers. "Maybe this is not the right time. Your boyfriend has died and you are sad. But if I don't ask now, I may never get another chance."

She started the engine.

"Jirí, I'm not ready to go out with anyone yet."

"I know that." Blood was beginning to crust his top lip, giving the illusion of a Chaplin mustache. "I wanted to ask if you can help me get a job. I'm happy to start off small. I am studying accountancy. I will graduate this year and I would like to stay in this country, but I need a better job. I thought maybe there might be something here. TV stations always need accountants."

Stevie forced a smile. "I'll put in a word for you if I can. The way things are going, I have a feeling there may be some vacancies coming up soon."

She dimmed the lights, put the car into gear and steered it out of the parking lot, into the darkness of the road beyond.

Fifteen

The adrenaline from the fight wore off about a mile down the highway. Stevie pulled on to the hard shoulder and surrendered herself to the shakes. Every part of her hurt. She dragged a tartan traveling blanket from the back seat and draped it around her shoulders. There was a packet of acetaminophen in her satchel. She dry-swallowed three and then ran trembling fingers over her face. Its contours were swollen and unfamiliar.

The attack had been so sudden and so determined that there had been no time for fear. But the sense of dread that had shadowed her since she had found Simon's corpse was stronger and Stevie realized that she was scared to look at her face. She took a deep breath, pulled down the sun visor and looked into the small vanity mirror.

She explored her face in portions: eyes, cheeks, mouth, chin. A collage of cuts and contusions. She didn't want to switch the Mini's interior light on but Stevie could see enough to know that she was a mess.

She whispered, "Well, kid, if your face is your fortune I think you may have blown it this time."

There was a bruise on Stevie's temple where the jar thrown by Rachel had met its mark. Her cheek was scuffed and there was a red bloom of broken veins across her nose. She looked at her hands. Her palms were grazed and stinging from where she had hit the pavement, her knuckles red and scraped. Stevie cautiously touched her ribs, where Jiří's boot had made contact. The pain made her gasp but she persisted, pressing into the tenderness, making sure nothing was out of place.

When she was satisfied that nothing was broken she leaned forward and ran her hands up each of her legs from ankle to thigh. Her jeans were ripped at the knee and her flesh felt mauve with bruises, but the thick denim had helped to save her legs from more abrasions.

"You'll live." Stevie gave a harsh laugh. "Talking to yourself . . . first sign of madness."

She slid the laptop from her satchel. It looked undamaged. Stevie considered taking it from its slipcase and switching it on to check but the thought of the screen's electronic glow illuminating her face stopped her. It struck her that if her attacker believed she already knew what was in the laptop, she might no longer have the option of walking away.

Stevie wondered if Simon had realized how dangerous a task he had set her. Had he genuinely thought it a simple courier job, a favor to release him from whatever intrigue he had been embroiled in, or had he been as careless of her safety as those men who secretly concealed drugs, or even bombs, in their girlfriends' luggage?

"Fuck, Simon," she whispered. "For a clever man you were a hell of an idiot."

Tears clouded her eyes. Stevie swore again and rubbed them away. There was no time for crying. She took a bottle of perfume from her bag, sprayed a little on the palms of her hands, and dabbed it on her cheeks and her exposed knees, to disinfect her grazes. It stung, but it was a small, sharp pain, a distraction from the rest of her hurt, and she welcomed it.

She wondered if the man who had attacked her was out there in the darkness, watching her now. The TV studio was on an industrial estate, badly served by public transport during the day, not served at all by it at night. He must have driven there. After Jiří had chased him off, her attacker could have made it to his own vehicle, waited for her to drive out of the parking lot, and then tailed her at a discreet distance. Leaving his headlights off might be risky, but it would guarantee that Stevie wouldn't spot him in her rearview mirror.

She checked again that the car doors were locked and then held her hands up in front of her face. Her fingers were still trembling, but not as badly as before and she reckoned she was fit to drive. She would go back to St. Thomas's and check on Joanie before she decided on her next move. She turned the key in the ignition, gunning the engine into life, and glanced again in the rearview mirror to make sure that the road behind her was empty. Her toe had just touched the accelerator when her cell phone buzzed with news of an incoming text. Stevie took her foot from the pedal, pulled on the handbrake, and fished her phone from her bag, glad of the distraction. Joanie's name flashed on the screen.

"Thank Christ."

Joanie had recovered enough to send a text. They would convalesce together, Joanie from the sweats and Stevie from her beating. Her friend made a convincing act of being sweetly stupid, but she was the cleverest person Stevie knew. Joanie would tell her what to do about the laptop. The phone lit up and she saw the start of the message scrolling along the top of the screen: *Joanie didn't make it . . . Joanie didn't make it . . . Joanie didn't make it . . . Joanie didn't make it . . .*

Stevie felt as if her own heart had stopped. She turned off the engine and pressed the speech bubble that opened her messages.

Joanie didn't make it.

I thought you should know.

Derek

Stevie put her head in her hands and took a deep breath. There were ashes in her mouth. She wanted to cry but the tears that had threatened only a moment before refused to come. She whispered her friend's name, "Joanie," but Joanie was dead, and Stevie had never believed in ghosts.

"Joanie."

Ancient Egyptians thought that repeating the names of the dead kept them alive, but no matter how many times you said their names, the dead were dead, and there was no bringing them back.

"Joanie."

Stevie put her head against the wheel and closed her eyes. She was glad of her bruises, glad of the flesh-and-bone pain. She drew in a deep juddering breath. Light blasted into the car's interior and Stevie's eyes jerked open. She turned the key in the ignition, and pressed her foot to the accelerator, racing the car along the shoulder. A horn sounded and she saw a truck speeding past, headlights ablaze. Stevie braked. She let the truck's lights fade into the darkness, and then steered the Mini on to the highway. It was best to keep moving.

The road before and behind her was dark, but the opposite side of the lane glowed with the headlights of cars driving away from the city. Stevie pictured herself sitting at the breakfast bar in Joanie's sunny kitchen, sipping a glass of the Cava she bought by the crate, telling her friend all that had happened. How Simon had looked, ungainly in death in a way he had never been in life; the spider that had brushed across her face as she had slid the laptop from its hiding place; the sympathy in Dr. Ahumibe's voice as he offered to take care of the package Mr. Reah could no longer receive.

Joanie's first question would have been, "Was Dr. Ahumibe handsome?" Stevie smiled a smile that squeezed tears from her eyes. It would have been a ruse to distract her, a prelude to more important, more frightening questions.

"Does the man who attacked you think you know what Simon was hiding in that computer, and if he does, how much danger does it put you in? Do you still believe that Simon died of natural causes, or do you think he was murdered?"

The questions conjured a memory of Joanie's laugh. The recollection was so strong that Stevie could almost smell her friend's perfume.

The Mini slid across the highway, sickeningly fast, and Stevie suddenly came to. She turned the steering wheel hard left, correcting its course away from the median strip and the stream of headlights blazing on the other side.

"*Jesus Christ. Fuck!*"

An LED sign above the highway flashed, TIREDNESS KILLS, and was gone. She sped on, laughing at the sign's perfect timing, though none of it was funny. She knew she should find a service station, pull over, and rest, but kept her foot hard on the pedal and let the car eat up the miles.

Stevie knew what Joanie would have told her to do. It was what she should have done when she first opened Simon's letter. She sailed down a ramp and off the highway, the edgelands slid away and London started to rise around her. Stevie glimpsed the glow of a twenty-four-hour grocer's, the shapes of the homeless curled in doorways, a young couple wobbling home, arm in arm, dressed in their nightclub finery. Joanie was dead, but the world was still going on.

She slowed to a stop at a red light and punched her destination into the GPS. The road behind her was still empty of cars. Joanie's death was final, as all deaths were, but the reasons for Simon's might yet be unraveled. She would try to make sure he received some kind of justice, and find protection for herself in the process.

Sixteen

The police station was a squat, two-story building, dwarfed by the trio of tower blocks that loomed behind it. The station had small high windows, barely larger than arrow slits, which combined with its breezeblock architecture to make the building look as if it was expecting a sudden siege. Joanie had nicknamed it "Precinct 13" and the name had stuck. Stevie imagined Derek sitting beside Joanie's body, holding her hand, and felt an unexpected stab of jealousy. She pushed it away. Derek had followed his dick, and broken Joanie's heart, but policemen were clannish and dropping his name to someone in his squad might mean Stevie was taken seriously, or at least given a hearing.

The police-station door was locked. Stevie swore. Derek had long complained that undermanning had rendered his station a part-time concern, but she had thought it was just another of his gripes. She pressed the doorbell anyway, and when there was no response hammered against the door's reinforced glass. There was a shadow of movement somewhere beyond the reception desk. She put her finger back on the bell, kept it there, and continued banging on the door with her other fist.

"Hello!" Her voice was still raw from where the man had tried to strangle her and it sounded weak in the early-morning darkness. "Hello!" Stevie's hand was aching, but she thought she could see a silhouette, vague in the gloom beyond the glass. "I want to make a statement."

There was another movement behind the reception desk, a white face hazed into focus and the lock buzzed open.

"Thank fuck."

Stevie pushed through the door and into the station. She had slipped her bare feet into the running shoes she kept in the trunk of the car, but something had happened to the muscles in her right calf and she was limping. The station smelled of cheap disinfectant and too many bodies sweating poverty and fear. There was a poster on the wall behind the counter stating the police's right to do their job without being subjected to violence or verbal abuse. The text was illustrated by a photograph of a trio of good-looking officers of assorted ethnicities, two men and a woman, each one blandly fit. Were they real, or recruited from some model agency? It was bizarre, the thoughts that came into your head when you were in fear of your life.

"Sorry, miss, normal service has been suspended."

Derek had often boasted that police officers retired early, but the man behind the counter looked beyond pensionable age. Stevie placed the bag containing the laptop on to the counter.

"I need to speak with someone. I've got evidence that might be crucial in a murder investigation."

"I'm sorry, darling." The policeman glanced at the bag but made no move to take it from her. "I can see you've been through the mill, but there's no one here that can be of use to you tonight. The best thing you can do now is go home, lock your doors and stay put."

Stevie clenched her grazed palms; the pain felt good.

"What do you mean?"

The policeman's stubble was a day or two old and a shade grayer than his hair.

"I mean there's no one here to take a statement from you."

It was an effort not to vault the desk and shake him.

"There's you."

"No," the policeman said with the kind of patience usually reserved for children or the mentally challenged. "I'm not here."

His hands rested on the reception desk, fingers splayed on the plastic countertop. Stevie touched one. The flesh was cold, but it was alive.

"Yes you are."

He slid his hand free.

"No I'm not. Everyone here is dead."

She looked into his eyes, and she could almost believe he was a ghost.

"What are you talking about?"

"I'd go now, if I were you. Before anything else happens to you."

His tone was gentle but Stevie thought she could detect a threat in his words. She shouldered her bag and took a step backward.

"I know an officer who works here, Derek Caniparoli."

"Yes," the policeman nodded, "he's dead too."

"No, he's not." Her voice was rising. "He sent me a text ten minutes ago."

The man's smile slid into a smirk.

"A lot can happen in ten minutes."

"Fuck you." Stevie turned on her heels. "Fuck you and fuck your police force." She halted at the door and faced him. "First sign of trouble and you fall apart. I've witnessed more shit in the last three days than you've seen in your whole career and I refuse to let it beat me."

"Good for you." The policeman's smile was the dead calm of a sea just before a tsunami, and Stevie was suddenly aware that they were alone. "But remember what I said: a lot of people are dying, one or two more's not going to be missed." He looked her up and down. "You're in a bit of a state, but you're still a good-looking girl beneath those bruises. I've been very patient but I suggest you go home now, before someone decides they'd like a last thrill."

This time Stevie didn't hesitate. The pain in her leg was still there, but she banged out of the police station and half jogged the short distance to her car, scanning left to right as she ran, like a soldier making for fresh cover.

Seventeen

Stevie slammed the driver's door, checked the locks, took out her phone and found Joanie's number. She hoped Derek still had his wife's cell phone with him and that it was turned on. She pressed call and listened, swearing under her breath as it rang out. She tried again. This time Derek picked up.

"Stephanie, yes."

His voice was brisk and she could hear a bustle of activity in the background.

"Derek, I'm sorry about Joanie."

"Me too."

There was nothing else to be said and not-quite-silence hung on the line for a moment, a blackbird starting off the dawn chorus at her end, a babble of voices at his.

"I'm outside your station."

"I'm not there."

"I know. There's no one there. Just an insane-looking policeman who told me he was dead."

"That'll be Phil. He should be on sick leave by rights." Derek gave a bitter laugh. "By rights most of us should be on sick leave, but it's all hands to the pump. The Guvnor reckoned Phil would be more of a hindrance than a help out in the field, so we left him to mind the fort. I take it he's not doing a very good job?"

"You could say that."

"Best to keep out of his way. Look, Stevie, it was good of you to call but I need to go."

"Wait a moment."

"I can't, sorry."

"Derek, someone killed my boyfriend."

His sigh sounded as if it had traveled across eons to reach her. Stevie remembered what the policeman had said of Derek, "He's dead too," and the back of her neck tingled.

"I'm sorry to hear that." His voice was heavy. "But things are in a bit of a mess, in case you haven't noticed. I'm afraid he's not the only one."

"This is different. Someone deliberately organized Simon's death and arranged things to make it look natural. Simon sent me a note, telling me he'd hidden a laptop at my apartment and to deliver it to a colleague he trusted at the hospital, but his colleague caught the sweats and died before I could get it to him."

"Repeat that more slowly for me, please," Derek said. She did as he asked and he gave another sigh. "Are you sure?"

The question bewildered her.

"What do you mean?"

"Joanie said you had a habit of hooking up with rich fuckwits, all flash and no heart was how she put it. Are you sure someone isn't playing a joke on you? Some Hooray Henries have peculiar ideas of what's funny."

"Simon wasn't a Hooray Henry, he was a surgeon and yes, I'm sure. I found Simon's body. I smelled him before I saw him. Is that authentic enough for you?"

She thought Derek was going to find another objection, but he swore softly, "Jesus Christ," and asked, "What's in the laptop?"

"I don't know. I can't get past the password."

"Stevie, this is what a psychiatrist would call displacement activity. You're fiddling while Rome burns. I'm sorry your boyfriend's dead. I'm even sorrier Joanie's dead. Whatever you think of me, I'd walk through fire to bring her back. But there's nothing any of us can do. Forget it. Go home and keep safe. Someone told me vitamin C is good for staving off the sweats. Buy a few cartons of orange juice and then lock yourself in."

"It's not as simple as that, Derek. I think someone's after me. I was attacked by a man outside work tonight. He pretty much kicked the shit out of me. I think he would have killed me if it hadn't been for the security guard. He saw what was happening and managed to beat him off."

"Are you okay?"

Derek sounded genuinely concerned and Stevie found herself blinking away tears.

"A bit bruised, but I'll live."

"What makes you think it wasn't a straightforward mugging? The sweats is a call to all the scum of the earth to crawl out of their holes."

It was the way Derek had always described the crowds he policed. Demonstrators, soccer fans, rioters; he reduced all of them to zombies. Easier to push people around, Stevie supposed, if you thought that joining a crowd neutralized your brain. She couldn't believe she was calling on him.

"It wasn't a random attack, Derek. There's nothing and no one around the studio. This guy wasn't just passing by, he was waiting for me. He wanted to get his hands on the laptop and he didn't care if he killed me in the process."

"You should have given it to him."

For all his shtick about law and order, that had always been Derek's advice: *If you can't outrun them, hand over your valuables and live to fight another day.* Stevie tried to keep the irritation out of her voice.

"Maybe I should, but he doesn't know I've not seen whatever it was Simon hid on it. As far as he's concerned, I'm in on the whole story."

She wanted to ask Derek to help her for Joanie's sake, but Joanie was dead.

"Hold on a minute, Stevie." She heard the faint sound of someone talking to Derek on the other end of the line. He said, "I'm going to put you on hold." And she was left with the hiss of dead air. When Derek returned he sounded out of breath.

"You found one body. That was my twelfth. We've been in and out of houses all night checking on people reported missing."

"I thought you would be excused, because of Joanie."

"I told you, all leave's canceled. That includes compassionate leave." Derek sighed. "Not that I deserve much compassion." There was a pause and then he said, "You were a good friend to Joanie. You were always there for her."

Stevie knew what Joanie would have wanted her to say and so she said it.

"She still loved you, Derek."

"I didn't deserve her." The policeman's voice was gruff. He cleared his throat and asked, "You really think you're in danger?"

"I wouldn't have called you otherwise."

"I guess not." He took the phone away from his mouth and Stevie heard him ask someone, "Have you checked the other rooms?" There was the sound of a dog barking. Derek shouted, "Could someone lock fucking Fido up?" and then he was back on the line. "Are you still living in Camden?"

"Yes."

"Go home, lock the door and don't open it to anyone except me. If the doorbell rings, ignore it, same for the landline. I'll get there as soon as I can, but it may not be for a while." Derek's voice had regained the sense of certainty that used to exasperate her. Now it was reassuring. "I'll call you on your cell phone, so make sure it's charged. I'm just a beat cop so don't expect me to be Sir Galahad. If you don't answer, I'll assume you've fucked off."

"Thanks, Derek."

"Don't thank me, I've not done anything."

The line died abruptly and Stevie was left alone with the sound of birdsong. She sat there for a moment, watching the sunrise turning the tops of the high-rises pink. They looked mystical, like giant standing stones deposited there by some cosmic ancestor. She wondered if there would ever come a time when people would marvel at the civilization that had created such giant structures, and ponder on what they had been trying to express.

Eighteen

A wind was rising and Stevie could hear the cord of the window blind *tap, tap, tapping* against the pane. She had kicked the covers off in the night and a chill had crept into her bedroom and across her body. She reached out blindly and pulled the covers up. *Tap, tap, tap*, the sound of plastic hitting against glass. She knew she should get up and close the window before the storm arrived and rain blew in, but she was wearier than the dead, and sleep kept towing her under. *Tap, tap, tap.* Stevie looked toward the sound. The blinds were raised, the window closed. Simon stood on the other side of the pane, his face pale and slack, his index finger tapping against the glass.

He mouthed, "Let me in."

Stevie made to move, but then she remembered that he was dead and floating miraculously outside her third-floor window.

"No!"

Stevie's head shot up. She was still in her car outside the police station. *Tap, tap, tap.* She looked groggily at the passenger-side window and came face to face with a young woman.

"It's my Nan." The woman's voice was muffled, her features absurdly close. "She's not well."

Stevie rubbed her eyes with the heels of her hands. The woman was still tapping on the window, an insistent rhythm. Her short nails had been tipped with French-polished falsies, a few of which remained.

"You've got to help me."

The stranger's pupils were tiny. She was strung out, though whether it was from fear or something more chemical, Stevie couldn't be sure. She lowered the window an inch.

"What's wrong with her?"

"I don't know, do I? I'm not a doctor. She needs to go to the hospital."

It was a scam, Stevie was almost certain of it, but a small sliver of doubt niggled at her. She took her bag from the well of the passenger seat. There were three tens and a twenty tucked inside her purse. She slid the tens free and posted them through the gap in the window to the woman.

"Take a taxi."

"The elevators are off. I need help to get her down the stairs."

The key was still in the ignition. Stevie started the engine.

"Ask a neighbor."

"None of those bastards will help me."

The woman had tucked the money into the pocket of her jeans. Her fingers were back at the window, not tapping this time, squeezing through the gap, trying to force the glass down.

"Let go." Stevie pressed the button to raise the window again, but the woman's hands were in the way and it refused to close. She looked around for something to swat them with. All she could find was the ice scraper that had sat in the pocket of the driver's door since last winter. She waved it at the woman. "I'm telling you to fuck off."

"Language." The woman was laughing now, a crazy sound, cutting through the dawn, but her fingers were persistent and the window shifted a little beneath their pressure. Stevie rapped the invading knuckles with the ice scraper and the woman shouted, "That fucking hurt."

Stevie took off the handbrake and let the Mini roll slowly back, but the woman was tenacious.

"Don't be like that." She hung on, laughing more wildly now, as if this were some game between the two of them. "You'll take me hand off."

"Let go."

Stevie rapped at the fingertips again with the scraper, harder this time, and saw one of the false nails detach and land on the passenger seat.

"Stop it." The woman laughed. "It hurts."

And then suddenly a second pair of hands was inserting itself between the car roof and the window, trying to pry them wider apart. Stevie couldn't see the person's face, just a stretch of T-shirt and tracksuit bottom, a Nike logo. These hands were broader, with patches of hair on their fingers. The window started to give. The woman fell back laughing, leaving the man to it.

"You're in for it now," she hooted. "Boots will get you. You should have ran me over."

Stevie put the car in gear and drove toward the road. There was a bellow of pain, a sound of something dragging and a scream of protest from the whey-faced woman, but Stevie kept her eyes on the view ahead, and her foot on the accelerator.

When she glanced through the side window a mile or so down the road, she saw familiar streets through a smear of blood. It was only a smear, Stevie reassured herself; much less than there would have been had she severed one of the man's fingers. She kept the window down the fraction she had already lowered it, letting the cool air hit her face, hoping it would be enough to keep her awake until she got home.

The pavements had the blighted look they took on after a heavy weekend, littered with the remnants of fast-food feasts and stained with piss and pakora sauce. Stevie stopped at a red light and a cleaner carrying a bucket and mop crossed the road. The cleaner's hair was concealed beneath a dark blue headscarf, her clothes covered by a neat tabard. It was hard to believe there could be anything seriously amiss in a city where such women went calmly about their business.

The traffic lights flashed and then shifted to green. Stevie drove on slowly. There were other cars on the road now, and she rolled the window open wider. This was one of the intersections of the day, when too-early-to-work businessmen and women crossed paths with the last of the staggering-home crew; the time when those easing themselves into the day, the early-morning joggers and sippy-cup-coffee crew, shared the streets with night workers and the beginning-to-come-down-from-whatever-had-kept-them-up-all-night crowd.

Stevie felt her eyes grow heavy and turned on the car radio. A farming program was on, the presenter interviewing a scientist about the likelihood of the virus crossing species. *We all remember the panic surrounding the H1N1 virus commonly known as bird flu. The fear then was that the illness would pass from birds to humans. Are you worried that this current virus, which has been christened V5N6, might infect cattle and other livestock?*

Stevie turned off the radio and stopped in front of another red light. A shoal of cyclists slid to a halt around her car. For the first time in ages she noticed the variety of the people, the assortment of skin color and styles that had secretly delighted her when she moved to London. A pink-faced man in a business suit and cycling helmet put a hand on the roof of the Mini and leaned insolently against it. Some other day she might have unlocked the handbrake and rolled gently forward just for the pleasure of seeing him wobble, but instead she gazed at the miracle of him: his crumpled fawn suit; the red sock revealed by his rolled-up pant leg. She glanced up at his face and saw a white cotton mask stretched across his mouth and nose.

On the other side of the road the proprietor of a Turkish café flung a bucket of hot, soapy water across the pavement in front of his shop and began sweeping it into the gutter. Shelf stackers were busy unpacking boxes inside the Tesco Metro. The sun was fully up now. The warmth of it on her face seemed to soothe her grazes. The lights changed again. Stevie let the cyclists dash ahead. She kept her eyes on the road, reached a hand into the glove compartment, found her sunglasses and put them on.

It was as if morning had recalibrated the world. Everything looked so normal that, if it weren't for her bruises, she would find it hard to believe the episode in the parking lot or her conversation with Derek had taken place. A bus stopped to let early-morning commuters aboard and Stevie glanced in her side mirror, beyond the smear of blood, checking that she was free to overtake. Something on the passenger seat caught her eye. She passed the bus and then took a tissue, lifted the false fingernail from the seat and dropped it out of the window.

She hated Derek's cynicism, his description of people as the scum of the earth, but suddenly she felt as if the wakening streets around her were an illusion that might be peeled back any time, to reveal another, shadow world that could suddenly drag you under without a word of warning.

"You're well out of it, Joanie," she whispered. "Well out of it."

But she wished she had asked Derek how it had been; if Joanie had suffered, or if she had slipped away without the panic of knowing that it was the end.

Nineteen

The door to her apartment was ajar. Stevie crept down the hallway and rang her neighbor's doorbell, but there was no response. She had been burgled once before, three years ago. When the police had eventually appeared, hours after she had called them, they had been coolly indifferent, as if their job was to verify the facts for the insurance company, rather than find the perpetrators. Stevie couldn't imagine that their response would be any swifter this time, even if she told them she was afraid that whoever had broken in might still be lurking there.

She leaned against the wall in the corridor. The best thing to do was to walk away, call Derek, and arrange to meet him somewhere else, or not to call Derek at all, just dump the laptop at the hospital, get in the car, and keep on driving. But if the man who had attacked her thought she was privy to whatever was hidden on the laptop, losing it might not be enough to free her of him.

Stevie took off her sneakers, pushed the door tentatively open and peered inside. The coat stand had been felled. It lay on its side among her scattered coats and hats, but the hallway was empty, the apartment silent. She thought again about walking away. There was a road-map of the British Isles in the car. It would be easy to close her eyes and stick a pin into a random destination, somewhere no one would connect her with, and drive there.

Stevie flattened herself against the lobby wall again, took out her cell phone and pressed Joanie's number. *Joanie, Joanie, Joanie* flashed onscreen but Derek didn't pick up.

"Fuck." Stevie mouthed the word.

She was tired, bruised and filthy, the grit of the parking lot mixed with blood and sweat on her skin. Joanie's death mingled with Simon's in her mind. Stevie knew she wouldn't win in a physical fight against her parking lot attacker but part of her wanted to give it a try. She pushed open the door to her apartment and slipped inside. Her satchel was heavy and awkward but she kept it strapped across her body. Somewhere outside a jackhammer started up; the soundtrack of the city. Stevie tiptoed along her hallway, breathing in as she passed each open door.

She shifted her bag to her back, stepped over the coat stand and crept into the kitchen. Cupboards had been swept clean, crockery and glasses shattered on the floor, but the knife block was still sitting in its place next to the cooker. Stevie trod carefully, cursing her bare feet, and slid the carving knife from its slot.

Outside the jackhammer rumbled on in sporadic bursts. She let its noise mask the sound of her progress, moving when it moved, freezing when it stopped, all the time holding the knife firmly in front of her.

Someone had taken her apartment apart. There had been no malice in the act. There was no graffiti on the walls as there had been last time, no turd coiled on the rug. The break-in had been carried out thoroughly and methodically, by someone looking for something.

Books and CDs had been spilled from their shelves in the sitting room, cushions tossed free of the couch and easy chairs, the furniture itself turned on its back to make sure nothing had been hidden below, or taped to its base. Drawers were pulled from the sideboard, their contents dumped on the floor. Stevie saw her mother's rings, her own checkbook and emergency credit card, and realized that nothing had been stolen.

Shirts, pants, and dresses were tumbled together in her bedroom like massacre victims. The duvet had been dragged from the bed, the mattress tipped to the floor. The wardrobe door was ajar, a few dresses still hanging drunkenly on their hangers.

The drilling stopped, and Stevie stopped too, holding her breath until the racket resumed. She managed three steps forward, three steps closer to the darkness behind the half-open door, before the drilling paused again. She primed herself, like a sprinter waiting for the starter's gun.

Her cell phone chirped news of a message, loud as an airplane crash.

Stevie lunged forward and yanked the door wide, holding the knife high above her shoulder, plunging it into the darkness, letting out a yell she had never heard before.

There was no one there.

She leaned into the wardrobe's empty shadows, laughter bubbling from within her. She wanted nothing more than to close the closet door and sit there in the must and the black, but she forced herself to check her office and the bathroom. When she was sure there was no one lurking anywhere in the apartment, she pulled her cell from her pocket. The message had come from Joanie's phone. It was short and to the point: *Take the laptop to Iqbal.* An address in Clapham followed.

Stevie texted back:

I'll get there ASAP
Thanks

The front door lock was beyond her ability to repair, the door itself splintered but still sure on its hinges. Stevie closed it and put on the security chain. She dragged the Ercol sideboard she had been so proud of from the living room and set it against the door. Some empty wine bottles had been dumped on the floor with the rest of her recycling. She gathered a few and put them on the table. The arrangement wouldn't stop an intruder but it would make a racket if anyone disturbed it.

Stevie undressed and stood in the shower, letting the water course over her body. She dried herself, smeared her cuts with antiseptic cream and swallowed two anti-inflammatory pills. Normally she would have walked naked through the rooms of her apartment, letting the air soothe her skin, but now she went straight to the bedroom and sorted through the muddle of clothes until she found underwear, a running vest and a black tracksuit. Even stripped of its sheets the bed looked like the perfect haven, but she ignored it, pulled on fresh clothes and went through to the shattered kitchen. There were two ill-assorted Lean Cuisines, a beef chow fun and a shrimp Alfredo, in the freezer. Stevie packed a dishtowel with ice cubes, blasted both of the ready meals in the microwave, and ate standing at the worktop, holding the ice to her swollen face.

The apartment had meant a lot to her. It had been her touchstone, the sign that she had made something of herself since she had first arrived in London, armed with only her journalism degree. Now she wondered if she would ever live there again.

It was half an hour since Derek's text. Stevie put a bottle of water, some energy bars, a packet of painkillers, her phone charger, and the carving knife in the satchel beside Simon's laptop. She covered the worst of her bruises with makeup, then went through to the living room, slipped her mother's rings over her grazed knuckles, and left the apartment. Stevie pulled the door shut behind her, but didn't bother to look back and check if it stayed closed.

Twenty

S tevie had just tucked her satchel under the passenger seat of
the Mini when her phone jangled into life. She scrambled it
free from the side pocket of her bag and saw a number she didn't
recognize flashing on the screen.

"Stephanie Flint?" The voice was male and unfamiliar.

Stevie had heard of spy software that could follow you via your
cell phone, tracing your movements across virtual maps, and an
image flashed into her head of her car parked at the side of the
road, while her attacker gazed down on it, huge and godlike. She
slid her key into the ignition.

"Who is this?"

"Alexander Buchanan from St. Thomas's Hospital. Is that
Ms. Flint?"

She remembered him. The pharmacist, Simon's other colleague, a pale man with translucent eyes, some kind of handsome
in his strangeness.

"Yes. Do you have some news about Simon?"

"In a manner of speaking." Buchanan sounded assured, but
there was an underlying hesitation in his delivery, as if he was

uncertain of how much he should tell her. "I wondered if you might be available to meet. As you may have gathered from the news, we medics are rather pushed at present, but I'd prefer to discuss this face-to-face if possible."

Stevie held the phone away from herself for a moment, trying to weigh her priorities. She had parked in a side street around the corner from her apartment, but she could see a glimpse of main road from where she was sitting, the parade of shops that the real estate agent had described as "convenient" when she had bought her apartment. She lifted the phone to her ear again.

"I'm sorry." She made her words crisply efficient, trying to match Buchanan's public-school-followed-by-Oxford-or-Cambridge confidence. "I have an appointment I mustn't miss."

"Afterward perhaps?"

"I'm not sure that will be possible. Can't you tell me what this is about over the phone?"

Now it was the pharmacist's turn to pause. Stevie let the silence hang between them. Buchanan had called her, and much as she wanted to hear what he had to say, that made him the seller and her the buyer.

After a moment he said, "I asked to be present at Simon's autopsy. The results were consistent with what I believe you were told when you found him."

"Sudden adult death syndrome?"

"Yes, but SADS is notoriously hard to diagnose; it can be a bit of a catch-all really. I felt an obligation to a friend and colleague to make sure that there were no underlying causes, so I asked to examine the body myself."

The body. Death had turned Simon and Joanie into objects. Stevie resisted the urge to press her forehead against the hard edge of the steering wheel.

"What did you find?"

"Simon was in good shape for a man of his age. He had no undiagnosed heart defects, and hadn't suffered an embolism or any of the other biological catastrophes usually responsible for sudden deaths."

"Does that mean there's no way of finding out . . . ?"

The pharmacist interrupted her. "Like I said, Simon was a friend as well as a colleague. I conducted some extra toxicology tests of my own. Simon's blood contained faint traces of a sedative, too faint for standard checks to detect."

Stevie scanned her memory of Simon's en suite. The bathroom cabinet had been neat and well stocked. She couldn't remember any sleeping pills, but he was a doctor and presumably able to acquire prescription drugs when he wanted them. She said, "If Simon was feeling under the weather he might have decided he needed a good night's sleep and taken something to help him get one."

"That's certainly possible, but the faintness of the sedative traces intrigues me. If Simon took a sleeping pill before going to bed and died within the next five to seven hours, I would have expected there to have been more left in his system. It could be that he lingered on in a coma and the sedative left his system during that time, but sudden death syndrome is usually swift and unexpected, hence the name. You found his body in bed, which suggested to me that Simon had died in his sleep. That set me wondering if he might have taken anything else, some narcotic that wouldn't leave any residue in his body."

"Simon wasn't into drugs. He didn't even drink much alcohol."

It was true. Simon had possessed so much energy that he often seemed a drink ahead of her, even when he had been sticking to mineral water for the sake of an impending operation.

"I realize that." The hesitation was back. It made the pharmacist sound like a man about to break bad news, reluctant to give voice to what he was about to say. "I wanted to ask if you'd noticed anything odd about Simon in the weeks before he died. Did he seem anxious? Depressed?"

It was the same question that Simon's cousin and the policeman who had interviewed her had asked.

Stevie said, "He was distracted, worried maybe, but if you're asking me if I think Simon committed suicide, then the answer is no, I don't."

"You sound certain."

"I am." Stevie had a sudden impulse to tell Buchanan that she was also sure Simon had been murdered, but he would be bound to interrogate her and any opportunity to draw out what he knew would be lost. Stevie looked beyond the window of the car. The street was empty, but it was lined with apartment blocks and whoever had searched her apartment might be hiding behind one of the anonymous windows, ready to follow her. She pushed the doctor, the way she might put pressure on a merchant in a souk, by pretending to walk away. "I'm sorry, but I'm going to have to go."

"Forgive me." The pharmacist took a deep breath. It was silent at his end of the line for a moment and Stevie wondered if the connection had been broken. Then he said, "Simon and I were at school together, and I still think of him more as a brother than a friend. He didn't really have any close family members left, and so it's up to me to find out as much as I can about how he died." Buchanan let out a short, embarrassed laugh. "I hope that doesn't sound too melodramatic. I still can't believe he's dead. I guess what I really want to ask is, did Simon leave anything that might explain what happened, a note or a diary?"

"No, nothing like that."

"Just the package for Mr. Reah?"

"Yes."

The pharmacist paused again, as if trying to decide what to say next.

Stevie turned the screw. "I'm sorry I can't be much help . . ."

Buchanan interrupted her, as she had hoped he would.

"I know you refused to let Dr. Ahumibe take responsibility for the package, but I wonder if you would consider allowing me to take a look at it?"

It would be a simple thing to hand the laptop over to Buchanan with a warning that someone was after it. Simon had been clear that she was to trust no one except Reah, but both Simon and Reah were dead, and there was no bringing them back.

It was as if the pharmacist sensed the uncertainty in Stevie's silence. He added, "Things are pretty bloody here, but I could send my son William to pick it up if you tell me where you are. He could be with you in no time."

It was silly to think she would hand the laptop over to a stranger. Simon had entrusted it to her and she had fought for it with her life. Stevie said, "Simon never mentioned you or your son."

"He was William's godfather." Buchanan sighed. "Simon had a tendency to compartmentalize. He never mentioned you either."

It was nothing she didn't know already, but Stevie was surprised by a quick throb of disappointment. She asked, "Was he good with children?"

"William's twenty-nine, not a child anymore, but yes, Simon was one of his more popular uncles. He wasn't the most attentive godfather, prone to forgetting birthdays and rather too inclined toward dangerous presents for my ex-wife's liking, but William adored him. He's pretty cut up about his death. We all are."

Stevie heard the grumble of a car engine and saw a blue Fiat speeding along the main road. There was something about the Fiat that bothered her, but she wasn't sure what. She asked, "What was Simon like as a boy?"

Alexander Buchanan paused for a moment, and then said, "Rather like he was as an adult: brave, inclined to recklessness, clever and—just as important—capable of applying himself. He had a silly sense of humor, but he was kind too, not a quality to be taken for granted in small boys. I joined the school as a day pupil when I was twelve. Simon was a boarder. Normally they looked down on us part-timers, but he took me under his wing. I lacked the charm to match Simon's popularity, but for some reason he took a shine to me and that won me a grudging acceptance with the rest of the boys. Maybe that's part of the reason I feel such an obligation to Simon now. I owed him a lot."

Another car sped along the main road and Stevie realized what had bothered her about the blue Fiat. At this time of day the traffic should have been too heavy to allow cars to travel much above a crawl. Somewhere a door slammed. Stevie scanned the street but there was no one in sight. She slid down the driver's seat, hiding her face in the dashboard's shadows.

"How convinced are you about your narcotics theory?"

"I'm not convinced at all. It's a working hypothesis, but without more evidence that's all it is."

"But supposing you are right, how would Simon have taken whatever it was?"

"Orally." There was the tiniest of pauses, the type that Stevie and Joanie had been trained to avoid when they joined the shopping channel. "Or by injection."

The pause had told her what she wanted to know, but Stevie asked, "Was there evidence of an injection on Simon's body?"

There was silence on the line again. Stevie could feel Buchanan trying to make up his mind whether to answer her or not. She already knew that he would. The pharmacist had been led too far for him to retreat now.

Buchanan let out a breath that was all acquiescence.

"There was a puncture between his index and middle finger that might have been consistent with a needle piercing his skin."

"Why didn't you tell me before?"

"If Simon did kill himself, and I'm not saying he did, but if he did, he went to a lot of trouble to make it look like he died from natural causes. Who am I to undo his last wishes? Look." Buchanan became briskly efficient, as if suddenly realizing he had given her all he could and had nothing left to bargain with. "I wish you'd let William pick up the laptop. All I want to know is whether Simon committed suicide, and if so why."

Surprise galvanized Stevie. She put her cell on speaker, turned the key in the ignition, and guided the car from its parking space.

"I never mentioned what was in Simon's package. What makes you think it contained a laptop?"

Buchanan's answer was fast and bewildered in its innocence.

"Dr. Ahumibe told me. Perhaps he guessed."

Stevie had been careful not to mention the laptop to Ahumibe. She said, "Thank you for your call, Dr. Buchanan. I take it you're still at the hospital?"

"No, I'm at my lab. I'm part of the international collaboration trying to find an antidote for V5N6. It would be a great help if you could let me see the package. It may seem silly with so many other lives at stake, but I'm finding it hard to concentrate. I keep wondering if Simon killed himself and if he did, what could have made him so unhappy." The pharmacist spoke quickly, as if he was afraid she might suddenly cut the call. "If you don't want to trust William, why not bring it here yourself? I promise it won't leave your sight."

"Tell me where your lab is and I'll think about it."

Buchanan gave her an address, sounding suddenly weary. "I'll be here for the foreseeable future. Where are you?"

"It doesn't matter. I'll know where to go, if I need you." Stevie might have been telling him to fuck off and die.

"Please don't hang . . ."

Stevie turned off her cell and stabbed the address Derek had texted her into the GPS. Iqbal's place lay on the opposite side of the river. She turned a corner, narrowly missing a taxi. She raised a hand in an apology that turned into a two-fingered salute when the driver pressed the horn and drew a finger across his throat.

"Better men than you have threatened to kill me," Stevie whispered, though she had no evidence that they were better men at all.

The near collision had shaken her and she drove slowly, keeping her eyes on the road, trying to work out what the conversation with Buchanan had revealed. One thing was clear. If the pharmacist's hypothesis worked for suicide, then it also worked for murder. A sedative could easily be slipped into a drink; warnings about nightclub predators with a penchant for Rohypnol had taught her that. Once it had taken effect, all that the killer would have had to do was inject Simon with whatever poison they had chosen, and then sit at his bedside and make sure he didn't wake up. It was a horrible image, the assassin waiting quietly in a chair by the bed, the murderer and victim caught in a pastiche of doctor and patient.

Turn left in one hundred yards, the chilly female voice of the GPS instructed. Stevie did as she was told, glad to surrender control to someone else, just for a moment.

Twenty-One

It said something about her own prejudices that she had expected Iqbal to be overweight, dressed in pizza-stained sweatpants, and pale from too many hours at a computer keyboard. The man who answered the door was young and slender with dark, long-lashed eyes. Stevie felt suddenly, ridiculously, shy.

"Iqbal?" The young man nodded and Stevie said, "I'm Stephanie Flint, a friend of Derek's, I mean PC Caniparoli. He said you'd be expecting me."

"Yes." He hesitated on the doorstep for a moment, as if wondering if their business could be conducted there, then stepped back and let her into the apartment.

"Could you take off your shoes, please?"

A magazine was neatly positioned inside the door. Stevie unlaced her sneakers and placed them on it.

Iqbal nodded at an empty coat rack. "You can hang your jacket there."

Stevie started to unzip her tracksuit top but remembered that she was only wearing a thin vest and sports bra underneath.

"It's okay, I'll keep it on."

Iqbal made a helpless gesture with his hands, as if he were the minion of a giant corporation, charged with a regrettable duty.

"I'd prefer it if you took it off, please."

Instinct told Stevie that he wasn't trying to get a better look at her breasts, but she asked, "Why?"

Iqbal gave an apologetic smile.

"To avoid infection."

Stevie shrugged off her jacket and put it on one of the pegs. Iqbal handed her a bottle of antibacterial gel. A blush was spreading across his cheeks, but Stevie guessed that he was tenacious, the kind of person who would follow through, even when it made him squirm inside. She washed her hands and made to give the bottle back, but he stepped away from her, neat as a ballroom dancer.

"Can you wash up to your elbows, please?" The nervous smile flashed across his face again. "It's what hospitals tell visitors to do."

Stevie did as he asked. The gel was cold, its chemical scent harsh in her nose and the back of her throat, as if it was also disinfecting the inside of her head.

"I've already had it."

"The sweats?"

"Yes."

She passed him the gel and this time he took it from her.

"Maybe you're immune, but that doesn't mean you're not a carrier."

The thought had not occurred to her. She asked, "Does it make it more likely?"

Iqbal frowned. "I don't know."

He walked into the apartment and she followed him. The place reminded her of a magazine feature on compact, open-plan living. The sleek kitchen was tucked neatly into a corner, a dining table sat in front of it and beyond that, a large couch faced on to a picture window. The apartment was decorated in a muted, natural palette of bamboos and stone grays. Books, CDs, and DVDs were ranked neatly on a bank of shelves, adding a flash of mismatched color. A floating staircase led up to a mezzanine where Iqbal's sleeping area presumably lay. The only glimpse of chaos was a workstation cleverly positioned beneath the stairs, its surface crammed with a confusion of computers, wires, and printouts.

A flat-screen TV hung to the right of the couch, somehow suggesting that viewing was a solitary activity, to be undertaken lying down, with your head propped against the armrest. The television was on, flashing images from a hospital ward somewhere in India, which were quickly replaced by similar scenes from somewhere in Europe and then Africa. The TV's volume was down and subtitles stabbed across the bottom of its screen.

V5N6 IS NO RESPECTER OF
AGE OR SOCIAL CLASS

The picture shifted to stock film of an anonymous scientist delicately inserting a dropper into a test tube.

SCIENTISTS ACROSS THE WORLD ARE
TAKING PART IN AN UNPRECEDENTED
COLLABORATION

The image made Stevie think of her defection from the lab in St. Thomas's, and of Joanie, lying helpless in a nest of tubes.

Iqbal went to the kitchen area, took a package of frozen peas from the freezer and handed it to her.

"Hold this to your face. It'll help the swelling."

"Does it look that bad?"

"Not if you've just gone a few rounds with Amir Khan." His eyes met Stevie's and glanced away. "You have a laptop you want me to look at?"

"Yes, it belonged to my boyfriend . . ."

"Can I see it, please?"

It felt odd to be surrendering the computer to a stranger, and Stevie hesitated.

Iqbal said, "You did bring it with you?"

"Yes."

Stevie pulled the laptop from her bag and handed it to him.

"What do you want me to do?" Iqbal slid it from its slipcase.

"Get past the password, if you can."

Iqbal took the machine to his workstation. He rearranged the laptops, tablets, and PCs on the desk, clearing space for Simon's.

"Is that all?"

"I don't know. I have no idea what's in it."

"Okay." Iqbal put the laptop on the desk and switched it on. He settled himself on a desk chair and pulled out its neighbor, indicating that she should sit too. "This won't take a nanosecond."

Stevie perched on the edge of her swivel chair. A headline screamed from the open screen of the PC in front of her.

CIA PLOT TO DISABLE CHINA

She asked, "Do you believe that?"

Iqbal looked up, his face gleaming in the glow of Simon's laptop.

"What?"

"About the CIA."

"I don't know. It's possible, I suppose. There are all sorts of rumors flying around on the Net. That's one of the more sensible ones. Some people believe the sweats was sent by aliens, a kind of cosmic chemical warfare." He reached beneath the desk and pulled out a plastic carton. "It's not called the World Wide Web for nothing. You can get sucked in and trapped there. CIA, FBI, MI5, the Jews, the Mormons, the Christian Scientists, God, Muhammad, Jehovah, blacks, homosexuals, the Chinese, the North Koreans, it seems like everyone wants to blame someone. I was almost relieved when PC Caniparoli called. I needed to be kicked offline for a while."

Iqbal turned the laptop upside down, looking for something among the bar-codes and serial numbers stickered on its base. Stevie tried to think of information that might help him work out the password.

"Simon was a doctor. He worked with sick children at St. Thomas's Hospital. His second name was Sharkey and he has a cousin called Julia who's also a doctor." She glanced at Iqbal to see if the information she had offered was useful, but he was occupied in unpacking a bewildering tangle of leads and devices from the carton. She said, "I'm not sure what else I can tell you."

Iqbal looked up from his task.

"Don't worry. It's none of my business who your boyfriend was, or why you want to access his computer. I'm doing this as a favor to PC Caniparoli."

"I thought it might help you come up with the password if you knew a bit about Simon."

"Is that how you think computer passwords are broken?" Iqbal looked amused. "Someone guesses until they hit on the right word?"

"I don't know." She was floundering. "What do you do?"

"This." He took a small silver box, which reminded Stevie of the card reader she used to transfer her vacation photographs onto her Mac, and plugged it into the side of the laptop. A window appeared on the start-up page, and Iqbal's fingers moved, light and fast, against the keyboard. "Here we go." The familiar jingle sounded and icons glowed into life on the desktop. "*Voilà!*"

Iqbal swiveled around, triumphant.

Stevie got to her feet. Now that the computer was unlocked, she was unsure whether she wanted to know what Simon had hidden there.

Iqbal's brow creased. "Do you want me to leave you alone for a moment?"

"I don't know."

"Tell you what." He pushed his chair back from the desk. "I'll make us a cup of tea. Give you a bit of privacy."

"Thanks."

It was an automatic response. Stevie felt detached, as if she too was a computer, a robot girl waiting to be programmed with her next task. She could hear Iqbal running the tap, filling the kettle, moving crockery around. The sounds belonged to another world. Stevie stroked the computer keyboard. Would this be her Rubicon? No, she had crossed that when the stranger had attacked her in the parking lot, or maybe even earlier, when she had found Simon. Perhaps there had been no going back after that.

She clicked on *Recent Places* and opened the first document listed: an Excel file headed *CP Study 001*. A bewildering register of numbers and percentages appeared on the screen and she let out a groan.

"What is it?"

Iqbal was cradling a teapot in his hand, rolling a splash of hot water around its belly, warming the china.

Stevie shook her head. "I'll never be able to decipher this."

"Let me take a look." Iqbal emptied the water down the sink, tipped three teaspoonfuls of tea into the pot and poured boiling water over it. He put the teapot on a tray beside two mugs and a metal tea strainer. "Do you take milk?"

Stevie wanted to tell him to forget the tea, but she said, "Yes."

Iqbal took a milk carton from the fridge, added some to both of the mugs, and carried the tray over to the desk. He looked over Stevie's shoulder at the open document.

"Minimize it and open the next one on the list." *CP Study 002* was another Excel document, another screed of incomprehensible data. Iqbal lifted the lid of the pot, stirred its contents, and strained tea into the two mugs. "And the next one." He handed Stevie a mug. "And the ones after that."

CP Study 003 and *004* were more of the same, but the documents that followed were of a different stamp: patients' notes, written in technical language that was difficult to follow. They scrolled through them, unsure of what they were searching for until Iqbal said, "Let's have a look at his downloads."

Iqbal lingered on an article headlined "The Breakthrough That Could Transform the Treatment of Cerebral Palsy," which had been published three years ago in *Archives of Disease in Childhood*. Scans of a series of contracts followed. The first was with a pharmaceutical company, TelioGlaxin©; the rest were a series of franchises licensing various organizations to carry out the treatment developed.

Iqbal scooted his chair closer. He leaned in, put his finger on the touchpad and moved the cursor down until he reached the part about money. He let out a low whistle and returned to the three names at the top.

"You know these guys?"

Simon's name was written above John Ahumibe's and Alexander Buchanan's.

"This is Simon Sharkey's laptop. He was my boyfriend. I've met the other two men once, recently. They were colleagues of Simon's."

"Did he do this to you?" Iqbal stretched a hand toward her bruised face, but didn't touch it. "Your boyfriend?"

"No, that was someone else."

He nodded to show he believed her.

"They had a lot of money coming in."

"Enough to incite murder?"

Iqbal raised his eyebrows. "How much is enough? Six months ago, a schoolkid was stabbed to death for thirty dollars, outside the shops at the end of my road. It can happen to the best of us." Iqbal looked at her. "But yes, these guys were making the kind of big money some people would kill for." He came to the end of Simon's downloads. "Okay, I think we may have exhausted this particular seam." He closed the computer window and scrolled the cursor down the start-up menu. "Last, but most certainly not least, let's have a look at the picture library." Iqbal clicked and Simon's gallery sprang on to the screen. There was one, solitary image saved there.

Stevie had forgotten the photograph's existence, but as soon as she saw it she remembered the afternoon it was taken.

It had been one of their few daytime excursions. They had shared a boozy lunch at the Charlotte Street Hotel and then walked to Russell Square. Neither of them had been dressed for lazing around on the grass. Simon had been at meetings that morning and was still in his suit, and Stevie had been wearing a dress more appropriate for fine dining than picnics, but they had sat together on the lawn among tourists with time to kill, and office workers grabbing a quick lunch.

Stevie remembered how Simon had suddenly leapt to his feet and accosted a passing couple. How he had handed the woman his phone, explained how to operate the camera function, and then sat nimbly back down on the grass and reached an arm around Stevie, drawing her close. It was a good photo. They were both laughing, trees dappling the sunlight behind them.

Iqbal asked, "Is that him?"

"Yes."

"Where is he now? In prison?"

"He's dead."

It was harder to say with Simon's face in front of her, his smile wide and reckless.

"The sweats?"

"No, I think he was murdered because of something to do with all of this." She closed the computer window, banishing the photograph to the archives. "Why did you ask if Simon was in prison?"

"That kind of money? It's too good to be true and in my experience, too good to be true can be a short cut to a long stay in the big white hotel. I learned that the hard way."

"You went to jail?"

"No, but I could have. That's the reason I do the odd favor for PC Caniparoli."

"He bribes you?"

Iqbal's expression had turned serious at the mention of murder, but he favored her with a smile.

"Derek's a decent guy. He gave me a break. I owe him big time."

"That's what I need, a break." Stevie gestured at the documents stacked together on the desktop. "I thought that if I could get into Simon's computer I'd know why he was killed and what to do about it. But all I've ended up with is a bunch of hospital notes I'll never be able to understand and an incomprehensible jumble of numbers." She got to her feet and closed the laptop's lid. "I'm more confused than when I arrived."

"No, you're not." Iqbal took a sip of his tea. It was cold. He made a face and set the mug back on its coaster. "You know your boyfriend was part of a major medical breakthrough. You also know there's big money involved and who the other two people included in the contract are. I'd say that's quite a lot of information to go on. As for the rest of the stuff." He shrugged his shoulders. "You seem like an intelligent woman. Maybe you wouldn't get the finer points of the scientific argument, but I bet if you read the articles and patient notes, you'd understand the gist of it."

"Maybe, but there's no way I can get to grips with the *CP* files, whatever they are. They're just a mass of numbers. I wouldn't know where to start."

"When you said all you wanted was to get past the password I guessed it would just be the beginning." Iqbal raised the laptop's lid and the files sprang back on to the screen. "My first degree's in math, but I took a postgrad in statistics. Raw data is a language I speak."

"You'll help me?"

"PC Caniparoli asked me to help you out and like I said, I owe PC Caniparoli. It might take a while though."

"How long?"

"I don't know, an hour or six, maybe more." Iqbal stuck a memory stick into the computer, saved the *Archives of Disease in Childhood* article and patient reports to it and then inserted the stick into his own computer and pressed print. A printer at the other end of the desk hummed into life and started to scroll forth pages. "Why don't you settle yourself on the couch and read through these while I spread out over here and do my best to make sense of all this?" He grinned at her. "You can put the kettle on and make us another pot of tea if you like. I've been preparing for a siege. There should be enough tea bags and cookies to last us through Armageddon and into the beyond."

Twenty-Two

Stevie woke unsure of where she was, and then she saw the lights of the city shimmering in the darkness beyond the large picture windows and remembered. She pushed herself upright on Iqbal's couch.

"How long was I out for?"

"Hours. I reckoned you needed it."

She ran a hand through her hair, pushing it away from her face. "I feel awful."

Iqbal went behind the breakfast bar, took the packet of frozen peas from the freezer and tossed them to her.

"I stuck them back in when I saw you'd fallen asleep."

"Thanks." Stevie held the pack to her face. The coldness hurt. "Do I look awful?"

"Better than when you arrived. You hardly remind me of Joseph Merrick at all."

"Thanks."

She lifted one of the cushions from the couch.

"Looking for these?" Iqbal held up the notes he had printed earlier. "How much did you manage to get through before you dropped off?"

"Not much."

She had passed out almost as soon as she had sat on the couch.

"It makes interesting reading. Put it together with some of the other stuff I've found and it becomes fascinating. Come and take a look."

Stevie gave the city lights a last glance. There was something different about them. Something she couldn't put her finger on. She turned her back on the lights and joined Iqbal at his desk. He swiveled around in his chair to face her.

"Okay, did you read the article about the breakthrough your boyfriend and his colleagues made?"

"A bit of it." Stevie was ashamed to admit she hadn't gotten beyond the first paragraph before sleep had ambushed her. "I'm not sure I absorbed it all."

"I think it could be one of the keys to the whole thing." Iqbal's eyes were bright with the triumph of discovery. "Put simply, Simon and his team, Buchanan and Ahumibe, had an idea that if they could work out a way to deliver anti-epileptic medication directly into the spinal tissue of children with cerebral palsy, it could be more effective than existing treatments. They looked at methods of delivering medication for other conditions, and Buchanan, the pharmacist in the crew, developed a form of anti-epileptic medicine that could be administered through a pump implanted in children's abdomens."

"It sounds like the cure might be worse than the disease."

"That's where you're wrong." Iqbal was as enthusiastic as a new convert. "Cerebral palsy is a horrible disease and these are sophisticated devices. The pumps deliver minute trickles of medication through a tiny tube implanted in the spinal cord. We're talking microsurgery."

"So, did it work?"

"According to the studies Simon and his team set up, it worked very well indeed, much better than they'd anticipated. There was only one problem."

Iqbal paused and Stevie realized that he was waiting for her to ask what the problem was.

"What?"

"The treatment was expensive. It would cost around seven thousand dollars to insert the pump, another two thousand three hundred dollars every three months to fund the drug, plus another twelve hundred dollars every three months to top up the pump. It could go on for as long as the child lived, into adulthood, into old age. People say you can't put a cost on a life, but these funding bodies in the National Health Service do exactly that. They have to or there'd be no money left for anything else. They ruled that the treatment was too expensive for the NHS to license. But the team had gotten their teeth into the project."

Stevie tried to push images of teeth and dissected spines from her mind.

"What did they do?"

"They found a pharmaceutical firm that would manufacture their form of the drug, set up their own company, Fibrosyop, and decided to offer the treatment privately."

It chimed with what Nurse Webb had said.

"So only rich people could afford it?"

Iqbal leaned forward. "Do you have kids?"

The question was unexpected. It made her think of Joanie and Derek, the IVF treatments Joanie had only told Stevie about after Derek had left.

"No." Stevie stretched her shoulders, trying to loosen the knot of muscles in her neck.

"Neither do I," Iqbal said. "But I know that if I did, I'd do anything for them."

"I guess that's the way it's meant to be."

"Exactly." Iqbal smiled. His teeth were white, and so evenly spaced he could be mistaken for an American. "So it wasn't only rich people who accessed the treatment. Parents raised money in whatever ways they could. Some of them more or less bankrupted themselves."

"A nurse I spoke to said that by offering the treatment privately, Simon and his colleagues hoped they'd find a way to make it cheaper."

"No doubt. But I'm betting they got rich in the process."

Stevie remembered Simon's exclusive apartment, the fast cars, five-star hotels, and expensive meals.

"I don't see where this gets us. It might not be the prettiest story, a bunch of doctors profiting from sick kids, but they weren't doing anything against the law."

"That's true. But the treatment wasn't foolproof." Iqbal flicked through the sheaf of papers. "The raw data on Simon's computer is a record of results of the trials they did. I haven't worked my way through all of it yet, but it seems straightforward enough so far." He pulled a page from the pile and handed it to her. "I did, however, take a break from the data to do a bit of extra digging. Have a look at this."

He maximized a window on the laptop and a website burst across the screen. The site was simple, an amateur job, but it had been made with passion.

DO NOT TRUST YOUR CHILDREN TO FIBROSYOP screamed the banner. A photograph of a smiling girl, wearing a party dress and glittery doodle boppers, took up most of the screen. It had been taken at Christmastime, and a silver tree, decorated with tinsel and baubles, sparkled in the background. The image was so full of color that it was an instant before Stevie realized that the girl was in a wheelchair, her neck supported by a headrest. The text surrounding the photo was a passionate invective against Fibrosyop.

Joy Summers had been seven years old when she had died after undergoing treatment by Simon's team. Her father was convinced that the doctors were to blame. Stevie wondered if Mr. Summers had written his report of his daughter's early death in the first throes of grief. His pain resonated in every accusation.

"This is the treatment that Simon helped to develop?"

"One and the same. I don't know if he was justified or not, but Joy Summers's father had a definite grudge." Iqbal clicked on a link to a newspaper article, with the air of a magician completing a trick. "After his daughter died, his wife committed suicide. They had already sold their house to pay for the treatment. He lost pretty much everything."

Stevie scanned the article. Polly Summers had taken an overdose. Her husband Melvin had found her lying in their daughter's bed, the child's photograph face down on the sheet beside her.

"Horrible."

"Imagine how it was for Melvin Summers. Maybe he decided he had nothing left to lose and took the law into his own hands."

"Simon was killed by someone with medical knowledge. They managed to make his death look natural."

Iqbal grinned. "Did I mention that Mr. Summers was a dentist? These guys are experts in anesthetics. He'd know the best way to knock someone out, and the difference between a long sleep and the big sleep."

"I don't know." Stevie spoke gently, not wanting to rain on his parade. "Mr. Summers may have had a motive, but why would that make Simon hide his computer in my apartment? I'm not sure it adds up."

Iqbal's smile faded. She could see his zeal waning, tiredness winning the battle. He balled up a piece of paper and tossed it in the trashcan.

Stevie asked, "What was that?"

"Summers's address."

Stevie fished the paper from the trashcan and smoothed it flat. It was a close-up of a leafy cul-de-sac taken from Google Earth. The street had been surveyed on a bright, sunny day. A woman walking a golden Labrador was frozen mid-step outside a red-roofed apartment block. One of the apartments was ringed in blue felt-tip. The street might have been anywhere in the city, were it not for the address printed neatly in the margin.

"How did you find it?"

"It was easy. Summers isn't such a common name and the report on his wife's suicide gave his age. I found him on the electoral roll and cross-checked against council tax records. It took less than ten minutes."

Iqbal picked a cluster of paper clips from a jar on the desk and started to thread them together. There was something self-conscious about the way he was avoiding her gaze. A thought occurred to Stevie and she asked, "Did you check up on where I live too?"

Iqbal let the chain of paper clips fall back into the jar. She saw a blush spreading across his face and laughed. It was a welcome release.

"I looked you up on the Web. I'm afraid *Shop TV* is a little loose with info about its presenters. It gave me more than enough to go on." Iqbal took a piece of paper from his pocket, crumpled it into a ball and sent it into the trashcan. "That's another problem with the Net. It's too easy to find out things you shouldn't want to know."

Stevie had a sudden urge to take his hand in hers. She clasped her fingers together.

"I'll check Melvin Summers out. You're right, he might be a lead." She laughed again. "Listen to me. I sound like a real detective." This time she reached out and touched him. "You should get some rest."

Iqbal looked beyond her, out toward the lights of the city. Now that he was no longer absorbed in the documents his mouth had a worried set to it.

"I shouldn't have looked up your address."

"It's okay." Stevie gave in to her impulse and sandwiched his hand between hers. Iqbal's fingers felt warm and dry. She squeezed them. "I'm flattered."

Iqbal returned her squeeze, a gentle pulse of flesh on flesh. He said, "There's something happening out there."

It was quiet in the apartment among the glow of the computer screens. Stevie asked, "Is it getting worse?"

"The official media is playing it down, but #sweats is just about the only topic on twitter. According to it and other sites I looked at while you were asleep, the sweats are spreading." Iqbal stroked the back of her hand. "I'm glad PC Caniparoli sent you here. Working through the data is just about the best distraction I could have had."

"Derek said that I was fiddling while Rome burns."

"What else is there to do?" Iqbal sounded hopeful.

Stevie let go of his hand.

"Watch television?"

She got up, took the TV remote control from its dock on the shelves, pointed it at the television and clicked. The same images as before flashed on to the screen: the hospital wards, the masked scientist staring intently at the test tube as he introduced something into it, drip by careful drip.

V5N6 IS NO RESPECTER OF AGE OR SOCIAL CLASS. SCIENTISTS ACROSS THE WORLD ARE TAKING PART IN AN UNPRECEDENTED COLLABORATION TO FIND A VACCINE.

**MEANWHILE PEOPLE ARE BEING ADVISED
TO TAKE SOME SIMPLE PRECAUTIONS.**

Stevie looked over her shoulder at Iqbal. "You were right. It's better not to touch." She turned her attention back to the screen.

**LIMIT TRAVEL TO NECESSARY JOURNEYS.
DO NOT HOARD FOOD OR GAS.**

Iqbal got up from his seat and stood behind her. Stevie could smell the fragrance of the fabric conditioner he washed his clothes with, and beneath that his own sharp scent. He rested his fingers gently on her shoulders, a feather-light touch more warmth than weight.

**REPORTS OF WIDESPREAD INFECTION
HAVE BEEN CONDEMNED AS ALARMIST
BY THE GOVERNMENT**

"The more I consider it, the more I think it might be worse not to touch." Iqbal squeezed her shoulders gently. Stevie felt his breath on the back of her neck and then the trace of his lips, dry and delicate, at the top of her spine. She felt her body respond and whispered, "I might be a carrier."

**THE MINISTER FOR HEALTH HAS URGED
INTERNET USERS AND THE MEDIA TO MAKE
CLEARER DISTINCTIONS BETWEEN HARD
NEWS AND RUMOR**

Iqbal pulled the left strap of her vest to one side and grazed her shoulder with his teeth.

"I know." His mouth continued its progress across her shoulder and his words were a murmur. "But maybe the news is right and reports of multiple deaths are much exaggerated."

"My best friend died of it."

He kissed the top of her head again. "Would you like me to stop?"

Stevie hesitated for a beat. Thinking about Joanie had made her remember how alone she was.

"No."

He shifted her other strap and ran the tip of his tongue along Stevie's right shoulder, making her gasp.

"The sweats has some positive outcomes." Iqbal's teeth found the sensitive spot between her neck and her shoulder. "It makes men bolder. I guess, in the end, all we are is a bundle of cells with the same needs as a mayfly."

Stevie shivered and leaned into him. Iqbal was slim and light compared to Simon's solid bulk, but the heat of him, his urgency, recalled Simon, and she found herself wanting to be overwhelmed. Stevie turned to face him, still in the orbit of his arms. She whispered, "Maybe we shouldn't."

"Maybe we should." Iqbal caught her hands in his, holding her embrace tight. "People like you are survivors. I'm just a computer geek, the kind of guy who gets shot in the first frames of the movie."

Stevie remembered her mother, the months of battling, the growing indignities that had turned her into someone else, and the final relief of defeat. She said, "It's not as simple as that. Life isn't like the cinema. No one's invulnerable, no matter how strong they are. We can't predict who'll live and who'll die."

Iqbal whispered, "This might be the last chance either of us ever gets."

Stevie laughed. "Do you hit every girl you meet with the please-make-love-to-me-before-I-die-of-the-plague chat-up line?"

He touched her hair with his face. She felt him breathe in her scent the way Simon had done when they were making love.

"Not usually."

"Good, because only an idiot would fall for it." Stevie raised her face and they kissed. She felt Iqbal's body tremble and knew that beneath his desire he was shy. The realization emboldened her and she pulled off her vest.

Iqbal ran his hands the length of her body, stroking her breasts through her bra, exploring the slide of her back, the slope of her rear. She whispered, "Are you sure?" and he led her up the floating staircase to his bed. Iqbal's body was smooth, his skin almost as soft as her own. She tried not to think of Simon's broad chest, the rough, gratifying weight of him, as she let Iqbal touch his lips to her bruises. He traced his fingertips across her body, his caress so light that when she closed her eyes Stevie was barely sure that he was there. She saw his hand on her thigh and thought, we are all flesh. Then Iqbal leaned across her, turned out the lights and they clung to each other in the dark.

Twenty-Three

In the hours they had spent in bed, it had grown obvious what was wrong with the view from Iqbal's apartment. There were fewer streetlights than there should have been, and whole districts of the city were now sunk in darkness.

Stevie stood at the window, trying to work out which neighborhoods were illuminated, but it was like trying to map an unfamiliar galaxy, and she gave up. Iqbal was still in bed, sprawled beneath the duvet, sleeping like the dead.

She had lain on her side watching the gentle rise and fall of his breaths, and been surprised by two contradictory emotions: a stab of guilt at being unfaithful to Simon, and an urge to close her eyes, give in and stay with Iqbal. It would be the sensible thing to do. Sit tight, tune into the TV and radio and wait until things worked themselves out. But it would be a kind of death too.

Stevie padded downstairs in her bare feet and got dressed. She copied Simon's files on to the memory stick Iqbal had given her and then printed out two copies of each. It might only be a matter of time before the electricity failed here too, or the Internet went down. She left one of the bundles of printouts on Iqbal's desk and tried to compose a note, but there was too much and too little to say. In the end she scribbled her cell number on a scrap of paper, added her name and a kiss: *Stevie X.* It would have to do. She hesitated over Simon's laptop, wondering if she should take it with her, but decided to leave it where it was. It was safer at Iqbal's, one computer hidden among many, the same way that Simon's murder would have been one small death among thousands, were it not for the letter he had left her.

Stevie had her hand on the front door when she suddenly turned back, booted the computer up again and printed out the photograph of the two of them laughing together in Russell Square. She folded it into a small square and slipped it into the zippered pocket of her tracksuit. The bottle of antibacterial gel was on the desk, next to a set of keys. She hesitated, and then shoved them both in her satchel and left, closing the door gently behind her, careful not to wake Iqbal.

The GPS instructed her to follow an unfamiliar route. Stevie obeyed its directions, slipping along residential roads and dual highways, passing parks and parades of shops, moving in and out of darkness like a restless sleeper sliding in and out of consciousness.

London had always been a city of contrasts, but tonight it seemed a place divided into light and shadows. She traveled through streets where every gate was bolted, every shop shuttered, every window a closed unblinking eye. Then she would turn a corner into bright lights and see drinkers crowding pavements outside pubs whose closing bell should have rung hours ago.

Stevie stopped at a red light and saw a man standing beneath a flickering lamppost, raising his arms in the air. She rolled down her window and heard him shout, "The four horsemen of the Apocalypse have saddled their horses and are galloping toward us." He put a hand to his ear. "Can you hear their spurs? Do you feel their breath against your neck? Soon the honest dead will rise from their graves and all sinners will be cast into Hell's fire." The man saw Stevie watching him and pointed at her. "You know the pain of burned flesh. Imagine the pain of burning all over your body, for all time, all eternity . . ."

The lights changed and she drove on, but it was hard to make headway. People spilled into her path as if, now that they had flung off the division between night and day, the boundary between road and sidewalk no longer existed. There was a holiday recklessness to the crowds, a sense of ragged revelry. She wondered if this was how it had been in the old days, when families packed a picnic and treated themselves to an outing to Newgate to watch the hangings.

A flock of youths on undersized bikes tore across the Mini's path, bandit-quick, hoods up, mouths and noses hidden behind scarves and surgical masks. They vanished up a side street, fast as thieves. A bag slid from one of the boys' handlebars as he rounded the corner. A bottle shattered, tins bounced and dented against the pavement, and Stevie realized that their booty wasn't from electrical stores, sportswear outlets, or computer shops, but a supermarket. She turned a corner and saw the supermarket, squat and shining, its parking lot jammed worse than any Christmas Eve. Men and women struggled to their cars, pushing ill-balanced carts heavy with supplies. Stevie paused to watch. The shoppers had an anxious edge, but assistants were still tidying away abandoned shopping carts, and it was clear that the customers were hoarders and not looters. A car tooted impatiently behind her, and Stevie moved on.

She was used to driving home in the early hours. The night-time city was a world beyond her windshield, the preserve of drunks and police, of prostitutes, insomniacs, curb crawlers, and shift workers. She was used to stumblers and head-down walkers.

But Stevie knew that London was unpredictable, a city that could explode into pitched battles, Molotov cocktails, burning cars, and blazing buildings.

She drove cautiously, keeping to the rules of the road, until three buzz-cut-bald men approached her car at a red light, put their weight against its roof and started to rock it from side to side. They were chanting something, a soccer song she didn't recognize. Stevie put a hand on the horn and her foot to the floor. Her right tire skidded against the pavement and she thought the Mini might roll, but the combination of horn and spinning wheels startled the men and they let go. After that she no longer bothered with traffic signals.

Busy streets held their terrors, but sliding back into the black, traveling the unfamiliar roads with only the glow of her headlights to guide her, was even more unsettling. The unlit pavements looked deserted, but once her eyes became accustomed to the gloom, she caught glimpses of people moving in the darkness, and was glad of the knife in her bag.

She only stopped once on an unlit road, when a fox stepped into the Mini's path and forced her to hit the brakes. The fox was skinny, its flanks hollow and scraggy, as if it had not quite recovered from a fight. But the creature stared at her, holding its ground, eyes gleaming like polished metal. Stevie tapped the horn. The fox blinked, gave her a last assessing look, and then trotted into the dark with no more haste than a family dog returning from a stroll. Stevie wondered if it sensed something afoot, a chance that it and its kind might soon have more sway.

She tuned the radio to Radio London and set the volume low, so it wouldn't drown out the voice of the GPS. The presenter was interviewing a reporter somewhere on the streets of the city. Stevie thought she could detect a sense of excitement in the broadcasters' voices, exhilaration that the news was right on their doorstep. The quiet hum of their words accompanied her journey: *curfew . . . power failure . . . lack of manpower . . . looting . . . army . . . rationing . . . closures of nuclear facilities . . . food shortages . . .* There was health advice too, instructions to stay at home, to drink plenty of water, to keep children indoors. Schools were closed and teaching suspended, though some had been reopened as official quarantine centers. There was a phone number for relatives of the sick to call, though once again the advice was to *stay at home*; going to hospital would only result in *further delays.*

The GPS instructed her to *turn left.* Stevie obeyed and the mechanical voice announced with a sense of pride that usually made her smile: *You have reached your destination.* She looked at the bonfire barricading the entrance to Melvin Summers's street and whispered, "Thank you."

Twenty-Four

Stevie had passed other fires on her journey, distant orange glows that had reminded her of Guy Fawkes Nights of her early childhood, the smell of rotting leaves, burning wood and gas, the thrill of sanctioned danger. She had been scared of fireworks, had held her mother's hand fast and refused to go near the front of the crowd for fear of flying embers.

The bonfire blocking her way was as high as any her local council had organized. There were figures moving around the blaze but the fire's glow was too bright to make out their detail. They might have been trying to guard the road, or raze it to the ground. One of them peeled away from the group and walked toward her car. The firelight illuminated the smears of blood and fingerprints on the passenger window. Stevie remembered the way the strange girl and her companion had tried to push it open. She felt in her bag for the knife she had taken from home and laid it in the shadows of the passenger seat.

The figure made a circling gesture with his hand, indicating that she should turn her car around and drive away. Stevie stayed where she was. The satellite image Iqbal had printed showed that Melvin Summers's street was a dead end. This was her only way in.

The figure stood still for a moment. She could see that it was a man now, though his features were hidden by a scarf tied around his nose and mouth, like a bandit in an old cowboy film. The man was short, his body square and stocky. His stance was less confident than the fox's. The creature had seemed to challenge her; the stranger looked hesitant, despite the stick in his hand. Stevie switched off the headlights so that the man could see her face. She scrolled the window down a smidgen and turned off the engine.

"I'm not going anywhere," she whispered.

It was as if the man heard her. He took a few tentative steps forward, stopped about a foot away from the passenger window and shouted, "This road is under lockdown. Turn your vehicle around and go away."

The formal words sounded stilted, as if they belonged to an unfamiliar script the stranger was following. Now that he was closer Stevie could see that what she had taken for a stick was actually a metal bar. She wondered where you would find such a thing.

"I'm here to visit someone." She leaned across the passenger seat, resting a hand on the hilt of the knife, and raised her voice. "Melvin Summers. He lives in this street."

"I'm sorry," the man said, shaking his head, "but there's no coming and going from here, miss."

His voice was muffled by the scarf tied around his face. It was hard to guess his age without seeing his features, but the leather jacket he was wearing was ten years out of fashion, the body beneath it broad and running to fat.

"What do you mean?"

"Everyone beyond this line is healthy. We want to keep it that way."

The man was still keeping his distance, and Stevie wondered if the improvised mask was intended to block infection rather than hide his features.

"What happens if someone inside your line gets sick?"

"We'll cross that bridge if we get there." The stranger paused, as if considering his answer, and added, "There's a quarantine center in the primary school." He pointed to somewhere beyond her car, out into the darkness.

A second man stepped beyond the glow of the fire. He was taller than the first, thin and rangy, and carrying a baseball bat.

"Are you a journalist?"

The newcomer had a soccer scarf wrapped around his mouth and nose. It made him look like a terrorist glimpsed on a CCTV camera, an already dead man, located after the fact.

"I just want to visit Mr. Summers. He lives here. He's a dentist. His wife died recently, his wife and his little girl."

"I remember him." The baseball bat hung loosely in the second man's hand. "He's not a dentist no more, gave it up after his missus offed herself."

"Does he still live in the street?"

"No, miss." The squat man rested the end of his metal bar against the ground and leaned his weight against it. "He lives in the bar, said he was spending his savings on drinking himself to death. The sweats would be a blessed relief if you ask me."

Now that they were talking the men seemed more relaxed, as if they had decided she posed no threat. Stevie gave them the smile that had won her countless sales.

"You seem pretty organized. Is there any way to find out if he's in your quarantine zone?"

"It don't make no difference if he is or if he ain't." The man with the baseball bat sounded defensive and she guessed they hadn't carried out a census of their small kingdom. "No one gets in. That's the rule."

"I've had the sweats. I'm immune." She smiled again. "Won't you let me through? It's important."

The man with the baseball bat took a step forward and for an instant she thought he might be about to name a price she wouldn't want to pay. But the man with the metal bar straightened his shoulders and put a hand on his companion's arm.

"Sorry, miss. Official advice is to stay at home, have contact with as few people as possible, and that's what we're making sure happens. We're just doing our best to protect our properties and our families. You should go home too. It won't do you no good to go wandering around at night, even if you have had the sweats. There are some funny people about."

Stevie thought he might have cast a look at the man standing next to him, but if he did, it was so fleeting she couldn't be sure.

"Where does Mr. Summers drink?"

"The Nell Gwynne, back the way you came and then first on the right." The tall man swung his baseball bat to and fro, a slow-moving pendulum. "He's more than likely there."

"Leave it alone, miss," the smaller man said. "It's after midnight and Nellie's isn't a place for a woman on her own, not tonight."

Stevie put the car into gear. She saw the man armed with the baseball bat take a bottle of spirits from the pocket of his jacket, as if talk of pubs had made him thirsty. His companion took a step forward, shouting to make himself heard over the noise of the car engine.

"Even if you find Summers, he'll be too far gone to know you're there."

Stevie turned the car around and drove in the direction of the pub.

Twenty-Five

The hanging baskets decorating the front of the Nell Gwynne had once been impressive, but the pub's clientele was intent on watering itself, and the begonias, geraniums, and trailing lobelia drooped limp as seaweed at low tide. Stevie pulled the zipper of her tracksuit top up to her chin and pressed through the crush of drinkers on the pavement, into the warm tobacco fug of the pub's interior. She detected the sweet, throat-sharp scent of marijuana beneath the cigarette smoke shelving the air. The pub was low-ceilinged and so noisy that at first it seemed everyone was talking at the tops of their voices. But as Stevie pushed her way to the bar she became aware of drinkers on the periphery, men and women, as limp as the pub's flower display.

Traces of the cozy pub it must once have been clung to the Nell Gwynne like a light shining in a half-demolished building. A menu was still chalked on the blackboard, offering steak pie, roast lamb, fish and chips, and other pub-grub staples. Black-and-white photographs of an older, more rustic London crowded the walls. Stevie noticed a horseshoe pinned above the door, arched end at the bottom, to keep the luck of the house from draining away.

"All right, dear?" A thin, rat-faced man nodded a gentle, absent greeting in Stevie's direction and then unzipped his fly and let go a long and hissing stream against the side of the bar.

Stevie stepped smartly backward, away from the rush of piss.

"For Christ's sake, Tony," said a man in scuffed jeans and a denim jacket. But no one made a move to throw out the drunk, and when he was finished he zipped up and continued taking steady sips from the beer glass, golden on the bar in front of him.

Iqbal had printed a photograph of Melvin Summers from the dentist's website. It was a head-and-shoulders shot of a neatly groomed, square-jawed man in a white coat. Stevie took the print-out from her tracksuit pocket and cast her gaze around the room.

The drinkers were mainly men, gathered in small huddles or settled determinedly on their own. Pensioners, intoxicated boys, and business types mingled with wired-up youths and shell-suited men sporting gold chains and sovereign rings, whose broad bellies suggested long, restful hours in front of flat-screen TVs. A middle-aged cyclist, his flesh squeezed firm by Lycra, shoveled change into the fruit machine, playing with chance as if his life depended on it; a laborer in a fluorescent jacket and work boots cradled his hard hat between his hands; a man with a young face and gray hair talked gently to a standard poodle who stared up at him with rapt attention. There were a few women too. Stevie saw that they were at the center of clusters of men and knew she would have to watch her step.

The man in denim whispered, "Help yourself to a drink, Princess. It's self-service. John and Doris won't mind, not where they've gone."

"A terror against tick, John was," Tony said. "You remember how he was, Django. Probably spinning in his grave."

There was an edge of bravado to his voice, as if mentioning graves was a mighty dare.

Django turned his weary gaze on him. "Show a bit of respect for the dead."

Perhaps it was Django's jeans and denim jacket that reminded Stevie of an urban cowboy, a man unsuited to the times he found himself in. Or maybe it was the casual way he propped himself against the bar, as if he had known all along that life would come to this desperate pass. She showed him the dentist's photograph.

"I'm looking for Melvin Summers. I was told this is his local."

Django continued to contemplate his glass. He spoke without looking at her.

"You're not a debt collector, are you, Princess?"

His neighbor laughed. "Get even, die in debt."

Django said, "Shut up, Tony," in the same calm voice he had used when he had invited Stevie to help herself to a drink. "What do you want him for?"

"I want to ask Mr. Summers about the doctors who treated his daughter prior to her death."

Django asked, "What are you then? A private eye?"

"A private dick," crowed Tony.

Django said, "You're a fool, Tony."

The other man grinned, as if he had just been given a compliment.

Stevie said, "I lost someone too. I need to find out why, while I still can." She was surprised to find her eyes welling up.

Django looked at the beer glass in front of him with distaste, and then took a long, deep swallow from it.

"I don't know if you've noticed, Princess, but people are dropping like flies. I'm all for justice, always have been, a tooth for a tooth and an eye for an eye, fair enough. But there doesn't seem much point in chasing after the death of one poor sap anymore."

"If we stop caring about the death of 'one poor sap' we might as well give up." Stevie saw a lazy smirk spreading across Tony's drink-dulled face and felt the futility of it all. "There's no sense in talking to you. You've already given in."

She turned to walk away, but Django caught her by the arm.

"Hold on a minute, Princess."

Stevie tried to shrug him off, but his grip held her, hard enough to bruise. The last time anyone had grabbed her had been in the TV station parking lot. Stevie kicked Django's shin and gave a swift uppercut to his chin that hurt her knuckles.

"Hey, hey, hey." Django caught her free wrist. Stevie tried to break away, but he was stronger. He brought his mouth close to her ear and whispered, "You shouldn't hit people, unless you're sure you can beat them," his breath warm and beery against her face.

Stevie pulled her foot into a kick, but Django let go before she had a chance to deliver.

"Leave her alone, Djang." Anxiety narrowed Tony's voice to a whine. "She looks like she's already taken a beating."

"Fuck off, Anthony."

Django's voice was barely more than a whisper. He rubbed the stubble on his chin where Stevie's fist had made contact.

Stevie said, "Touch me again and I'll show you just how capable I am of fucking you up."

To her surprise Django started to laugh, a dry, unhappy sound, barely audible over the noise of the bar.

"What is this? Christ, I'm your mild-mannered janitor type, but suddenly everybody thinks I'm going to go postal." He wiped his mouth on the back of his hand and placed a coaster on top of his pint. "Keep your eye on that for me, would you, Tone?" He nodded to Stevie to follow him and walked toward a door labeled *Lounge Bar*. "Melvin's through here. But you'll be lucky to get any sense out of him. I'm guessing if you know enough to look for Melv, you already know what happened to his wife?"

It was as if the altercation had made them allies. Stevie said, "I read about it."

A cheer gusted from the gents' bathroom where a small huddle was spilling out of the door. Django put a hand on Stevie's elbow and guided her past the rabble, toward the lounge, but not before she had glimpsed a blur of white flesh in the center of the knot of men, moving to a familiar rhythm.

"It's like Hitler's bunker in here," Django said. "I'd kick the crowd out, except there's too many of them. They'll vanish when the drink does." He tapped the pocket of his denim jacket, somewhere near his heart. "I've got the key to John's secret supply. Once this group is gone I'll lock the door, dig out the special stuff, go up to John and Doris's apartment and wait for things to improve."

"Do you think they will?"

"What?"

"Improve?"

He shrugged his shoulders. "Depends what you mean by improve. I reckon there'll be a lot more jobs to go around. Some people might think that's a good thing. On the other hand, there are jobs your average man can't do. Like being a brain surgeon or operating a nuclear power station, so life might get a bit less sophisticated. I can guarantee you one thing though."

"What?"

"If I survive, I'll be spending less time in the bar."

Stevie said, "I heard this place has become a refuge for Mr. Summers."

"That's one way of putting it. Another would be that when he got tired of getting hammered at home, he got hammered here instead." Django paused in the center of the busy room and looked at her. "Funny, Melv came in here a lot, but it was always a shock to see him, know what I mean? Like seeing a dead man step through the door. We're all on borrowed time, but no one really thinks about it until something like this happens, then getting hammered seems like the best thing to do. I guess Melv was just a step or two in front of the rest of us. He's been a dead man walking since he found his wife."

A disheveled man in a no-longer-smart business suit staggered over and put an arm around Stevie's waist. He leaned his head against her chest and slurred, "Why don't you and me go somewhere where we can be kind to each other?"

Django gripped the stranger's shoulders and turned him in the opposite direction. "Fuck off, man, she doesn't want to know." He gave the man a gentle shove that sent him staggering toward the bar, in the broken mechanical walk of the soon-to-crash drunk.

Stevie said, "Thanks, but there was no need. I could handle him myself."

"Is that how you got those bruises? Handling things yourself?"

Django stretched a hand toward her face, but Stevie stepped beyond his reach.

She said, "I saw Melvin's website. He blames his daughter's doctors for her death."

"Not just her death, his wife's too. He wanted their licenses revoked."

"Did you ever get the impression that he might go further than that?"

"What do you mean?"

"Go outside the law."

Django's face was furred with stubble, his jowls soft and puffy from drink and late nights, but his expression hardened.

"Why would you want to know that?"

Stevie forced a smile. "I'm not the police."

"Sorry." He ran a hand over his face. "I forgot you lost someone too. Was it your kid?"

"I'd rather not talk about it."

Django gave a small nod. "It looks like we're all going to learn a lot more about losing people."

"How about you?" she asked. "Have you lost somebody?"

Django looked away. Someone had decided it was too dark and set tea lights on the tables. The scruff of stubble on his chin glinted against the candlelight, gray speckling sandy red, an intimation of old age.

"I guess it says something about my life that the people I'm missing most are John and Doris." He gave her a sad smile. "Up until now, the only thing I ever lost was chances."

Twenty-Six

The tables in the lounge were cluttered with a Manhattan sky-line of wine goblets, tankards, tumblers, and shot glasses. It was obvious that some time earlier it had been the scene of heavy drinking. Now it had become a chill-out room, where people could escape the chaos of the main bar and marshal their resources for their next bout. A couple of sleeping drunks were curled on the banquette, using their jackets as pillows. Another lay beached on the floor, next to the empty fireplace, his breaths raw and labored, his brow slick with perspiration.

Django nodded toward the other side of the lounge where a man was slumped in a corner seat, his shaggy head resting on the table in front of him. "That's Melvin. Come the future, he might be your only chance of root canal treatment." Django crossed the room, put a hand on the sleeper's shoulder and gave it a rough shake. "Melvin . . . Melv . . ."

Melvin Summers's head lay in the crook of his right elbow. His other arm was stretched across the table, his hand still curled around an almost-full tumbler of beer, the way a sleeping child might clutch a favorite toy. Django eased the glass from Summers's grip and poured its contents over the dentist's head. At first

Summers reacted at the speed of a mollusk, then the liquid met its mark and he sprang to his feet, toppling the table.

"Wha the fuck . . . wha the fuck . . . fucking . . ."

Django put a hand on the other man's shoulder and pressed him gently back into his seat. He righted the table and set it back in place.

"You woke me up." All the grimy wrinkles in Melvin Summers's face creased. It looked like a fetish mask carved from some pale, moon-grown wood. "Do you know what it takes for me to fall asleep?" His voice was too weary to hold a threat. "Christ Almighty."

The dentist let out a groan and started to bang his forehead against the table.

Stevie leaped to stop him, but Django was quicker.

"Fuck, Melv, don't do that." He grabbed the collar of the dentist's jacket, holding his head upright, like an executioner who had forgotten the formality of the guillotine. "I wouldn't have woken you, friend, except that this lady here said she might be able to help with your little Joy."

Summers bore no resemblance to the neat professional who had graced his company website. His shirt hung open, exposing chest hair matted with beer and sweat. Remnants of dried blood were jeweled around his nostrils, and Stevie guessed this wasn't the first time the dentist had pounded his head against the table.

"Behave yourself." Django ruffled Summers's already ruffled hair.

Melvin Summers's mouth hung slackly open. He turned his eyes on Stevie and said, "Joy's dead."

It sounded like a verdict on the state of the world.

"We know, friend, but . . ." Django looked at Stevie as if suddenly realizing he didn't know her name.

"Stephanie."

"Stephanie here is going after those doctors that let Joy down, and she wants anything you can give her on them."

"Fuck off."

Melvin Summers rested his forehead on the table and covered his head with his hands. Django looked at Stevie and shrugged.

"I told you."

"Mr. Summers." Stevie sat next to the dentist. He reeked of stale sweat, sour beer, and urine, but she leaned in close and asked, "Why were you so sure that the doctors were responsible for Joy's death?" The dentist kept his head buried beneath his hands and his reply was muffled. Stevie put a hand on his shoulder. She felt him shrink beneath her touch, but he didn't pull away. "What convinced you?"

The dentist raised his head and looked at her.

"Because she died."

"It wasn't just that, was it, Melv?" Django had settled himself on a stool on the opposite side of the table. "She'd been ill a long time, your girl, since she was born. There were reasons you didn't think it was natural causes, weren't there?"

"Fuck off, Django. Go and get your hole and leave me alone."

Django gave Stevie an apologetic look and said, "Keep it clean, Melv."

The dentist rested his chin on his knuckles, as if the weight of his head was too much to carry unaided.

"Where's my drink?"

Django held up the empty beer glass.

"If I get you a refill, will you have a chat with Stephanie?"

Melvin Summers's face was still sticky with the beer Django had poured over him but he looked at his empty glass with bemusement. He thrust a hand into his pants pocket and pulled out a bundle of bills.

"S'okay, Melv, put your money away. It's on the house." Django looked at Stevie. "What's your poison?"

Stevie thought it might be nice to drown in a river of vodka or an ocean of gin, but she said, "I'm driving."

"Way things are, I doubt anyone's bothering about the drunk-driving laws and I know where Doris kept the champagne."

"She said she didn't want anything, Django." The dentist's voice was knotted with desperation. "Now fuck off, please, and get me a beer, like the good man that you are."

"What did your last servant die of?" Django said, but he sauntered toward the bar, looking like a man who could face anything, as long as he had a whisky in his hand.

Stevie wondered if she should wait for the drinks to arrive and lubricate the conversation, but the carriage clock on the mantelpiece chimed five. Time was draining away.

"I'm sorry to dredge up painful memories, but like Django said, I'm looking into Fibrosyop, the doctors who treated Joy."

Melvin Summers stared at her. He had handsome, symmetrical features beneath the blood and stubble, but his eyes held a recklessness that might not be entirely due to alcohol. Stevie wondered whether he would have been a happy family man if his daughter had lived, or if alcoholism and bitterness had always been lurking somewhere, ready to trip him up.

He asked, "Who are you representing? A rival drug firm?"

"No one. Myself."

"Why?"

One of the crashed-out drinkers mumbled something in his sleep and turned over.

Stevie said, "I lost someone too."

It was the answer she had given Django, and not quite a lie, but the taste of it was sour in her mouth.

Melvin Summers massaged his eyes with the heels of his hands.

"Fuck, my brain hurts." He leaned back in his chair and stared at her. "It won't do you any good. They all back each other up."

"Who?"

"The drug companies, the doctors, the money men."

Summers looked toward the door of the lounge and Stevie followed his gaze. In the bar beyond, a woman was dancing on her own. The woman raised her hands in the air and wiggled her fingertips, like someone miming rain. The dentist gave a deep sigh. "Django's taking his time." He tapped his fingernails against the table in a restless military beat that turned into a clenched fist rapping against wood. Stevie bore it for as long as she could and then put a hand over his.

"I need your help." Now that Melvin Summers's fist had stopped its banging Stevie could hear the carriage clock ticking off the seconds, beneath the snores of the sleeping drinkers. "And I might be the only other person still interested in what happened to your daughter."

"What difference will it make now?" Melvin Summers closed his eyes and Stevie thought she had lost him, but after a moment he opened them again. "I'm like the damn ancient mariner. I've got one fucking story and a compulsion to ruin everyone's day with it. Poor guy had a thirst on him too if I remember rightly."

He looked again at the door connecting the bar to the lounge.

Stevie said, "Don't worry about ruining my day. It's already hit the skids."

"It's early. There's still time for things to get worse." Summers rapped his knuckles against the table again, and then settled back in his seat. "Parents of sick kids get to know parents of other sick kids. I guess in the old days you would have run into each other in waiting rooms, or maybe at support groups, if you could find the time to go to a support group, but these days the Internet connects us all." He spread out his hands, like a conductor getting ready to rouse the orchestra, and then slumped back in his chair again. "Joy wasn't the only child the treatment didn't help. She also wasn't the only one who died while she was undergoing it. Okay, so Joy was ill, and there were no guarantees, I understood that, but children with cerebral palsy can live well into adulthood." Melvin Summers ran a hand through his hair. It flattened beneath his fingers and then sprang up into the same wild tangle as before. "After Joy died, I followed what happened to other children on the program. The death rate was higher than in the general population of children with cerebral palsy, and the ones who did survive just didn't improve, not in the way the research suggested they should have."

He gave Stevie a defiant look, inviting her to contradict him.

"Sounds like you knew a lot about Fibrosyop's research."

"Of course I did." Melvin Summers's eyes had lost their glassy sheen, as if talking about his daughter's case had sobered him. "It didn't matter to me that the treatment was expensive. I didn't care about that, neither did Carol, but I wanted to be convinced that it had a better-than-average chance of being effective. Joy had been through a lot and this was an invasive procedure." Django returned and set a pint next to the dentist's elbow, but Melvin Summers ignored it. He leaned forward, his eyes on Stevie's. "You meet parents who would do anything in the hope of making an improvement to their child's condition, however slight, even if it involves putting the child through more suffering. I didn't want that." Summers lifted his pint and took a long deep swallow that left a foam mustache on his top lip. "Carol said she felt the same way." He wiped his mouth with the back of his hand. "She did feel the same way. But the heart and the head don't always agree. My wife would have done anything for Joy. She wanted to rush into the treatment, but I insisted on time to research it. I read everything available—the prognosis was amazingly good." He looked at Django. "What is it they say? If it sounds too good to be true then it probably is."

The other man nodded. "So you reckon it was like some Nigerian prince wanting to share his fortune with you. All you need to do is give him details of your bank account and he'll make you a millionaire."

Summers said, "Substitute sick kid for bank account and you've got it in one."

Stevie wished Django would go away and leave them to talk in peace. She touched his arm, hoping he would take the hint and keep quiet. "You think the doctors deliberately went out to con you?"

The dentist grinned and she saw the reckless gleam in his eyes again. It made him look like a pirate, or a murderer. He said, "Let me ask you a question. What do you do for a living?"

"I sell stuff."

"What kind of stuff?"

"Various things."

"Various things." Melvin Summers raised an eyebrow. "Well, maybe selling various things is an honest profession, but I've been a dentist for almost twenty years, and I can tell you, dentistry has its share of crooks. There's money to be made from medicine and, as far as I'm concerned, wherever you find an opportunity to make money you'll find villains. Anyone who thinks otherwise is a fool."

Stevie smiled to soften the sting of what she was about to say. "The doctors who founded Fibrosyop tried to get their treatment licensed for use by the National Health Service. They didn't turn to the private sector until after the NHS rejected it."

"I'm not saying they planned it. But mistakes happen and sometimes they work to people's benefit. By the time Joy was undergoing treatment, those doctors were making so much money I reckon they didn't want to stop, even if they knew their miracle cure was a piece of painful and expensive shit."

Stevie said, "Did you take your suspicions to the authorities?"

Summers's voice was boozy with contempt.

"They're all in league with each other. I needed numbers if I was going to get anywhere. The website was just the first move. My plan was to rally as many parents as possible and then get the media on our side. One fucked-up dentist wouldn't convince anyone, but a group of parents with media interest would have a chance." The dentist looked at her. "What's the fucking point?" He put his pint to his mouth and took three deep swallows. The liquid was low in the glass and Stevie wondered if he was about to finish it and leave. "I've told you what I know. If you don't believe me, you can fuck off."

Django leaned forward. "Stephanie only wants to know what makes you so certain."

Summers ran his fingers over his skull, roughly kneading his head. It was a long time since the dentist had had a haircut and his hair was thick and coarse, like an animal's winter pelt.

"After Joy's death, one of the doctors came to see Carol and me in the hospital, to give us his condolences. I saw his face." He shook his head. "That doctor knew the treatment was a crock of shit and he was ashamed."

Stevie said, "He told you?"

"No, but it was written all over him."

Summers looked straight at Stevie, challenging her to disbelieve him.

She asked, "Did you say anything to him?"

"Not then. Carol was with me and she'd been through enough. I tried to tell myself how hard it must be for a doctor to lose a patient, especially a young patient. But I knew it was more than that, and it ate at me. Every time I closed my eyes and tried to go to sleep, I'd see that doctor's face, the shame on it. Other children were being subjected to the same useless procedure, and other parents were lying awake in their beds, praying that everything would work out, when what they should have been doing was enjoying the child they still had." He lifted his pint and emptied the last of the dregs from his glass. "I knew there was no point in trying to make an appointment to see him. He'd just find reasons not to meet me. So I staked out the hospital."

Django pulled a bottle of beer from his pocket and struck its cap against the edge of the table. A slice of cheap veneer splintered from the tabletop and the metal cap bounced on to the carpet. He handed the frothing bottle to the dentist. "What happened?"

"I saw him swanking across the foyer with another couple of doctors, all white coats and stethoscopes. I didn't say anything, just walked up and stood in front of them. He recognized me right away. It was obvious I'd been waiting for him, but he was smooth. You don't get to that level without being smooth. He actually seemed pleased to run into me." The dentist grinned again and tilted the bottle to his mouth. "Looking back, I can see he was desperate to get me out of the building in case I'd come to make some kind of public scene. A *brouhaha*. He suggested we went for a drink." Summers flicked a fingernail against the rim of the beer bottle and it made a small *ping*. "I guess he got my measure pretty quickly. I seem to remember that I drank three malt whiskeys and he had one beer which, now that I look back, might have been nonalcoholic." Summers smiled at Django. "Never trust a man who drinks nonalcoholic beer."

"Unless he's operating on a sick kid the next day," Django replied softly.

"God forbid." Melvin Summers spat on the carpet. "I laid it all out in front of him. My observations, the way the research and the reality didn't stack up, and he listened patiently."

Summers paused again and Stevie said, "I'm sensing a 'but.'"

"There was no 'but.' Not right away. He was tight-lipped, but you'd expect that. Britain's becoming as litigious as the US. No one admits to anything unless they're forced to. The doctor told me he was just one of a small team who made up Fibrosyop, and that as far as he knew the trials were watertight. Nevertheless, he said, he took my concerns seriously and would initiate a review of the treatment's results."

Django said, "Sounds reasonable."

"I thought it sounded like a pile of shit, and I was right." Melvin Summers grinned, like a man about to lay his trump card on the table. "That evening two police officers came to my house. They told me that the doctor had been clear that he didn't want to file an official complaint because of my 'obvious and understandable distress at my recent bereavement,' but if I persisted in harassing him, he would seek an injunction. It was all rather gentle." He shook his head. "They were your typical coppers, big guys. The kind you suspect might have turned to crime if they hadn't joined the force, but it was like a little bit of Dr. Sharkey was in the room with us. Apparently he had called in at the station personally to make sure there were no mix-ups. He'd obviously impressed them."

Stevie started at the sound of Simon's name, but neither of the men seemed to notice.

Melvin Summers let out a sigh. "I'd already put the website online. That may have been one of the reasons the police didn't take the case seriously. They thought I was some kind of Internet vigilante." He took another swallow of his beer. "I let Joy down twice. First when I handed her over to Fibrosyop, then when I confronted Dr. Sharkey. I should have held fire and got everything in place before I showed my hand."

Django patted the dentist's shoulder. "You shouldn't blame yourself, friend."

Stevie said, "Grief makes people do all sorts of strange things."

Melvin Summers took a cell phone from his pants pocket and handed it to Stevie. A photograph of his daughter beamed out from the screensaver. Joy Summers was sitting bolt upright, her neck and head supported by her wheelchair's pillowed headrest. The girl's hair was dark and tied in a silver ribbon, her eyes framed by glasses. Her smile was a hundred watts.

"She was beautiful," Stevie said, and she meant it.

"Carol and I knew about our daughter's condition from the start. We knew the name Joy Summers would sound silly to some people. But it suited her. She was a joy and quite frankly I don't care if it sounds corny to you or anyone else. She brought sunshine into the life of everyone who met her."

Django leaned forward and said gently, "She wouldn't want you to be like this though, would she, friend?"

The dentist picked up his bottle of beer and drained it. He threw it at the fireplace. The bottle glanced against the mantelpiece, dislodging the carriage clock and clinking loudly as it bounced unbroken on to the hearth. One of the drinkers opened his eyes, got to his feet, and then sat down again.

"Take a look around," Summers said. "I think the moment for joining AA might have passed."

The two men laughed. Django took another beer bottle from his pocket, knocked the cap free and set it foaming before the dentist.

Stevie said, "Dr. Sharkey is dead."

Melvin Summers stopped laughing. He lifted his beer bottle in the air.

"May he rot in hell, and may all those whom he loved join him there before too long."

The curse sent an electric current along the back of Stevie's neck.

"Someone killed him."

"Nothing to do with me, dear. I wish it was."

Django put his hand over Stevie's, and she realized why he had sat patiently with them while Melvin had recounted his story.

"Stephanie didn't come here to accuse you, Melv," Django said.

The dentist snorted. "Christ, you always did have a tendency to get cuntstruck, didn't you, friend? Look at her face. That's exactly what she came here for."

A sound of splintering wood and raised voices came from the other bar. The three of them glanced toward the lounge door, but they remained in their seats. Django turned his gaze on Stevie and squeezed her hand more tightly than was comfortable.

"Is he right?"

"Not exactly . . ."

Django repeated, "Not exactly?"

The pressure on her hand increased.

"Dr. Simon Sharkey was my boyfriend. He was part of Fibrosyop. I think someone may have murdered him. I want to find out who and why."

Django pulled her close. Stevie smelled beer, sweat and desire. He whispered, "You told me you'd lost a kid."

"No I didn't."

He tightened his grip on her hand. "You let me think you had."

Another crash came from the adjoining room. A woman screamed, a dog started barking, and a rumble of male voices clashed with the confused protests of the drinkers.

Django knocked Stevie's stool from under her as he got to his feet, toppling her to the ground. She thought he was about to kick her and braced herself to roll away from his boot, but he gave her a look of contempt and said, "Be careful who you make a fucking fool of in the future."

The noise in the next room was louder. Django went to the lounge door, glanced into the other bar, then slammed the door shut and bolted it. "Fuck, you'd think the police would have better things to do with their time." He pulled on the denim jacket he had hung on the back of his chair and patted the two beer bottles he had slipped in its inside pockets. "Sorry, Melvin. I wouldn't have brought her over if I'd known."

Stevie got to her feet holding the stool in front of her, ready to hit Django with it if he came too close. Glasses were shattering in the bar beyond, and someone began battering their fists against the other side of the connecting door.

"Don't worry about it." The dentist seemed unaware of the chaos in the next room. He nursed the dregs of his pint like a man who had been felled by yet another bereavement. "She brought good news."

The curtains in the lounge were closed. Django pulled one open a crack and peered out of the window. "Usual stupid pigs, they're concentrating on the front entrance." He looked at Summers. "If we go now we might make it out through the back." The drunk who had woken was already at the door that led out to the street. Django shoved him out of the way.

"You're at the end of the line."

He unbolted the door, opened it a crack and peered out.

The dentist leaned back in his seat and looked at Stevie.

"My old gran used to say, 'The Devil knows his own.' When I was a kid I used to wonder what she meant by it. Now I know. Look at you, fucking invincible."

Django said, "It's now or never." He gestured to Melvin Summers, but the dentist shook his head and raised his empty beer bottle in tribute. Django returned the salute with a nod. He stagewhispered, "Geronimo," and slid outside, the newly woken drunk at his heels.

A swell of rising voices came from the street. Stevie stayed where she was.

"Did you kill Simon Sharkey?"

The dentist shook his head. "No."

The banging on the connecting door had grown more desperate. One of the sleepers woke, stiffly unfurled his body, and staggered to his feet, his footsteps sure as a zombie's.

Stevie said, "You had a good motive."

"So did a lot of people."

"Perhaps, but you're a dentist. You work with anesthetics; you had the means to kill Simon and make it look natural." The drunk was still struggling with the bolts, but he would master them soon. Stevie forced herself to be cruel. "Plus I'm guessing you lost more than most, your wife and your child."

Melvin Summers flinched.

"If I'd killed your boyfriend, do you think I'd deny it? Believe me, I'd be fucking boasting."

There was a clunk and a small exclamation of satisfaction as the drunk managed to slide the bolts free. Stevie looked at the dentist, as if staring at him could uncover the truth. The bar door opened and she ran for the exit.

Twenty-Seven

Outside was a commotion of black-uniformed police officers and dazed civilians scuffling in the weak, tobacco-colored dawn. Stevie saw Django in their midst, tussling with a policeman. One of the bottles of beer slipped from his pocket and shattered, foaming against the pavement. He let out a roar and smashed a fist into the policeman's neck. The roar turned to a scream and Django crumpled to the ground, Taser wires snaking from his thigh.

Stevie flattened her body against the wall of the pub and edged her way along the side of the building. When she reached the corner she broke cover and ran, bracing herself for the electronic sting of a Taser. Her limp had returned but she could see the Mini, parked where she had left it, on the other side of the road. Stevie took the key fob from her pocket and unlocked the car, still running. She threw herself into the driver's seat, slammed the door and turned the key in the ignition. The daylight dimmed, as if the engine's grumbling start had leached power from the rising sun. She looked up and saw a policeman at her window. The policeman grabbed the handle of the driver's door and pulled, but Stevie had already clicked the lock home and it held tight. She crunched the gearstick into first, swearing under her breath. Her foot hit the clutch too hard. The car bucked and stalled, dead.

The policeman banged against the window with a gloved hand. Stevie turned the key in the ignition again, slid through the gears and pressed her foot to the floor. The Mini accelerated forward, just as the policeman brought his baton down hard, against the glass. Stevie had skewed his aim, but he caught the side window a glancing blow that cracked the glass like ice beneath a stone.

Stevie looked in her mirror as she sped away. The policeman had tumbled to the ground, but he was already getting to his feet, and she hoped that only his pride was hurt. She wondered if it mattered that he had probably got her license plate, or if things had gone beyond that.

Somewhere deep in her bag her phone started to ring. Stevie unzipped it and felt blindly inside, keeping her other hand on the wheel and her eyes trained on the road. The phone wasn't in the side pocket where she normally stowed it, and her fingers scrambled against her water bottle, hairbrush, and makeup bag, things recognized and unrecognized, until eventually it stopped its jaunty tune and Stevie abandoned her search. She turned the car radio on, unsure of where she was going but determined to put as many miles as possible between her and the Nell Gwynne.

Classical music was playing, soft and somber, on the radio. Stevie wondered if it indicated a new phase in the crisis, or if it was the kind of thing that always filled the airwaves in the early hours. She shifted through the stations until she found a news broadcast. The sweats had slipped from headline position, and the news was dominated by riots that had spread across Britain's southern cities and into the north as far as Newcastle.

She was back in suburbia. The houses scrolling past were neat-edged, the sidewalks beyond them punctuated by overflowing dumpsters and piled with trash. The car's windows were closed, but the smell of something rotten slipped inside, the scent of a fruit-market gutter at the end of a long hot day.

Shops had been looted, the radio announcer said in a distant voice, as if making clear that it was nothing to do with him; cars and buildings set on fire, people driven from their homes. Police resources had been stretched, he warned, but with the help of the Army, the authorities were reestablishing order.

The streets beyond the car windows were empty, the only movement the wind ruffling the trees and trembling the tops of privet hedges in need of a trim.

"Reestablishing order," Stevie repeated under her breath. The impact of the policeman's baton had shaken the whole car. Even if she managed to discover who had murdered Simon, Stevie wasn't sure what she would do with the information. Save it, she supposed. Collect the evidence and store it until things returned to normal.

"At least it was the police and not the Army," she said out loud to comfort herself.

Her words might have conjured the soldiers. Stevie turned the corner and saw four of them, standing in front of a barrier blocking the road. She considered turning back, but they were cradling machine guns and though Stevie couldn't quite believe they would shoot her, she slowed the Mini to a halt and rolled down the window, hoping the shattered glass would hold.

Twenty-Eight

The soldier who approached was young and dressed in desert fatigues.

"There's a curfew."

He was Scottish, with an accent that made her think of slums and razor gangs; his eyes were framed by wire-rimmed glasses, his chin speckled with acne. The combination made him look like an intelligent schoolboy who had been pressed into service.

"I'm sorry." Stevie glanced at the clock on the dashboard: 6:30 a.m. "Doesn't it end when the sun comes up?"

"You're thinking about vampires." The soldier's expression was serious. "They knock off at sunup. The curfew ends at 7:00 a.m."

"I'm heading home." In the past few days, lying had become second nature. "I spent the night at a friend's."

Someone said something into the soldier's headpiece and he looked away, toward the lightening dawn, as if the instructions were coming from above. The tinny voice stopped and the soldier bent toward her window, still keeping his distance.

"Is it more than three miles away?"

"No."

It was another lie, as smooth and automatic as the previous one.

"Okay, turn off the engine and step out of the car."

The gun was still resting in the soldier's arms. It was turned away from Stevie, toward the empty street, but now that she could see it up close, it was all too easy to imagine him putting his finger on the trigger and aiming it toward her.

"Why?"

"I need to check your trunk."

"What for?"

"Okay?" one of the soldiers by the barrier shouted and the boy by the car called back, "Aye fine, just the usual twenty damn questions." He squatted down on his haunches and looked at her. "You can get into big trouble for breaking the curfew. Did you know that?"

"No."

"You should, it's all over the news. Now stop making me look like an ass and get out of the car."

Stevie turned off the ignition. Her hands were still trembling, but she didn't shift from the driver's seat.

"I'm not moving until you tell me why I should."

"For fuck's sake," the soldier said. "Do you see what I'm wearing?"

"Yes."

He tapped the barrel of his machine gun.

"And do you know what this is?"

"Of course." Stevie kept eye contact with the soldier. There were lines and shadows on his skin at odds with his youth. "I'm not trying to be awkward. I just feel safer inside the car."

Some of the defensiveness went from the soldier's face, and for a second he looked frail. It was like glimpsing the interior of a house from the window of a train. A sudden intimate view, gone before you had time to register the details. He glanced at the barrier where his comrades were waiting and when he turned his attention back to Stevie, his toughness was restored.

"No one's going to hurt you. I just need to make sure you've not been looting, and then you can go on your way."

"You promise?"

The soldier drew a finger diagonally, one way and then another, across his chest.

"Cross my heart and hope to die." He made a face and looked upward to where high command or God was watching. "I take that second part back."

Stevie opened the door and stepped onto the road. The sky was flushed rosy pink, and there was a scent of bonfires in the air, as if summer had vanished and autumn arrived early.

The soldier asked, "What happened to your window?"

"Someone threw something at it."

He nodded, as if it was only to be expected, and walked around to the back of the car. Stevie followed him and opened the trunk. There was nothing inside except for a half-empty bottle of screen wash, a traveling rug, and a bundle of newspapers destined for recycling. She shoved it all into a corner and rolled back the bottom of the trunk to reveal the spare tire and jack stored beneath.

"Can I go now?"

The soldier's radio was squawking again. He held up a hand, palm outward, commanding silence.

"Roger that." It was as if the radio controlled the official part of him. It died and the soldier muttered, "Fuck," beneath his breath. He looked at her. "Pull over to the side of the road and wait in your vehicle." He must have seen the rebellion in her face because he said, "This road has to be kept clear for priority traffic." He raised a hand to the men at the barrier and shouted, "They're on their way." One of them waved to show that they had heard, and the three soldiers set about shifting the hurdle that formed their barricade.

Stevie got into the car. The soldier slapped her roof with the flat of his hand and pointed to where he wanted her to park.

She said, "How long will I have to wait?"

"You're asking the wrong man. This was meant to go through hours ago. It'll take as long as it takes."

"Can't I go back the way I came?"

"You're not much of a listener, are you? If I were you I'd sit back and get a bit of shut-eye."

"I'd rather sleep in my own bed."

"Wouldn't we all?" The soldier grinned. "Do you know where I'm meant to be right now?" He didn't wait for her to reply. "Up in Glasgow with my wife and three-year-old. The wife's mother's sick, and she insists on looking after her. I've told her to keep the boy well away, but it's a small apartment and my wife's never been a great one for following orders, unlike me." He looked at her. "The guys over there are the same. Straight back from a three-month tour, no decompression time, all leave canceled. We're nice guys. Peace lovers, but it's not a good idea to go around breaking curfews and arguing with soldiers. If my commanding officer tells me to shoot someone, I shoot them and they stay shot, understand?"

Stevie nodded.

"Don't look so worried." He gave her a smile that made him look like a child soldier, young, but already marked by symptoms of an old age he would never reach. "I doubt it'll come to that."

Stevie maneuvered the car into place, checked the fuel gauge and then turned off the engine. The tank was half full, but supplies might be getting low and she should think about refueling if she was to stay mobile. She made sure the door was locked and then stretched back in the driver's seat and closed her eyes.

Cell.

Stevie opened her eyes and rummaged in her bag for her phone. Iqbal's number was logged under missed calls. She stared out at the soldiers. They were still standing beside the open barrier gazing straight ahead, unsmiling, as if each one was encased in his own distinct world. Stevie wondered what "priority traffic" they were waiting for.

She pressed call-back and lifted the phone to her ear. Iqbal answered on the third ring.

"Are you okay?"

He sounded anxious and Stevie felt a jolt of regret. It had been a mistake to sleep with him.

"Yes, fine."

"The government's declared a curfew."

"I know." She heard the remoteness in her voice and tried to inject some warmth into it. "Is the Internet still working?"

"Yes," Iqbal said. "It's weird. It seems like half the city has lost power and the other half's going on as if nothing unusual is happening."

"That's a good sign, surely."

"Maybe, but if everyone stayed at home there'd be less chance of the virus spreading."

Stevie wondered if it was a comment on her early-morning defection from the warmth of his bed.

"People need to come out sometime, if only to get food."

There was silence on the line. Stevie imagined Iqbal sitting at his desk in the not-quite-sterile apartment he had stocked for a siege.

He said, "People need to avoid contact with each other to give scientists enough time to come up with an antidote or a vaccine, before the virus spreads too far."

She remembered what Dr. Chu had said about doctors' failure to cure the common cold.

"That could take years."

"So what would you suggest?"

"I don't know. We carry on and hope for the best?"

Iqbal's laugh sounded as if it belonged to an older man.

"This is war, Stevie. The virus is the enemy. We have to wipe it out before it annihilates us."

One of the soldiers at the barrier had taken out a pack of cigarettes. He offered them to his comrades, but the Scot said something to him and he shoved the pack back in the pocket of his uniform jacket, without lighting up.

"What would your solution be?" Stevie asked. "Paint crosses on victims' doors, or lock them up in concentration camps?"

"Phrases like concentration camp are over-emotive. Infected people should volunteer for isolation. Anything else is selfish."

Stevie saw Simon's face again, the way his mouth had hung open, gums receding to reveal the length of his teeth, the unnatural smile grinning at her from the rumpled bed, familiar and strange.

Perhaps Iqbal also remembered Simon's death, because his voice softened.

"At least that way they wouldn't take anyone with them."

Over by the barrier, the Scottish soldier was saying something into his radio. Stevie rolled the car window down a crack. She smelled the autumn scent of smoking wood and, beneath it, something sweet and familiar that made her think of compost and rotting leaves. The trees shifted in the wind and whatever the soldier was relaying was lost in the sound of their gusting branches. She slid the window back in place and asked Iqbal, "Do you think that's why they've imposed a curfew? To avoid the sweats from spreading?"

"I think the curfew's about public order. The government don't have the balls or the manpower to order people to stay in their houses indefinitely. Right now they seem more concerned with protecting property than lives." Stevie wondered how Iqbal, who had isolated himself in his home, knew more about the situation than she did. "I've got some good news for you." His voice was eager again. "I managed to hack into Dr. Sharkey's e-mails."

The sound of a diesel engine and heavy wheels rumbled into the early-morning stillness. Stevie looked up and saw an army truck driving through the open checkpoint. The truck was olive green, unmarked, and without windows. One of the waiting soldiers removed his cap and lowered his head as it passed. The others followed suit.

Stevie wondered if Iqbal had read any of the messages she had sent to Simon, but kept the thought to herself and asked, "Is there anything that stands out?"

"It's mainly medical stuff, way above my head, but Dr. Sharkey kept an online scheduler that sent daily reminders of appointments to his inbox. I hacked into it too and cross-referenced his appointments with his e-mails, to see what he was up to before he died."

The ease with which Iqbal had managed to shatter the illusion of privacy appalled her, but Stevie asked, "What did you find?"

"Dates with you were awarded an emoticon, a smiley face."

"Anything else?"

"Three days before his Web presence ceased, Dr. Sharkey was meant to meet a journalist, Geoffrey Frei."

"I've never heard of him."

"No?" Iqbal sounded surprised. "He's an investigative journalist who writes popular science pieces on medical corruption. His last book concentrated on the drug industry. It was a bestseller. I read it." Stevie heard the sound of paper being shuffled. "I compared some dates and discovered that Geoffrey Frei was in the news a lot the week Dr. Sharkey died."

Stevie could still see the truck in her rearview mirror, traveling at the slow pace of a funeral cortège. The Scots soldier left his companions by the barrier and walked toward her car.

"Iqbal, I'm sorry, but I'm about to be moved on," she said. The soldier pointed toward the road and mouthed something that might have been *straight home*. Stevie gave him a nod and gunned the engine into life. "I'm going to have to call you back."

Iqbal kept talking. "Frei was mugged somewhere near King's Cross Station the night before he was due to meet Dr. Sharkey. He was a big guy, a rugby blue, whatever that is. It looks like he tried to fight the muggers off, but it would have been better if he'd just given them his wallet. They stabbed him in the neck, the jugular to be precise. By the time he was found, he'd already bled to death."

The soldier slapped the roof of the Mini, and she jumped.

"Jesus!"

Iqbal said, "What was that?"

"Don't worry, it's nothing." Stevie was already rolling down the window. "I'll call you back."

She killed the call and looked up at the soldier.

He said, "You're free to go. If you take my advice you'll stick to the main roads."

Stevie nodded. "Good luck."

"Same to you." The soldier grinned, revealing a set of bad teeth, the bottom row as crowded and overlapping as drinkers in a station bar. "Here's hoping neither of us end up priority traffic."

Twenty-Nine

It was eerie, driving alone through the violet dawn blush, her car engine announcing her presence to the otherwise silent streets. Stevie took the Scottish soldier's advice and kept to main roads. She found herself scanning the windows of houses and apartments, trying to fathom life from drawn curtains and lit rooms. She thought about the army truck. Priority traffic, no one wanted to be; that had prompted the soldiers to bow their heads and remove their caps. She wondered where it would put its load to rest.

Stevie had been fresh from college and working for a tabloid when foot-and-mouth had hit Britain. She was too green to get the assignment, but the crisis had been headline news, and she had followed it, impatient for the day when her name would be a byline on the front page. Stevie remembered television footage of bonfires stacked with burning carcasses, plumes of black smoke drifting across villages. She wondered what arrangements Derek was making for Joanie and pushed the thought away. It was better not to dwell on these things. She had her task. It would be her compass through this crisis.

A trio of teenage girls, weighed down with hastily packed shopping bags, were ambling along the pavement. The girls' languid, after-the-party gait made her wonder if they were sick, or simply worn out by the excesses of the night before. Stevie glanced in her rearview mirror as she passed and caught a fleeting impression of gray skin cowled in shadows.

A gas station gleamed up ahead, but when she got closer she saw that its entrance was coned off, its pumps clamped, and marked OUT OF SERVICE.

"Shit."

Stevie glanced at her fuel gauge again. The tank was still more than half full, but she thought the dial had slipped a little. There were more cars on the roads now, though still a shadow of the traffic that would usually gridlock them at this time of the morning.

Stevie thought about Geoffrey Frei, the proximity of his death to Simon's. She wondered if the police knew of the two men's assignation. There had been a spate of stabbings and Underground station muggings that summer, and the journalist's death might easily have been another random attack that had ended tragically. But the coincidence remained: Frei and Simon had been due to meet, and now both of them were dead.

Stevie pulled over, turned off the engine and tapped Frei's name into the Internet search engine on her iPhone. The connection was painfully slow, but eventually a list of options appeared on the small screen. Stevie clicked on an obituary in the *Sunday Times*. It was as Iqbal had said: the journalist was the author of a regular column exposing scientific misrepresentations and scandals. His most recent book had been a crusade against corruption in the pharmaceutical industry. It had topped the nonfiction charts and he had been in the process of researching a follow-up. Geoffrey Frei was survived by his wife Sarah and twin sons.

She returned to the search engine and found a report of Frei's death in the *Evening Standard*. A photo of an open-faced man headed the article. Stevie took in the generous smile, the trendy, heavy-framed glasses, and curly hair. Then she scrolled down and read that Frei had been discovered by garbagemen, slumped between rows of trashcans, at the back of the railway station. The area around King's Cross bristled with CCTV cameras; the journalist had been captured crossing the station concourse and in the street beyond, but his encounter with the muggers had taken place off camera. Police were reported to be investigating, and there was a call for witnesses, but once it had disposed of the journalist's celebrity, the article took on the weary, dead-end air of a much retold story whose conclusions were already known.

Stevie wished that Simon was there to tell her what was going on. She leaned back in the driver's seat and took from her pocket the photograph of the two of them laughing together in Russell Square. She traced a finger around the edge of Simon's jaw, trying to remember the scent of him, the timbre of his voice.

"Fuck, Simon," she whispered. "What were you up to?"

Simon had been a good-looking man, with a responsible job, who had known how to play the fool. He had thick dark hair, a pleasantly broad body and lines at the corners of his eyes that suggested hard work and a good sense of humor. He had been clever too, of course. But it had been his faults, as much as his attributes, which had drawn her to him. The sense of style that had flirted with, but never completely embraced, vanity. The too-fast cars and gregariousness that had threatened to embarrass Stevie, even as it amused her. And then there had been the sex.

At first she had thought Simon's profession might put her off, that when he touched her she would be reminded of the snap of silicone gloves or the texture of blood. But Stevie had discovered extra assurance in the touch of hands that knew the secrets of flesh and bone.

"You know how I look inside," she had once said to him, lying naked in the middle of his bed. He had traced her organs with his fingertips, here her heart, here her liver, gall bladder, stomach, rolling her on to her front so he could run his fingers around the outline of her kidneys, her lungs, and then trace a line down her spine that ended with his teeth sinking gently into the cheeks of her "gluteus maximus," until she had laughed and turned onto her back; a move that he had rightly taken as an invitation.

Stevie scrolled down the search engine results again. Frei's death had prompted editorials on societal decay and a feature that charted his background and education against that of a youth convicted of stabbing a stranger to death. Frei had been born to parents who were both doctors. He had attended the same top public school as a former prime minister, and then followed in the family tradition, obtaining a medical degree. After he graduated, Frei had worked in a London hospital for a while, and then changed direction, taking a postgrad in journalism at the London School of Economics. A regular column in *The Independent* had followed. It had formed the basis of his first book.

A movement outside in the street snagged the corner of her eye. Stevie looked up to see a group of dogs trotting along the pavement, so smartly paced that they gave the illusion of keeping in time with each other. She counted five of them, a motley selection of breeds that might have made a cute assortment, had they been drawn by a children's illustrator. Each of the dogs was wearing a collar, but the pack occupied the pavement with an assurance, a dogged doggyness, that gave them a feral edge. A bichon frise let out a yelp and the rest of the pack set up a frantic chorus of barking. The dogs upped their pace, a slender greyhound at their head closely followed by a sleek Dalmatian. Stevie watched, glad she was in her car, as they dashed around a corner. A tiny chihuahua that was probably worth a lot of money was the last to vanish.

She looked at her smartphone again, ready to close the Internet down, but a name she recognized jumped out at her from the list of hits. Dr. John Ahumibe had written an obituary of Geoffrey Frei in *The Lancet*.

The doctor began by saying that he wrote as a medical colleague, an admirer of Frei's journalism, and "finally as a friend." He briefly mentioned their membership of the same rugby team at school and their subsequent friendship at college. Although in later years they had kept in "more sporadic touch," Dr. Ahumibe went on to say how much he had admired Frei's work. The doctor's prose was starched with formalities that might have indicated grief or respect or simply a poor writing style.

Stevie breathed on the windshield, fogging it with her breath. She drew a neat triangle on the hazed glass with her fingertip and added a name at each corner.

She wrote Dr. Ahumibe's name in the middle, and after a moment's hesitation put Buchanan's beside it. Reah had died of the sweats and it wasn't unusual for people who had gone to school together to enter the same professions and keep in touch. But Dr. Ahumibe had known all three men, and now all three of them were dead.

Stevie took a tissue from the glove compartment, rubbed the diagram away and then pressed dial on her phone. Iqbal picked up immediately and she said, "I'm sorry I hung up." She wanted to ask him if Frei's death could be related to Simon's, but any answer he could give her would only be speculation and so she said, "Do you think you could find Frei's address?"

"If you promise to come back in one piece." He gave a faint, awkward laugh. "I don't mean come back to me. Not necessarily."

"I know." There was silence on the line. Stevie thought she could hear Iqbal willing himself not to ask her where she was. She could still see the faint outline of the crude diagram she had drawn on the windshield: Simon, Reah, and Frei constellated around Dr. Ahumibe. She said, "If there's an answer to why Simon died, I think it's somewhere in the computer. Simon was determined to get it to Reah, and someone else was equally determined to get it off me."

"So why don't you come back here and help me work through the data?"

It was a good question. Stevie closed her eyes and tried to picture herself at Iqbal's desk, trawling through computer printouts. She had managed to calculate her sales figures and commission percentages without any trouble on *Shop TV*. Perhaps she would discover a talent for a different type of statistics. The idea of a siege made her chest tighten, but that wasn't the only reason she was focused on staying on the road. She spoke slowly, trying to order her thoughts.

"Simon obviously believed Reah would understand the information on the computer right away. I thought Simon was trying to tell Reah something, but what if he already knew what the computer held? The data you're examining might be evidence that supports something both Simon and Reah were already aware of." Realization quickened her voice. "The laptop is crucial, but we may never know why, without putting it into context. That's what I have to focus on."

"I know it's none of my business, but I don't like you being out there on your own."

"We're a team. You're the brains and I'm the foot soldier." Stevie injected a smile into her voice, to hide her irritation at the paternal edge in his, and related a version of her meeting with Melvin Summers that excluded the pub lock-in and police raid. "Summers was bitter, and he had the means, but I'd be surprised if he was the killer. He struck me as the kind of man who would give himself up if he'd done the deed. Broadcasting the reasons why he'd murdered Simon would be part of his revenge."

"Killing the man wouldn't be enough. He'd want to kill his reputation too? It sounds like your boyfriend knew how to make enemies."

Stevie considered telling Iqbal there was no point in being jealous of the dead, but she knew from experience that jealousy, like love, didn't conform to reason. She said, "Perhaps Melvin Summers simply needed someone to blame for his losses and Simon was the obvious target." A convoy of army trucks rattled past, green tarpaulins shivering on their frames. Stevie asked, "How is it going with the data? Have you made any progress?"

"I'm working my way through it, but the only way to go is slowly if I'm going to avoid errors. I can tell you one thing though. I did a search and it looks like the team didn't submit all of their studies for publication."

"What do you mean?"

"Some of the trials showed more positive results than others. They ditched the negative ones and only published outcomes that endorsed their treatment. Those are the ones I'm concentrating on."

"Is that legal?"

"According to Geoffrey Frei's book, inconvenient results are routinely suppressed. I wouldn't have thought to look for it otherwise."

"What's the difference between only publishing positive results and publishing false ones?"

"Limiting your publications to positive results is legal, but being caught publishing false results would be professional suicide. You could end up in jail."

Stevie knew Simon would never have done anything that might endanger his career. She said, "Simon would never have risked harming children," and wondered at the gap between what she had thought and what she had said aloud.

She could hear Iqbal's fingers rattling against computer keys.

"In that case, maybe he had faith in the treatment and didn't want to cloud its chances of being approved by publicizing trials that were less than a hundred percent." The key strokes stopped. "It looks like Frei was unlisted, but here's his address." He read out a street and house number in Swiss Cottage, and Stevie punched it into her GPS. Iqbal said, "Will you keep me updated on where you are?"

"Philosophically or geographically?"

His voice was serious. "Both."

Stevie hung up and turned on the engine. Only a moment ago she had felt close to Simon, but now she was losing her picture of him. The man she thought she had known was fading, and a new one was taking his place. Did her hunt still make sense if he was someone else?

She was kidding herself. It had never made any sense. Nothing did.

The route suggested by the GPS would take her close to Simon's apartment block. Simon had loaded the laptop with coded data he had wanted her to deliver to Reah, but perhaps there was information he was less inclined to share still stored in his apartment. Stevie checked her mirrors, steered the car away from the curb and started to drive.

Thirty

The streets around Simon's building were lined with parked cars. Stevie drove a slow circuit in search of a free space, taking left turns that drew her gradually farther from her destination. She had tuned into Radio London, hoping for local news, but a panel of people she didn't recognize were discussing prisons.

"Criminals are incarcerated because they're a danger to society," a plummy female voice said. "To truncate their sentences would not only be an affront to justice, it would be dangerous."

A male voice broke in, a tired drawl: "So you would leave people to rot, rather than release prisoners who've been convicted of nonviolent crimes?"

It was turning into a bright morning, but the sun was still low in the sky and the streets were cast in shadows. Stevie glanced in her rearview mirror. There was no one on the road, or the pavement, behind or ahead of her. The district was usually busy with commuters battling their way toward the city center, and mothers ferrying their children to school, but today it had a dull, Sunday-morning feel that deadened the spirits.

"There's no question of people rotting," the female voice said. "All we're proposing is that prisoners give up some of their privileges . . ."

"Privileges." The man stretched the word into a sneer.

Stevie saw a space. She guided the car into it, turned off the radio, flipped down the sun visor and examined her reflection in the vanity mirror. Even if she had wanted to, her face was still in too much of a mess to appear on TV, but her bruises were shifting from blue-black to an easier-to-camouflage yellow. She ran a gentle finger across her skin, testing it, thinking for some reason of Rachel, her scarecrow body and fashion-sharp haircut. The memory of the producer's plea for Stevie to stay and help broadcast another program was touched with guilt. It had been an appeal for normality, a future to stay alive in. Her own quest to uncover the truth about Simon's death was similar, except that it wasn't only the virus Stevie was afraid of.

She took her makeup purse from her bag, applied a smear of foundation, and then a layer of powder to her bruises. It was getting increasingly hard to care about the way she looked, but her face was a weapon that had served her well, and it was important for her to maintain it, just as it was important for a soldier to maintain his gun.

A row of homeless people lay in the lee of a building, wrapped in sleeping bags like war dead zipped in body bags. Stevie's running shoes were silent against the pavement but she could hear the sound of her own breaths, the blood pumping its way through her heart. It was as if a hum that had been part of the city for so long no one noticed it anymore had suddenly been switched off, leaving an unnerving, white silence in its place.

The sign on the door of the twenty-four-hour grocers declared it OPEN, but the shop had an empty, dead-eyed look. Stevie thought about going in, buying a newspaper, and asking the shopkeeper if he had heard any news of the sweats, but some instinct told her to walk on.

The top of Simon's apartment building appeared up ahead, rising sharp-cornered above the others. Stevie took out her cell and called his landline. She imagined the abandoned interior, the phone ringing unanswered in the neat living room, and in the bedroom where Simon had died. After a while an automated voice invited her to leave a message. She hung up, knowing it was no guarantee that the apartment was empty.

When she reached the path outside the tower block, Stevie pulled up the hood of her tracksuit jacket and quickened her pace, aware of the hundreds of windows staring down at her. Somewhere a trashcan had been overturned and garbage was strewn across the green. A scattering of papers lay becalmed next to discarded tins and scraps of food. Stevie bent and lifted an official-looking document from the ground, but it was someone's bank statement, nothing to do with her or Simon, and she let it fall again.

She looked up to the twentieth floor. The building swooned toward her, and it was as if she could see the earth moving on its axis. Stevie shook her head and fell into a slow jog, trying to outrun her own insignificance.

A large man dressed in black cargo pants, a leather jacket, and a knitted cap at odds with the sunny morning, bolted from the entrance, almost knocking her over as he barreled past. He had a handkerchief wrapped around his mouth and nose. All she saw of the man's face was a pair of gray-blue eyes, a fringe of straw-colored hair, and a scrap of white skin, but Stevie's throat tightened with the memory of strong hands twisting her scarf around her neck. She hunched her shoulders and kept her head lowered, hiding it in the shadow of her hood, hoping he wouldn't identify her.

She had read that people who had been assaulted saw their attackers everywhere, their features imprinted on strangers' faces, like the ghost of a loved one conjured by a distant relative's smile. But she knew without a doubt that the man who had just run past was the stranger who had tried to kill her in the *Shop TV* station parking lot. She stepped smartly into the shadow of the doorway and watched until the figure disappeared around a corner.

"Fuck, fuck, fuck, fuck, fuck, fuck, fuck." Stevie closed her eyes for a second and wondered if now might be a good time to take up smoking, then she pushed one of the buzzers at random. When there was no response she tried the one above, and then the one above that, her eyes on the road outside, watching in case the man came back. Her finger was pressed to yet another buzzer when the intercom crackled and a voice trembled, "Hello?"

Stevie made her own voice bright and efficient.

"I'm a doctor on call. I'm here to visit a sick patient, but they're not answering. Could you let me into the building, please?"

"A doctor?"

The voice was high and distorted by static. She couldn't tell if it was male or female.

"Yes." Stevie suddenly wished she had chosen a different identity: a meter reader, a florist or a postwoman, laden with packages from Amazon. But she knew that none of these would command the same authority. "I'm visiting a patient. I need to get to them as soon as possible."

"If I let you in, will you see me too?" The voice was rushed and desperate. "Please, I think I'm dying."

"Shit." She swore under her breath and then assumed her "doctor's voice" again, the edge of authority. "I'm sorry, but you'll have to contact your own GP. Tell me who they are and I'll call them for you."

The static on the intercom hissed and swelled into a snowstorm of sound and Stevie realized that the person on the other end was laughing.

"Do you think I haven't called my own GP? They're not picking up." The blizzard of static died and the person on the other end said, "No one's picking up." The coughing resumed, harsh and uncontrolled, and Stevie pulled back from the intercom, as if she was in danger of catching the virus. When the voice spoke again it was breathless but determined. "I won't let you in unless you promise to see me."

"I'll do my best."

"Best isn't good enough. Promise."

"Okay, I promise."

The lie was almost a whisper, but the person on the other end must have heard it because they said, "Apartment twelve, fifteenth floor," and buzzed her in.

Stevie ignored the elevator and started the long climb up the deserted stairwell to Simon's landing. It had been a mistake to jog the path to the high-rise. Her legs were still sore from the scuffle in the parking lot, and the weight of the broken promise made every step an effort.

Thirty-One

Tape was still strung across the entrance to Simon's apartment: POLICE. DO NOT CROSS. The door was ajar, as Stevie had hoped and feared it would be. She stood on the landing, her ears straining for any sound, but the building was as quiet as the street outside. She reached out and pushed the door. It swung open, a sly invitation. Stevie took a deep breath, ducked beneath the police tape, and slid into the apartment, pulling the door shut behind her. The lock refused to click into place and she silently cursed Simon again for not getting it fixed.

The gauzy, white curtains in the lounge were drawn across the large picture window and the room was drenched in soft, pearlized light. Some uninvited visitor had reduced the apartment to the same chaos as hers, but Stevie had been expecting that too. She trod cautiously, careful not to step on the mess of papers, CDs, books, and photographs, the detritus of Simon's life.

A breeze cut across the room and the papers on the floor quivered. Stevie froze, like a deer sensing itself in a hunter's sights, and looked toward the balcony. The white curtains fluttered and Stevie saw that the door was open a fraction. Too late she remembered the knife she had left in the car. She cast around, looking for something she could use as a weapon. Simon had decorated his apartment in a sleek minimalist style and there were no ornaments or convenient sporting trophies that would act as a club. She picked up a table lamp and tiptoed to the balcony door, holding its base level with her shoulder, ready to strike.

The curtains blew softly toward her. Stevie reached out a hand to stop them and saw the sky beyond, pale blue and hung with clouds. A hawk was reeling high above. She watched it swoop and turn, allowing a dangerous dreamy vagueness to creep over her. All things must die, she too one day. It needn't be a tragedy unless you were forced to go before your time, like Simon and Joanie. The hawk rose toward the clouds. She watched it climb across the unbroken blue and realized that there were no airplane trails scarring the sky. The curtains caught on the same gust of air that lifted the bird and pulled away from her. The balcony was empty. Stevie closed the door and turned her attention to the apartment.

The thought of going into the bedroom where she had found Simon was like a stone in her chest, and so she went there first. A faint smell of decay still lingered. The sheets were the same ones she had found Simon swathed in, though they had been dragged from the bed and abandoned in a careless heap on the floor. Stevie checked the en suite, noticing for the first time the crack in the porcelain sink, where she had dropped her bottle of perfume. She ran a finger along it, avoiding the sight of her own face in the mirror.

The other rooms were empty, all in confusion. She gave the walk-in closets and wardrobes a quick check, the lamp still in her hand, her heart still in her mouth. There was no one there, but Stevie had a sense that the search of Simon's apartment hadn't been as thorough as the one conducted on her own place. There was something haphazard about the half-emptied drawers in Simon's desk, the defeated suits hanging like suicides in the wardrobe, the mattress still square upon its frame. The red-and-purple dress she had come to pick up the day she had found Simon, hung lopsidedly among his suits. She touched it and a memory stirred of her old self in the silk. Then she drifted back through to the sitting room, unsure if she was looking for evidence of why Simon had been murdered, or of who he had been beneath the charm.

She was certain that the man who had run from the building was the person who had wrecked the apartment. What would he have done to her if she had arrived earlier? Would there have been a point when she gave in and took him to Iqbal and the laptop? She sank down on to the floor among the mess. They hadn't spent a lot of time together in Simon's apartment. Simon could make a mean breakfast, a heart-attack special, but he had never invited her around for a dinner party or a romantic meal. Restaurants were for eating in; the apartment was for predinner drinks on the balcony and late-night drinks that ended with the two of them tangled together on the couch.

Stevie pushed a muddle of books and papers aside, and lay back on the cleared strip of carpet, stretching her back against the floor. Simon had come to her place too, and twice he had booked them both into spa hotels, but most of their lovemaking had happened here. She ran a hand down her body, trying to replicate Simon's sure touch.

Stevie remembered a television show she had once seen about the London Blitz. The presenter had explained that during bombings strangers had coupled with each other in doorways and air-raid shelters, driven to lust by grief and fear. Were people all across the city getting down to it right now, compelled by a primal urge to make new life in the face of death? Stevie thought about the unlocked front door, but the apartment was silent, the building so still it might have been abandoned. She slipped a hand below the waistband of her tracksuit bottoms, wondering at herself.

Was this what she had come here for? She stretched her back and opened her eyes wide, looking at the upside-down living room. And suddenly she felt as if her heart had stopped.

Whoever had searched the apartment had pushed Simon's large couch up against the wall. Protruding from it, stretched out slim and languid, as if its owner were sunbathing in some sheltered cove, was an arm. Some reflex was tightening a band around Stevie's chest, but her lungs had been arrested, the air inside them held there, drowning her. Maybe it was the overload of oxygen in her lungs, the lack of it reaching her brain, that gave the scene a 3-D clarity. She took in the fingers curling from the palm like the fronds of a spider shell, the two plain silver rings, one on top of the other, the pink polish so pale it made the fingernails look like flesh.

Stevie slid her own hand out of her pants. She rolled on to her side, pulling her knees up to her chest, and breathed in and breathed out, breathed in and breathed out. The fingers remained still and outstretched, as if frozen in the act of beckoning someone closer. Stevie felt an urge to run away, out of the apartment and back to her car, before the owner of the hand came to, alive and deathly. She fought it down and scrambled to her feet, almost falling as her foot slid on a framed photo of two young boys whose names she didn't know. She righted herself against the arm of the couch, and dragged it away from the wall. The body flopped from its hiding place, soft and rag-doll limp, leaving a smear of blood against the white paintwork. Stevie averted her gaze, but not before she had seen the mass of blood, black and vital, coating the back of the skull. It looked desperate, but there was still a slim chance that the stranger was alive and so she dropped to her haunches, turned the woman on to her back and placed a hand against her cheek. The skin was cold and taut, the flesh beneath it spongy and swollen.

Come on, come on, come on, come on . . .

Stevie didn't know if she was muttering to herself or to the stranger. She put her hand between her own breasts, found the frantic thud of her heartbeat, and then pressed her palm against the same point on the other woman's chest. There was no answering rhythm. Stevie felt the stillness within the body and knew it was dead, the same way that you can tell a house is empty simply by entering it, but she pressed her fingers against the inside of the woman's right wrist and then her left, feeling for a pulse. There was nothing.

Stevie leaned back on her heels, her own breathing harsh and ragged in her ears. She had been close enough to the man to feel his slipstream as he ran from the building.

"Christ," she said to the woman, "what did he do to you?"

It was a stupid question and Stevie realized with shame that what she really meant was, *It might have been me.* She took another deep breath and slid her hands into the pocket of the woman's jeans, looking for something that might identify her, but the jeans were slim-fitting, their pockets empty. It felt wrong, touching the corpse so intimately, another violation after the indignity of murder.

The woman had probably been good-looking, but death had done her no favors. Whatever mechanism kept the muscles of the face in place had stopped working and the skin slumped softly away from her features, giving the corpse a blurred look. Stevie forced herself to stare, wondering if she had seen the woman somewhere before. Some ghost of a recollection flickered palely in her mind, but it was too insubstantial to grasp. After a long moment she went through to Simon's bedroom and took a clean sheet from a pile tumbled on the floor.

It was as she came back into the living room and saw the body from a distance that Stevie realized who the woman reminded her of. The two of them shared the same athletic build, the same coloring. The woman's hair was a similar length to Stevie's, almost, but not quite, touching her shoulders. Their faces and dress sense were different, the woman around a careful decade older, but a killer in a hurry and unfamiliar with both of them might not have had time to notice that.

"Who are you?" Stevie whispered and then, ridiculously, "I'm sorry if I got you killed."

She unfolded the sheet, shaking it in the air, the way she might shake bedclothes fresh from the washing line, and draped it over the dead woman.

"Sorry," she said for a second time. "Sorry."

Stevie found a pair of scissors in Simon's kitchen drawer, took them into the en suite and slowly began to chop careful slices from her hair.

Was the dead woman another of Simon's secrets? The sight of her ruined skull had made jealousy impossible. Instead Stevie felt the kind of pity a wife might feel on discovering that her husband's mistress had been tricked into thinking he was single. The woman could be her way out, Stevie realized, her chance to slip away and wait for the sweats to take their course.

Stevie hadn't given herself a haircut since she was a teenager, and the result looked like a hatchet attack, but the short crop brought out the angles in her face. She had lost weight in the past few days and now her features seemed to be a series of corners: sharp cheekbones, hinged jaw, and bright eyes set deep in their sockets. It was a skull face, without the grin, her expression nervous in a way that skulls have no need to be.

Somewhere in the high-rise a door slammed. Stevie gripped the scissors in her fist like a knife, her heart pumping. She looked at the room beyond the mirror, ready to react to the first sign of movement, but the building sank back into silence. Stevie let out the breath she had been holding in and caught sight of her reflection in the mirror. She saw the panic on her face and realized that this was how it would be if she ran, a life shadowed by fear.

Stevie went back into the bedroom and took one of Simon's white shirts from his wardrobe. She put it to her face and breathed in, but it was freshly laundered and held no consoling scent of him. She pulled off her tracksuit top, put the shirt on over her vest and then flicked through the hangers in the wardrobe until she found a lightweight, black linen suit she had never seen Simon wearing. It was an inch too long and several sizes too wide, but she rolled up the pant legs, belted the waist tight and let the shirt hang loose on top. The combination looked absurd.

Stevie pulled off the shirt, replaced it with a dark blue V-necked T-shirt and put the suit jacket on top. The effect was early eighties New Wave, hip and androgynous, not Stevie's style at all, but she no longer looked like herself, and that was what she was aiming for.

Would the killer continue to look for the laptop even if he believed that he had murdered her? Stevie wondered if he would try to discover what Geoffrey Frei had known. Maybe he would get ill and die, or take fright of the sweats and leave town. That would be the best solution. It would save her from having to kill him.

Thirty-Two

An album stamped with the name of some long-defunct photography studio lay half in, half out of Simon's wardrobe. Stevie picked it up and carried it through to the lounge. The shape of the woman was still there, beneath the white sheet, and so she took the album out on to the balcony and rested it against the railing, squinting against the sun. A lone helicopter hovered in the distance, lingering magically in midair. Stevie stared at it, trying to work out whether it was the police or the press, but then she saw that it was flying away from City Airport and wondered if it belonged to some oligarch fleeing infection. She watched until it flew overhead, a rattling roar of propellers and engine that quickly faded back into silence, and then opened the album's cover and peeled back the protective layer of tissue paper beneath.

The album began with photographs of Simon as a baby. The first showed him cradled in his mother's arms, a tiny face peeking from a white blanket that looked as if it had been crocheted by teams of spiders with a flair for detail. Simon's mother's hair was set in stiff curls and she was dressed in a formal suit and high-heeled court shoes, a combination that reminded Stevie of city hall weddings and going-away costumes. The new mother looked proud and worried. Stevie tried to see beyond her prematurely aging perm and prim outfit and realized that she had been young when she had brought Simon into the world, in her early twenties at the most.

Stevie flicked through the album, watching Simon growing from baby to toddler, the photographs going from black-and-white to Kodacolor. A second boy entered the pictures. Simon's mother's hair grew longer and loosened into honey-tinted waves. She had been a good-looking woman, growing younger as she aged, as had so many of her generation. The box-pleated skirts and twinsets she had favored were replaced by flared pants, cheesecloth blouses, and miniskirts, which were in turn replaced by maxis. There was the occasional photograph of Simon's father too, a smiling man wearing black-rimmed spectacles, who seemed to have a cigarette permanently clamped between his fingers. He had clearly preferred the other side of the camera: most shots were of his wife and two boys, at home, on vacation, posed in front of his Alfa Romeo, as if recording all of his prized possessions in one shot.

It had been a privileged early life, but the photos stopped abruptly when Simon was around seven years old, leaving the final pages as blank as his suddenly curtailed future. Stevie turned to the back cover and found a cardboard pocket designed to hold photographs that were yet to be stuck into the album. Tucked inside was a series of school photos. Someone had filed them in the order they were taken, the earliest first. Row upon row of little boys in identical school uniforms, all aged about six or seven, posed in front of a castellated building, which reminded Stevie of Hampton Court. The boys' ties, white shirts, and blazers made them look like a shop display of ventriloquists' dummies, stiffly alive and sinister. She searched for Simon among the faces but found it difficult to tell the boys apart; they were too young, their features unformed and lacking distinction.

It wasn't until she was several photographs in, that Stevie found him. Simon was standing in the back row near the center, his face a miniature version of the man she had known, his features already marked with the combination of mischievousness and intelligence that had drawn Stevie to him. She remembered Buchanan telling her that he had joined the same school when he was twelve and flipped forward, drawing a finger along the lines of straight-backed boys until she found what she thought was him.

A thin boy, taller than the rest, Alexander Buchanan looked as if a growth spurt had robbed him of blood and energy. He was standing, pale and unhappy, at the end of a row and next to him, glancing away from the camera, was a boy who might have been John Ahumibe.

The next image in the series confirmed it. This time the three boys were standing in the same row, Buchanan on Simon's left, a curly-haired, bespectacled boy on his right, and next to him Ahumibe. Stevie slipped the school photos from the album and went back into the apartment.

The drawers of the writing desk Simon had kept in the corner of the sitting room had been tipped out, their contents dumped in a pile on the floor. Stevie knelt, looking for an envelope to put the photographs in, and saw a dash of gore on one of the desk's sharp corners. She followed its progress to where it slid, oil-slick black, across the floor.

Simon's rug had been a bold geometric statement, intended to counter the minimalism he had favored elsewhere. Its pattern could have been designed to camouflage blood, but Stevie wondered how she could have missed the drips and spatters, the roadmap of her almost-twin's death.

You didn't need to be a forensics expert to reconstruct what had happened. The woman had been standing in the middle of the floor, or perhaps sitting on the chair by the window, when the man had entered the sitting room. Whichever it was, Stevie was sure that she had already been there when he arrived. Was she waiting for Simon, not knowing that he was dead, or had she also come in search of something?

Her death had been an accident. Nothing else made sense. The man was desperate to acquire the laptop and though Stevie had felt his willingness to kill her in the twist of silk around her throat, there was nothing a corpse could tell him.

He had hit the woman, to show he meant business, and she had fallen badly, smashing her skull against the unforgiving corner of the desk. Stevie wondered if the man had been sorry, or if he had merely felt the impatience of someone who had cocked up at work, the fuck-shit of a bad day at the office, and the embarrassment of having to report to the boss that things had gone out of kilter, sales figures were down, productivity lower than it should be, the bid rejected, a woman dead.

There was bile in her throat, and Stevie realized that it was her own head she saw slamming against the desk, her own blood soaking the carpet.

"You're alive," she whispered. "So get on with it, before you really do end up with your head staved in."

She rooted gingerly through the mess on the floor, careful to avoid the traces of blood. For an instant she thought she had found an envelope, but even before she touched it she saw what it was: a small, beige clutch bag. She opened it and found a lipstick, a card wallet, a set of car keys, an iPhone and a small, old-fashioned-looking snub-nosed revolver. Stevie tried to remember how movie gangsters and detectives opened their guns to check their bullets, but the only image that came to mind was a spinning chamber; a game of Russian roulette.

The wallet contained a clutch of credit cards in the name of Mrs. Hope Black and several business cards bearing her name and an address in Kentish Town. Stevie knew the street. It was the home of a deli where she had sometimes bought olives and wine to share with Simon.

Stevie stood at the foot of the woman's veiled body, like a priest about to say a prayer. She whispered, "If I get the chance, I'll kill him for you."

But in her heart Stevie knew that if she killed anyone, it would be to make herself safe.

Thirty-Three

Hope Black's Jaguar had leather seats, a walnut dashboard, a full tank of gas and a GPS that had been carefully stowed in the glove compartment. Stevie walked the pavements around Simon's building, pressing the key fob she had found in the dead woman's bag, until she heard an answering chirp and saw the tell-tale flash of indicator lights. There was no one there to observe the theft, but the empty streets made her feel exposed, and Stevie was glad when she was in the driver's seat with the door safely locked.

Better Bets was in the middle of a small parade of shops. She parked in an adjacent road and walked the final stretch, nervous of what might happen were someone to spot her driving Hope Black's car.

A man and a woman were walking along the street toward her, both of them wearing white surgical masks over their mouths and noses, like Beijing citizens on a poor-air day. They saw her and crossed to the opposite sidewalk, the man's hand cupping the woman's elbow, as if to encourage her to walk faster. The woman had her head lowered but the man made eye contact with

Stevie, and then quickly looked away, as if he couldn't afford to risk any more empathy.

Stevie took out her phone and called Iqbal, and then Derek. Neither of them picked up. It meant nothing, she reassured herself, nothing. Batteries faded, people fell asleep, mislaid their phones, or simply chose not to answer. A missed call was not an intimation of death.

An elderly man was sitting on the pavement outside Better Bets, his back resting against the shop's shuttered window, his cap lowered over his face. He was smartly dressed, in a brown jacket, checked shirt and tweedy pants, as if he had set out for a long autumn walk rather than a summer stroll in the city. Stevie had passed by hundreds of homeless people, beggars, drunks, and junkies in her years in London, but the old man's carefully put-together outfit reminded her of her dead granddad. She saw that the scuffs on the old man's jacket were recent and squatted down beside him.

"Are you okay?"

A wisp of white hair had escaped from beneath the man's hat. It bent in response to the breeze, but his head remained sunk on his chest. Stevie had touched enough corpses for one day, but she thought she saw a faint flutter beneath the old man's eyelids. Joanie, Simon, and Hope had each been beyond help, but if the man was alive she might be able to do something for him. Perhaps there was an anxious relative she could call. Stevie lifted his wrist and felt for a pulse. There was nothing.

"You're doing it wrong."

"Christ!" Stevie jolted backward. She remembered the way Django had leaped when the Taser hit him and hoped he had found his way back to Doris and John's champagne. "Sorry, you gave me a fright."

"You need to press further down, on the artery." The old man's voice was a raw whisper, catgut-stretched and dried. "You won't feel nothing dicking around up there," he croaked.

"Sorry." Stevie had jumped at the sound of his voice, but the knowledge that the man was dying didn't shock her the way it would have done before. "Can I get you something?"

"A blow job." His laugh was a wheeze of old bones and stale air. "Sorry, dear. Good of you to ask." He narrowed his eyes in an effort to focus on her face. "You healthy?"

"Yes."

"Keep away from infected people like me."

"I've had it."

"Don't matter. I was an ambulance driver. I know about these things. Pretty soon there'll be rats, then cholera, typhoid, who knows what. Do yourself a favor. Keep your distance."

"Are you sure you wouldn't like me to get you some water, or call someone to come and get you?"

"You just do as I told you. Being a Good Samaritan's all fine and well, except for when it kills you." He gave her a smile that was all death. "You got any kiddies?"

"No."

"Neither did we. Would have liked some. Now I reckon it's a blessing we never did, things being as they are."

She had seen very few children since the crisis began, Stevie realized. She imagined them, huddled in their houses, hidden from the sweats by their parents, the way Anne Frank's mother and father had hoped to hide her from the Nazis.

"It's not so bad at the end," the old man said. "I saw it with my wife. You think you're getting better, you stop being sick and the headaches take a back seat, then you realize you're on your way out anyway. Another of nature's little jokes. But it ain't painful anymore. That's about the best you can hope for in this life, an easy death." A tear slipped its way down his cheek. "Fuck off and give me peace to look at the sky."

Stevie touched his shoulder and got to her feet.

The door to the betting shop was closed, its metal shutter rolled halfway down. Stevie banged against it and when there was no reply, pushed the shutter up and tried the door. It was locked. She rapped against the wood, then took Hope Black's clutch from her bag, fished out her keys and tried each of them, until one turned smoothly in the lock.

"Hello?"

She pushed the door open and stepped inside. The shop was dark. It smelled stale, like the house of someone who had become too old, or too ill, to take care of themselves.

"Hello?" She took another cautious step.

The flat-screen televisions ranged around the room glowed blue and silent, lit with error messages. The space behind the screened counter, where bookies must have calculated the odds, was empty. Stevie had stuffed the leather clutch at the bottom of her bag, wary of the awkward questions that might be asked should someone recognize it. Now she wondered if she should have slipped the gun into her pocket. It was too easy to imagine someone leaping out from behind the deserted counter. She pushed against the door that would take her into the bookmaker's stall and the private sanctum beyond. It was locked tight.

"You need the code number."

A man was standing in the doorway beyond the counter. He took a drag from the cigarette in his hand and said, "You another joker wants to bet on whether you're going to make it or not?"

"Have you had a lot of those?" Stevie smiled, as if it was normal to meet strange men in unlit betting shops, but her voice wavered like a flame caught in a sudden draft. The bookmaker held Stevie's gaze for a moment, and she had a feeling of being weighed and measured, then he shrugged. He was handsome, if you didn't mind your men scruffy and over fifty.

"Some. More betting they'll make it than not. Not much point otherwise. There's a few wanted to bet the Queen would snuff it. I told them to beat it and learn a little respect. I did lay a few that the Prime Minister wouldn't come through. He's fair game. I even took an accumulator that the PM, the mayor, and the chancellor would all shuffle off to Buffalo in the same week." The man's voice was slow and monotone, as if he had been drinking. "Should have given it lower odds."

Stevie said, "I'm not here to place a bet."

"We're not taking any right now, as it happens." He looked at the cigarette as if he was surprised to see it in his hand and then took another drag. "What are you here for?"

"I'm looking for Hope Black."

"She's not here." His face was half hidden in smoke and shadows, but she thought the bookmaker might have smiled. "I'd say come back later but . . ." He let the unfinished sentence hang in the air.

"But what?"

He shrugged again. "She may not come back, or I may not be here when she does."

Stevie couldn't think how to ask why the woman had been in Simon's apartment. She said, "Do you mind me asking where she's gone?"

"Ask away."

This time there was no doubt that the man was smiling, a small, unhappy twist of the mouth with nothing of joy in it. He lifted the cigarette to his mouth again and she saw that it was a joint. Stevie wondered if she should tell him that Hope was dead and that she had found her. She asked, "Are you Hope's husband?"

The bookmaker took another drag from his joint, narrowing his eyes against the smoke.

"Do I look like I'd want to get hitched to an Irish-Jamaican bookie? Hope and me are strictly colleagues, or should I say strictly boss and lackey, no prizes for guessing which is which. She inherited this place from her dad and me along with it."

Stevie detected injury in his voice and wondered if he was closer to his boss than he was admitting.

"I found her card in my boyfriend's apartment. She must have put it through the letter box. He's dead. He died before all this happened, but he wasn't into betting, and I wanted to know why she had left it there."

The man was wearing an antiquated beige cardigan that seemed more holes and tears than wool. He leaned against the doorjamb and pushed a hand deep into one of its pockets.

"You know the best bit of advice I could give a young person like you?"

"What?"

"Learn when to take advice." He glanced toward the street, the sun blazing against the pavement. "I never took any when I was your age, but I could have saved myself a lot of bother if I had. See this scar?" He leaned forward and turned his face to the side so Stevie could see the white line that ran from the outside corner of his eye to the edge of his mouth. "I got that because I didn't listen to a piece of advice."

"What was it?"

The bookmaker shook his head, as if she had missed the point.

"It doesn't matter what it was. My advice to you is, cherish good memories while you can and don't go looking under too many stones. So Hope left her card at your boyfriend's apartment? So what? There's enough trouble in the world—don't go looking for more."

"I need to know."

"Why?"

"Because . . ." She paused, trying to think of an answer that would make him want to help her. "Because the past wasn't the way I thought it was, and if I don't find out what really happened I might go insane."

Stevie didn't bother to add that she was scared whoever had killed Simon and Hope might yet find her.

The man snorted. "Sanity's overrated."

Stevie held his stare, giving him the half-promise smile that had won her countless sales, and he let out a sigh and stepped out of the doorway. The security screen between them was grimed with a thin layer of dust and he looked spectral behind its fog.

"People always think they need to know. What's the betting the sweats were made in a test tube by someone who needed to know something?" The bookmaker slid open a cupboard in the wall. "Just like Eve with that damn apple. Look where it got her." He squatted and tapped a code into the small safe concealed inside it. "Flung out of Paradise, didn't know a good thing when she had it. Like the rest of us, as it turns out." He took a ledger from the safe and set it on the counter. "Hope went out to collect outstanding debts." He must have seen the surprise on Stevie's face because he said, "An excellent example of someone not taking good advice. I told her to leave it and sit tight until all this was over, but Hope got nervous at the prospect of creditors leaving town, especially the ones that were leaving in wooden boxes. She reckoned that even if they couldn't take it with them, they sure as hell wouldn't leave it behind to pay their gambling debts."

"I told you, Simon wasn't a gambler."

"He was, if Hope paid him a visit. What's his full name?"

"Simon Sharkey. I thought perhaps he and Hope were seeing each other."

"Simon Sharkey the doctor?" The man stared at her as if she had suddenly grown more interesting.

Stevie nodded.

"No," he said. "They weren't seeing each other."

Stevie smiled with relief. A thought occurred to her and she asked, "Did Hope have a sick child?"

The man shook his head. "Not so's you'd notice." He leaned closer, the screen still between them, the ledger still resting on the counter. "I've got good news and bad news for you. Bad news first. I did know your boyfriend, knew him pretty well at one time. He was what you might call a regular. The good news is that I hadn't seen him for a while. He made a heroic effort and kicked the habit. We did our part by agreeing, at his own request I might add, that we wouldn't serve him again, even if he begged us to."

"And did he?"

"Not to my knowledge. Which still leaves the question, given that she wasn't one for social calls, why was Hope at his house?" The bookmaker flipped open the ledger and began turning its pages.

Stevie asked, "Are your computers down?"

She thought again of Iqbal, a life half-lived on the Web, and hoped he was okay.

The bookmaker gave her a grin. His face was long and thin, the kind of face Stevie realized she had always instinctively mistrusted, though she could think of no reason for her prejudice.

"As the boss says, a book can be tossed in the furnace. A computer has magic ways of holding on to information that you might not want to share."

"Why write it down at all then?"

"Even Old Nick makes you sign a contract, or so I've heard." The moving finger paused, and he raised an eyebrow in an expression that made him look as if he might be on intimate terms with the man himself. "Okay, this is interesting. Naughty Hope."

"What?"

"It appears that my boss isn't the cold-hearted harridan I cursed her for all these years. She seems to have lent the doctor rather a lot of money."

"How much money?"

He turned the ledger around so that Stevie could see the entry his finger was resting on.

"Over forty-five grand."

Simon's share of Fibrosyop had guaranteed big returns. He had his own apartment and a secure job. There had been no need for him to seek out back-street loans.

Stevie said, "Are you sure it wasn't payment for a lucky bet?"

"I don't make mistakes about money. It looks like the good doctor stuck to his resolution, though a man who needs to borrow 45Gs from a bookie might not be entirely lily-white." He grinned. "No offense meant."

Stevie whispered, "So that's why Hope was there. She'd come to collect."

The man looked up, all trace of cannabis mistiness gone.

"You seen her?"

"I meant that's why . . ." Stevie stumbled on the lie, ". . . that's why she went there."

"No you didn't." The man closed the ledger gently and said in a dangerously soft voice, "How did you get in? I thought Hope had forgotten to lock the door, but she didn't, did she? You've got her keys."

Their eyes locked and there was a moment when she might have been able to lie, but it passed.

"I'm sorry." Stevie backed away from the counter. "She was dead when I got to Simon's apartment. Someone killed her. It was fast. She wouldn't have felt a thing."

The man's features buckled, but his voice was the same quiet whisper.

"You stood there, chatting to me as if she was still alive."

"I didn't know what else to do."

"So you consulted your sense of decency and found you didn't have one?" His voice had been rising, but he paused, as if struck by a sudden thought, and whispered, "What did you do with her body?"

Stevie looked at the ground, ashamed.

"I covered it with a sheet."

"You cold bitch." The man went to the door that separated the front shop from the back counter, stabbed at the security buttons and pulled the handle, but the lock stayed tight. "Fuck! Fucking thing!" His voice was hoarse, and he might have been crying. "I told her not to run around with cash on her. Told her and fucking told her." He slammed a fist against the door and stabbed another combination into the keypad.

"Sorry." Stevie was still backing away, her eyes on the man, as if she could keep him there by strength of will. "I'm sorry."

Her feet entered a shaft of sunlight stretching across the betting shop's dingy floor. The heat of the day touched her shoulders and the spell was broken. She turned and ran. For an instant, the brightness outside robbed her of her sight, then she saw it all: the empty road, the shuttered shops, and the drawn curtains in the apartments above them. The old man was still slumped against the side of the building, but this time she didn't pause to check on him. Stevie kept on running until she reached Hope's car, not daring to look back to see whether the bookmaker was chasing her.

Thirty-Four

S imon's school photographs were tucked safely in her bag next to Hope Black's gun. Stevie felt sure that whatever had happened to Simon was connected to the past, old loyalties reaching across the years to snare him in a scheme that had somehow resulted in his borrowing a small fortune from Hope, and finally, in his death.

She tried phoning Iqbal again, but the only response was from his voicemail so she left a message: *Iqbal, it's Stevie. Please call me when you get this, I'm worried about you.* She wondered if she should head south, return to Iqbal's apartment and check that he was okay. She had programmed the GPS with Geoffrey Frei's address in Swiss Cottage. It told her to *turn left* and she turned left. Iqbal had seemed keen enough to hope for more than a one-night stand. She couldn't imagine him deliberately ignoring her calls. The GPS directed her to *drive straight ahead for four hundred yards.* Stevie kept her hands on the wheel of the Jaguar and her eyes on the road.

Even if the key to Simon's death lay in the past, instinct told her that the only way she would uncover it was to press on. The man who had attacked her, and killed Hope Black, might have come to the same conclusion and already be on his way to the

Freis' house. Even if she eluded him, the journalist's wife might flee the city or succumb to the sweats, and then any chance of discovering what Frei had known would be lost. Stevie pushed Iqbal from her mind and kept on driving, a small knot of shame hardening in her chest.

Geoffrey Frei had lived in the kind of house beloved of British sitcoms. There were rows of them, as anonymous and indistinguishable to a stranger as the lines of little boys in Simon's early class photographs. The houses made Stevie think of a lost London where bowler-hatted men in pinstriped suits wielded umbrellas rolled as tight as their emotions as they headed for the 06:45 train. And of wives who stayed at home, gearing up for the first consoling gin of the day.

The respectable-at-all-costs suburbanites had been replaced by a new type of middle classes. Journalists and TV producers, pilot fish to media sharks they mostly despised; senior lecturers hoping to make professor; Web designers and MBAs, looking for the next big app/craze/.com miracle, all passing through on the way to their next property upgrade, and all praying that the market didn't collapse before they got there.

The curtains were drawn in many of the houses, as if they were homes in mourning, or occupied by honeymooners who had decided to stay in bed all day. But there were also pockets of activity: men and women in crumpled Boden and GAP casuals, loading their four-by-fours and station wagons with children, supplies, and pets. It would have looked as if the district had decided to go on a sudden vacation, were it not for the grim stares and drawn faces. Stevie drove past a man sitting on the edge of the sidewalk, his face shocked free of expression. She saw doors and windows clamped with steel shutters. She heard screams and saw a woman being forced into a car by two men. Stevie slowed the

Jag, wondering if she should intervene, until she saw that there were tears running down the men's faces too.

An oversized Subaru sat outside Geoffrey Frei's house. Stevie parked alongside it, allowing other traffic a lane to pass by, but boxing in the Subaru. She opened the gate to the Freis' yard just as a tall woman came out of the house carrying a box of groceries. Her task was made more difficult by the blond, curly-haired child clinging to her neck, his thin legs clamped around her waist in a way that confirmed Darwin's theories about evolution. The child looked at Stevie with wide eyes and then buried his face in his mother's chest, wrapping himself even more closely around her. Stevie said, "You look like you could do with a hand. Would you like me to take the box?"

Sarah Frei had frozen on the doorstep, but the sound of Stevie's voice galvanized her.

"Get out of my garden and keep your distance."

She sounded as if she had the authority of an army at her heels, and Stevie took an involuntary step backward.

"I've had the sweats." Stevie held up a hand, remembering that Geoffrey Frei's obituary had mentioned he was the father of twins, and wondering where the other child was. "I'm not contagious."

"I can't afford to take that chance."

"I understand, but I've traveled quite a long way to see you. My name is Stephanie Flint. My boyfriend knew your husband and I think their deaths might be connected. If I promise not to move from here, can I ask you a few questions?"

Sarah Frei was wearing a pair of cropped jeans and a floral blouse over a dark blue vest. She was broad-hipped and large-shouldered, the kind of woman that men with a bit of land and a yen for descendants must once have prized.

"Geoff was mugged. It was a random attack." The box was threatening to slip from the woman's grasp, and she bent and put it on the ground. A can of tomatoes tumbled free, rolled across the garden path, and into an overgrown border. She stared at the escaped tin, as if it was a problem beyond her capabilities, and then raised her eyes to look at Stevie. "I can't tell you anything. I wasn't there when Geoff was killed." She looked tired beyond tears, but there was a crack in her voice. "He was on his own."

"I think your husband was researching a story that somehow involved my boyfriend. They were due to meet the week Mr. Frei died. Two days after your husband died Simon was dead too. I think their deaths might be connected."

Sarah Frei had pinned her hair up in a careless knot. She pushed a strand away from her face.

"Almost everyone has lost someone. I'm sorry you've had a wasted journey, but I have responsibilities." She lifted the box and took a step forward. "Get out of my way, please."

The front yard was tiny, the only exit through the gate. They were all lepers now. It was a weapon of sorts, the force field of infection. Stevie held her ground.

"My boyfriend didn't die of the sweats. Someone killed him and tried to make it look like he died of natural causes. I only realized he'd been murdered when I discovered that he'd left me a laptop full of data. I couldn't access it at first, and when I did it was too technical for me to understand. The problem is, the person who killed him doesn't know that. They're after me now. If they think you know something, you could be in danger too."

The child whimpered. Sarah Frei jogged him up and down in her arms, in a dislocated, jerky fashion.

"Don't you get it? We're all in danger."

"Your husband might have been murdered. Don't you want to find out the truth about why he died?"

"What the fuck does it matter anymore?" The child heard the emotion in his mother's voice and started to cry. A man carrying supplies to his car down the path of an adjoining yard looked across at them, but he made no effort to intervene. "Shhhh, it's all right." Sarah Frei resumed the jerky rocking. The child's cries grew louder and more fractious. His arms and legs still stretched tightly around her, like a spider trying to subdue a much larger prey. "Shhhh." Sarah Frei put the box back down on the path and sank on to her doorstep. "See what you've done?" She threw Stevie a defeated look, opened her shirt and put the child to her breast. "Shhhh."

Stevie couldn't stand the not-knowing anymore. She said, "I read you had twins. Is the other one okay?"

Sarah Frei rested the child on her knees, cradling his head in the crook of her arm. She gave a small smile as he settled, and Stevie caught a glimpse of the person she had been before the crisis: an untidy, capable woman, sexy despite her ample rear, rough heels, and unshaven legs.

"He's with my mother." The child had quieted and the process of comforting him seemed to have soothed Sarah Frei too. "She was going to take both of them but Felix had a cold. We decided it was better to leave him with me and let Alex go with her. It was a mistake. I hadn't realized how bad things were going to get." She looked at Stevie. "Can you believe what's happening?"

It was a pause in hostilities, a Christmas soccer match before the fighting resumed. Stevie squatted on the ground. She saw Simon's face, his eyes rolled back in his head, Joanie in her nest of tubes, Hope's shattered skull.

"No, it feels unreal."

"That's where we're going now, to my mother's place in the New Forest, as soon as you let us." Sarah Frei reached into her jeans pocket and took out a pack of cigarettes. "Geoff would go crazy if he could see me smoking and breastfeeding at the same time, but right now I think it's the least of our worries." She lit up and took a long drag. "You've got until I finish this and then we're leaving."

The sun caught her strawberry-blond hair, highlighting flecks of silver-gray among the gold. They looked like a mark of her widowhood, and the sight of them made Stevie feel ashamed.

"I'm sorry." She ran her hand over her own rough crop, surprised at the jaggedness of it against her palm. "I wouldn't normally behave like this. It's like I'm trying to outrun a landslide."

"We all are." Sarah Frei took a pull at her cigarette. "So you'd better get on with it. You only have until I finish my cigarette."

"Can you tell me anything about the story your husband was working on when he died?"

Sarah Frei took another deep drag. Stevie watched the tip of ash glow and grow, the cigarette shrink.

"Normally Geoff doesn't . . ." Sarah Frei gave a dry smile. "Didn't talk much about his work. He liked to leave it behind when he came home, but that last case blurred the boundaries between Geoff the family man and Geoff the journalist." Sarah Frei tapped the cigarette with the unconscious ease of a practiced smoker and the ash crumbled to the ground. "He'd known one of the people involved. He didn't tell me his name, but Geoff said they had gone to the same school; they even trained together for a while, back when Geoff still thought he wanted to follow in his father's footsteps." The child had fallen asleep. She fastened her blouse and then ran a hand softly over his curls. "He was too squeamish to be a doctor, not that he'd ever admit it to anyone except me. Geoff was a gentle man. I was the tough one in the relationship. He couldn't stand pain." She looked up and her eyes met Stevie's. "But he could kill with his pen, if he thought the cause justified it."

Stevie opened her bag and flicked through the bundle of school photographs. She found the one that showed the trio of doctors together in the same row. The curly-haired boy in the glasses was sandwiched between Simon and Dr. Ahumibe. She held it up so that the other woman could see it.

"Is this your husband?"

"I don't know. It might be."

Stevie took a step closer and held out the photograph.

"Here, the boy wearing glasses?"

She pointed at the serious face beneath the Harpo Marx curls.

"I think so. He looked so like Felix and Alex when he was little. It's like fast-forwarding to how they'll be when they're ten or eleven." Sarah Frei grimaced as if she had just realized that she had spoken as if the future was assured. "Geoff was big on nurture over nature, all that *Give me a child until he is seven and I will give you the man* stuff. He reckoned the person you became was determined by how you were brought up."

"So, bad luck if your parents let you down."

"Very bad luck indeed, according to Geoff."

Stevie looked at the turrets and dreamy spires of the school in the photograph's background.

"I guess your husband's family didn't let him down."

A speck of steel entered Sarah Frei's voice.

"They worked very hard to help Geoff be what he eventually became, a good man."

It was how the newspaper column had styled Geoffrey Frei: a good man, a campaigner against corruption.

Sarah Frei went on, "Don't assume things were easy. His father worked overseas, his mother went with him, and Geoff was sent to boarding school. He was horribly bullied. He hated it."

Rich people always tried to assure you they had had it rough, Stevie thought. It was part of the way they misunderstood the world.

She said, "Perhaps that's what helped him have empathy with people when he grew up. What did your husband tell you about the case?"

Sarah Frei formed her mouth into an O and breathed out a perfect smoke ring. It was a schoolgirl gesture, tough and sulky, but when she spoke her voice had lost the edge it had taken on when she had talked about her husband's bullying.

"Geoff had been contacted by a whistle-blower. That was often how it started. Someone who was aware of something going on in their workplace that they couldn't stomach, but who didn't know how to stop it, would contact Geoff. This whistle-blower was high up, but scared. They were implicated somehow and wanted Geoff to help them find a way out that wouldn't wreck their career."

"What was he going to do?"

"That was the problem. Geoff couldn't expose the scandal without exposing his source, and he wasn't sure that he wanted to spare him anyway. He didn't drink much, but we had wine with our dinner one evening, after the boys were in bed. Geoff got quite morose about the investigation. He didn't go into details; like I said, he tended to keep the darker side of his work separate from family life, but it was something nasty." Sarah Frei stroked her child's curls. "All the same, he had known the man when they were both children. They'd been friends when they were at school. That was why the whistle-blower had gotten in touch with Geoff in the first place." She shrugged. "Geoff was going to write the article and alert the relevant authorities, but he didn't feel good about it."

"Did he say whether he was going to warn his source of what he intended to do?"

Sarah Frei put the cigarette to her lips, but drew on it less hungrily.

"Geoff was Geoff. He liked to think he was very twenty-first century, but he had this big private-school chip on his shoulder about doing the honorable thing. I used to tell him, forget the honorable thing. Just do the right thing."

"Did anyone else pick up the investigation after he died? Any of his colleagues?"

Sarah Frei paused and Stevie became aware of the noise in the street, the growl of engines as cars drove away, the burble of subdued goodbyes. Sarah Frei raised her hand in farewell to a departing Volvo and gave a sad smile. "That's Max and Abigail's mom and dad gone. We should leave soon too." She glanced at her cigarette and then turned her attention back to Stevie. "The newspaper was going to send a courier to take Geoff's computer and notes to his editor. I think they thought it would be insensitive to send one too soon, but they should have been quicker off the mark. The house was burgled while we were at Geoff's funeral." Sarah Frei shook her head. "Can you believe it? At the very moment we were putting my husband into the ground someone was in our home, going through our things. Most of the neighbors were at the funeral so the burglars couldn't have chosen a better time."

Stevie said, "That's terrible." But she was remembering her own torn-apart apartment and Simon's ransacked apartment. "Did any of your neighbors get burgled too?"

"No. I think some of them felt bad that they weren't, as if it would have made things better if they'd lost something too." She gave a small, bitter laugh. "What I wanted was for one of them to have lost her husband instead of me. I wanted Geoff to be here so we could both lend a sympathetic ear while someone else tried to pick up the pieces of their life." Sarah Frei glanced at the child and then raised her eyes to meet Stevie's. "I'm sorry, that sounds terrible." She took an angry pull at her cigarette. "Geoff's editor described the burglary as the last straw, but quite frankly I found it hard to care. The burglars took quite a few things of value, including Geoff's computer, but so what? The boys were safe and they were all that mattered."

"Didn't your husband keep a backup or store files online?"

"Real people with real reputations were involved in Geoff's investigations, so he was careful about where he stored his research. He had a flash drive that he kept in his jacket pocket and a laptop that he kept mainly at home. If he'd stored his research on the newspaper server his editor could have accessed it, but Geoff didn't consider that secure enough." Sarah Frei rolled her eyes. "It's lost. All of it."

"Did your husband say anything about the whistle-blower, anything that might help to identify them?"

"Like I told you, Geoff was always anxious not to expose his sources, even to me. But he was at the angry point in the investigation. The doing-it-in-sorrow-rather-than-anger stage would have come next. He told me that the people he was investigating thought they could apply a scale to suffering, as if life was an accounts ledger and relieving the pain of one group offset inflicting it on another." She shrugged. "Geoff loved being a journalist but I'm not sure it was the best job for him. He felt things too deeply. He'd had a couple of episodes of depression, not so bad that he was hospitalized, but bad enough. I felt it was my responsibility to protect him from that." She took another drag at her cigarette, smoking it down to the nub, like a homeless person unsure of where their next cigarette would come from. "I'm afraid I didn't make a very good job of things that night. I tried to add a sense of proportion by pointing out that it was just what happened everywhere: big companies destroying the environment, or exploiting their workforce, then trying to make themselves look good by sponsoring some sexy charity. I made a bad joke about how it was essential that the charity be sexy—after all, no one wants a logo highlighting victims of anal fissures on their product. Geoff lost his temper and shouted at me. It was unlike him."

"What do you think he meant about scales of suffering?"

The child stirred in Sarah Frei's lap, and she stroked his head again.

"I'm not sure. I got the impression it wasn't simply whatever the people involved had done that had infuriated him, but some warped morality that they'd used to justify it." She dropped the cigarette on the ground and crushed it beneath the toe of her sneaker, even though it was already dead. "We need to go."

"One last quick question, please." Stevie held up the photograph again and pointed to Simon, Buchanan, and Ahumibe.

"Do you recognize any of these men?"

"They're not men, they're boys." Something caught Sarah Frei's attention and she leaned in closer, putting her arms around her son to stop him rolling from her lap. "Is that John Ahumibe?"

"Yes."

"He was the only person from school that Geoff kept up with. They weren't close—the occasional drink, the odd exchange of e-mails—they were both busy, but they touched base from time to time." She looked at Stevie. "Geoff said the whistle-blower was someone he'd known at school, but I got the impression that it was someone he hadn't seen for a long time. It never even occurred to me to ask if it was John. Was it him?"

"I don't know." Stevie pressed her finger beneath the young faces of Simon and Buchanan. "What about the other two?"

"It's hard to be certain, but I don't think I met either of them. Like I said, schooldays weren't the happiest days of Geoff's life. Are they the people Geoff was investigating?"

"I think so."

"Including John Ahumibe?"

"Yes."

"Who are the others?"

"One of them was my boyfriend." Stevie stroked the face of the youth that had been Simon. "The other was their colleague, Alexander Buchanan."

"Was your boyfriend involved?"

"Maybe. I don't know. But if he was, I think he was doing his best to fix it when he died."

"Would you still think that if you hadn't been in love with him?"

It was on the tip of Stevie's tongue to say that she hadn't been in love with Simon, but she whispered, "I don't know."

Sarah Frei blew on her son's face, gently wakening him. He grumbled and turned away and she whispered, "Time to go now, Monkey." She looked at Stevie. "If you'd told me a week ago that Geoff had been murdered, I wouldn't have rested until I'd found his killer, but things have changed. I still care, I care deeply, but the new priority is to stay alive. We're leaving London until this virus or whatever it is burns itself out. You should do the same."

"There's someone I need to check on first."

"Don't leave it too long." Sarah Frei got to her feet, lifting her sleepy child with one arm and struggling with the box of groceries with the other. "Things are falling apart. Soon the sweats won't be the only thing we have to worry about."

Thirty-Five

"Stephanie, are you okay?" Alexander Buchanan had known that it was Stevie on the other end of the line, before she said a word. The thought of her name blinking on the pharmacist's phone was disquieting, and Stevie wished she had acquired an anonymous pay-as-you-go cell. Buchanan asked, "Where are you?" His voice was as urbane as ever, but there was a note of anxiety beneath his charm.

Stevie had forced her way through the jam of departing four-by-fours, urban jeeps, and station wagons in the streets around Sarah Frei's house and now the Jaguar was eating up the miles. She put him on the speakerphone and glanced at the GPS's map, checking that she was on the right road for Iqbal's apartment. Buchanan was the third person she had called. Neither Derek nor Iqbal had picked up and she had an increasing sense of her life burning away, like a fuse on a bomb steadily fizzing toward an explosion.

"What were you and Simon up to?" Stevie didn't bother with niceties or preliminaries.

"We were helping sick children get better."

Buchanan's voice sounded self-consciously reasonable, like the voice of a man who considered he had every right to be offended, but was refusing to rise to the bait.

"There was more to it than that. You were making a lot of money."

Stevie had expected to hear the bustle of the hospital in the background but Alexander Buchanan might have been answering her call from a soundproofed booth.

"The treatment generated a profit, yes, but we put most of that into research, in the hope that we could eventually make it more readily available. I'm at my lab. If you come here I can show you some relevant paperwork."

"I'd prefer you to e-mail it to me."

"All I have is hard copy, and right now I don't quite have the time to scan and send it." The pharmacist's voice had lost its veneer of tolerance. "Normally I'd ask one of our technicians to help out, but they seem to be either dead or otherwise occupied. So if you can't examine it yourself, I'm afraid you'll have to take my word for it."

"My sense of trust has taken a bit of a battering." Along with the rest of me, she thought, but didn't say.

Stevie had expected to be snared in lines of traffic, but the roads were all but empty. Normally it would have been a relief, but she found herself hoping she would turn a corner and see a stream of vehicles, each one containing healthy, pissed-off travelers. Up ahead, traffic lights glowed red. Stevie slowed to check that there was nothing about to cross the intersection and drove through. She said, "Simon didn't die of natural causes. He didn't kill himself either. Someone murdered him, but perhaps you already know that."

There was a pause on the line. The only sound the expensive purr of the Jaguar's engine. After a moment Buchanan said, "It crossed my mind."

"It crossed your mind?" She pressed her foot to the accelerator. "So all that guff about the possibility Simon had committed suicide was just an attempt to distract me. Who killed him?"

"I said I suspected the possibility of foul play." He spat the words like a schoolteacher infuriated by a stupid answer from a bright pupil. "I didn't say I was positive, and I certainly didn't say I had a suspect in mind."

"But you seem to be extremely well informed."

Somewhere in a quiet place beyond the car, beyond her imagination, Alexander Buchanan sighed.

"I knew Simon for over thirty years. I also knew he had a weakness for exotic company, of a kind that could get you into trouble. Nothing personal, but you're a case in point. At the risk of sounding like a terrible snob, surgeons don't normally go out with salesgirls."

Something dashed in front of the car, black and swift, a blur of legs and fur. Stevie swerved, bracing herself for the impact, but there was no bang, no sickening swell beneath her wheels, and when she glanced in the rearview mirror she saw a dog running along the white lines in the middle of the road, as if they were a map that would guide it home.

She took a deep breath and said, "Going out with salesgirls isn't a crime. Exploiting the families of sick children is."

"Agreed, but that's not what we were doing."

"I heard otherwise."

"A-h," the doctor stretched out the vowel, like a dawning realization. "You've been talking to Melvin Summers."

"He thinks you killed his daughter."

"Yes, he does. It's a common delusion. Recently bereaved parents often find it impossible to absorb the senselessness of a child's death. Some of them resolve their confusion by becoming convinced that the doctors were responsible. I wouldn't say you get used to being a scapegoat, but for the most part you learn how to deal with it. Mr. Summers is to be pitied. His wife committed suicide and he resorted to alcohol, not the best form of medication for a man already under great emotional strain, but he was a serious thorn in our sides. I'm afraid our diplomatic skills had failed and we were discussing the possibility of taking out an injunction against him."

She was approaching another crossroads, another red light. Stevie pressed a foot to the Jaguar's brakes again and, when there was no sign of an oncoming vehicle, sailed through. She said, "I might have bought that, if there weren't other accusations against your team. Did you know Geoffrey Frei was investigating you?"

"No, but he was perfectly welcome to do so."

There was a school up ahead. A sheet drooped from its railings, QUARANTINE CENTER painted across it in red. Whoever had made the sign had loaded their brush with too much paint and the letters were tailed by drips that made the words look as if they were bleeding. Stevie slowed the Jaguar to a crawl. The door to the school was open, the playground crammed with carelessly parked cars, but there was no other sign of life.

She put her foot back on the accelerator and said, "Frei's investigation was brought to an abrupt halt. He was murdered and then someone broke into his house and stole his research."

"I heard about his murder, but I didn't know about the burglary. Tell me, was that all that was taken, his research I mean?"

The sun cut into Stevie's eyes, blinding her for an instant. She flipped down the sun visor. The Jaguar's air conditioning was on, the space inside a comfortable sixty degrees, but she had an urge to open the car windows and feel the air outside on her face. She kept them closed, the car sealed tight, like a space rocket speeding toward the unknown.

"Other valuables were stolen, but that doesn't prove anything. The killer would want the murder and burglary to appear unrelated."

Buchanan gave a dry laugh. "That's the thing about conspiracy theories; they rely on speculation and that makes them endlessly adaptable. Conspiracists can always come up with an explanation because they don't have to stick to inconvenient facts. Tell me, what do you know about Frei?"

"I know he went to school with you, Ahumibe, and Simon. I spoke to his wife. She said he hated it. He was bullied."

"I'm afraid that was true. Frei was one of those boys that seemed to attract bullies. I never met his wife, but I'm glad to hear he found some happiness, even if he did intend to persecute us. Frei was a strange fish. Ahumibe kept up with him, but the rest of us had cut our ties long ago. He dropped out of medical school and seemed to have transformed his disappointment into a grudge against the profession."

"I don't think there was anything personal about it. His wife said he was torn between old loyalties and an urge for justice."

Buchanan let out a guffaw that made her sit back in the driver's seat.

"You're right. He was torn, but not for those reasons. It used to make me laugh when I saw his column in the newspaper, his 'good man' image, a crusader for the forces of justice in an unjust world. Oh, I daresay Frei did some good, but the man was a congenital liar. His whole life was predicated on deceit." Buchanan took a deep breath, as if considering what to say next. "Frei was a rather old-fashioned creature, a closeted, married homosexual with children. He and Ahumibe may have had an on-off dalliance; there were certainly rumors to that effect when we were at school. It was the source of some of the bullying. I don't care what people get up to in their private lives. But I do know Frei had a weakness for casual pickups. When I read the news of his death, I couldn't help wondering if it was the result of a brief encounter that had gone awry."

"You're lying."

"Ms. Flint." Buchanan's voice was exasperated. "I am getting rather tired of being called a liar. If you don't believe anything

I say, there doesn't seem to be much point in our having this conversation."

"Please, don't hang up." An army truck passed her, headed in the opposite direction. Its sides were dusty and mud-spattered, as if it were in the middle of some campaign. Stevie stared at the road ahead, determined not to make eye contact with the other driver. She heard Buchanan breathing on the end of the line and wondered what was keeping him there. She said, "If there's no truth behind Summers's allegations or Frei's investigation, why would anyone want to murder Simon?"

"Let me ask you a question. How did you and Simon meet?"

It had been an Internet date. A week of late-night flirting online, that had led to a drink in Soho and ended in the bed of a hastily booked hotel room.

Stevie said, "We were introduced at a party."

"Did he tell you much about his background?"

"Bits and pieces."

"I'll interpret that as not much. Didn't it strike you as funny that he never introduced you to his family or friends?"

"Not really. I didn't introduce him to mine."

"In that case perhaps it was a marriage made in heaven."

"We weren't married."

"No, Simon wasn't really the marrying kind. None of us were, although I had a disastrous attempt at it. Our little gang were the lost boys, the ones whose parents boarded them through the holidays because it was too far to fly us to wherever they were. None of us found it easy to make relationships, but we became some kind of family. Later we shared an apartment and then, later still, we worked together. Simon was best man at my wedding. When my son was born I asked Simon to be his godfather, and when I got divorced he let me move into his apartment for a while."

"Where did Frei fit into all this?"

Stevie was driving along an avenue of trees, sunlight strobing between the leaves, turning her progress into a cartoon of alternating bright and dark. She wondered if the journalist really had been gay. His wife had made a big thing of his gentleness, but that meant nothing. Some of the gay men Stevie had met had been manly, some of the straights fey.

"I told you, Frei went his own way." Buchanan's voice was too tired for impatience but she sensed his frustration. "What I'm trying to say is, the three of us shared a history. We looked out for each other."

"You also shared a business."

"Yes, we had a shared endeavor, to help sick children."

"You still haven't told me why you thought Simon might have been murdered."

An old man in a bathrobe and slippers was shuffling along the pavement, slow and determined, like a corpse making its own way to the grave. Stevie glanced in the rearview mirror as she passed and thought his eyes had been blackened, though it may just have been the effect of shadows, settling in the hollows of his face. Buchanan's sigh seemed to carry into the car, so close she could almost feel it against her skin.

"I'm telling you this because it's obvious you're not going to give up easily. But it's important you know that, if Simon was killed, trying to uncover the reason why could put you in danger."

"Are you threatening me?"

"Quite the opposite. I'm warning you." Perhaps Buchanan realized that his answer sounded like intimidation because he sighed again. "Lots of boys envied Simon at school. He was handsome, good at sports and managed to excel in his studies without being a bore about them. I'm repeating myself." The doctor paused as if picturing his friend's gilded youth. "I've already mentioned how popular Simon was. He made the most of his time there, worked hard, gained excellent grades, went up to Cambridge, but deep down he hated it. Simon always felt that there was something more real beyond the bourgeois confines of our world. He wasn't fool enough to throw away his advantages, but he became a social tourist. He sought out interesting company."

"Like salesgirls."

"That was unfair of me." Now that he had started, Buchanan seemed keen to get on with his story, like a university don aware of the ticking of the lecture-theater clock. "At first it was people in the arts: musicians, poets, writers. He even dated a rock singer for a while. A strange-looking girl, all skinny legs, multicolored hair, and black eyeliner; like an angry parrot. I got the impression it was the world these people inhabited, rather than the work they did, that attracted Simon. After a while, unfortunately, their exoticism seemed to fade. I suspect Simon discovered that most of the arty crowd were hard-working and middle class, rather like him."

Stevie asked, "Why unfortunately?"

A car was traveling slowly on the road ahead, its rear window jammed with bags, as if heading for the start of a family vacation. She overtook, and caught a glimpse of the car's occupants. An elderly white lady was at the wheel, a small Asian boy in the passenger seat. Their mouths were moving in a song, the boy waving his arms in accompaniment.

Buchanan said, "When their appeal started to wane, Simon drifted toward an edgier set." His voice softened and Stevie realized that he had reached the point her ex-editor had called "the golden axis," the moment when the story took over and the interviewee needed to go on. "We were at a school reunion when it struck me for the first time how deep Simon was in. It was the kind of boozy all-male affair you'd probably imagine: black tie, comfort food, lots of back-slapping and blue jokes. Simon regaled us with stories of his expeditions into the seamier side of society."

"The sex industry?" Stevie touched a foot to the brake, not trusting herself to steer the Jaguar straight. "Do you mean he slept with prostitutes?"

"I very much doubt it." Buchanan spoke slowly, as if weighing his words. "Simon may have met people who were involved in the sex industry. If you turn over a stone you have no control over what crawls out, but that wasn't what I meant. Surgeons need to be able to cope with risk. Not everyone can take a knife and cut into someone else's body. Simon was cool under pressure and fascinated by people who had the same ability. No doubt that was what attracted him to you."

"My job isn't dangerous."

"Perhaps not, but you present a show on live television with only the barest of scripts. Most people would find that impossible. And look at the way you've responded to this crisis. You could have run away, but instead you ran toward it. I'd give odds you're the kind of person who undertakes extreme challenges for charity."

Soon after her mother had died Stevie had rappelled down the Forth Railway Bridge in aid of Cancer Research. The thrill had hijacked her, the rush of air and sea, the moment when she had lost all of her thoughts and been no more than one of the gulls swooping above the iron girders.

"No," she said. "I always thought those sponsored challenges were ego trips."

Buchanan made a sound that might have been a laugh.

"Simon preferred the kind of woman who would contradict him, strong women who weren't afraid to rise to a dare. I daresay he had the usual moral objections to the sex industry, but it was also the wrong kind of risk-taking for him. He was drawn to people who put themselves on the line. He was especially elated the weekend of the reunion because he'd recently been introduced to a bank robber. 'One more specimen for *The Newgate Calendar*,' was how he put it. Everyone else found his exploits hilarious. Simon was a natural storyteller. But the way his adventures were escalating worried me. I took him aside and warned him that sooner or later these people would want something from him, most probably access to drugs."

Stevie passed an office block spray-painted with massive green letters: SO LONG AND THANKS FOR ALL THE FISH. A week ago it would have made her smile. She asked, "What did he say?"

"He thanked me for my concern and told me to drink up. I was falling behind and was in danger of becoming a bore." The pharmacist paused and took a deep breath, as if marking a change of chapter, and Stevie realized that he too was a natural storyteller. Buchanan continued, "Around seven years ago Simon met a woman called Hope Black. I think her background excited him. Her father had been a bookie, as had his father before him, back in the days when gambling was illegal. The Black family tree was intertwined with the family trees of people most of us would cross highways to avoid. Hope was as proud of her connections as Simon was fascinated by them. They started to see rather a lot of each other. At some point Hope introduced him to backroom poker; illicit matches, high stakes, and the potential to win the jackpot or lose your skin. Simon was fond of Hope, but he fell in love with gambling. He told me later that he felt like he'd found the thing he'd been waiting for all of his life."

The mention of Hope's name had chilled her. Stevie tightened her grip on the Jaguar's steering wheel, Hope's steering wheel.

"Didn't you try to stop him?"

"I might have, if I'd known what was going on, but it was only when things reached crisis point that Simon told me the full story."

"What happened?"

"It was so predictable I'm surprised you need to ask. Simon was out of his depth. He got into a bit of hot water, and Hope dropped him. Perhaps she didn't have any choice in the matter. He came to Ahumibe and me with his tail between his legs, and we helped extricate him, mainly through a fucking great loan to repay the money he'd borrowed from some rather demanding creditors. We hushed it up, Simon went for treatment with a colleague in Harley Street, who is almost as well known for his discretion as for his ability with addicts. All seemed well, for a while anyway. I thought I'd noticed a certain reckless edge to him over the last few months and wondered if he might be about to suffer a relapse. But when I confronted Simon, he assured me that everything was okay. He was in love, he said, and being in love made him silly. I told him not to be too silly, and we left it at that. Now I wish I'd pursued it. If you're looking for someone with a grudge against Simon you're more likely to find them among his gambling associates than at the hospital, though as you'll already have worked out, my advice is to let sleeping dogs lie."

It fit with what the lonely bookie in Better Bets had told her. Stevie thought of the forty-five thousand dollars Simon had borrowed from Hope Black. It was as if Buchanan read her mind. He said, "Have you spoken to Hope yet?"

"Hope Black is dead."

"Ah, that's a shame. She was an attractive woman."

His reduction of the woman to her looks irritated Stevie, but she asked, "You met her?"

"Oh yes, we all met Hope."

The doctor's voice was cool, as if no one was dead, no brains leaked into the carpet, no body cold between soiled sheets.

"Hope didn't die of the sweats. Someone bashed her brains in." Stevie made her words deliberately crude, wanting Buchanan to picture the blood, the ruined skull. "I think they thought she was me."

There was a roundabout up ahead. Stevie ignored the yield lines, remembering the way Hope Black's hand had seemed to beckon her. There was a blur of movement and her stomach swooped. A Honda Civic was traveling from the right and it was almost upon her. The other car had the right-of-way but Stevie put a hand on the horn and pressed her foot down hard on the accelerator, metal touching metal. She saw an open mouth, a blur of fear and wide eyes, heard the blare of the other vehicle's horn and the screech of rubber against pavement, and then she was away, the Honda a reflection skewed across the road in her rearview mirror.

If Buchanan heard the commotion of skids and warning blasts he ignored it.

"Hope didn't look anything like you. She was at least ten years older. She was taller and darker as well."

He sounded faintly amused. Stevie could imagine his smile, the pale lips stretched in the white face.

"She resembled me enough for someone who didn't know either of us to get confused."

"Hope lived life on the edge. That's what drew Simon to her. It's very probably what drew her death too."

"It's more complicated than that. Someone's been chasing me ever since I tried to deliver Simon's package to Mr. Reah."

"You mean the laptop?" She heard a faint smile in Buchanan's voice, as if he had caught her out in some gaucherie. "Get rid of it then. Hand it in to the authorities, or bring it here and allow me to dispose of it for you."

"I don't have it anymore."

"In which case, you're off the hook. What did you do? Hand it in to the police?" Stevie let the silence hang between them, and after a pause Buchanan asked, "Did you manage to read what was in it?"

"No." It was only a half lie. "I couldn't get past the password."

The pharmacist's voice became serious. "It's possible the laptop might contain confidential information about our process . . ."

The sentence trailed away. Stevie could almost hear the faint murmur of the pharmacist's thoughts, potential scenarios turning over in his head. ". . . but that wouldn't have prompted anyone to want to get their hands on it so desperately that they would threaten you. Simon must have encoded other information there. If he had gotten involved with Hope again, then it could well have been something injurious to his health."

Stevie pulled Hope's Jaguar over to the side of the road. She could imagine Simon as a reckless, put-the-whole-stake-on-red gambler. She realized that she believed Buchanan, and that if Simon was with her now, she would tell him that whatever there had been between them was over. Tears filled her eyes; she wiped them away with her sleeve.

"If I bring the laptop to you, you'll be in danger too."

"Perhaps." Buchanan's languid sophistication seemed more brittle than sinister now. "But you're forgetting I've dealt with Simon's creditors before. They belong to a small world, smaller since the advance of the sweats, no doubt, and unlike you I'm a known quantity. People can't go around killing respected research pharmacists without some questions being asked."

"They managed it with Simon."

"Simon crossed the line. I haven't. I'm not compromised and I've got nothing to hide. I'll make it clear that I'm going along with things in order to get them off your back, but that if they harm either of us, the full force of the law will come down on them."

"Assuming there's any law left."

"That's something we can only pray for." Buchanan no longer sounded smug.

"Aren't you afraid I will give you the sweats?"

"My granddad flew Spitfires in World War Two. Fighter pilots used to say, *If your number's on it* . . . I've adopted that as my motto for this particular conflict. The priority now is to try and find a cure. Scientists all over the world are online, pooling ideas and information." Buchanan sounded resolute. Perhaps he was still thinking about his grandfather, a young man running across the airfield toward his Spitfire, ready to embark on another mission that might be his last. "I can't leave the lab, but I took the precaution of holding on to the contact numbers of the people I dealt with last time Simon was in trouble. They're probably out of date, but it's a place to start."

Stevie wondered at his willingness to interrupt his research to help her, but then Buchanan asked, "Are you still healthy? No reoccurrence of symptoms?" And she decided that he was more confident of saving her from Simon's creditors than of finding a cure for the sweats.

"Yes," she said. "I've had lot of exposure to people with the virus and so far I'm fine."

"Good," he said. "That's extremely good news. I heard it's getting a little hairy outside. Tell me where you are and I'll send my son William to pick you up."

"I've managed on my own so far."

"That's the kind of thing Hope would have said."

"I'm not Hope."

"No, she's dead."

"And I have no intention of joining her. There's someone I need to check on. As soon as I'm through I'll deliver the laptop to you."

"It would make more sense to let William . . ."

Buchanan started to make some objection but Stevie killed the conversation and ignored the melody of his return call. She recognized the streets now, she was only a block or two from Iqbal's apartment, but she turned on the robot voice of the GPS and let it guide her. The sound of a familiar voice, even a recorded one, was a comfort.

Thirty-Six

I t was like going back to the beginning again, the smell of decay, the silent apartment, the slow patrol through empty rooms, except this time there was music softly playing, a repetitive not-quite melody she had never heard before, notes crisscrossing, as haphazard as colors on a harlequin's costume. Everything in Iqbal's apartment looked as it had on her previous visit, its contents tidy and tastefully arranged, but the air was tainted. Stevie took Hope's gun from her bag. The weight of it unnerved her, but she kept it in her hand, the barrel pointing away from her.

"Iqbal?"

Stevie had meant to shout his name, but it came out barely above a whisper and was lost in a tide of notes.

The screens of the computers ranked along the desk beneath the stairs were dead. Stevie noticed Simon's laptop among them, a small pile of printouts stacked neatly by its side. She ignored it.

"Iqbal?"

The room was almost white with light, the brightness of the day cutting through the picture windows. She lowered the blind and saw that the reading lamp beside the couch was on, although the couch itself was empty, its cushions plumped as if no one had sat there for a while.

"Iqbal?"

Stevie ran the tips of her fingers along the surface of the breakfast bar, raising a thin coating of dust. She brushed a hand along the wall as she climbed the stairs, though she had never been afraid of heights.

"Iqbal?"

The music was fainter upstairs. Years ago she had gone on impulse to a boyfriend's house and found him in bed with a woman she had never seen before. For some reason the moment came back to her, the feeling she had gotten when she had walked into his hallway, the sense that something was out of balance, the world not as it should be.

Iqbal's bed was hidden behind a Japanese screen, white paper stretched on a cherry wood frame. A lamp glowed softly behind it. She said his name again softly, "Iqbal?" The music rose in a wave and shattered, notes splashing around her, but nothing broke the gleam of light beyond the screen.

"Jesus." Stevie ran a hand over her hair, still surprised to find it shorn. She could go downstairs, collect the laptop, bundle the papers Iqbal had left into her bag and head for Buchanan's lab. If she went now, she might be able to convince herself that Iqbal was waiting out the sweats in comfort somewhere else. Stevie took a deep breath and stepped behind the screen.

In life, Iqbal had been lean, with features clean enough to be carved in stone. Death had robbed him of his beauty. Stevie saw the empty pill bottles on the bedside table and whispered, "Stupid. Stupid, stupid, stupid." She had an urge to kick the bed, to shake his body back to life and slap some sense into it. "Why would you do this?" She felt a pain in the palms of her hands and realized that she had clenched her fists so tightly her nails were

digging into them. "Stupid." She had thought the sweats sense-
less, but to submit to the dark rather than taste even the first tide
of suffering was worse.

Stevie pulled the sheet over the face that was no longer his
and went downstairs. The music was coming from an iPad resting on one of the bookcases. She tried to close it down but the
small screen confused her and the music rattled on, unbear-
able and pointless. Stevie took the tablet out on to the balcony,
looked at the empty street below and then cast it down on to
the concrete. She went back indoors and sank on to the couch.
The gun was still in her hand. She stowed it in her bag, took
out her cell, and called Derek. An automated voice informed
her that the number she was calling was no longer available. He
had gone to Norfolk, she told herself, to be with Francesca, the
woman who had stolen him away from Joanie.

Somewhere on the other side of the city a pyre of black smoke
was reaching into the sky. She watched it for a while and then
went to Iqbal's kitchen and searched through his cupboards.
Although they were packed with enough tins and dried goods to
keep a family for several weeks, there was no alcohol.

"Stupid." She wondered why she hadn't taken a bottle of malt
from Simon's apartment. Why hadn't it occurred to her that at
some point she would need to get drunk? "Stupid, stupid, stupid." It was becoming a mantra. She went to the desk and looked
at the printouts piled next to Simon's laptop. An envelope neatly
labeled with her name lay on top. There was déjà vu in that too.
Stevie ripped it open and took out the letter inside.

Dear Stevie

Please don't go upstairs. I have the sweats. I knew from the start that I
wanted to have some control over the way I die, and so tea and cookies

weren't the only things I stockpiled. Meeting you has made these last days better. It also makes leaving harder, but I've read how the final stages go. I hope you'll mourn me a little, but please don't be too sad. You gave me a wonderful gift. My gift to you is beside the laptop. I think Simon and his team made a genuine mistake, the kind that might happen to anyone. They tried to do something good. I feel jealous of Simon, but you can be proud of him, even though he got some things wrong. It's the intention behind the act that counts, right?

I lost my faith a long time ago, but recently I've been thinking there might be something beyond all of this after all and that if there is some kind of deity they won't mind whether we believe in them or not. What they will care about is whether we tried to do good in this world. I'm glad I had the chance to be some help to you before I go. Who knows, it might open a door in the afterlife.

Please pray for me.

Iqbal

Stevie found an unopened bottle of bubblebath at the back of the bathroom cabinet. Its label was decorated with a jolly Santa Claus holding a sprig of holly in his hand. She wondered if it had been a Christmas present and, if so, who had given it to Iqbal. Had he simply never got around to opening it, or kept it for some other reason? She couldn't find a basin and so she took a large bowl from the kitchen, carried it upstairs to the bathroom and filled it with warm water. She poured a capful of bubblebath into the bowl and splashed a hand around in the water. Foam frothed on its surface, the bubbles horribly festive. A familiar, clean scent rose from it, more suitable to a child's bathtime than to a corpse's laying-out.

Stevie set the warm water at Iqbal's bedside, soaked a fresh wash-cloth, and began to wipe his body with it. He had asked her to pray for him, but her mother and she had never been churchgoers. She didn't even know what religion Iqbal had belonged to. In the end she settled for the Lord's Prayer, stumbling a little over the final lines,

> *For thine is the kingdom,*
> *the power, and the glory,*
> *forever and ever.*
> *Amen.*

When she was finished she patted Iqbal's skin dry with a towel, and then found a clean sheet and wound him tightly in it. Were it not for the whiteness of the cotton, his body would have resembled a mummy's, lifted free of its sarcophagus. Stevie had taken a piece of paper and a marker pen from the desk. She wrote his name clearly, IQBAL, and placed the paper on top of the body.

"Not exactly a good send-off, I'm afraid, but the best I can do."

Stevie touched her fingers to her lips and placed the kiss she had been too squeamish to give his dead skin, on to Iqbal's parceled forehead. She felt calm, as if the act of washing and binding him had soothed her.

There was a typewritten letter on top of the small pile of pages that Iqbal had left next to Simon's laptop. Stevie saw a faint reflection of herself in the desk's glass surface and slid the papers closer, erasing the gaunt face, the ragged hair. She set the letter aside, uncertain that she could survive the sound of Iqbal's voice in her head again, so soon after reading his suicide note. The rest of the pages looked impersonal, reams of numbers cumulating into calculations. Stevie recognized the layout and realized that Iqbal had printed the data from Simon's laptop. She worked her way slowly through it, careful to keep the pages in order. Iqbal had highlighted particular numbers and lines of figures, perhaps thinking that would make it easier for a non-statistician to understand.

Despite his efforts, Stevie found it impossible to make sense of what was in front of her. She turned to the letter, dread in her belly, but as soon as she started to read, she knew that Iqbal had written it before the sweats had touched him, back when he had thought he might survive. There was no greeting and no leave-taking, no plea for her affection. This was the computer guru and statistician speaking.

A BRIEF SUMMARY OF FINDINGS

The research team analyzed their original data in the usual way.

i.e. they attempted to ascertain whether positive results were due to their new treatment, or simply owing to chance. After studying the data, they concluded the possibility that the positive results were mere chance was one in a thousand. Drugs have been licensed on far lower probabilities. It was as close to proof that the treatment was effective as they could have hoped for.

What I believe Simon eventually realized, and what I discovered when I redid the team's calculations, was that along the way someone had made a catastrophic statistical error. The error had been absorbed and repeated. There was in fact only a one in ten chance that the treatment had been effective, way below the balance of proof required.

This appears to have been a genuine mistake, a miscalculation in the figures.

I was helped in my own calculations by a coded
mathematical summary Simon included among the
documents, a sophisticated text it was a pleasure to
grapple with. This suggests to me that he wanted
to keep what he had found secret, but detectable to
someone who would know how to look for it in the
right way.

Stevie leaned back in the chair and looked up at the ceiling. Simon
had made a mistake, a costly, devastating mistake, but a mistake
all the same.

She turned on the laptop and scrolled through the documents,
searching for something else that might have made the computer
a target, but it appeared that Simon had acquired the machine
purely for the purpose of storing the drug trial data. The only
unrelated document was the photograph of the two of them
together in Russell Square,

Stevie looked up at the ceiling again. A small cobweb she was
sure Iqbal would never have allowed hung gossamer-high above
her head. She had seen photographs of Chernobyl: abandoned
homes, factories and schools that had been overrun by nature
until they looked as if they had belonged to some lost civilization.
It was easy to imagine London's pavements cracked by weeds, col-
onies of deer roaming Oxford Street, dust gathering on the tables
of Caffè Nero and Starbucks, posters for action movies wilting
from billboards and Underground tunnel walls. She sat up. Those
kinds of thoughts had the potential to drag her into the same
shadows that had claimed Iqbal.

Buchanan had insisted that, if Simon had been murdered,
then the blame lay with his gambling associates, but the pharmacist had also been adamant that the treatment was effective. If he
was wrong about one, then he might be wrong about the other.

The question was, did Buchanan genuinely believe what he had told her, or was he lying?

She still had Hope's gun. She could go to the lab, put the barrel to Buchanan's head and demand that he tell her the truth. Stevie tried to imagine what it would be like to use it and remembered the way Hope's skull had bloomed red against Simon's floor. Anyone who pointed a gun must be prepared to fire it.

Alexander Buchanan had been quick to push himself forward, quick too to provide explanations and offer help, but there had been a third man in the research team. Dr. John Ahumibe had been more reticent. He had lost two friends and a work colleague, but Stevie wondered if there had been another dimension to the pediatrician's reserve and if, behind the quiet façade, lay something he wanted to hide.

Thirty-Seven

The streets around Westminster were a jam of cars, abandoned every which way, as if their drivers had not paused to think about how to make their exits. Stevie was forced to park the Jaguar at least a mile from St. Thomas's Hospital and make the rest of her journey on foot. It was eerie, threading a route through the empty vehicles, some with their engines still running, gas fumes clogging the air. She passed a young man slumped across the steering wheel of a hatchback. His dark hair hung over his features like a curtain, and if it weren't for his broad shoulders, Stevie might have mistaken him for a girl.

A week ago she would have wrenched open the door, tried to revive him, and called for help. Now she quickened her pace. It was too easy to imagine the youth sitting up, drawing back his hair, and reminding her of what death could do to a face.

The Houses of Parliament still loomed solid and stately by the side of the Thames. Police barriers blocked the roads and sidewalks around the building, as if to protect the motorcade of some high-risk dignitary, but no officers were in attendance and Stevie slipped between them. Her feet wanted to break into a run, but she forced herself to keep to a steady pace.

She crossed Westminster Bridge remembering the tourists who had cluttered the sidewalk on her last visit. The London Eye was stalled, the streets deserted of everyone except her. Union Jack bunting fluttered above the closed door of a souvenir kiosk and postcards rippled on a pavement stand. A handwritten sign declared the postcards: THREE FOR £2.00. Stevie slid a view of St. Paul's from the stand. She had walked past the cathedral countless times, but had never been inside. She wondered if people were gathered there now, praying for relief from the sweats, or if fear of infection had discouraged even the religious from congregating. Big Ben struck the quarter-hour, as if nothing had changed and time still mattered. Stevie slipped the postcard back into the rack.

Something rumbled loud and mechanical from the river below. She leaned against the parapet and saw a lone barge pushing its way through the water toward her, iron and steadfast. Stevie waited until it disappeared from sight beneath the bridge, and then watched it glide away from the city, raising plumes of spume in the oil-black water. The sound of its engines held her. She raised a hand to the vanishing barge, but its captain was busy correcting course to avoid an unmoored tourist ferry and there was no answering wave.

Stevie wondered if Dr. Ahumibe would still be on duty, or if she was walking toward another corpse. Life was a losing race. The trick was to steer a straight path, choose a target and keep making toward it for as long as you could.

The front of the hospital was a gridlock of army trucks, ambulances, and police cars. A group of soldiers stood on the pavement outside the entrance, smoking cigarettes. It was unclear if they were guarding the hospital, or had been ordered to contain infected people inside. They looked up as she passed, their faces gray and battle-weary, and she saw that they were armed. Stevie kept on walking, aware of their eyes on her, glad of her ugly hair-cut and Simon's suit. She turned right, skirting the outside of the building. Apart from the soldiers, she had not seen a living soul since she had left the Jaguar. Were it not for the abandoned cars, the streets would be as empty as those of a small town on match day, after their team had unexpectedly made the League. Even if the guards let her through, the thought of the hospital's foyer, and what she might find there, frightened her.

Somewhere a woman started to sing. She had a full-throated voice that could hit the high notes and then swoop so deep it might have belonged to a man. The tune sounded familiar, like a song Stevie had known and then forgotten, but the words were in a language she didn't recognize. It was unsettling, the hidden singer, the lure of her voice, the words that might have been Scan-dinavian, or Arabic, or a language invented just for this song, glid-ing through the empty streets.

St. Thomas's Hospital was even larger than Stevie remembered. She tried a side entrance, but it was locked tight. The door's glass window had splintered into a web of cracks, as if someone had tried to smash their way through. Stevie peered through the mazed pane, but all she could see was an empty corridor and a sign pointing the way to X-ray. Stevie's ears strained for the slam of a car door, the sound of footsteps coming toward her, but there was nothing.

Not everyone had the virus, she reminded herself. She had passed other cars on her way to the hospital, had heard the singer and seen the soldiers, each one unquestionably alive. Dr. Ahu-mibe had looked like a survivor. He would be waiting inside St. Thomas's and she would make him tell her what he knew about Simon's death.

The loading bays around the back of the building were on a lower level from the pavement. Stevie kept close to the barrier and peered down into a parking lot reserved for emergency vehicles.

Lines of abandoned ambulances snaked their way from the road to the hospital's doors. Stevie caught a flash of movement and saw a soldier leaning against one of the vehicles. Even from a distance she could tell that he was sick, but instinct warned her to steer clear of men in uniform. She jogged on, keeping her body low.

Finally she found what she was looking for. A catering truck had been backed up to a delivery entrance, its rear doors open as if it was in the process of being unloaded. The driver, impatient with opening the delivery door each time he entered with a load, had used a brick to jam it open. A wedge of darkness was visible in the building beyond. Stevie waited for a moment to make sure that the driver wasn't going to suddenly reappear. Then she stepped into the shadows, took Hope's gun from her bag and slipped it into the pocket of Simon's pants. She had no idea if she would be able to shoot someone, even in self-defense, but it comforted her to know that she was armed.

Stevie edged slowly into the gloom of a dimly lit corridor, letting her eyes adjust to the darkness, ready to bolt at the first sign of danger. She was glad of the low light. It made her feel safer, her clothes black against the darkness, the gun in her pocket. Stevie took deep breaths, remembering her yoga classes, breathing in through her nose and out through her mouth. She could feel the weight of the building above her. The corridor's low ceiling was lined with exposed pipes, and the space hummed with white noise, as if it was the powerhouse of some oversized cruise ship.

A set of double doors, each fitted with a small porthole, lay ahead. Stevie peered through one of the windows. There was nothing in the corridor beyond, except for a metal cart that looked as if it was used for ferrying patients' meals. She slipped into the passageway. The white noise was louder here and Stevie wondered if she was nearing the boiler or some control center. The thought made her wary. Her object was to get to the upper levels without being waylaid by anyone, and from there to Dr. Ahumibe's ward. She could see other rooms leading off the corridor now, pale doorways shining faintly in the gloom. She upped her pace. It smelled bad down there in the dark, a Third World stink. Stevie slipped her silk scarf from her bag, wrapped it around her nose and mouth, and took the gun from her pocket.

Something flitted, fast and sure, along the side of the wall and a small scream escaped her. Once she had seen one rat, she saw the others, a swift-moving river of sharp noses, undulating spines, and sliding tails. She faltered, her back pressed against the wall, the gun still in her hand. The corridor was filled with the sound of claws scuttling against concrete and it was all she could do to keep her finger from squeezing the trigger. The loading bay was a small scrap of light at the end of the corridor. A rat ran over her foot. Stevie kicked out hard and started to sprint, away from the light and toward the next set of double doors. The rats parted to let her through and for a moment it was as if she was one of them. Stevie felt Simon's pants flapping at her ankles and let out a moan, imagining a rat scurrying up her leg. She grappled her phone from her bag, found the flashlight function, and turned it on. The corridor ahead shone with light and the rats seemed to pause for an instant, like an interrupted pulse in an electric current, and then she was through the double doors and into the next section of the building.

There were creatures there too. Stevie could hear them darting into corners, but she had left the pack behind. A set of stairs waited at the end of the corridor. Stevie paused to tuck Simon's pants into her socks. Her heart felt as if it was about to batter its way out of her chest.

"Easy, easy, easy, easy." Her words were all breath.

The flashlight beam juddered against the walls and Stevie realized that her hands were trembling too much to hold the gun safely. She shoved it into her bag, took a deep breath, and leaned forward, her hands on her knees, gasping for air. Something moved in the dark, she straightened up and the light sprang through an open doorway illuminating the room beyond. Stevie gave a gasp and swung the beam away, but the scene had imprinted itself on her eyes, like a digital photograph, captured in an instant.

Less than two weeks ago she had been a presenter for a TV shopping channel. It wasn't her dream job, but the pay was good, and Stevie had liked it well enough. She had had a boyfriend too, a nice guy, a doctor. He had been a little too inclined toward spontaneity for Stevie to be sure that their relationship would last, but he had been good fun, especially in bed. She knew that if their romance fell apart, she could turn to Joanie, a fine friend who knew what it was like to lose a man, and who would laugh about it with her, because what else could you do? It was gone, all of it, but her losses were nothing compared to what waited in the room ahead.

Stevie took a deep breath. Then she tracked the beam slowly across the wall of the corridor and through the open door. Bodies stretched all the way from the entrance to the far wall, laid out head to toe; a mosaic of corpses.

An attempt had been made to preserve the bodies' dignity. Those at the far end of the room had been covered by sheets, but at some point linen had grown scarce and the people closer to the doorway lay exposed, wearing the clothes they had died in. The humming sound made sense now. Bluebottles battled in a busy haze above the rows of dead.

Stevie saw an old man, his feet bare, his soles pink and vulnerable, his mouth agape. She saw a girl with tomato-red hair whose roots were showing. She saw a Rasta man with gray dreads and a black dready beard. She saw a girl with braids that were secured by hair clips shaped like daisies. She saw an elderly woman whose wig had slid sideways, exposing the bald skull beneath. She saw a child of no more than three years old. She saw a fat man with cheeks like slabs of boiled ham. She saw a man with a hennaed beard, bushy and piratical. She saw a girl with a Vidal Sassoon bob and almond eyes. She saw a youth in a yellow Space Invaders T-shirt. She saw a large man with his hair pulled back in a ponytail. She saw a girl in a summer dress and green sandals. She saw an elderly man wearing an EasyJet-orange-colored turban. She saw a skinny white boy with tattooed sleeves. She saw a soldier whose arms were tucked tight by his sides, as if he had died on parade. She saw a middle-aged woman in a red-and-gold sari. She saw a bald man with a sunburned head. She saw a nurse wearing stained scrubs.

She saw.

She saw.

She saw.

There was a whine louder than the droning flies, a sinking mechanical moan. Stevie knew what it was, but the sight of the bodies had driven everything else from her head and its name escaped her.

She had never grasped the miracle of distinctness so clearly before, had never truly understood death's vastness. Each hanging limb and lolling head had belonged to a person. Each one of them had felt the approach of death and feared it. And now they were gone, leaving a husk of flesh behind. Nothing connected the dead except their deaths. They were lost to themselves, and to the living.

Stevie felt a horrible sudden urge to laugh. She clamped a hand over her mouth, shaking her head, as if denying what was in front of her could make it go away.

The machine hum was building. Its vibrations touched Stevie and she realized that it was the sound of an elevator descending from the floors above. She clicked off her flashlight and ran for the stairs. The elevator doors breathed open just as she reached the landing. A hospital cart rattled in the corridor below as someone pushed it, slow and weary, toward the makeshift morgue.

Thirty-Eight

Stevie's sneakers scuffed against the stairs leading to Dr. Ahumibe's ward. The hospital's fluorescent lights seared into her brain. She paused and pressed her knuckles to her eyes, wondering if this was the return of the sweats, the blessed bout that would carry her off.

A scrambling sound that was all movement made her look up. A rat was scurrying down the stairs toward her, fat and sleek, busy as a working mom in her lunch hour. Stevie's kick made contact. The rat gave a high scream as it skidded across the step, paws splayed seeking for purchase, then it tumbled, tail twisting, rump over belly, into the stairwell and landed somewhere below.

She tried to erase the memory of what she had seen in the basement, but reminders lined the walls of the hospital's wards and corridors. People in white coats and green scrubs lay among the dead and the doctors and nurses still on their feet had a tranquilized look. None of the medics challenged her, but a man slumped on a chair reached out a hand and caught Stevie by the sleeve.

"You don't have it, do you?"

"No," she said. "I did, but I recovered."

He gripped her wrist tight, his fingers digging into her flesh, bruising it. Stevie tried to pull away but the stranger held on tight, with a hand that felt all bone.

"They should be experimenting on you." The man lifted his head and shouted, "This girl has the answer." It was as if one of the corpses from the basement had risen up and started to talk. He was sick, his face glossy with sweat, skin that might have once been a rich copper now sunk to khaki. She could see death on him, but the man raised his voice loud enough to turn some heads. "The antidote is in her blood."

Stevie chopped at the sensitive part of his wrist with the edge of her hand and pulled free.

"I'm sorry."

"You can save us," the man whispered.

"No, you're wrong."

Stevie could see the stairs to Dr. Ahumibe's ward up ahead. She broke into a run.

"Stop her," the man shouted. "She's the antidote."

But his voice was weaker than his grip, and if anyone heard him they paid no attention. After that, the quiet of the stairway came as a relief.

Stevie heard the sound of sobbing. A woman of about her own age sat hunched on a landing, her face buried in her hands. Stevie touched the woman's hair as she passed, but she didn't stop. There was nothing to say.

Dr. John Ahumibe was in the small office where they had first talked. He was sitting at the desk, his head slumped across its surface. For a moment Stevie thought that he was dead, then she heard the sound of his breaths and saw the matching rise and fall of his ribs, and realized he was asleep. She took a chair from the other side of the desk, shut the door, set the chair against it, sat down, and closed her eyes.

Stevie woke with a start, unsure of where she was. Dr. Ahumibe's head was still resting against the desk, but his eyes were open. He blinked and said, "You're still alive."

"You were right. I'm a survivor."

The doctor didn't bother to lift his head.

"I killed them all."

"Simon, Frei, and Hope?"

The doctor rolled his head from side to side. His pupils were magnified, his eyes almost all black, and she wondered what he had taken.

"The children. I killed them."

There was no one there to hear her, but Stevie's voice was a whisper. "Do you mean Joy Summers?"

"No." The doctor rolled his head against the table again awkwardly, as if some mechanism had broken inside. "The children. It was my job to make sure that they were okay, and so I took care of them, one by one."

Stevie got to her feet and looked through the small window in the door, out into the ward beyond. The lights were low, but she could see the closed doors of the side wards. She imagined the drawn sheets and the motionless swell beneath each one.

"All of them?"

"All that hadn't been taken by their parents, or already died, yes."

Stevie touched the glass. She felt an urge to open the doors and draw back the sheets, but stayed where she was.

"Couldn't you have taken them somewhere?"

"Where?"

She turned to look at him.

"I don't know. The countryside?"

"It would only have extended their deaths. It was better this way." The doctor sat up, dragging a hand across his face. His complexion had turned the gray of a riverbed after long months of drought. Stevie saw his features properly for the first time, and recognized the signs of the sweats on him. He asked, "Why are you here?"

"I want to know what happened."

"No one knows." He yawned, and Stevie saw his teeth, the wet tongue and soft inside of his throat. "Sometimes viruses just appear." The doctor's voice was cracked with grief and tiredness. There was a bottle of water on the table beside him. He poured a measure into a glass and took a small sip, as if he was unsure whether he would be able to hold it down. "I heard a theory, way back in the beginning when we had only just started to get seriously worried. An astrophysicist suggested that the virus might have been caused by space dust, brought in on a fallen asteroid. For some reason that still appeals to me. Outer space gave us life, now it brings us death."

Falling stars and children dead beneath their sheets, the bodies laid together in the basement. For a moment the images in Stevie's head threatened to overwhelm her. She gripped the armrest of the chair.

"I want to know why Simon died."

"Why Simon died." Dr. Ahumibe repeated her words as if they were in a foreign language he was in the early stages of learning. "There was no reason. It was just one of those things. Sad at the time . . . devastating . . . but now I think, lucky bastard, 'to die upon the midnight with no pain,' and miss all of this."

"He was murdered."

"Is that why you're here? Because you think someone killed Simon?" The doctor opened a drawer and took out a clutch of white paper boxes. His hands were shaking but he stacked the boxes patiently on the desk, one on top of the other, concentrating on the task as if it was important to get their edges straight, their corners aligned. "Everyone liked Simon. No one would want to murder him." He looked up and met her eyes for the first time. "You must have loved him a lot, to still care."

"Don't you care?"

"I told you, I think he was lucky to go when he did. Simon always was lucky."

"According to Alexander Buchanan he wasn't lucky at cards."

"Xander told you about that?" Dr. Ahumibe gave a sad, vague smile. "It seemed like a big deal at the time, thousands of dollars owing, criminal types creeping into the hospital in search of Dr. Sharkey." He shook his head. "Simon used to say, 'What's life without a little danger?' It made me angry, but now I realize he was the only one of us who really knew how to live." He flicked a finger at the tower of boxes, toppling them across the desk. "A short life, but a merry one."

From somewhere inside the hospital came the sound of screaming and running feet. Dr. Ahumibe reached into his pants pocket, took out a set of keys, and pushed them to the edge of the desk.

"Lock the door and turn out the light. People may be looking for drugs." He pulled off his white coat, his movements slow and awkward, as if the pockets had been weighted with stones. "It's best no one knows I'm a doctor." He shoved the coat under his chair. "I can't help them anymore, and there are better ways to go than being beaten to death."

Stevie turned the key and clicked off the room's fluorescent light. The dusk was coming in, another day drawing to its close, with no clue of what tomorrow would bring. She wondered fleetingly where she would sleep that night. The sound of pounding footsteps built until they passed the office door and faded down the corridor. She waited until she was sure they were gone and then said, "I think Simon died because the revolutionary treatment you were peddling was a con."

"We never set out to deceive anyone." Dr. Ahumibe shook his head. "All I ever wanted to be was a good doctor."

He started to stack the boxes back into their neat piles.

Stevie said, "Tell me what happened."

The doctor's voice was Mogadon-calm. "It doesn't matter anymore. Nothing does."

Stevie wanted to hurt him. To get a knife, cut through his bristled cheek, and hear him scream. She got to her feet and swept a hand across his desk, knocking the boxes of pills to the floor.

"All of these people, the ones who caught the sweats, they didn't want to die, but no one could help them, no matter how hard they tried.

"There were too few of us left to keep the children alive. I gave those who could drink a glass of orange juice, the others I injected, and then I walked from bed to bed and watched them fall asleep." He looked up at her, his eyes tunnel-black. "It was peaceful."

"If Simon had been here he might have helped to keep them alive." She wouldn't think of the children, the bodies in the basement. "Simon's death could have been avoided. Okay, he might have caught the sweats, but at least he would have had a chance, and who knows? He might have been immune like me." Stevie could feel all the emotion she had tamped down beginning to rise, treacherous, in her throat. "He might have been here now."

Dr. Ahumibe bent and calmly began to pick up the scattered pill packets. His movements were slow, like a pearl fisher diving deep against the tide.

"When did you speak to Buchanan?"

Stevie sank back into the seat. The silk scarf she had wrapped around her face, in an attempt to mask the stink of the basement, was still strung around her neck. Even so, Stevie supposed the air smelled bad, but she had grown used to it. She slid off the scarf and wiped her eyes with it.

"I don't know. A few hours ago."

"I called him but he didn't pick up. I thought maybe . . ." Ahumibe shook his head. "Was he still uninfected?"

She blew her nose on the scarf's hem.

"He didn't say."

The doctor's eyes met hers. "Some people live for up to three days, others go within hours. I should take these soon." Ahumibe glanced at the packs of pills. "Once the vomiting starts they're less reliable."

Stevie watched his trembling fingers, the tower of boxes growing.

"The package I was to deliver to Mr. Reah was a laptop. It contained data that proved your research was flawed."

"I know." Dr. Ahumibe put the final box on the top of the pile. It looked like a miniature version of Simon's apartment block, white and modernist. "Simon told me."

"Did you kill him?"

The doctor stared at the tower he had made and then retrieved the topmost box, opened it and slid out a blister pack. He dropped the empty box in the trashcan, as if it was still important to be neat, and laid the slim pack on the desk.

"Simon died of natural causes."

"Buchanan attended the autopsy. He said that he found evidence Simon had been injected with something shortly before his death."

Dr. Ahumibe looked up. Sweat prickled his brow but his eyes looked less drugged, sharper than before.

"That doesn't necessarily mean anything."

"Maybe not on its own, but Simon was about to give Mr. Reah data that proved the treatment you had collaborated on was worthless. You and Buchanan both had a vested interest in stopping him."

The pharmacist had insisted that the treatment was effective, but Dr. Ahumibe didn't bother to contradict her. He said, "Simon had as big a stake in the business as we did."

"Did he know that it was worthless?"

"It wasn't worthless. There was a glitch, a temporary glitch."

"A glitch." Stevie remembered the photograph of Joy Summers, the big box-office smile framed by the wheelchair headrest. "Did Simon know?"

"Not at first. None of us did."

"Whose fault was it?"

"We were a team. We were all equally responsible."

Ahumibe glanced away. It was the kind of feint that lost you the sale and Stevie knew that even though Death had both hands on his shoulders, ready to push him into a grave, the doctor was dissembling. She scooped the packets of pills from the table, shoved them into her satchel, took the gun from her pocket and pointed it at him.

The doctor looked at the gun, unmoved. "You'd be doing me a favor."

"Not if I shot you in the legs and left you to bleed to death."

She wondered if she would be able to do it and decided that perhaps she could.

"Go ahead. If there was an easy way out, I've already bypassed it."

"I could still make it harder for you."

"Do you really think so?" The doctor held her gaze. "Put the gun down." He brushed the air in front of him with his hand, as if trying to flap something away. "Killing people makes you feel bad."

"I told you. I'm not threatening to kill you." Stevie slipped her finger from the trigger and rested the gun on her lap, her hand still tight around the grip. "The person who analyzed the data on Simon's laptop said he thought there had been a genuine mathematical mistake."

Dr. Ahumibe sighed. "We were all responsible," he repeated.

"We don't have time to waste on some Spartacus routine. Someone made the initial error. Who was it?"

The doctor rested his head on the desk again.

"It doesn't matter anymore."

"Tell me and I'll leave you alone. Otherwise I'm here till the bitter end, and believe me, I will make it as bitter as possible."

Ahumibe muttered something she couldn't make out.

Stevie said, "I won't give your pills back until you tell me."

"Buchanan." He raised his head and spat out the name. "Buchanan made the initial error, but Simon and I should have spotted it. Medicine is like the law: ignorance is no defense. We were all equally to blame."

"When did you realize?"

"I spent the most time with the children." The doctor closed his eyes for a moment. His skin looked solid, as if it was made of wax or resin, some other substance than flesh. A bead of perspiration trickled down his brow and Stevie saw that the sweats were gaining ground. He said, "They weren't responding as I'd expected. People think of science as being exact. In reality there are too many factors to predict results precisely, but nevertheless the general level of improvement among the children we treated wasn't anywhere near as good as it should have been."

"Didn't Simon notice?"

"Simon was a good surgeon, but medicine wasn't his life. He left most of the aftercare to me."

"Why didn't you just stop operating?"

"That was my first instinct. I called a meeting of the three of us. Buchanan turned up, Simon sent his apologies." A howl echoed along the hospital corridor. It sounded both animal and human; crazy in its abandon. Dr. Ahumibe sipped his water and gave a small shudder. "There's no point in going over any of this.

It's getting dark. We've had armed guards on the doors for the last few days but it sounds like they've surrendered us to the fates. You should leave."

"I promise I'll go, as soon as you tell me what happened."

The doctor leaned back in his chair and closed his eyes. For a moment Stevie thought she might be losing him, but then he said, "At first Buchanan denied that there was anything wrong, but when I hit him with the cold facts, he was forced to admit that he already suspected something was awry." Dr. Ahumibe opened his eyes and fixed his stare on her. "That was the word he used, *awry*, as if we were talking about a squint necktie or a badly hung picture."

"But you could have pulled the plug on the whole business. Why didn't you?"

Dr. Ahumibe was still gazing at the ceiling.

"I made a promise to myself when I was a child. I remember it very clearly. I was lying in my bed at school, listening to one of the boys in my dorm crying himself to sleep, and I pledged that when I grew up, I would remember what it felt like to be an unhappy boy."

"Very Peter Pan."

He looked at her again. "You're wrong. Peter Pan didn't want to grow up. I was desperate to reach an age when I would be in charge of my own life, my own destiny. But I kept my promise. I never forgot the misery of childhood and when I became a doctor I knew that I wanted to specialize in pediatrics." His voice cracked. "I have helped to save a lot of children's lives."

"You also gave several children operations they didn't need, and charged their parents money they couldn't afford."

A tear leaked down the doctor's cheek, but for the first time he sounded angry. "Every single one of them went home healthier than when they arrived."

"Including Joy Summers?"

"Joy's death was nothing to do with the treatment."

"How can you be so sure?"

"Because I'm a fucking doctor." Dr. Ahumibe buried his face in his hands as if he couldn't bear her to see his expression. His breath juddered. After a moment he whispered, "The treatment may not have had the results we initially calculated, but it did no harm and it was on the cusp of doing a lot of good." He dragged his hands down his face. His cheeks stretched beneath the pressure and Stevie saw the red of his lower eyelids, the bags beneath, formed from a weight of sleepless nights. Dr. Ahumibe splayed his fingers against the surface of the desk and stared at them. "The basic premise was sound but Buchanan needed to refine the drug. He was worried that if we suddenly withdrew, our sponsors would lose confidence. We had put everything we possessed, including our reputations, into Fibrosyop. We couldn't afford to suspend the company."

"So you decided to subject already sick children to operations that you knew would be ineffectual, in order to protect your reputations."

"We operated on a very small number of children compared to the potential good we would be able to do in the future." He turned to face her. "In the very near future. It was only a matter of time before Xander found the correct formula."

"You were experimenting on children."

"You make us sound like Josef Mengele. It wasn't easy, but in the end we acted for the greater good."

His tears were gone. In their place was the closed face of a disgraced MP, ready to fight his corner.

"Where did Simon fit into all of this?"

Pain puckered Dr. Ahumibe's brow, but he managed to inject some malice into his voice.

"Simon had a hot date and didn't turn up for the meeting, so we made the decision to continue without him. When he eventually checked in, a day or so later, I told him there was nothing to worry about. It was what Simon wanted to hear." Dr. Ahumibe bent forward, clenched by some kind of spasm. The howl sounded again somewhere in the hospital, this time shadowed by a chorus of crazy laughter. "No one murdered Simon. I would have laid down my life for him. Both of us would." A crash of overturning furniture shook the floor. He said, "Aren't you scared?"

"Terrified, but I can't afford to give in to it. Not if I'm going to survive." Stevie fingered the handle of the gun. "You keep telling me that the three of you were best buddies, but Simon's note insisted the laptop went to Reah and no one else. He was adamant I wasn't to trust you or Buchanan."

"All Simon was worried about was covering his own back. Xander and I took the strain for months before Simon noticed. He should have gotten down on his knees and thanked us for bearing his share of the pressure. Instead he threatened to go to the authorities or the press."

"And so you killed him."

"I never killed anyone, until today." Dr. Ahumibe took another sip of the water on his desk and then held a hand out toward her. "I need the tablets." Stevie ignored his outstretched palm, and after a moment he said, "Buchanan would have brought Simon around eventually. Si was the squeaky wheel, the one that demanded the most attention, but Buchanan always persuaded him in the end."

"What if he couldn't, this time?"

Dr. Ahumibe took a handkerchief from his pocket. He splashed some of the water from the bottle on it and then held the handkerchief to his forehead.

"It was the only way." He doubled over and retched into the trashcan. "Simon would have recognized that, eventually."

Stevie looked away, trying not to gag. Ahumibe said, "Give me the tablets."

"I will. I promise you." She paused to let him recover and then asked, "What happened to Geoffrey Frei?"

The doctor retched again. He looked up, his face puddle-gray, and whispered, "You're torturing me."

"Your treatment cut sick children open and pumped them full of a useless drug. That was torture."

Ahumibe was slumped forward in his chair now. He whispered, "People like you see the world in one dimension. Things are either good or bad, no muddied waters. If it were up to you, there'd be no progress." The doctor wiped his mouth with his damp hanky. "I don't know what happened to Frei. He was mugged. Or perhaps it was a pickup gone wrong. Geoff loved his wife, but he needed other forms of release. He knew cruising was risky. He would give up for a while, but sooner or later old habits always reasserted themselves."

"He was investigating you."

"So what?"

"You don't think it's a coincidence? Frei and Simon were both in a position to expose you and Buchanan and they both died under suspicious circumstances. Hope Black is dead too. I found her lying on the floor of Simon's apartment. Her head had been smashed in."

"The whole world is dying. Everyone except for you." Dr. Ahumibe leaned over and retched into the trashcan again. The sounds he made were dry and painful and Stevie felt her own stomach clenching in response. When the doctor looked up there was spittle on his chin. He wiped it on the sleeve of his shirt. "Xander was devastated by Simon's death. He came to the hospital to break the news to me. At first he was too upset to speak. We've known each other most of our lives but I'd never seen him like that. I thought perhaps something had happened to William, his son. Later, after he'd broken the news, Xander told me that when he saw Simon curled up dead in his bed, it was like seeing him again as a boy, back when we shared a dorm at school. The image haunted him."

Stevie leaned forward.

"Buchanan said he saw Simon dead in his own bed? Are you sure he wasn't referring to when he saw him at the morgue?"

"No, it was before Simon was brought to the morgue. Xander told me there was a picture of the three of us, taken when we were students, hanging on the wall of Simon's bedroom. He found it deeply moving. We were as close as family."

Stevie remembered something Derek had been fond of repeating, one in a series of self-composed homilies Joanie had christened "Sayings from the Policeman's Notebook." She said it out loud.

"Families are the most dangerous units known to society. Most abuse, violence and murders happen inside families."

Stevie unlocked the door and glanced into the corridor. The lights had gone out and darkness shrouded the ward, hiding the bodies still tucked tight beneath their sheets. She reached into her satchel, took out the boxes of pills and dropped them on the desk in front of John Ahumibe.

The doctor looked up at her. "I keep seeing the children's faces. It was my duty. I couldn't leave them to suffer on alone."

Stevie turned her back on him and closed the door quietly behind her.

Thirty-Nine

The hospital was a nightmare of darkened corridors. Stevie had told Ahumibe that she could not afford to give in to fear, but terror fluttered in her chest. The building felt alive, as though the people who had died in the hospital wards had slipped into the fabric of its walls and were watching, and waiting.

Stevie wrapped her scarf around her face and counted each turn beneath her breath, trying to focus on the challenge of navigating her way to an exit. She kept her flashlight off and her hand on the gun. The sound of howling echoed up ahead and she corrected her route to avoid it. She saw other people ghosting through the dark, and pointed the gun straight ahead, both hands gripping the stock, so there could be no mistaking her urge for solitude.

Rats moved, swift and busy, along the walls, and Stevie knew that she would have to leave London soon, before other diseases took hold. Sudden footsteps charged along the corridor, and she pinned herself flat against the wall, melting into the darkness, until the runner rushed by, a panicked breeze of pumping arms and pounding legs.

The dead were everywhere. They were slumped on waiting-room chairs, like a Tory indictment against NHS inefficiency, stretched out on beds, sprawled across desks, or lay where they had fallen, limbs tangled in positions impossible to hold in life.

Moans and harsh rattling breaths echoed from the shadows of abandoned rooms, and Stevie knew without a doubt that there was no God. If there were, he or she would have saved a better person than her, one who was ready to sacrifice themselves to the care of the dying, rather than continue a quest for the truth about an already dead man.

A man stepped out of the shadows, leading a little girl of around six or seven years old along an empty corridor. Stevie moved into the center of the hall and aimed the gun at his head.

"It's all right," the man said. "She belongs to me."

Stevie looked at the child and asked, "Is that true, sweetheart? Is this your daddy?"

The girl had one hand gripped in the man's. The other was wrapped around a disreputable-looking toy monkey whose fur was matted from overloving. She stuck her thumb in her mouth and shook her head.

"I'm her uncle," the man said, his eyes on the gun.

Stevie looked at the little girl, who kept her thumb in her mouth and whispered, "Uncle Colin."

"Are you happy to go with Uncle Colin?"

The girl had the stunned stare of a road-accident victim. She nodded and the man looked relieved. He said, "You can come with us, if you like. There might be safety in numbers."

Stevie thought he was probably right, but she shook her head. "No thanks." The man glanced nervously at the gun again and Stevie wondered if he was considering making a grab for it. "You'd best keep on going," she said, her finger on the trigger, the barrel still pointing at the man's head. She watched until they vanished into the dark, like phantoms, the sound of her own breath loud in her head.

Once, a hand reached out, pale against the black, and a woman whispered, "Water," but when Stevie returned, with a plastic cup filled from a water cooler, the woman was gone. Her disappearance troubled Stevie and she upped her pace, holding on to the banister as she ran down a darkened staircase toward the hospital exit, aware that to trip and break a leg now would mean a slow death.

Forty

The GPS had stopped working. Stevie drove toward the industrial estate that housed Buchanan's lab, slowing the Jaguar frequently to consult a dog-eared *A to Z* she had found in the glove compartment. She had sealed the car's vents and made sure that its windows were closed tight, but an acrid smell that tasted of burned cinders and melting plastic slipped inside and caught the back of her throat. The sky was full of fluttering lights and strange glows, and she was forced to alter her route twice to avoid fires that had taken hold of whole city blocks. There were fewer looters now, though traces of them lingered in smashed windows and abandoned booty. Shoals of shopping bags cartwheeled along empty streets, like plastic tumbleweed. Once she saw a man hanging from a railway bridge. The bridge spanned a main road and she had no choice but to drive beneath, aware of his body gently swinging above her, his feet pointing toward the earth like the arrow of a compass directing the way to Hell.

Stevie had programmed the car radio to scan the stations, but there was only one voice on the airwaves, a recording of a Scottish woman repeating a mantra about the need to *remain calm . . . stay indoors . . . drink fluids . . . avoid contact with anyone showing signs of infection . . . observe the curfew . . .* Stevie turned the radio off.

Dusk was shifting to full dark. The occasional streetlamp still glowed warm and miraculous, like a message from God, but most were out, and Stevie navigated by the beam of the Jaguar's headlights. She wondered if John Ahumibe had been right about the virus originating in outer space, and pictured an asteroid plummeting to earth, the way it must have lit up the sky. Stevie wished that she had witnessed the thrill of its arrival, before anyone knew what it would bring. Occasionally her headlights picked out figures by the side of the road, but she didn't alter her speed, except once, when a man who looked like Simon stuck out a hand, hailing her as if she were a cab, and her foot hit the brake of its own accord. The man ran toward the Jaguar, but Stevie saw that he was a stranger, and left him behind in the darkness.

Her cell phone sat charging on the dashboard. It glowed with calls from Alexander Buchanan, but she left them unanswered. She wanted her visit to be a surprise.

The industrial park was a series of warehouses, factories, and outlet stores housed in ugly low-rise buildings. Stevie dipped her headlights and slowed the Jaguar to a crawl. The park looked deserted, like a vision of death: the nothing that followed the pain and convulsions of dying. But she was sure Buchanan was inside his lab, fussing over a cure he would never find and waiting for her to arrive. The pharmacist was a poisoner, a creep who killed slyly or got others to do his dirty work for him. She could feel his cowardice in his reluctance to admit his flawed calculations. She would do what she should have done before, point the gun at his head and make him tell her the truth about Simon's death.

It took her a few circuits of the industrial park, but finally she found Buchanan's lab, the name FIBROSYOP discretely etched on a sign attached to a locked and bolted gate. The laboratory was guarded by high railings that looked more permanent than the kit-built box they enclosed. A security camera, fixed too high for her to throw a blanket over the lens, was trained on the entrance. Stevie hoped it had succumbed to the power failures sweeping the city. She got out of the car, walked to the gate, and examined the padlock securing it. A heavy bolt cutter might be able to bite through the chain, but she had not thought to arm herself with one. Stevie felt a quick tremor of fear at the thought of all the things she had left undone. The city was falling apart and she was as unprepared as a lamb trotting blithely behind a Judas goat.

Stevie got back into the car and drove to the fence's perimeter, hoping for a gap to slip through, but she had kept her headlights off and the fence was just a presence in the blackness. She whispered, "Fucking useless," her words a hiss in the dark, but even as they escaped her lips, she saw a way in.

A truck loaded with a shipping container was parked next to the perimeter fence. She drew in beside it and closed the Jaguar's door quietly behind her. The only tool in the trunk was a wheel jack. Stevie shoved it in her bag and climbed on to the hood. The moon was full, the stars visible in a way she had never seen in London before. Stevie looked up at them for a moment, wondering if their sparkle heralded more asteroids, more viruses, and then scrambled on to the car's roof. It was a stretch, but she managed to hop from there on to the hood of the truck. A man's head was resting against the steering wheel, his features slack, his mouth and eyes open. Stevie's balance wavered and for an instant she thought she might fall, but she managed to regain control and clambered on to the top of the cab. She took a deep breath, climbed up on to the shipping container and ran along it, her footsteps ringing against the metal. She was level with the railings now. Their prongs curved away from her, hard enough to bruise, too blunt to impale. It was a long drop onto the pavement on the other side, and once she was over, there was no guarantee that she would be able to escape. Her phone buzzed in her pocket. Stevie took it out, saw Buchanan's number glowing on the display and knew that he was inside, waiting on her. She left the phone unanswered. Let the pharmacist wait. It was her turn to set the agenda.

Stevie tossed her bag over the fence, took off Simon's jacket and spread it over the railings. Then she moved back, as far as she dared, to the edge of the truck's roof, stepped into a short run and launched herself over the fence in a rolling leap, half recalled from high jump at school. Stevie landed on her feet, staggered and fell flat against the pavement, skinning her hands and knees. Simon's jacket was snagged on the railings above. A breeze caught the sleeves and it twisted gently, a broken silhouette, too much like the hanging man on the railway bridge for her to look at it for long. Stevie spat on her palms, trying to get some of the dirt out of her grazed skin. There was no point in regretting things that were beyond reach. She swung the strap of her bag over her shoulder and jogged toward Buchanan's laboratory.

Forty-One

S tevie had intended to smash one of the building's rear windows with the wheel jack, but when she got closer she saw that the windows were barred. She cursed and tried the fire escape and then the front entrance, but the doors to Buchanan's lab were locked, as she had known they would be.

In movies, people picked locks, spun their tumblers home with a credit card, or took out a gun and blasted them into irrelevance. Stevie squatted in the doorway's shadows, trying to plan her next move. The wheel jack was heavy in her bag, the gun snug beside it, but even if the door gave way, smashing it would take a while and make too much noise, and shooting at the lock was an invitation to a ricochet, a bullet in the face.

Her cell phone buzzed with news of a text. Stevie took it out of her pocket and pressed the small speech bubble on the screen: *Knock if you want to come in.* She cursed. Buchanan must have spotted her on the surveillance cameras but his message gave a surreal, Alice-down-the-rabbit-hole edge to her fear. She tensed, unsure of whether to run, or wait for the pharmacist to come to her.

The door opened. Stevie reached for Hope's gun, but strong hands grabbed her around her waist, pinned her arms behind her back and dragged her into a cocaine-white corridor that smelled of bleach. Stevie kicked and bucked, but her assailant held firm. She barely had time to register that he was dressed in protective overalls, his head and neck helmeted by breathing apparatus, like an investigator in a nuclear disaster zone, before a handkerchief was pressed over her mouth and nose, and a line of darkness sucked her down.

Stevie jerked awake. Her knees were drawn up to her chin and her eyelids felt as if they had been weighted with pennies. The thought forced her eyes open.

She was lying on a single bed in a small, white-painted, windowless room. The light was a searing fluorescent bright. Her head was foggy from whatever the stranger had sedated her with and her throat was Sunday-morning dry. Stevie massaged her temples with her fingertips. She looked up, saw a camera peering at her from a high corner, and resolved not to cry.

The collapsing world had made her think that Buchanan would give up his secrets as readily as Dr. Ahumibe had, like a ship dropping its ballast as it neared port, but it seemed that the pharmacist was as obsessed with keeping his secrets as she was with uncovering the truth. Stevie looked up at the camera and said in a voice creaky from lack of fluids, "You win. Let me go and I promise to mind my own business." There was no sign that anyone had heard her.

She swung her feet on to the floor and sat on the edge of the bed until she was sure that she could stand up without falling over. Her legs felt numb and insubstantial, as if she had been on a bumpy long-haul flight that had confined passengers to their seats, but Stevie managed the three steps to the door. It lacked a handle but a small, reinforced window looked out on to a deserted, equally white corridor.

The only hiding place was beneath the bed, or in the small shower room attached to her cell. Stevie checked them both, but it was clear that her satchel had disappeared. She searched her pockets, but she had already registered the absence of the gun's comforting weight and was unsurprised to find her cell phone gone.

A second security camera observed her in the shower room. Stevie gave it the finger, then washed her face, used the toilet and drank some water from the tap.

The madness of the last few days crashed over her. If she had fled the city, as Derek had told her to, she might be holed up somewhere safe, ready to sit out the sweats. The thought brought hot tears to Stevie's eyes, but she felt the surveillance camera shift and blinked them away. She looked into the lens and repeated her offer: "Let me go and I won't bother you again." But the camera maintained its mute, unblinking stare. "Okay," she muttered. "Fuck you." Stevie went back into the bedroom, stripped the sheet from the bed and started to fashion it into a noose.

She had just managed to string her handiwork over the bathroom door when the man in the protective suit entered the cell. He shoved her on to the bed and swept the sheet away. Stevie had left the duvet lying on the floor and he scooped that up too. It was an awkward movement to make in the bulky suit and Stevie grabbed her chance. She kicked the stranger in the stomach, knocking him off balance, and dashed for the door. For a moment she thought she might make it, but her jailer flung out a gloved hand and caught her by the ankle, felling her smack against the floor. The fall knocked the wind from her and Stevie lay there for a long time after he had locked the door behind him.

The unwavering fluorescence of the overhead lights absorbed all concept of time, and Stevie wasn't sure how long it was before the man returned. She was sitting on the edge of the bed, looking at the floor to avoid the camera's stare and the dazzle of the lights, but raised her head when he entered. She ran her fingers through her hair, trying to coax it into some kind of a style. The man threw a tracksuit and some underwear on to the floor and said, "Shower and put these on."

His voice was muffled by his head mask, but Stevie had felt his strength and knew that he was young. She gave him a modest version of her killer smile.

"I'm not showering beneath a camera."

"Do it yourself, or I'll make you." The mask made him sound like an asthmatic Dalek. "If you'd looked in a mirror lately, you'd realize no one's interested in your skinny ass." He tossed a cell phone on to the bare mattress. "When that rings, answer it."

Stevie looked directly at the man's mask. She could see her reflection in the visor, her head cartoon-large on its curved surface. She kicked her running shoes beneath the bed, pulled off Simon's battered pants and T-shirt, and stripped away her underwear. She forced herself to stand there for a second, naked and defiant, goose pimples rising on her flesh, and then scooped the fresh clothes from the floor and went through to the shower. She felt the man's eyes following her. Her body trembled with fatigue and the uncertainty of whether his interest could be worked to her advantage, or if that would only add to the danger she was in.

Forty-Two

"I didn't think you'd come." Alexander Buchanan looked like a man who had won the lottery but was worried taxes might decimate his winnings. He stood outside her room, his face framed by the door's small window, a cell phone to his ear. "I'm sorry for the clumsy welcome, but you didn't give us many options."

Stevie put the phone the man had left her on speaker. She faced the window and said, "There's usually an alternative to chloroforming a girl and locking her up under surveillance." She tried to summon the woman she had been on *Shop TV*: the unflappable babe, smart but unthreatening. "We were both friends of Simon's. I thought that might make us friends too."

Buchanan grinned and shook his head, as if she were incorrigible. The strain of the days since they had first met showed on his face, but his voice remained as smooth as a late-night disc jockey's.

"So why turn up unannounced, armed with a tire iron and a gun?"

"It's chaos out there. I needed to protect myself."

"Perhaps."

"There's enough death in the world." Stevie paused, to give her words more weight. "Dr. Ahumibe has committed suicide."

"John left me a message before he took care of the remaining children. He told me his plans. A great pity."

She had hoped the news would be a weakening blow, but the pharmacist might have been talking about arrangements for a working lunch. She said, "Dr. Ahumibe told me about the mistake you made with the cerebral palsy treatment, and your decision to continue."

The pharmacist shook his head. The glass in the door's small window was strengthened with checkered wire. It gave the illusion that his skin was rippling as he moved.

"John's weakness for confessing got Simon and me into trouble more than once when we were boys. I hope he also told you that continuing with the treatment was the quickest way to resolve the difficulty we were having with the formula."

"He told me you persuaded him that it was the best way forward, but that Simon didn't agree."

Buchanan made a face that might have been intended to convey regret.

"Disagreeable is the last word one would apply to Simon, and yet he often did disagree. We always managed to persuade him in the end."

"But not this time." Stevie's legs were sore, but there was nowhere to sit except for the floor or the bed, and she wanted to be able to see Buchanan's expression. She leaned against the door, putting her face next to its small window. "When Simon refused to go along with the cover-up, you killed him. I'm guessing Frei died for similar reasons."

Buchanan put his face against the window, close to hers. He lowered his voice, as if they weren't speaking from opposite sides of wood and glass, and putting their heads together was a prelude to a confidence.

"A neat theory, but not what happened."

This time the pharmacist's smile was like a closing door. Stevie straightened her spine and looked Buchanan in the eyes. This was not a moment for soft selling or subliminal messages, this was a do-or-die deal. She put an edge of command into her words, as persuasive as a TV mesmerist.

"Let me out of here so we can talk properly, like human beings."

"William and I have to be meticulous, if we're to avoid infection."

"William?"

"My son, Simon's godson. You met him earlier."

Alexander Buchanan's grin infuriated her. So many people were dead, some of them at his hands, but the pharmacist still had a son he could keep close. Stevie touched her throat.

"Was it your son who attacked me outside the TV studio?"

The pharmacist's smile tightened.

"I'm sorry if William frightened you. All he wanted was to save me embarrassment by getting hold of the material on Simon's laptop. My son is young and lacks finesse, but he wouldn't have hurt you."

"Did William tell you that I managed to pull off his balaclava when he attacked me? It meant I recognized him when I saw him running away from Simon's apartment block, just before I discovered Hope Black's body. William mistook Hope for me and murdered her. He would have strangled me if he could."

"Hope's death was an unfortunate accident."

"That wasn't the impression I got."

Color bloomed in Alexander Buchanan's cheeks, and Stevie saw that her jibe had met its mark. There was a dreadful pleasure in baiting the pharmacist. She felt a surge of adrenalin, the last power of the defenseless.

He said, "You're hardly the best judge of character . . ."

Stevie thought Buchanan had hung up, but then she saw the look of frustration on his face and realized that the phone signal had died. The pharmacist slipped his useless phone into his pocket and turned away. Stevie banged her fists against the door and shouted, "LET ME OUT." But the pharmacist was striding down the corridor, his back straight, footsteps swift and steady, like a man with lots to do.

Forty-Three

Stevie slept and dreamed, not of the disintegrating city, nor the dead she had known, but of food: steaming pasta rich with pesto; forbidden crusty bread, warm from the oven and dripping with butter; Cornish pasties, swollen and succulent. She woke, hungry and ashamed, to the sound of a key turning in the lock. Buchanan's son William entered, still clad in his protective suit. The room seemed to shrink around him. He showed her Hope's gun.

"Any crap, and I'll shoot you."

Stevie sat up in bed and smoothed her hair with her fingertips. Perhaps she was adjusting to the way the mask distorted William's voice, because this time she could make out his accent, a public-school drawl. His pronunciation should have been at odds with the gangster-speak, but working on the edges of the media had brought Stevie into contact with enough swanky people for her to know that the upper classes were not necessarily strangers to an uppercut.

Stevie swung her feet on to the floor. "Let me go, and I promise to walk away. No one cares anymore about how or why Simon died, or whether Fibrosyop acted unethically. I'm sure your father had his reasons for what he did." She let a tear roll down her cheek. "We need to look forward, not back, if we're to survive."

William Buchanan gestured toward the door with the gun.

"That's exactly what we are doing."

Stevie shifted to the edge of the bed, ready to get to her feet if it looked like William might hit her.

"No, it's not. I don't know what your father's told you, but he's obsessed with covering up his involvement in Simon's murder."

"You're the only one who's obsessed with Simon. Everyone else is concentrating on staying alive." William paused. "Except my dad, I suppose."

Stevie leaned forward. "And what is your father concentrating on?"

"Finding a cure. That's why he was so keen to get you to come here. I thought you would have worked that out for yourself by now."

And in that moment Stevie realized her true worth to the pharmacist.

Buchanan's lab was in a large room punctuated by rows of workbenches. Its windows were high and small, but they offered a glimpse of summer sky, Marian blue and dotted with white clouds so perfect they might have been painted on silk. Stevie thought of the metal railings guarding the building, the unscalable height of them.

Buchanan had also donned a protective suit and mask. Panic fluttered in Stevie's chest. She asked, "What are you going to do to me?"

"Just a few tests." The mask obscured Buchanan's face, but she thought that perhaps he was smiling. "Nothing to worry about."

Stevie took a step backward but William reached out and gripped her by the elbow. Hope's gun was in his other hand. She wondered if she should make a lunge for it, but the barrel was pointing at her forehead and she caught a glimpse of its tunneling depths, the blackness waiting for her there.

The pharmacist glanced at the expression on her face and said, "William, the gun is persuasion enough." He turned his attention back to Stevie. "It's been a stressful time." He might have been talking about a threatened redundancy that had failed to materialize. "I didn't get the opportunity to ask how you've been, healthwise that is, since we last met."

Stevie pulled herself free of William's grip. He let her go, but stayed close enough for her to feel his presence, the heat of his body inside the suit. She said, "Can I have a glass of water, please?" She wasn't thirsty, but it seemed important to make her jailers do something for her. Buchanan turned on a tap at the sink built into the workstation next to him. He let the water run for a moment, then filled a small paper cone and handed it to her. Stevie took a sip. "I've been fine."

Buchanan nodded. "Have you come into contact with many sufferers?"

The laboratory smelled drily of chemicals. Stevie had imagined that the pharmacist's quarters would resemble the labs in cosmetic commercials, shiny and wipe-clean, but the room had been caught up in the chaos of the outside world. Its countertops were littered with the detritus of Buchanan's work: flasks crusted with mysterious crystals, reams of paper, evil-looking Bunsen burners and abandoned Petri dishes, some of them clouded and staring, like sightless eyes.

"You can't be out there and not come into contact with people who have the sweats." She took a step to the left and looked at William, including him in their conversation. "Ask your son."

"I'm asking you. How close?"

"Close."

"Close enough to touch?"

"Yes."

"To share a meal?"

Stevie remembered the tea and cookies Iqbal had given her.

"Yes."

"To have sexual intercourse with?"

She drank the last of the water, crushed the paper cone and dropped it on the floor.

"That's none of your business."

William said, "Answer the question." But Stevie heard the discomfort in his voice, and hugged it to herself, like a prison shank.

"Once, with someone who subsequently died of the sweats."

It felt like a betrayal to describe Iqbal's death so casually.

"How soon afterward did the other person die?"

"I'm not sure." She let her eyes run over a weird arrangement of glass pipes and beakers, like the skyline of some futuristic city. "I left, and when I came back, he was dead. Two days at the most."

Buchanan nodded as if she had given the right answer. He slid open a drawer, took something out and started busying himself with it. His heavy gloves hid the object from view.

"I'm grateful to you for seeking us out, Ms. Flint. You saved us a lot of effort." He looked directly at her. "Come here, please."

Stevie glanced at William, at the revolver in his hand, and wondered how good a grip his gloves allowed him. She walked toward Buchanan, aware of the gun following her, and saw the cot, low on the ground behind the workstation. She saw too what the pharmacist was holding in his hands: a syringe.

"I'm not the only survivor." Her voice wavered. "There are lots of people out there."

Buchanan said, "Perhaps, but you're the only one who came to us. Don't worry. I have no intention of harming you. I just need to find out what it is that makes you immune. Roll up your sleeve

and lie down on the bed, please. It's a little difficult to be dexter-
ous, gloved up like this, so I'm going to ask you to stay very still."

Stevie wrapped her arms around herself.

"What are you planning to do to me?"

"Nothing drastic. I'm going to take a blood sample." The pale
face inside the helmet smiled. "I'm afraid I'm a little rusty at this
so you'll have to bear with me. When we were students, nurses
used to joke, 'Just a little prick with a needle,' whenever Simon or
I attempted to give an injection. I'm not sure I've improved much
since then."

Stevie hugged her body tighter. Instinct warned her that once
she was on the bed she would be lost. She said, "It was never about
the children for you, was it? You wanted the glory of making a
medical breakthrough. When you discovered you'd made a mistake and the treatment was no good, instead of coming clean you
faked the results." She turned to face Buchanan's son. "You must
have lost people too, William. We all have. Everyone is grieving,
except for your father. He thinks the sweats are an opportunity
to turn himself into a god, but he'll screw this up, just like he
screwed up before."

"You talk too much." William pushed Stevie against the workbench and pinned her there with his body. Stevie stamped on his
toes but he was wearing heavy work boots and her feet made no
impact. William peeled her left arm free and shoved her sleeve
up beyond her elbow. A cough rumbled in his chest. Stevie felt it
shudder against her spine. She kept her eyes on his father.

"You killed Simon to protect your work." William's weight was
forcing the air out of her, and her words came in gasps. "But your
work was shit, it wasn't worth protecting."

The pharmacist swabbed the crease on the inside of her elbow,
tapped it gently to raise a vein and tightened a tourniquet around
her arm.

"You talk about Simon as if he was incorruptible but he was as flawed as the rest of us. I told you he always came around in the end." Buchanan looked up and his eyes met hers, still blue behind the protective visor. "This time was no exception."

The needle pierced Stevie's flesh and she gasped. William's groin was pressed against her rear. Stevie felt his excitement, and bile rose warm in her throat. She swallowed and said, "I promise to cooperate, if you tell me what happened."

The pharmacist withdrew the syringe, leaving a small valve attached to her vein. He inserted a tube into it, and then looked beyond her, at his son. "William, can you help Ms. Flint on to the couch please?"

Stevie said, "I'll do it myself."

The pharmacist nodded and William let go, but Stevie had already felt a tremble in his body that might have been arousal, or something else. She sat on the camp bed. A small, clear plastic bag was resting on top of its mattress. Buchanan attached the tube in her arm to it. He said, "Simon always had an impulsive side. When he was young he had the energy to work as hard as he played, but he'd become careless, one might even say, lazy. No amount of brilliance can compensate for complacency. Simon was a good surgeon, but he was a shade short of brilliant."

The blood was leaving her arm, darker than Stevie had anticipated. It was as if she could see her strength deserting her. But she could also see the perspiration behind William's mask and knew that it was vital to keep the pharmacist's attention focused on her. She asked, "How much blood are you going to take?"

"An armful," the pharmacist joked. "Don't worry, we're not vampires. We won't drain you."

William made a small spluttering sound. He said, "This damn suit is too warm."

"It's necessary." Buchanan squatted in front of Stevie, his bed-side manner at odds with the gun still pointing at her head. He said, "Clench and unclench your hand. It will make the blood come quicker."

Stevie made a fist and released it, made a fist and released it; fist, star, fist, star, fist, star. Her arm ached. She said, "Why did you poison Simon?"

She had expected a denial, but the pharmacist asked, "Why do you care so much?"

"Because I loved him." It was the first time Stevie had said it out loud, and the words surprised her.

The pharmacist glanced at his son.

"There is a theory that believing yourself to be in love can subtly alter the chemical compounds of the body." He looked at Stevie. "It's possible that your *love* for Simon is a factor in why you're still alive."

William had been staring at her face, as if trying to decide whether he would prefer to kiss Stevie or shoot her, but he glanced at his father.

"If she fell out of love, would she lose her immunity?"

"That would be an extreme reaction, but who knows, it might be possible." Alexander Buchanan's voice was amused, as if he had long come to terms with his son being a fool. He touched the bag, warm with her blood, and looked at Stevie. "Are you willing to risk destroying Simon's spell?"

Stevie nodded. William's plastic visor was beginning to mist up. She wondered if Buchanan had noticed. Harvesting her blood had given the pharmacist a boost of energy. His face beamed inside his helmet, making him look like a spaceman who had managed to slip into the orbit of a planet he had feared he would never reach.

"Simon never dated what my mother would have termed his social equals. He preferred the kind of girl who would be impressed by the fact that he was a surgeon."

Stevie asked, "You didn't find it impressive?"

William said, "Dad thinks a sawbones is one step up from a car mechanic."

"Harsh but true." There was a dreaminess to the pharmacist's voice. He glanced at his son and Stevie wondered how he could miss the fog of moisture, the glistering skin. He said, "Simon was a good surgeon, but outside the operating theater he left most of the work to John Ahumibe and me. He was willing to take a third of the credit, but was too busy having a good time to do a third of the work. Perhaps that was why our arrangement was a success. I liked being in control and he was happy to leave me to it."

Stevie looked at the bag, almost full of her blood.

"Shouldn't you unhook me?"

Buchanan said, "In a moment."

William coughed again. "Forget the bedtime story." Buchanan smiled at his son. "Aren't you curious to discover whether the truth about Simon will have an effect on Ms. Flint's health?"

William said, "I don't see what difference it makes, given what comes next."

Stevie asked, "What comes next?"

Buchanan's voice was soothing. "Nothing you need worry about." He slid the needle from Stevie's arm and passed her a pad of cotton wool and a band-aid. "Here, hold this over the puncture." The pharmacist lifted the bag of blood and looked at it. "We should offer you a cup of sweet tea and a cookie, but this is the best I can do under the circumstances." He reached into the pocket of his overalls and tossed her a cereal bar. "Stay still until you get your strength back."

Stevie glanced at William. His shoulders had lost their bold stretch. He was looking at the floor and she thought she could hear the sound of his breathing. Her appetite had deserted her, but Stevie unwrapped the paper, peeling it slowly, the way Joanie had taught her would hold an audience's attention. She took a bite, chewed, and swallowed.

"Tell me what happened to Simon, and I promise to stay as still as a mouse."

William said, "Mice aren't still."

"As still as a stone," Stevie said.

William sank on to the bed beside her and took her hand in his gloved one.

"Stone dead."

Buchanan said, "Leave her alone, William." But his son stayed where he was. The pharmacist hesitated, as if considering whether to press his point, but then he looked at Stevie and said, "I would have refined the formula before Simon noticed anything was amiss, but we had a setback. A child died." He shrugged his shoulders. "Sick children do occasionally die, but the girl's family took it badly. Her father confronted Simon."

Stevie took another bite of the cereal bar. William's hand trembled in hers. Dr. Ahumibe had said the sweats could be on you for days before they hit home, or they could fell you in an hour or two. She said, "I'm assuming the parent was Melvin Summers."

"You've done your homework."

"I met him. His daughter's death killed his wife and destroyed his life."

"If you met him, then you'll know that Mr. Summers is . . ." Buchanan hesitated, as if something had just occurred to him. He raised an eyebrow and asked, "Is or was?"

"I don't know."

". . . is, or was, an unstable alcoholic. I doubt very much whether Summers would have managed to muster the self-control to put together a convincing case, but somehow he ruffled Simon's complacency enough to inspire him to reexamine the original research results."

Stevie said, "So perhaps he wasn't as lazy as you thought?"

The pharmacist shrugged. "On the contrary, Simon proved he was a lazy thinker. He went into a blue funk and threatened to down tools."

"Down scalpel," William muttered.

Buchanan threw his son an irritated glance, and Stevie realized that the pharmacist was building toward his punch line, the revelation that would show she had been wrong about Simon. She prompted him, "But . . . ?"

Buchanan snorted. ". . . but as usual Simon didn't consider the consequences. We had borrowed from our sponsors to set up Fibrosyop. If we called the treatment into question, not only would we have been bankrupt, but our professional reputations would have been destroyed. Worse than that, if it could be shown that we had knowingly continued, after we'd realized the treatment was compromised, we might well have faced criminal prosecution and prison."

Stevie said, "But Simon didn't realize that the treatment was no good until Summers alerted him. You and Ahumibe had already discovered it was useless and decided not to tell Simon because you knew he would call a halt to the operations."

Buchanan put his head on one side. It was a coquettish gesture, sinister combined with the protective suit and headgear.

"Simon should have worked it out. He would have, if he'd been doing his job properly."

William looked up at his father. "You killed him. End of story. Who cares?"

"Ms. Flint cares," Buchanan said, softly enunciating the words, as if explaining an obvious fact to an imbecile. "Because she loved him, which is rather beautiful considering all the destruction going on around us. I loved Simon too."

William said, "Fuck Uncle Simon." He got to his feet, stood behind Stevie and lifted the bag of blood from the bed. "Shouldn't this be in a fridge or something?"

Buchanan whispered, "Careful, William."

His son flopped the blood bag back on to the mattress. A soft red-black jewel that reminded Stevie of sea urchins she had sometimes seen attached to rocks at the bottom of cliffs.

William remained standing behind her. The back of Stevie's skull, the bit she thought might make a good target, tingled, but she asked, "What did Simon do, after you pointed out the consequences of coming clean?"

Alexander Buchanan's laugh was so abrupt that Stevie suddenly wondered if he had dipped into his chemical supplies.

"He tried to buy himself out of Fibrosyop. God knows where Simon got the money from, but he presented me with what he referred to as 'the first installment,' in cash, as if actual bills would be more persuasive than the promise of a funds transfer."

Stevie said, "He borrowed it from Hope Black. That's why she was at his apartment the day William went there looking for me. She wanted her money back."

William muttered, "I didn't see the signs on her until she was on the ground." He stroked Stevie's head. "I was wearing gloves, but I was in the same room. I breathed the same air." He looked at his father. "You were working on the vaccine."

William's touch made the hairs on the back of Stevie's neck rise.

Buchanan said, "Simon took sick leave. I thought he might bolt, so I asked William to keep an eye on him."

Stevie slowly turned her body and looked at William. The tremble in his gun hand echoed the flutter in her stomach. She said, "You and your father were close, even before the sweats."

"We've had our differences, but blood is thicker than water. Uncle Simon was scared. You could see it in the way he walked. He kept looking over his shoulder. I didn't bother to hide myself. I thought, let him see me. Let him be scared."

"I would have preferred a little more subtlety, but never mind." Buchanan glanced at the clock on the laboratory wall and then back at Stevie. "I think we'll give it another minute before we move you. We don't want you fainting on us." He leaned against the worktop. If it wasn't for his protective mask and overalls he might have looked like a man at a party, shooting the breeze over a few beers. "What really hurt was Simon's lack of faith. We'd known each other since we were boys. I'd already explained that all I needed was a little time. I was so close to perfecting the formula. I dreamed about it every night."

Stevie said, "You told me that Simon had come around to your way of thinking, but he hadn't, had he?"

"You're wrong. After I refused to let him off the hook by buying himself out, Simon agreed to allow me three more months to work on the formula. He also agreed to undertake the operations we already had scheduled. If you really knew him, then you'd know that was the way it always went with Simon, a compromise, which was generally followed by another compromise, until finally he was convinced that whatever it was he'd initially disagreed with had been his idea all along."

"But you killed him?"

"Yes." Buchanan's ebullience left him. "Yes, I'm afraid I was forced to."

William said, "This fucking suit is suffocating me."

His free hand went to his protective helmet. Buchanan snapped, "Keep that on." But William pulled it free and Stevie saw his face close up for the first time. His hair and eyes were the same watery pale as his father's, but his cheeks were flushed scarlet, his skin drenched in sweat.

Buchanan said, "Put your mask on."

"What's the point?" William held out a hand to his father, but Buchanan took a swift step backward.

"We need to get you into isolation."

"You won't leave me again, will you, Dad?"

William's gun hand shuddered. It was the moment Stevie had been waiting for. She grabbed the bag of blood from the bed, slammed it into William's face and threw herself on to the floor. The plastic split on impact and her blood arced in a spray around the room, splattering all three of them. Stevie smelled herself, rich and iron, tasted her life force sharp on her lips. The gun rattled on to the laboratory's tiled floor. She wiped her eyes and scrambled to where it had landed.

Stevie expected Buchanan to race her, but there was no hand at her heels, no harsh breath or panicked shouts, just the sound of William groaning. She seized the gun, spun on to her back, and pointed the muzzle in front of her, ready to shoot whichever of the Buchanans came at her first.

Forty-Four

Alexander Buchanan wiped the blood from his visor. His white overalls and mask were splattered with gore, as if he was a chainsaw killer fresh from a spree. He lifted a glass beaker in the air and said, "An extreme game of rock, paper, scissors. Acid versus a bullet."

Stevie was still on the ground. She scooted backward, through the slick of blood, until she felt one of the workstations at her back and propped herself against it, the gun pointed at Buchanan.

William had sunk on to the couch. He whispered, "Dad, I'm scared."

Stevie said, "You should look to your boy. He's dying."

Buchanan kept his eyes on Stevie.

"William, I want you to take the gun from Ms. Flint, give it to me, and then go to bed. I'll come and see you soon, I promise."

Buchanan's son had taken the worst of the blood bag's impact and his white-blond hair, flushed face, and overalls were drenched scarlet. He put his head in his hands and coughed as if he was trying to expel his lungs. Stevie felt an unexpected stab of pity.

"Don't let your father send you on another suicide mission, William. He could have kept you safe from the sweats, but he sent you out to do his dirty work instead. You're going to die soon. It'll be sooner if you take a single step toward me."

William wiped a hand across his face. He looked at his father. "What you were working on might cure me."

"It's not ready yet."

"Then make it ready. I don't want to die."

"I can't, son, not while Ms. Flint is pointing a gun at me." The acid shimmered in its flask, so clear Stevie thought that if she didn't know what it was, she might drink it without a thought. Buchanan said, "Take the gun from her, and I'll see what I can do."

"If your father was capable of making a cure, he would have done it by now," Stevie said. "I saw signs of the sweats on you hours ago, William. Your father must have seen them too. But he wanted to use you, the way he's used you all along." She got to her feet, keeping the gun trained on Buchanan, ready to switch aim if his son made a move toward her. The only exit from the room lay behind the two men. She said, "Get out of my way."

Stevie caught a cartoon glimpse of how it would be if she managed to shoot the flask of acid, the pharmacist dissolving from the feet up, his mouth and eyes the last to go, his scream sizzling to a fade.

Buchanan said, "Has anyone ever told you how impressive you are?" His voice was like silk. "You're astounding, far too good for Simon."

Stevie stepped slowly toward the other side of the room. The rows of workbenches hampered her escape, and so she moved in a straight line, her back to a counter littered with equipment. She asked, "Why did you kill him?"

It was the question that had driven her, but now that Stevie was on the edge of finding an answer, it seemed unimportant. Simon was dead and there was no resurrection in sight.

"I didn't have any choice."

"This virus, the sweats, whatever it is, is programmed to kill. It doesn't have any choice. You did."

She had reached the middle of the room. Someone had been looking at samples in a microscope, and slides were scattered across the surface as if the viewer had suddenly been interrupted. Buchanan was straight ahead of her, three workbenches away, the acid still cradled in his hands. He said, "Why don't you ask me about Geoffrey Frei again?"

"Did you kill him too, or was he another of your son's victims?"

"Neither." Buchanan held up the flask, as if admiring it. The light hit the liquid and projected a small rainbow against the wall. "Frei was Simon's conquest."

Stevie could feel the pharmacist's eyes on her, watching to see what effect his revelation would have.

She said, "I don't believe you."

Buchanan looked at his son. "Ms. Flint never believes anything I tell her."

Stevie glanced quickly at the door, wondering if she should make a run for it, or keep her back toward the wall and continue her slow progress. She shouted, "How are you doing, William?"

Buchanan replied for his son, "William's strong. He'll pull through."

Stevie marveled at the jocular note in the pharmacist's voice and wondered again if he had been self-medicating.

"Why would Simon kill Frei?"

Buchanan swirled the acid in the flask and held it up to his visor, regarding her through the eddying liquid.

"I would have thought that was obvious. Frei had gotten wind of our little difficulty, via Mr. Summers. It was Frei's wet dream. A chance to get back at the boys he hated at school."

The blood was crusting on Stevie's skin and hair, turning to powder on her eyelashes.

"I thought he was one of your set."

"Every schoolboy gang needs a whipping boy. Frei was ours. He was John Ahumibe's pet really. That was the reason we tolerated him at first, but he found his place. Simon was our noble leader, I was his deputy, and John Ahumibe was my faithful lieutenant. We were all officers and no men. Without Frei we would have had no one to lead."

Stevie rubbed her cheekbone and felt the dried blood crumble beneath her fingertips. "You told me, Ahumibe and Frei were lovers."

"*Lovers.*" Buchanan laughed. "That's rather dignifying it. Most of us put these practices away when we grow up, but for some, like Ahumibe and Frei, it becomes a habit they can't break. I found it childish, but I ignored it."

"Did you use Frei sexually when you were at school? Is that the real reason he was so keen to destroy you? Or was it just that he cared about justice and helping children in a way you never have?"

"Ms. Flint," Buchanan's voice was mocking. "What a mind you have." But instead of answering her question he said, "I don't think Simon had an inkling that Frei disliked him, until the night he killed the boy reporter."

Stevie was almost at the end of the workbench. When she reached it, her only option would be to make a dash, past Buchanan and his son, for the door. She paused, hoping that some crisis would hit William and distract the pharmacist from her escape.

She said, "Simon wasn't a violent man."

"No," Buchanan conceded. "Not normally, but guilt does strange things to some people." The pharmacist looked directly at Stevie, and she thought he might be smiling. "Or so I've heard." He placed the flask of acid on the workbench in front of him. Stevie willed him to walk away from it, but he picked it up again.

"Once Simon agreed to more time for me to refine the formula, we decided he would visit Mr. Summers and convince him that his concerns about the treatment were unfounded. 'Blind him with science' was the phrase I think we used. Being Simon, of course, he put off the task. In the meantime, Summers must have gotten in touch with Geoffrey Frei because he was on our case sooner than you can say British Medical Association. He got in touch *as a courtesy*, he said. His story was ready *to go to press* but he wanted to give us an opportunity *to give our side of the story.*" Buchanan shook his head. "Even as a boy he was pompous. Simon and I arranged to meet him in a bar near King's Cross."

Stevie said, "Simon had a meeting with Frei marked in his diary for two days later."

"That was typical. Simon was always punctual when he had surgery to perform, but outside of the hospital, his timekeeping was chaotic." The pharmacist now held the acid flask in his right hand. He let it go, and caught it with his left. It was a risky move and Stevie realized that he was gearing himself up for action while trying to lull her with his story. He said, "I called Simon to make sure he'd be there. When he arrived it was obvious he'd been drinking. It was unlike him, but then again, he was under a certain amount of strain. Geoffrey was waiting for us in the bar, but whatever he'd said about hearing our side of things, it was soon clear he'd only come to rub our noses in it. Simon and I tried to persuade him to hold off. We even offered to suspend operations, but he was determined to ruin us." Buchanan shrugged and the liquid in the flask trembled. "Geoffrey was a cunt. He deserved everything he got."

Stevie took another step. William was slumped on the bed, his breaths harsh and jagged. But Buchanan's eyes stayed on her.

He said, "It happened in the parking lot. It was so out of character that I'm afraid I didn't see it coming, but when it did I

thought, why not let him have it? Simon punched the little fag
in the face and he went down as fast as a sleeping pill. I thought,
'In for a penny, in for a pound,' and landed a kick or two, but
Simon was a man possessed. He took out a scalpel and stabbed
Frei. He'd been transformed into a different person, a thug, but
he was still a surgeon and he made every cut count. When it was
over, there was no doubt that Geoffrey Frei was dead." The pharmacist did his trick with the acid again. This time he held it in his
left hand and caught it with his right. "I suppose it was selfish of
me, but my first thought was that now I'd have the time I needed
to perfect the formula." The pharmacist gave a small laugh. "How
wrong I was. Simon wanted to call the police. He would have
called them there and then, but his hands were shaking so much
he dropped his phone. I took it from him. I was wearing a long
raincoat. I made Simon put it on over his jacket, to cover the
bloodstains. He'd gone into shock and it was like dressing a man-
nequin, but I slapped his face to wake him up and made him help
me move the body to a more sheltered spot."

"Behind some garbage cans."

The pharmacist nodded. "It seemed appropriate. I drove
Simon to his apartment, poured us both a brandy, and tried to
talk some sense into him. I thought he would see my point of
view—after all, I'd made myself an accessory to murder in order
to protect him—but killing Frei seemed to have made a new man
out of Simon. He continued to insist that we phone the police.
I knew him well enough to see that for once he wasn't going to
be swayed, but I argued with him anyway. In the end it became
clear what I had to do." Buchanan took a deep breath. "I had no
choice. He would have landed us both in prison. I told him that
I would make some coffee to help sober us up, and that when
we had drunk it, he could call the police. I laced his drink with
a sedative and when he was asleep did the hardest thing I've ever

done in my life." Buchanan shrugged. "I killed Simon, I admit it. But he was no better than me; he was a murderer too."

"You must have gotten a fright when the door wouldn't shut behind you."

"Typical of Simon not to get the lock fixed. What could I do? I took the keys to the apartment from his jacket pocket, locked the door, and hoped for the best."

Stevie had intended to make a sprint for freedom, but she stepped out from the shelter of the workbenches and said, "I spoke to Sarah Frei. She told me that her husband had been alerted by a whistleblower. You're also forgetting the note Simon left me, and the laptop he intended for Mr. Reah. I may not have grown up with Simon, but I loved him, and in the short time we were together, I got to know him better than you ever could." She took a deep breath. "I think the truth is that, out of loyalty, and against his better judgment, Simon tried to give you time to resolve things. When it became clear that you were going to persist with the treatment, he got in touch with Frei, told him what was going on, and gave him enough evidence to back the story up. You killed them both, and then you got your son to break into Frei's house during his funeral and steal the evidence." Stevie smiled as if she was giving the pharmacist a compliment. "Nice touch."

William bent into a spasm. Buchanan stood motionless beside him, his eyes still on Stevie. He said, "Don't make the same mistake Simon made. Work with me. If we can isolate whatever it is that makes you immune to the sweats, I'll be able to make a vaccine, maybe even a cure."

Stevie shook her head. "All you want is another shot at glory." She took a step forward. "I should shoot you, but I don't want your death on my conscience. Put the acid down, and give me the keys to the building and the front gate." She stepped closer. "Do it quickly, before I change my mind. You make a very good target."

Buchanan placed the beaker on the workbench. He reached into his overall pocket, took out a set of keys and tossed them to her, but the gun was in Stevie's right hand and they landed on the floor with a clatter.

"Touch me and you're dead." Stevie lowered herself cautiously, keeping her eyes on the pharmacist. She groped blindly on the floor with her free hand, seeking the bundle of keys, and when she didn't find them glanced quickly at the ground.

The pharmacist's first kick sent the keys speeding away from her. His second caught her in the ribs and hurled her after them. Stevie rolled with the kick, letting its energy propel her across the room. She slammed against a workbench, raised the gun and pulled the trigger. It gave a harmless click.

The sight of the gun had startled the pharmacist and he had thrown himself to the floor. But suddenly he was all action. He clambered to his feet, as fast as the clumsy overalls would allow, and started toward her.

Stevie swore. She lifted the gun again and took aim.

William Buchanan whispered, "I took the first bullet in the chamber out, in case it went off by mistake."

Stevie squeezed the trigger and fired.

The pharmacist looked down at the blood spreading across the chest of his white overalls. For a moment she thought that one bullet wouldn't be enough, but then Buchanan pulled the helmet free of his head and fell backward, his descent as sure as death.

Epilogue

Hope's Jaguar was parked by the truck, where Stevie had left it. She turned the key in the ignition and steered out on to the main road. It was still dark, but there was a glow on the horizon that might have been the city burning, or a promise of dawn. Stevie drove away from it into the blackness, glancing occasionally at the blaze of light in her rearview mirror. Dr. Ahumibe had been right. Killing people made you feel bad.

Stevie wished Joanie was in the passenger seat and wondered that she hadn't thought of Simon first. She had shot a man and left another to die. And killing people made you feel bad. The streetlights were dead. It was hard to see the road ahead, but Stevie kept her headlights off. She leaned forward and pressed her foot to the accelerator. She knew now why killers ended massacres with a bullet to the head or a noose in their prison cell.

The speedometer climbed. Stevie closed her eyes, saw the blackness deepen, and then opened them again. She let the speed drop to a steady forty and drove on, into the dark. Breathed in and breathed out. Breathed in and breathed out. Breathed in and breathed out.

Acknowledgments

The inspiration for *A Lovely Way to Burn* goes back to my early childhood, a mild obsession with "the bomb," the television dramas, *Threads* by Barry Hines and *Survivors* by Terry Nation. The idea that the collapse of civilization is imminent has been around since ancient times. Personally, I am amazed that we have survived this long, and while I don't exactly look forward to the end of the world as we know it, the knowledge that it may be just around the corner probably enhances the way I live. Many people have helped with this book. Sincere thank-yous go to Audrey Rae and Jennifer Scammell, who helped with medical research but are most definitely not responsible for any inaccuracies or flights of fancy that I may have added. Eleanor Birne has been an outstanding editor, and I have also benefited from the advice and support of my publisher Roland Philipps and my agent David Miller (who hates to be thanked). My partner, the writer Zoë Strachan, was once again my first reader and frequently set aside her own work to look at mine. I should also thank my family, who never complain about the amount of time I spend at my desk, even though it means I often shamefully neglect them.

I would also like to thank everyone at Cove Park, where I spent a very happy month and where I began this book, especially Peter and Eileen Jacobs, Polly Clark, and Julian Forrester.

About the Type

Typeset in Adobe Garamond at 11.5/15 pt.

Adobe Garamond is named for the famed sixteenth-century French printer Claude Garamond. Robert Slimbach created this serif face for Adobe based on Garamond's designs, as well as the designs of Garamond's assistant, Robert Granjon.

Typeset by Scribe Inc., Philadelphia, Pennsylvania.